OTHER BOOKS BY THE SAME AUTHOR

The Covenant – Published 2021

The Barbarossa Secret – Published 2022

FISSION

CHRISTOPHER KERR

The Book Guild Ltd

First published in Great Britain in 2023 by
The Book Guild Ltd
Unit E2 Airfield Business Park,
Harrison Road, Market Harborough,
Leicestershire. LE16 7UL
Tel: 0116 2792299
www.bookguild.co.uk
Email: info@bookguild.co.uk
Twitter: @bookguild

Typeset in 11pt Adobe Garamond Pro

Printed on FSC accredited paper
Printed and bound in Great Britain by 4edge Limited

ISBN 978 1915603 913

British Library Cataloguing in Publication Data.
A catalogue record for this book is available from the British Library.

This book is dedicated to the estimated six million Jews murdered in The Holocaust with some estimates much higher and thirteen million others including:

Russians, Slavs, Poles, Roma (Gypsies), those with disabilities, holders of certain religious beliefs, homosexuals, repeat criminal offenders and opponents of the Nazi regime, who perished in the genocide committed by the Nazis between 1933 and 1945.

"Each life is one precious individual"

Preface

Albert Einstein
Old Grove Road
Peconic,
Long Island

August 2nd, 1939
F.D. Roosevelt
President of the United States
White House
Washington, D.C.

Sir:

    Some recent work by E. Fermi and L. Szilard, which has been communicated to me in manuscript, leads me to expect that the element uranium may be turned into a new and important source of energy in the immediate future. Certain aspects of the situation which has arisen seem to call for watchfulness and if necessary, quick action on the part of the Administration. I believe therefore that it is my duty to bring to your attention the following facts and recommendations.

In the course of the last four months it has been made possible to set up a nuclear chain reaction in a large mass of uranium, by which vast amounts of power and large quantities of new radium-like elements would be generated. Now it appears almost certain that this could be achieved in the immediate future.

The United States has only very poor ores of uranium in moderate quantities. There is some good ore in Canada and former Czechoslovakia, while the most important source of uranium is in the Belgian Congo.

In view of this situation, you may think it desirable to have some permanent contact maintained between the Administration and the group of physicists working on chain reactions in America. One possible way of achieving this might be for you to entrust the task with a person who has your confidence and who could perhaps serve in an unofficial capacity. His task might comprise the following:

a) to approach Government Departments, keep them informed of the further development, and put forward recommendations for Government action, giving particular attention to the problem of securing a supply of uranium ore for the United States.

b) to speed up the experimental work, which is at present being carried on within the limits of the budgets of University laboratories, by providing funds, if such funds be required, through his contacts with private persons who are willing to make contributions for this cause, and perhaps also by obtaining co-operation of industrial laboratories which have necessary equipment.

This new phenomenon would also lead to the construction of bombs, and it is conceivable – though much less certain – that extremely powerful bombs of a new type may thus be constructed. A single bomb of this type, carried by boat and exploded in a port, might very well destroy the whole port together with some of the surrounding territory.

I understand that Germany has actually stopped the sale of uranium from the Czechoslovakian mines which she has taken over. That she should have taken such early action might perhaps be understood on the ground that the son of the German Under-Secretary of State, Von Weizsäcker, is attached to the Kaiser-Wilhelm-Institut in Berlin where some of the American work on uranium is now being repeated.

Yours very truly,
Albert Einstein

Letter from Albert Einstein to President Franklin D. Roosevelt – August 2nd 1939

Prologue

Monday 2nd August 1943 – 10am

Treblinka SS Sonderkommando Vernichtungslager (Extermination)
Camp II, Occupied Poland

The day was unusually warm, the sky clear, but he felt no warmth, only a steely ruthless determination to survive. In fact, he was no longer sure he felt anything anymore as his world no longer had relevance to who he was or how he had once perceived life.

Three months before, he had been in Warsaw and part of the Ghetto, taking some comfort in being amongst those of his background, despite being herded by the Germans, along with nearly 500,000 others, into a 3.4 square kilometre area reserved for Jews. That was until they learned of the killings from deserting guards, initially volunteering to work for the Nazis, who had fled the camps of Treblinka, Bełżec and Sobibór. They had told their stories to the Polish resistance of extermination taking place in camps which were not built for forced labour, but for the sole purpose of the eradication of all inmates on an industrial scale. At first, they had not been believed, but mass deportations were taking place from the Ghetto with no evidence of destinations ever being reached.

Resistance fighters had passed messages into the Ghetto of the stories emerging, which were of staggering, unimaginable bestial cruelty, including random shootings, and barbaric brutality by guards assaulting, abusing, and mocking the inmates before execution. As a result, plans had been adopted for an uprising. Inmates of the Ghetto were being herded daily in their thousands onto trains and were never heard from again.

Antoni Zielinski was just seventeen years old but had already experienced horrific changes in his life that would have been unimaginable only four years before. Now, he scarcely remembered the days of his youth, which seemed a lifetime ago. Then, he had lived in Nowy Dwór just thirty kilometres from Warsaw. His family were well-to-do. with his father owning an engineering business whilst his mother was a librarian. He had attended the local school but after the German occupation in 1939, everything changed. First, they were required to wear white armbands with the blue Star of David denoting that they were Jewish and thus treated as inferior; then his father announced his business was in trouble because people were frightened of trading with Jews for fear of reprisals by the Germans. In mid-1940, his mother was dismissed from her job, then his father had to surrender his business to the Germans, who placed a ban on Jews owning businesses, and he was told that he would be required to do labour for the Reich. One day, in October 1940, a German SS unit arrived led by some of the villagers Antoni knew, who identified his family as Jewish. As they were being rounded up, Doctor Krokowski, who had a local practice, pleaded with the SS officer that he had patients, amongst those being rounded up, who needed him. The man in the smart grey uniform looked at him with a sneer, drew his pistol and shot him in the head. That was the first time Antoni had witnessed a killing but the shock had become numbed over time by his experience.

They were taken away with their Jewish neighbours in a

lorry and transported to Warsaw, where they were forced to share cramped accommodation with three other families. The part of the city in which they lived was surrounded by walls and barbed wire in which Jewish families were imprisoned. Food was in short supply and within months of their arrival, people were lying in the streets and dying of starvation. Antoni was adept at scouting and scavenging for food. He found gaps in the wire and begged from those outside, gradually becoming known to the local partisans who sought information from him about conditions and German movements in the Ghetto. In July 1942, people began being rounded up and taken for 're-settlement' but the rumours speculated that the deportees were being murdered. Partisans told Antoni a few weeks later that they were being taken to death camps where they were being exterminated in gas chambers or in mass shootings. Antoni reported this to his parents, who refused to accept the stories, dismissing them as exaggeration. However, his father had taken him to the Jewish Council on Grzybowska Street, where he related what he had been told.

Although then only sixteen, he became involved in planning an attack against the Germans to prevent further deportations. Using gold given by the Council, he, along with others with contacts, obtained small arms, some grenades, and a small number of automatic weapons from the partisans who, whilst sympathetic to their cause, would not join in any insurgency as they stated it was not the right time for them. By late 1942, hundreds of thousands had been deported by the Germans and there was growing desperation. Food supplies had diminished, with many thousands dying of starvation whilst the Germans would carry out random shootings in order to stamp their ruthless authority on the population.

In January 1943, as Antoni had returned from foraging for food, he came across a sight he would never forget nor ever forgive. A line of vehicles was outside his dwelling with German soldiers and police shouting orders at terrified residents, some of whom were being dragged screaming from their accommodation. He watched from a corner thirty metres away, helpless, as he saw his parents being roughly pulled out on to the street. His mother was kicked by a soldier, at which point his father stepped in to shield her. An officer walked over, taking a rifle from the soldier, which he then used to club his father to the ground, who then appeared lifeless. Antoni was boiling with rage as he heard his mother scream, then sob as his father was thrown into the back of a lorry. The procession of trucks was driven away and that was the last Antoni ever saw of his parents.

The following day, he took up arms alongside many others, not fighting for victory, but for their dignity, for their race, for their right to choose the time and place of their deaths and for humanity. As the Germans drove a convoy into the Ghetto, shots rang out and Antoni, equipped with a Luger handgun, walked calmly from a side street towards an SS officer who had dismounted from a truck. He felt no emotion as he pulled the trigger, watching the shock register on the man's face before he fell. Seconds later, the truck exploded as grenades were lobbed into the back, flames enveloping the vehicle, and the Germans retreated, taking more casualties as they did so.

There had been odd skirmishes following this but the partisans informed them a major build-up of armoured vehicles was being assembled for an attack on the Ghetto, which started on 19th April. For three weeks, Antoni had fought alongside diminishing comrades against a vastly better equipped force, which began burning the Ghetto down, building by building, systematically destroying everything in a hellish inferno. In the first week of May, he had been hiding in a sewer when a grenade was dropped in. The blast killed two of his friends but he was thrown clear, regaining consciousness to face the barrel of a gun held to his forehead. By then, he had killed many, losing all sense of himself other than a hatred of all that these angels of death represented.

They did not kill him on the spot, but forced him to march

from the Ghetto to the *Umschlagplatz* (holding area) adjacent to Warsaw train station. On the way, some city dwellers would run to the slowly moving column to hand over bread or water before German guards would shout a warning or fire a weapon in the air. As they neared the station, one he recognised as a resistance fighter ran over to him, pressing a loaf of bread in his hand, whispering, *"niech Bóg cię chroni"* (may God protect you). As he ran away, Antoni felt around the bread to the heavier object without looking down, recognising that he was holding a hand grenade. At the station, he was loaded into a cattle truck for a two-hour journey crowded in with so many others; it was suffocating, whilst the lack of sanitation meant that the smell was overpowering. Many were sobbing, children were crying, and the overriding sense was one of impending dreadful catastrophe.

Antoni had determined that, before his demise, he would ensure he caused as many deaths as possible amongst his captors, concealing the grenade in a pouch on his belt that had formerly held ammunition. He felt no fear, nor sorrow, but was still driven to survive despite the hopelessness of his position, yet he knew he had to do whatever he could, never accepting the inevitable.

As the train jolted slowly to a grinding shrieking halt, there was the noise of chains being pulled away from the doors; then they slid open blinding the occupants with sudden light. The guards outside had dogs, which snarled and strained at their leashes, as they ordered the occupants to dismount the train with shouts of *"Raus raus!"* (get out). As he climbed out of the cattle truck, his hand clutched the grenade hidden inside his coat ready to use it irrespective of the consequences. On the platform, they were faced with a surreal sight of a small railway station with signs saying they were at '*Ober Majdan*'. There were more signs showing ongoing destinations and Antoni began to wonder whether they were, as they had been informed in Warsaw, being re-settled in labour camps in other parts of the country. They were addressed by a German officer with a loudspeaker whose words were translated by a Jewish man into Polish. As they listened Antoni noticed that the clock on the station did not move and, as he looked, he realised it was merely a painted representation. They were told they were to have a shower before being taken to camps in the Ukraine for re-settlement. Men with white coats walked down the line of people, with one stopping in front of Antoni. "You will come with us now, as we have work for you here." Inside a hut there were showers and he was told to strip with others who had been selected. As he did so, he noticed a gap between the bottom of the hut and the floor where he managed to slide the grenade unnoticed by the guards. He was not to realise until later that of the 10,000 people transported there that day, only twenty survived who were selected for work details. Later that night in the barrack hut, he was informed that he was a prisoner in Treblinka extermination camp.

Over the ensuing days, he became a *Sonderkommando*, initially tasked with gathering anything of value from those arriving at Treblinka, which might include jewellery, money, clothing, glasses, and even shoes, all of which would be carefully listed, before being sorted into piles for processing. He became immune from the desperate, sometimes pleading looks on the faces of those he 'processed'. He simply worked, doing what was required, and trying not to be noticed. From time to time, he would witness gratuitous acts of barbarity by the camp guards, including the random shooting of prisoners, or worse, which he affected not to notice. The hatred within him seethed and grew, yet, on the outside, he appeared calm, compliant, and supplicant. One day, he was chosen to work on the *Himmelstrasse* (road to heaven), as the SS called it, which was the walkway to the gas chambers. He heard the cries, and the screams, witnessing the collapse of some of those waiting. Despite steeling himself for what followed and becoming numb to all he was witnessing, he could not bear to look into the eyes of those facing their last minutes of life. After each 'batch' had been processed, he would clean and clear the walkway of what resulted from the gripping fear of those taking those terrible steps to their deaths, including the removal of bodies of any victims that had been disposed of by the guards. There were days when he was assigned to the *Lazaret* or infirmary, which was painted with a red cross. Prisoners causing problems or too infirm were taken to this building, behind which they would be executed. Unlike many who became resigned to their fate, he developed a desire to avenge what he witnessed. His hand grenade, which he had retrieved two days after his arrival, was now hidden in the base of a hut timber support by his bed, and just knowing it was there became a comfort to him. He slept at the bottom of a three-tiered wooden bunk in an over-crowded barracks crammed in with 600 prisoners despite having only being designed to house 250.

As Antoni worked, he became aware that there were plans for a revolt, which had been under consideration for some time. He recalled his impatience in Warsaw when plans for resistance seemed to be frustrated by delays and he urged those who confided in him that delays could cost them the opportunity for freedom, or simply the choice of how to die. Marceli Galewski, who occasionally worked with Antoni, asked why he could be trusted. as there were those who would give information to the Germans in the forlorn hope their lives may be spared. As they wheeled a cart carrying corpses to the newly formed fire pit created to destroy the remains, they stopped alongside the barrack hut where Antoni slept at night. He took Galewski to his bed, removing a cloth wedged against a wooden support, and extracted his grenade. "This is my Samson," he said "for this gives strength against Goliath and with Samson, I will slay evil."

After that, he became involved in furtive exchanges on how the revolt could succeed. By mid-1943, the privileged children in the camp who worked directly for the SS guards, carrying out menial tasks, had obtained an impression of the key to the armament store, from which a copy was fashioned. The plan was that arms, ammunition, and grenades would be smuggled to the prisoners;

individual guards would be summoned to see problems in various buildings and workshops around the camp where they would be killed. On a given signal, the armed revolt would begin and the gates overrun. Blankets and boards were made ready in order to help escapees traverse the barbed wire perimeter fence.

At 10am, the sun beat down that Monday morning in July and, as this was the day designated for rest from processing Jews, a number of German guards had gathered near the gates and were planning to go swimming in a nearby river together with some of the *Trawniki* (guards recruited by the SS from prisoner of war camps, normally Russian or Ukrainian). Antoni noted that there were at least fifty men laughing and joking as they mounted trucks noisily talking of their planned day. *At least that was fifty less to worry about*, he thought, as he gathered cleaning materials for the reception area, which it was his duty to maintain. As he passed the rear of one hut out of sight of the watchtowers with machine guns, he met a youth of about thirteen years of age pushing a cart in which there were two sacks, one containing a rifle, and the other a handgun and grenade. *"Bóg jest dziś z nami, Samuel"* (God is with us today), he said gently to the boy, as he put the sacks onto his own cart, patting Samuel on the back. Risking discovery, he knew he had to get the weapons he now carried to the gas chamber area, but no-one challenged him as he wheeled his cart down the *Himmelstrasse* to waiting, smiling, co-conspirators. Smiles were a rare commodity at Treblinka, but that day they felt a sense that they were seizing control of the hell they lived in. He continued delivering to various areas that morning, a process slowly being carried out in other areas of the camp. By 2pm, he was still cleaning the compound, ensuring he was noticed by the guards in order not to raise suspicion, but, by then, he had completed his part in the mission of smuggling arms. The tension in the camp was palpable as 700 inmates knew the hour was almost upon them.

At 3:30pm, as Antoni was moving to the barrack huts to remove both rubbish and the inevitable bodies, he heard a commotion. Then two Jews he knew were propelled out of one hut semi-naked; SS Scharführer Heinrich Matthes, the deputy Kommandant, pointed his pistol at their heads whilst guards stood by with sneering looks of disdain, their rifles also pointed at the hapless victims. "You see," the SS officer shouted, his voice echoing around the square, "We always discover anything you pathetic Jews try because we are the masters, and you will always obey because that is your duty. You will work without question. These Jews have been found with money and unless they tell us why and talk, they will die. If you wish to spare them, you must now speak out. If you do not give us information, we will begin reprisals which will result in many deaths this day."

Across the square, Antoni saw an accomplice, who he knew as a fellow conspirator, Rudek, with a bag under his arm. The officer now hit each of the men from behind with the butt of his pistol, both falling to their knees. One they feared walked around them. Unterscharführer Willi Mentz, known as a brutal camp assassin, kicking each of them in turn whilst holding his handgun outstretched. The tension grew as inmates crowded around the square, many either with carts, bags, or blankets covering what they carried. Antoni clutched 'Samson' to his chest and knew that the moment was approaching; a sack in his own handcart concealed his rifle. It was too early, as the conspirators were not yet in their allotted places, but Antoni sensed the inevitable. To his right, he watched the young man who deloused the German and Ukrainian quarters wheeling his spray delousing truck slowly forwards and there was an unmistakeable smell of gasoline in the air. It was all unreal, as though they were involved in a theatrical scene, but there was a terrifying gut-wrenching sense of reality too, with events creating an unstoppable momentum.

One of the guards began beating each of the prisoners in turn with the butt of his rifle, and they collapsed to the floor. Matthes strode around the square. "You all know I hate untidiness, and I do not wish to litter the ground with corpses, but I will have these Jews beaten until either they talk, or you talk. If you do not, one prisoner in every three will die until I have the truth." Antoni's hand reached inside his tunic for his precious 'Samson', feeling the time was nigh. The moment came in a sweeping slow motion of Rudek's arm as he reached into his bag, extracting a Luger pistol which he raised at arm's length, as Antoni grasped his hand grenade, reaching for the safety pin. There was the crack of the handgun and the guard who had been beating the prisoners crumpled, at which point Antoni lobbed his grenade amongst the guards who had been mocking from the side. There was an explosion and several men fell to the floor. Within seconds there were shots all around the camp as prisoners reached for their hidden guns. Some slipped into areas occupied by *Trawniki* guards, attacking and killing them with their bare hands before seizing their weapons. Wooden buildings were in flames as gasoline stolen by the inmates was ignited as part of the plan to incinerate the camp. A tank containing petrol by the camp garage was now blown up, throwing a huge fireball skywards and outwards, rapidly spreading an inferno.

As the shooting grew in intensity, there were shouts encouraging other prisoners to join in and rush the gates as Antoni saw the Deputy *Kommandant* run towards the SS guard area. Picking up his rifle, he took aim, but felt a harsh pain as his leg gave way and he looked down in disbelief to see blood pouring from a bullet wound.

Suddenly, there was a roar and a flash of flaming light shot into the air as the delousing cart full of gasoline ignited, showering its contents over surrounding buildings which were engulfed with massive flames sending heat waves across the camp. Thick smoke filled the compound; shouting mixed with screams, and guards were falling, whilst some ran trying to escape. Antoni had been blown backwards by the gasoline explosion and sat dazed for a moment until a fellow conspirator, Rudolf Masaryk, was by his side, tying a tourniquet around his thigh. "Go, please," Masaryk shouted, "Tell the world about this hell, and live, please live. Today, I choose to die with my brothers. My only sin was to fall in love with a Jew. Do not tell anyone, but until today I was not even Jewish but now, I feel I am." He grinned at Antoni, helping him to his feet, then propelled him towards the perimeter. Black smoke billowed across the camp and the bodies of guards littered the ground; when he turned back to Masaryk, he had gone and he never spoke to him again. Some guards were standing with their hands on their heads, surrendering, but inmates shot them as they ran past. Machine guns in the towers were firing and lines of men began falling over, whilst others continued to run, stumbling, picking up weapons from the fallen.

There were dead and dying everywhere and many screams; but still the staccato noise of the machine guns continued. Antoni lifted his rifle, took aim, and rejoiced as he saw the head of a guard manning one of the guns flip to one side and fall spread-eagled over the barbed wire below. Prisoners were climbing over the fallen to seek escape and Antoni followed them. As he approached the fence, a guard stood in front of him, challenging him. In an instant, he brought his rifle to the waist and fired, seeing the man double over in shock. By now, the whole camp was engulfed in fire, and the wave of prisoners continued towards the gates and the wire. Antoni climbed over bodies, using them as a bridge as he crossed the barbed wire, feeling nothing other than a desire to survive. As he ran, he heard a voice scream, "This is for my wife and my child who never saw the world!", turning briefly to see Rudolf Masaryk standing on the roof firing at the line of SS guards attempting to regain control, some of whom he saw fall. He was running on to the ditch beyond the wire, spurts of earth shooting upwards as the deadly machine gun fire traversed the escaping lines of men. More fell but no-one could stop to help them in the face of the incessant firing from the towers. Despite the pain from his injury, he raced towards the forest beyond, with many falling to the right and to the left of him. Suddenly, he was in the trees, his breath coming in rapid gasps, his heart pounding, and then he shouted, "I will survive!" Within a few minutes, he had joined a handful of others. Looking skywards they could see a thick pall of black smoke and they embraced one another, not with any feeling of triumph but in a grim bond of brotherhood.

Much later Antoni learned the true cost of that day. Out of approximately 800 inmates of the camp, it was estimated that around 300 had managed to escape. However, the Germans had mounted a massive troop concentration in an operation to round up the escapees, shooting many on sight, and executing the others on their return to Treblinka. Although detached from emotion, he harboured a hatred that only grew deeper as he learned that of the 800, under 100 had survived. Many sought shelter in the 'Aryan' side of Warsaw, the former Ghetto having been destroyed and raised to the ground. Antoni's desire for revenge took root as a need at this time and he sought out others who shared a deep survival instinct, born out of the camp experience, combined with the same need to avenge and protect the Jewish race.

1

Genesis

Saturday 2nd May 1931 – 11:30am
Grunau Flying School, Lower Silesia, Germany

When she entered, she was laughing, tossing her shoulder-length blonde hair and he noticed her immediately. She was petite, yet her bubbly personality seemed to captivate and fill the room with her energy. She was talking animatedly to one of the directors of the school, Wolf Hirth, who was also a flying instructor. "I want to do more with aerobatics," she exclaimed loudly, "That is where the thrill is, finding the limits of the aircraft and pushing the barriers of what is possible."

Hirth gently admonished her, "My dear Hanna, you are so crazy; you say you will fly for one hour, then we lose you for three or four hours. I don't think I have ever seen you fly in a straight line."

He waved across the room and smiled, "Wernher, you must come and meet my worst pupil, who never does what I tell her. May I present Hanna Reitsch to you? *Mein Leiblings*, this young man is Wernher von Braun. He is already a brilliant scientist

1

studying flight but not in gliders; no, he is a man of the future specialising in rocketry."

Her blue, dazzling eyes took Wernher's breath away as she greeted him. "Maybe I could fly a rocket, Herr Braun, can you arrange this?"

"Please," he stammered back, suddenly feeling nervous, "please call me Wernher, and I regret we have no rockets in which man, or woman, can fly yet; but one day, we will fly into space in rockets, leaving the atmosphere, discovering a new freedom." His passion for his subject had recovered his confidence and the room had fallen silent as others took interest.

She replied, enthusiastically, "Then you must tell me all about this rocketry because I want to fly everything and that is my life's passion."

"This is not yet possible, Fraulein," Wernher said, "But I will one day make it so."

Hirth cut in, "You know what she did last year, she took one of the new Grunau Baby gliders up, and disappeared. How long for, you might ask? Five and a half hours no less, not only driving us crazy with worry, but she succeeded in breaking the world record for endurance."

Hanna laughed, "It was because I was deliriously happy and I simply love being in the skies. I think flight is just so liberating and we are learning so much. We are breaking new barriers all the time and we are the trailblazers of the future."

"Bravo," responded Wernher, "but I think rocket flight will bring more to mankind in the future when we learn to conquer space."

A tall, jovial-looking man in his late thirties, smartly dressed in a tweed jacket, but wearing flying boots, walked over to join them. "Please forgive me, I could not help but overhear you and learning of your interests. May I introduce myself; my name is Robert Ritter von Greim and I am most interested in meeting those that I hope Germany may rely on in the future. I am a flyer myself and fought in the Great War. I am also a member of the *Nationalsozialistische Deutsche Arbeiterpartei* or the Nazi Party as we are now becoming called. May I please buy you a drink?"

He escorted them to a table and ordered a bottle of Riesling from the steward and a Schnapps for himself. After informing them of his service with the *Fliegertruppe*n (German air force), he went on to describe what had attracted him to National Socialism. "We should never have agreed to the Treaty of Versailles which is bankrupting our nation, and which takes away our dignity. The war was not lost on the battle front but because we were betrayed by unrest back home from communists, Jews, politicians, anarchists and the Kaiser's weakness. I met Adolf Hitler after the war and he spoke of rebuilding our national pride and of creating a strong, unified Germany with a vibrant economy in which all would have a stake. We are seeking young talented people like you because we are now the second largest party in the Reichstag and we believe we shall soon form a government. Our plan is to bring order, restore our strength, rebuild our armed forces, and that means new aircraft which will require skilled pilots like you, Hanna. We will embrace science to help improve our economy and enable us to have a powerful military supported by the latest innovations and that, Herr Braun, is where you fit in."

Hanna cut in, "Tell me about the machines you flew in; I just love hearing about the pioneers of flying."

Von Greim was delighted in the interest and told them stories of his time flying in Flanders over the trenches and of the duels in the sky. He said he was proud to have fought for the Fatherland and had scored 28 victories, for which he had been awarded the *'Blauer Max'* (the Blue Max or *Pour le Mérite* honour). He undid his shirt top buttons and proudly showed them the blue and gold medal suspended on a black and white ribbon. "I always wear this to remind me of my proudest days. Now, Germany has lost its way, but we will rise again with an invincible will inspired by our leader." His enthusiasm was infectious and they listened to his stories about legendary flying machines they had heard of including the *Pfalz, Albatros,* and *Fokker.* They warmed to him and both discussed their career aspirations with him, in which he took great interest.

Hanna was nineteen years old and had grown up in the town of Hirschberg, Silesia, which was set in a picturesque location nestled amongst the Riesengebirge mountains. She had always had an adventurous, mischievous, and irrepressible spirit since her earliest years. Her parents, who were conservative Germans, believing in old values of discipline and duty, despaired of her but, despite his strict values, her father, Willi, doted on her. He was a specialist ophthalmologist, whilst her mother, Emy, was an aristocrat who spent much of her time doing charitable work. They gave her a secure upbringing in a stable, ordered, family with her older brother, Kurt, and her younger sister, Heidi. Although Hanna could never be described as easily compliant, she had grown up respecting order, efficiency, and tidiness. Yet she was audacious, loving the thrill of adventure as a child and the attention this brought to her. She was fearless, seeking to climb higher, run faster, swim for longer, or ride horses more wildly than her peers. Her father had a *Mercedes-Benz* and she would shout at him to drive at the highest speeds, relishing the thrill of danger. She loved books, and from her youngest days, she would stare at pictures of daring pioneer flyers in balloons or the early flying machines.

One day, when she was out climbing with her brother at the age of six, they saw a red triplane flying machine, with black crosses painted on the wings, diving down from the peak of the mountain overlooking the valley near their home. Her brother had shouted excitedly, "*Oh mein Gott,* it is the Red Baron, von Richthofen," waving his arms wildly, as the aircraft screamed towards them. As the triplane neared, the pilot rocked his wings circling them. Then he had flown so low that his wheels were skimming the grass, then roaring over their heads and turning once more, this time waving at them, and flying so close they could see him smiling broadly. A long scarf fluttered down as the flying machine shot up in the air executing a loop before, once again, the pilot rocked the wings, climbed, and disappeared over the next peak. They ran to the spot where the scarf had fallen and Kurt picked it up. Made of silk, it was light blue in colour but had the letters M and R intertwined, embroidered in red on one corner. Her brother tied it around her neck and she could smell the aircraft gasoline mixed with the scent of the pilot. As they returned home, her parents were excited by the story, her father confirming that it was the scarf of Baron Manfred von Richthofen, the legendary German air ace, whose family home was in Kleinburg, near Breslau, not very far away. This planted the seed within Hanna for flying, her enthusiasm for which would never be dimmed. The scarf remained with her as a treasured possession, even more so, as they learned that a few weeks later, von Richthofen had been killed flying over the Somme on the Western Front in France.

After that, Hanna had never stopped talking about flying, saying that, one day, she would take to the skies and fly above the clouds. She collected pictures of aircraft, gliders and famous aviators with pride of place reserved for von Richthofen, who, she insisted, she would have married. After accepting that she would go to a *Koloschule* (finishing school for colonial families) to learn essential skills of cooking, cleaning, and farm work, she exacted a promise from her father, in return, that she could go to the Grunau flying school.

She explained to their luncheon host that she was now enrolled at medical school but that her heart was not in it. "I am a woman breaking into a man's world," she said earnestly, "and let me tell you, Herr Greim, I have already broken many flying records set by men, so if your Mr Hitler wants a flyer, then I will be available. I want to fly faster, higher, and further than anyone because flying is my first love."

Von Greim smiled at her, "Maybe I will challenge you to a duel in the sky, but we will be flying real aircraft, not gliders. Perhaps,

I will let you both into a secret; the Party Führer has decreed that we shall defy the Treaty of Versailles. Already, we have engineers who have joined us and they are designing new sleek and modern machines. For those we will need pilots with skill who can test and advise us in creating a new German air force, which will be called the Luftwaffe. You may have heard of a fellow flying ace, Hermann Göring, who is now a member of the Reichstag. He will be the leader of this Luftwaffe, which will be the most powerful air force in the world. We may even have use for rockets, Herr Braun, which could one day become great weapons."

Wernher laughed, saying that he was more interested in the possibilities of developing flights into space, but he conceded that there was enormous military value in his research too. He stated he had been fascinated by rockets from a young age, just as Hanna was by flying. He had been born into a family with aristocratic roots, with his mother related to a number of European royal families. His father, Magnus, was a politician and civil servant moving the family from Wirsitz in the Posen Province to Berlin in 1915. His home life was dominated by the care and attention lavished on him by his mother, Emmy. His elder brother was more interested in the work carried out by his father in politics, leaving Wernher to spend time with his mother. As a young boy, he had become interested in music under her influence, developing into an accomplished cellist and pianist. He began composing music and that became his main interest, inspired by Bach and Beethoven, whose works he could play effortlessly, without sheet music, by the age of 10. His mother then inadvertently became the catalyst for a new interest, astronomy, after he received a telescope from her as a present. His excitement in the study of planets grew and he dreamed of one day being transported to another world, powered in a rocket-propelled space craft. In his later school years, he developed a passion for physics and mathematics inspired by his dream of space flight. He became a dreamer, mixing his scientific interest with a deep imagination, which spurred him on with what he termed 'creative *passion'*. During the school holidays, in May 1929, his parents took him to the Avus Speedway near Berlin to see the new rocket cars being demonstrated by automobile manufacturer, Fritz von Opel. He recalled his overflowing excitement as he watched the car being prepared from their seating close to where the launch of the Opel was to take place. His father used his influence to gain Wernher an invitation to inspect the vehicle. He watched, fascinated by the complexity of wires being attached to the twenty-four rocket exhausts at the rear of the car in order to synchronise the ignition. Fritz von Opel enthusiastically explained to him how he had created his concept and that he had developed rocket-propelled gliders too. Wernher asked whether Fritz had yet experimented with liquid fuel, explaining how much it would increase the efficiency and thrust. Fritz was astonished at his knowledge as the 17 year-old explained the physics, informing him that flights were being successfully made by Robert Goddard, a scientist in the United States. Wernher glowed with pride as Fritz looked up at his father, saying prophetically, "This boy has an astounding depth of knowledge and enthusiasm and he will achieve great things. I believe he should apply to the *Technische Hochschule zu Berlin* (Technical University of Berlin known as TH Berlin) where he will flourish." Shortly afterwards, the bespectacled Fritz, clad in his overalls, waved to Wernher as he climbed into his rocket vehicle, which was named Opel RAK III, and, after a few moments, there was a thunderous roar and huge clouds of thick white smoke poured from the rear rockets. Then the car shot forwards, building speed rapidly, and Wernher's heart thumped with excitement as he watched. That day, Fritz Opel hit a speed of 230 kilometres per hour in front of a cheering crowd and Wernher turned to his parents saying, "One day, we will fly in a craft powered like that into space and visit other planets."

One year later, he was admitted to *TH Berlin*, and, within weeks, his remarkable talents were spotted and he joined a research team developing liquid rocket fuel led by Dr Willy Ley. The whole concept of rocketry had become a passion within him as he yearned to develop the technology, utterly absorbed in its possibilities. That year, he went to the picture house to see the movie made by Fritz Lang, *Die Frau im Mond* (woman on the moon), which depicted a rocket travelling into orbit, then to the moon and back. He turned to the girl he had taken with him and said, "That is how it will happen and the rocket you see is based on the research I am doing. One day, I will create such a rocket to carry men to the moon."

As he explained his interest in rocketry, Hanna watched his boyish enthusiasm and could feel the passion in his words. He was, she thought, awfully handsome and dashing looking in his leather flying jacket with its woollen collar under which he wore a smart striped tie. His hair was thick and wavy, giving him film-star looks, with a ready smile and wide, attractive blue eyes. He also displayed impeccable manners, which was a trait she admired, and she began to be aware that she was drawn to him. "Wernher, it all sounds so wonderfully exciting and I want to fly one of these rockets. Can you arrange this?"

He laughed, responding, "Fraulein, with your reputation, you would probably reach the moon in one. We are working on aircraft ideas too and one day we will need test pilots."

Von Greim interjected, "We will be building all kinds of new aircraft when we take power and you both are young representing the future of our Fatherland. I think you should meet some people who may assist by giving you backing for your careers and in this, I can help you." He turned to Wernher with a grin – "I can also confirm that the Treaty of Versailles says nothing about building rockets, so we can be quite open and maybe we shall become leaders in this field. That would shake the world and make them wary how they treat Germany. I would like to invite you both to hear the Party Führer speak and when we take power, there will be marvellous new opportunities for you. Adolf Hitler is speaking at the *Sportpalast* in Berlin on 19th May and I hope you both will agree to attend as my guests?"

They looked at one another, and, although they had only just met, each sought the other's approval, which was given by a mutual laughing nod of their heads. After taking their contact details, he stood up, clicked his heels, and kissed Hanna's hand before firmly shaking Wernher's. "I look forwards to seeing you in Berlin and maybe, Herr Braun, you might play the piano or the cello for the Führer; but please, only Beethoven, because regrettably, Bach was Jewish."

2

'Lead by example and serve as a source of inspiration'

(Mossad's published values)

Saturday 15th May 2021 – 10am
Mossad HQ aka 'The Office' – King Saul Boulevard,
Tel Aviv-Yafo, Israel

David Stern walked briskly through the glass doors, flashing his pass, removing his covid-19 mask briefly at the reception before taking the elevator to the fifth floor. Although forty-two years of age, he looked considerably younger, aided by a passion for tennis, which he played regularly at the Maccabi Tennis Club. As a boy, he had been tipped as a possible international player having shown outstanding promise, but his heart was set on becoming an officer in the military. His parents ran a small chain of men's fashion stores, which had given him a comfortable childhood, a private school education, and a home complete with a tennis court.

From his military days, he still liked to dress smartly and preferred light suits and ties to the more common jeans and open-neck shirts now worn by so many, although on this day, he was wearing a blazer, with light grey trousers. He was tall, with black, slightly wavy, neatly parted hair giving him a distinguished air. After serving fifteen years in the army, he had developed a clothing wholesale business, which now virtually ran itself, whilst still carrying out freelance clandestine missions for Mossad, especially on business trips abroad, many of which masked assignments. During the last five years of his army service, he had been seconded to Intelligence to carry out various covert operations, travelling extensively across Europe and in the USA. As he approached the panelled door of the Director's office, he felt some apprehension as this was not a normal summons, having received a call late the evening before requesting that he report to HQ in the morning. He had rarely met the Director, although he was a well-known figure as former National Security Advisor, and was often seen in the company of Prime Minister Benjamin Netanyahu, especially on meetings of international importance.

The Director welcomed him with a firm handshake, gesturing him to a comfortable chair by a small meeting table, then signalling him to remove his mask. "David, *naim meod,* (nice to meet you) you are welcome, thank you for coming and do please join me." The informality of the greeting took him by surprise, but the Director's air of authority could be felt, and his eyes and expression reflected his well-known reputation for uncompromising efficiency. He was immaculate in his appearance, wearing a well-tailored mid-grey suit and blue and white striped silk tie. "Well, *Rav Seren,* (Major) how does life outside of the army suit you? I hear your business is prospering with customers in many countries? I'm surprised you have time with your reputation on the tennis court." David smiled, feeling the warmth of a man who had clearly checked his background before the meeting.

"I never like to be beaten in anything, Yossi, as I am sure you will be equally well informed about."

The Director laughed. "That is my job, David, and I never attend a meeting unless I know everything I need beforehand.

Limonana or *Nes* coffee?" They both settled for a *Nescafé* espresso, which was brought in by a secretary minutes later after they had swapped anecdotes about their respective sports, the Director being a keen runner. Then the Director retrieved a tablet from his desk, sitting back down and looking from the screen to David as he clicked through to the file he sought.

"David, we seem to have an issue with some of our former colleagues from this organisation who have disappeared or whose lives have come to an end unexpectedly. As you know, we always look after our own, and there is something happening out there about which I need to find answers. Too many coincidences, and I have never believed in coincidences, especially when it impacts people I have known."

He tapped the screen, reading -

"Moshe Levi, born 1929, served with our Intelligence overseas on a number of assignments, attached to our embassy in New York City from 1960 – 1966. Fought against the British in 1945 and was a member of the militant Lehi group, reportedly involved in assassination units as he was a skilled shot. Retired from service in 1980 and died in hospital three weeks ago when recovering from successful heart surgery.

"Ben Herzl, born 1939, seconded to Mossad in 1961 from the army as a bright young soldier, an outstanding rifle marksman, and a reputation for ruthlessness. Served abroad on assignments, attached to our embassy in Washington DC from 1962 to 1964 before returning to the military front line and fighting with distinction in the Six-Day and Yom Kippur Wars. He never fully retired and was called upon from time to time for more deadly duties. Committed suicide five weeks ago.

"Antoni Zielinski, born 1925, the oldest but most interesting. A secret survivor of Treblinka, a fact which was only known to us. In 1944, he was appointed head of the Jewish section of the Polish resistance in the Warsaw Uprising after which he escaped to Palestine. During the latter stages of World War Two, he served in an elite commando unit for the British with a reputation as a deadly sniper, but then fought them during our struggle for the establishment of Israel. He became a militant Zionist, joining the extremists in Irgun, and had friends in high places including Prime Ministers' Yitzhak Rabin, Menachem Begin, Yitzhak Shamir and Shimon Peres. He was arrested for marching on the Knesset inciting violence against our own government in 1952; an event organised by Menachem Begin. He joined Mossad and became involved in hunting and assassinating former Nazis, in what was known as *Operation Damocles*, especially those selling their services to the Arabs. He actually befriended a former German SS officer he had been sent to either despatch, or force his agreement to co-operate with us. This was one Otto Skorzeny, a German war hero who, ironically for a committed Nazi, ended up helping and advising the Israeli military. Antoni was still healthy at 95, but died, purportedly from food poisoning, just three weeks ago.

"Simon Gerin, born 1942, was a decorated career soldier who stayed in the army until his retirement as a *Tat Aluf* (Brigadier General) of the Paratroopers Brigade at the age of 60 in 2002. He was an outstanding rifle shot as a young soldier whose skills were useful to both Mossad and the army, in which he had a brilliant career, also serving with distinction in the Six – Day War, Yom Kippur, Lebanon and the First Intifada. He was last seen a month ago driving out of Be'er Sheva, heading through the Negev desert for Tlalim Kibbutz. He never arrived and his car was found abandoned."

David took the last sip of his coffee, then held his forefinger up – "Accepting that you do not believe in coincidences, Yossi, what specifically has raised your interest here?"

"Yesterday, there was an attempt at a break-in here in Tel Aviv at the home of another old soldier, one *Aluf* (Colonel) Tzadok Berkowicz. He was born in 1953, and is the youngest of those involved. He was a pilot with the Israeli air force and then served abroad as an Intelligence officer working with our embassies in

London, Paris, and Washington. Later, he became an electrical engineer pioneering electronic weapons research for Mossad. He fought back against the intruders, opening fire with a machine gun, but his attackers got away, although he is certain he hit at least one of them. I am seldom, if ever, wrong, David, but addressing the coincidences, there is a uniting factor in that their files show that all five knew each other and all five were militant Zionists."

"Any evidence of a joint interest, political or military, or an operation in which they were involved together?" David asked.

"Sadly no," the Director responded, "but there is evidence that all of the files have been tampered with or made more classified at some stage and even I am unable to track down certain information. Ultra-classified periods have to be accessed using both the prime minister's electronic key combined with the Director of Mossad and I do not wish to involve Netanyahu. My concern here is not to create too many waves which may frighten off those responsible and so I do not want any of my regular agents working on this. I want to know what is going on, who is involved, and why? I do not like not being aware of all that happens in Israel but my greatest interest is to establish there are no old scores being settled by our Arab neighbours and, more specifically, ensuring that Iran is not involved."

"Maybe one of their Mullahs has issued some kind of Fatwa?" David suggested.

"Well, I can tell you, if they have, our PM, Benjamin, will authorise more military action, which would escalate tensions massively. God help us if they ever have a nuclear weapon because I am certain they would use it."

"Why Mossad and not *Shin Bet*?" David asked. "Surely, this is an internal security matter and I normally deal with foreign intelligence matters."

"Two reasons, David," came the reply – "All of the agents involved had worked for Mossad and all had worked abroad. Secondly, I do not want to use internal security resources for reasons of secrecy. The last thing I need is *Shin Bet* crawling over our work plus there may be external forces at work here."

"So, you want me to have a poke around, see what I can find out?" David asked.

The Director leant forwards, speaking earnestly, "I need you to operate with absolute stealth, reporting only to me. I have not even informed the PM of this and so you are under the radar. However, you are working under my personal command and you have authority to use lethal force, if necessary."

"Any police leads?"

"All of the deaths apart from the disappearance have been accepted as non-suspicious so nothing to go on there."

"Can I see their files?"

The Director stood up and walked to a cupboard, returning with a number of folders. "Crazy, I know, but not all files have been transferred onto the database, particularly the older ones. Take these to one of the spare offices and look through them all you wish. There is not much but references from here may give you access to other information which is held electronically. I will authorise you have the highest code level access. For that, you will have a unique key that will need to be activated with variable numbers each time you attempt to gain access. Good luck, David, I am hopeful your mission does not take too much time up as I would not wish to interfere with your on-court success."

An hour later, David was in an office that the Director had allocated to him in which he was able to work without interruption, free from the curiosity of others who respected this as normal practice in the secret world in which they operated. He studied the files in turn, briefly sifting through each and then cross-referencing information held in the databases of Aman (military intelligence), Shin Bet (internal security), and the central Mossad database. He was searching for common unifying areas between each of the men, noting these down with headings. The men had all lost parents or grandparents in the Holocaust and their roots were in Poland, Germany and Czechoslovakia. The oldest, Antoni, had survived a German death camp, and after Warsaw had been liberated in 1944, he came to Palestine to join the fight for independence from the British. Two had fled Europe to Palestine with their parents when the Germans had invaded Poland. Simon Gerin was born in the British Mandate territory and his parents had fled Germany in 1938 after *Kristallnacht*, during which his father's tailoring business was attacked and set on fire by marauding Nazis.

He turned to look at the data on screen for the youngest, Tzadok Berkowicz, discovering that his parents had been born in a small Polish village outside Warsaw and there was a file note. *'Assisted in their escape from Warsaw by the Betar (Zionist youth movement) through Menachem Begin, then the leader of Betar in Czechoslovakia and Poland'*. The link to the former Israeli prime minister was there for the oldest of the five men, confirmed by the Director's description, and now the youngest. There were other similarities in that at least three of them had served overseas in the USA, all were ex-military, displayed militant traits, and three were marksmen.

There were many gaps in the files relating to the specifics of operations, which was not uncommon. However, what was uniquely puzzling was that there were notes recorded that information had been removed as highly classified on the orders of Israeli prime ministers on separate dates. In a large script were the words 'Ultra Secret – Subject Classified' in red. This was common on looking up the service record of each of the five, which gave full reports for periods, but it was the missing elements in which David found commonality. All five records were on the personnel database, and all five had similar annotations. Four of them related to missing periods between 1962 and 1968, and were authorised by former Prime Minister David Ben-Gurion after he had left office, but endorsed by Prime Minister Levi Eshkol subsequently. The youngest of the deceased had records removed covering a period of service in the USA in 1999, classified on the direct orders of Prime Minister Ehud Barak. Earliest access or release dates for the classified information had been extended in 2019 by the current prime minister to ninety years. As such records were in the secret intelligence arena in any event, it was unlikely that they would ever, in reality, become accessible.

Finally, as he looked into the military service records; he could see that all had been working for *Caesarea*, or *Kidon*, as the organisation was now known. This was the unit responsible for exposing, despatching or 'taking out' undesirables across the world who posed a threat to the Israeli state. He noted that all five files had a similar prefix code, which was Unit 235, but this was embedded and non-searchable as a query within the database. He had not heard of this unit previously but was fast reaching the conclusion that he was dealing with something that had connections that went to the height of the Israeli hierarchy of power. He decided to enlist the help of an old friend and within seconds, he was using a coded greeting that he had not employed for five years. *"Aleichem shalom*, this is David S, how is Galilee? Could we consider the new wine crop in our office? There is a pressing issue if you are free? Today, yes, at 3pm. *Lehitra'ot"* (see you later) The voice at the other end calmly acknowledged the contact but David sensed the surprise and excitement of his former commanding officer. Moshe Gellner had also been his contact when he had first been recruited into Mossad, at which time his unique greeting had always started with, 'How is Galilee?' The reference to 'our office' would always mean that David would come to Moshe's home, avoiding any connection between them in front of others.

An hour later, he headed down Highway 2, his mind a turmoil trying to think through a motive behind the deaths of former Mossad operatives. The organisation was like a brotherhood and, despite the sensitive or violent nature of some of the work, there was a camaraderie wherein agents looked out for each other. The worst of the killings, which he felt a strong connection to, was for the oldest of the five. '*The poor bastard fought in the Warsaw Ghetto, took part in the Treblinka death camp uprising, then fought to gain independence for Israel. If he was to die, it should not have been a murder*' – He tried to put personal thoughts and emotions out of his head, which was something he had never been good at.

He looked in his mirror, becoming aware of a white Toyota that he sensed was following him. As an experienced agent, it had become second nature, in such circumstances, to accelerate, overtake vehicles, then slow down keeping a close eye on his rear-view mirror. He had followed three such manoeuvres, and the Toyota had remained either directly behind him, keeping a distance of twenty five metres, or one car behind. '*He's had the same training I've had*'- he mused, – '*Let's see just how good you are and, maybe, who you are.*' David was competitive in everything he did in life and winning was always his only option, which had helped him achieve success on the tennis court. In the army, too, he had excelled in every aspect from leadership to completing arduous training exercises in faster times than his comrades. He was also credited as being a successful strategist, and in shooting he had gained a reputation as an outstanding marksman. He had served in various military conflicts including commando raids, the Second Intifada from 2000, and the invasion of Southern Lebanon in 2006, after which he began work initially for Aman (military intelligence), and then, after showing considerable skill in his covert work, he transferred to Mossad. Whilst a ruthless operative, he never lost a sensitivity to the plight of others, including some adversaries. Unusually, this included some sympathy for those in the Palestinian Authority often caught up in conflict inspired by fanatics, such as Hamas, who would employ barbaric practices in pursuit of their goals. However, he was acutely aware of the fact that Arabs formed 20% of Israel's population and he had become disillusioned with his country's settlement policy in land that Israel continued to occupy in contravention of International Law. Yet his parents had drummed into him the brave fight for a Jewish homeland, which had taken place in their lifetimes, and that had followed the world turning a blind eye to the atrocities committed by Nazi Germany in the Holocaust.

There existed in David's life a conflict between his loyalty to the military and Israel, and an inner conscience about the Palestinian question. He rarely raised it with others as it was a contentious issue, exciting deep feelings that he knew would inevitably result in passionate adversarial exchanges, which he preferred to avoid. His cousin, Benjamin, had settled in Britain and whilst they had always been close, they had furiously debated the solution to the unresolved Palestine issue. Benjamin had joined *Na'amod*, a Jewish group committed to ending the Israeli role in the occupied territories and the establishment of equality and justice for both Israelis and Palestinians. He had been recruited by British Intelligence to work in MI6 seeking out those holding extremist views, areas of antisemitism, and on the investigation into sensitive areas relating to Arab/Jewish issues. David had found that he had little argument to utilise against his cousin's beliefs other than the security of Israel, which was always under threat in the region from both outside and within its borders. Occasionally they had shared intelligence, which provided a useful source to both Mossad and MI6. As a result of his conscience over the Palestinian question, he had been relieved to leave the army and avoid further conflict in the Gaza Strip, concentrating on the somewhat easier world of espionage. This still carried an element of excitement and danger but without the same inner moral contradictions.

On this day, as he sped down the highway from Tel Aviv to Caesarea, a journey of about an hour, with the Mediterranean sparkling to his left, he was puzzled by the fact he was being followed. He had only called his former boss and his phone was highly secure, yet it was too much of a coincidence that someone should be tailing him. He reasoned that there must have been a breach in security and that someone had been alerted that he was on a mission. As he approached the junction at Netanya he had selected, he instinctively checked his weapon, a *Glock 19*, an easy to operate handgun which had become his favourite since leaving the army. It was light, accurate, and easy to conceal when he carried it under clothing. Withdrawing it from the glove box, he took his hand off the wheel for a second, giving him the chance to check it, despite always keeping it loaded; his military training had stood him in good stead to double check. He placed it on the seat next to him, then, as he began to slow for the junction, he suddenly wrenched the wheel hard over to the right, his tyres shrieking with the violence of the manoeuvre into a minor turning before the junction. There was a blast of a horn sounding behind him as he sped down the small side road, his eyes narrowing as he observed the white Toyota still tailing him about 100 metres behind. His suspicions now confirmed, he pressed his foot down and the engine roared as his Jaguar F-Type leapt forwards, sending a cloud of dust off the small road behind him. He carefully watched to ensure his pursuer was still behind him, being careful not to lose him but merely using the power in his 575-hp supercharged V-8 engine to gain a larger distance between the vehicles. He wanted to give the impression he was playing with his car rather than trying to escape his pursuer. Eventually, after shooting down a long straight road, he joined Highway 4 running parallel to the main road he had left 10 minutes earlier, then took another exit heading back towards Natanya, speeding up then deliberately dropping back in order not to raise the suspicions of his pursuer that he had been noticed. He followed a long straight road towards the ocean at high speed, slowing at the end, and turned into the Hotel Seasons car park, which he knew well from meetings he had attended there. Finally, he drove past a line of cars towards the perimeter, then slowly back to an area near the rear entrance knowing he was being observed. He slipped his gun into a jacket pocket, exited the car slowly, in a relaxed manner, and walked towards the door aware of the Toyota now pulling up nearby.

He entered the door, then stepped rapidly to the left into

a small alcove, containing a table on which there were tourist information leaflets, from which he could see the car-park and his pursuer leaving his car and walking towards the hotel. Within seconds the door opened and a thickset man with dark curly hair entered in dark glasses. He had a neat beard and moustache and was wearing a t-shirt and jeans. He looked up sharply as David walked from the alcove, arms outstretched aiming his gun at the man's forehead. "OK, *ben-zona* (son of a bitch) you will turn slowly around, put your hands behind your back, and walk to your car in front of me. Try anything and I'll kill you. I don't know you, so I'm *zrikat zayin* (not giving a damn): The man looked shocked, then did as David requested, turning just once to see that the weapon was being openly exposed and levelled directly at him. When they reached the car, David commanded sharply, "Point to where the keys are, *tzair.* (novice) I work for Mossad; if you die, no-one will ask questions – *kabish?*" As the man indicated his jeans pocket, David barked the order, "Unlock the doors, open both of them, then you will climb in the passenger seat with your hands behind your head. What is your name?"

The response came back in a sullen tone as he climbed into the passenger seat – "Mehedi Saleh."

David walked around the front of the Toyota and leant into the driver's side, training the Glock at Mehedi's head. He demanded the keys and opened the car window before stepping back, shutting the door and leaning back in with his arms rested on the door frame. "OK Mehedi, are you Arab?"

"I am Negev Bedouin" came the curt response.

"Right, let me make this simple, if you want to live, you will answer my questions. I have served all my life in the military and I love my country. I do not like being followed by anyone, especially an Arab, so I will ask this once, who do you work for? Hamas?"

The reply, when it came, took David by surprise – "I too love Israel because this is my country. I served in the army and I am now with Shin Bet. I was ordered to watch you but was not aware you were with Mossad. I am a *sanjeran* here (stuck with unwanted task). Check me out."

Within seconds, David had placed a call and given a secret code requesting an identity check, before Mehedi's bona fide was confirmed, but he kept his gun pointed at him. "So, *chofer* (annoying person) – who ordered you to tail me and when?"

"I have nothing to hide from you." Mehedi said with a little less rancour now. "I received a coded message which gave me orders without identifying the source. I was given your name, a photograph, and not even informed you were with Mossad. I was merely told where you were and that when you left the building, I should follow you. I have no instructions other than to file a report to my source on your whereabouts and any contacts you make. I am not even armed, David, my weapon is still in its holder under the driver's seat. Check if you do not believe me." David opened the door, reached under the seat, and found the gun, at which point he lowered his own, slipping it back into his pocket. He climbed into the car, started the engine and switched on the air conditioning.

"Well, my friend, it looks like we are both on the same side but with different motives. I wonder just what is going on here? What military unit did you serve in?"

"Two years in the *1ˢᵗ Golani Brigade* then *Sayeret Matkal Unit 269 Special Forces* for 13 years, reaching the rank of *Sgan aluf*" (Lieutenant Colonel) came the reply.

David whistled in admiration, for this unit was the elite of the Israeli Defense Forces, responsible for commando-style operations and direct military action, manned by the toughest, highly trained personnel. Then, he said jokingly, "Oh my God, they are letting Arabs in there now? The standards are slipping. I did *Egoz Unit 621*, then *Maglan Unit 212* with a lot of guerrilla and undercover stuff until I was seconded for the Military Intelligence service, Aman. I finished as *Rav Seren* (Major) after 15 years."

There was an instant thaw in the atmosphere between them, both recognising a common bond from their military service.

David extended his hand in greeting, "*Shalom,* now at least we know we are on the same side. I think, maybe, we might help each other because I sense something big is going on."

Mehedi grinned, "Maybe I can be more Jewish than you; it depends on the deal, *shachtzan* (slang meaning 'know all'). Forgive me, but you did call me both a *chofer* and *ben-zona.* Something tells me you are not just sightseeing; perhaps, we can share a little more over a drink?"

3

Gleichschaltung

(Nazi term to describe organisation of total power)

Monday 18th May 1931 – 4pm
Hotel Kaiserhof, Wilhelmplatz, Berlin

They had arrived separately but both had been provided with rail tickets and were informed that their rooms and all expenses for two nights at the Kaiserhof had been paid for by the NSDAP. Hanna had protested to von Greim that she wanted to fly to Berlin but he said would not hear of it, joking that her reputation for aerobatics would put civilian air traffic at risk.

She had arrived first and was utterly dazzled and enchanted by the glamour of Berlin; the bustling in the streets, big department stores, and the sheer energy she felt, contrasting with her quiet rural life in her home town of Hirschberg, Silesia. The taxi drew up through a covered archway to the palatial entrance reception of the Hotel Kaiserhof and a uniformed concierge with a pillbox hat opened the car door and bowed. Hanna had never experienced such treatment and felt quite elated, a feeling which increased after she had informed reception of her identity when she was presented with an enormous bouquet of flowers. Escorted to her room, she was even more surprised to find she was in a suite comprising a seating area, with a separate bedroom and bathroom. There was a note on the table on headed paper with the words 'Nationalsozialistische Deutsche Arbeiterpartei' in bold black script at the top and an eagle centred beneath clutching a swastika. In a handwritten note beneath were the words, 'On behalf of the Führer, Adolf Hitler, welcome to the future of Germany in which your extraordinary talents will be given the opportunity to flourish. I have taken the liberty to order Champagne on the condition you will not be permitted to fly immediately afterwards. Heil Hitler!

Mit freundlichen Grüßen, (Kind regards)
Oberstleutnant Robert Ritter von Greim

As she took the suite in with its sumptuous patterned wallpaper interspersed with wood panelling, she felt a thrill of excitement at what was happening. She had heard a little of Hitler on the radio and seen him in cinema news reels but, although others were becoming captivated by this man as an icon, she had not really been swept up in the enthusiasm gripping those around her. Her consuming interest and passion lay with her flying, for which she, herself, was building a reputation for daring and outstanding ability. Nevertheless, she was aware that there was enormous excitement beginning to sweep across the nation about the new Nazi movement with its promise to transform Germany and restore national pride with strength.

As she peered through the window, she could see red flags being erected at one side of the hotel bearing a black swastika in a white circle. There was a knock at the door, announcing the entrance of a waiter, dressed in a white jacket, carrying a silver ice bucket in which there was a bottle of Krug Champagne on a tray, together with two cut coupe glasses and an envelope with the words neatly typed on the front, 'Guest Reception Briefing'. The waiter bowed, then deftly removed the cork, asking her if she wished the Champagne to be poured. She responded, "Danke schön but who is the second glass for?" The waiter replied he had merely been given orders but that he believed she was to be joined shortly. She allowed him to pour one glass, then hurried to the mirror as he left to tidy her blonde hair, which was naturally curly and difficult to control. She re-applied her make-up, added some perfume and then glanced sideways at herself in the full-length mirror, checking her puff white sleeves beneath a maroon velvet short-sleeved jacket, over wide-legged light grey trousers. She wondered whether she should have worn a hat but hated them with her customary dislike of conforming with all that was expected of her. '*Verdammt, they can take me or leave me. I am the guest, after all*', she thought, as there came another knock at the door.

She crossed the room, hesitating one more time in front of the dressing table mirror, then waved it away with disdain as she headed purposefully to the door, and, as she opened it, her heart fluttered for a moment as a smiling Wernher von Braun greeted her with a dramatic mock bow before kissing her hand. "*Guten Tag*, I wanted to go to the bar but was informed that you had ordered drinks," he started with a mischievous look.

Hanna was immediately very aware of him, as she had been on the first occasion they had met. "Wernher, you come here to beg a free drink and gain entry to a lady's private room? How utterly scandalous! I am not sure I dare let you in." Then with a spontaneity that surprised even her, she hugged him. "*Mein Gott*, they are spoiling us. Have you a room like this?" She gestured her arm out as she ushered him in. Wernher was dressed in a dark brown double-breasted lounge suit, with a striped necktie, white breast pocket silk hankie, and two-tone shoes with a light tan top contrasting with the darker colour matching his suit. As he poured his own glass of Champagne, he just exuded a film-star-like appearance with his thick wavy hair. '*Gosh*,' she thought, '*he looks utterly dashing.*' He appeared so cute to her with his boyish good looks combined with a cheeky, mischievous smile reminding her of Ronald Colman in the film, "*Raffles*", which she had seen a few months earlier, in which Colman played an aristocrat doubling up as a jewel thief. '*If only I had bewitching eyes like his co-star, Kay Francis*' – she wistfully thought for a second before being brought back to reality as Wernher raised his glass with a wicked grin, "A toast to our futures, and, with that, perhaps, to our benefactor, Herr Hitler." They clinked their glasses together.

"Do you think Hitler is good for Germany?" Hanna asked, already sensing that Wernher was more informed than she on such issues.

"We need strong leadership," Wernher responded, "This man is inspiring the masses like no other before him. He has vision where there has been none, and is not frightened of speaking out against the injustices we have suffered after the Great War, imposed by the Versailles Treaty. Our country has been in a state of confusion, anarchy, and threatened by communism with Russia looking on, ready to attack us. Many say that Providence has sent this man, which I do not care to believe, but such is his extraordinary passion and belief in our destiny as a race, it is almost impossible not to want to follow him. Germany will rise again and command respect from those who have trampled on our misfortune and I want to be part of the new, not stagnate in the shadows of the past."

Hanna stared at him in awe of his grasp and self-assured nature, finding that she could not help but be fascinated and attracted by his sheer magnetism. She struggled to find the words, not wishing to appear foolish, but managed, "I think I want that too but I've never really dwelt on such matters. I do wish Germany was a prouder nation and it does seem to me that there has been so much uncertainty and lawlessness. When I fly, I forget such things and hopefully, if this chap, Hitler, does become Chancellor, there will be the opportunities that von Greim spoke of."

Wernher refilled their glasses and raised his to her, "I think, *meine liebe* Hanna, many questions may be answered at dinner tonight because we are to be introduced, I am informed, to some of the people of influence in the Nazi Party who may help our careers. There are two guests of honour. The first is Hermann Göring, who you should take to as he was a fighter pilot ace in the Great War and people see him as like a number two to Hitler. The second is Joseph Goebbels, who is reputedly a great speaker and who looks after Party publicity. They are both members of the Reichstag. Have you opened your guest reception briefing yet?"

She had completely overlooked the envelope the waiter had brought in earlier and which she had left unopened on the dressing table. "I honestly have not even looked yet", she replied, – "Have you had one?"

Wernher smiled at her warmly, attracted by her bubbly nature and her almost childlike enthusiasm, which he had witnessed when they had first met, contrasting with his more measured and logical approach to life. That said, he had held a fascination for his interest in rocketry from being a boy and his dream of space travel now amplified through his university studies, which in many ways was not dissimilar to her obsession with flying. "Mine was in my room and I opened it as soon as I arrived. It seems everything is meticulously planned. I am to be introduced to three incredible people tonight, all of whose work I have admired greatly and all appear to be enthusiastic about the Nazi Party. They are Dr Walter Dornberger, who specialises in my main interest, rocketry; Karl Becker, a professor of military sciences, and Otto Hahn, who is a wonderful physicist. These Nazis are clearly focussed on efficiency and detail, which is a trait I relate to."

Hanna walked to the dressing table to retrieve her envelope, suddenly feeling an inner sense of excitement. Then, as she opened it, "What do they want with me? I have spent a year in finishing school being taught how to be a lady, learning how to cook, clean, and muck out animals." As she pulled out the card from inside the envelope, she said with a giggle, "Do you think maybe Hitler is seeking a good wife?" As she looked down at the neatly printed script below the eagle and swastika, she stopped, wide-eyed, intaking a deep breath of surprise, putting her hand over her mouth, "*Mein Gott*, Wernher, I have been asked to join the top table as the personal guest of Hermann Göring. We are to be joined by Ernst Udet, the fighter pilot ace, and their Director of Press Communication, Joseph Goebbels."

Wernher let out a whistle of surprise, "Maybe you are being groomed as a potential bride then," he grinned, "stolen from my attention before I have hardly got to know you."

"Oh dearest, Wernher," the words tumbled out before she could stop herself, "I would simply adore getting to know you better." He was just so, well, utterly irresistible.

"Well, that's settled then," he said without showing any surprise, "Cocktails before dinner, and, most definitely afterwards, when we have finished impressing everyone." Her eyes met his, and they both felt the moment, as they were held by one another. Then he smiled, pouring them both another glass of Champagne before saying in a somewhat cheeky way, "I think we are going to enjoy each other's company enormously," adding flirtatiously, "which will be rather fun, don't you think?" He handed her the glass, and, as she reached for it, he took her hand and kissed it softly. She giggled again then remonstrated, "Herr von Braun, how very forward of you; now drink up as I have to get ready for a very important date." Within a few minutes, he had left and Hanna felt the happiest she had been for some time.

At 6:30pm, her room phone rang and, as she answered, she was met with, "Fraulein Hanna, I trust you are enjoying our hospitality?" She recognised the voice of von Greim and immediately responded energetically, "Herr von Greim, thank you so much for all of this and the flowers too. This is all so overwhelming."

"Please, call me Robert, and that is because you are not only my guests but also guests of the Führer. Now, I must ask if you would do me the honour of accompanying me to dinner?" Without waiting for an answer, he continued, "Shall we say in one hour?" Upon her reply that she would be joining von Braun in *der Friedrich Keller* cocktail lounge, there was a chuckle in the response, which was slightly disconcerting, "I would not have expected anything else from Herr von Braun, who, it seems, has the eye of the ladies. I will, er, rescue you in one hour."

When she entered the lounge, she attracted many admiring glances, not least from Wernher seated by the circular bar, who was utterly dazzled by her appearance. She was wearing a long cream shiny silk gown, chosen with her mother's guidance as Hanna was not at all at ease with such fine clothes that she had little experience of. The dress was low cut and closely draped, clinging to her body in a sinuous and fluid manner creating a sensuous look, over matching satin high heels that helped in making her taller in appearance. Around her neck she wore a lightly feathered stole, whilst her blonde hair was fashionably curled short to her neck. Long earrings and a pearl necklace hung low added to the look and she had applied heavy eye make-up, which gave her a sultry appearance, completed with a clutch bag in black velvet embroidered in a rich golden pattern.

"Oh my darling, you are simply breathtaking." Wernher greeted her, in a black tuxedo with matching bow tie and silk white top pocket handkerchief. "Forgive me, but you look utterly ravishing," he further enthused, kissing her hand before leading her to the bar. She smiled demurely, not used to such compliments. In turn, she looked at him with admiration, cutting a dashing appearance with his wavy light-coloured hair swept back yet with a hint of a centre parting, smiling at her with intense Prussian blue eyes. "I think I am more at ease wearing a flying jacket than all this finery," she responded – "I must confess, this is the first major formal event I have ever attended. We rehearsed them at finishing school, but I somehow do not think I will be walking across the room here with a book on my head, as we had to then, learning deportment." Wernher laughed as he turned to order them two *sidecar* cocktails, instructing the bartender to go light on the Cointreau and Cognac and heavy on the lemon. He turned to her, explaining, "We have a long evening ahead and I think we need to be on our best behaviour, but, perhaps not later." She knew he was flirting but she was unashamedly enjoying it.

They remained at the bar, discussing their hopes, sharing their excitement about the future and their dreams of realising ambitions to combine their careers with their passionate interests. Perhaps this was the providential moment that would give them the opportunity they both sought. More people were arriving, some dressed in the brown uniforms of the Nazi Party, and the bar tender informed them that a band was assembling in the main reception area. There was a growing air of expectation and they watched brown-shirted officials scurrying around who appeared to be giving instructions and organising matters. Guests were moved away by uniformed security from the entrance to the cocktail bar to make way as von Greim entered. The guards immediately snapped to attention and raised their right arms in salute as did a number of other guests, Hanna noticing that many women also did the same. A beaming von Greim dressed in a dinner jacket approached them, wearing his Blue Max cross at the neck. He bowed before raising Hanna's right hand to kiss it. "I trust you have survived the undoubted attentions of this '*Valentino*'. I am afraid, Herr von Braun, I must steal this lady from you over dinner but I pledge to return her safely. Please come this way as the guests of honour are due here shortly."

They ascended the grand steps to the main reception area where there was a crowd of guests and a band positioned near the double doors leading to the restaurant. A line of people was forming on one side, which von Greim explained was made up of VIP's who had the privilege of being selected to greet the guests of honour. There were armed guards forming up at the entrance doors to the hotel and von Greim led them to join the line. "As my guests, you will be presented personally and then, Wernher, I will introduce you to Dr Walter Dornberger, who is most interested to hear of your studies." There was an air of expectation and the hum of lowered voices, then they saw a man in a brown uniform and black boots marching towards the hotel entrance, who von Greim informed them was Reichsführer-SS Heinrich Himmler, the head of a growing elite security organisation, who had been elected as a member of the Reichstag a few months previously. He barked an order and the entrance doors were held open for him to exit. A Master of Ceremonies stepped forwards in 18th century costume complete with a white wig, long coat and neck ruffle, banging a silver-topped staff on the floor three times. *"Meine Damen und Herren*, the Führer's Deputy Speaker, decorated fighter pilot ace awarded the *Pour le Mérite*, and Reichstag Member, Hermann Göring." The band struck up playing the Nazi Party anthem, '*The Horst Wessel Song*', and the six guards by the door snapped to attention. Seconds later, Himmler re-entered, then stood to one side as Göring made his entrance, smiling broadly, and acknowledging the many right arms which were raised in salute. Hanna took a deep breath, whispering excitedly to Wernher, "He looks magnificent, like a royal prince." Göring was dressed flamboyantly with a shoulder cloak, and a long black evening jacket with four military-style buttons down each side; a gold chain was suspended across the middle over a low white waistcoat, beneath which he had a blue sash worn diagonally across the chest matching his *Pour le Mérite* or 'Blue Max' medal, which was at his neck. His thick dark hair was swept back and he began walking slowly down the line of people, shaking hands and stopping occasionally to exchange a few words. Hanna gripped Wernher's hand, then, looking up at him, she whispered again urgently, "What am I going to say?" to which he replied, "I believe it will be he who does the talking. He has a reputation for charm, so be yourself."

The band was now playing the national anthem, '*Deutschlandlied*', and people joined in with the words, "*Deutschland über alles*" as Göring approached where they were standing, opening to von Greim with "Ah, Ritter, you old rascal, how are you?" He slapped von Greim on the back, "I never have forgiven you for scoring 25 victories against my 22 in the war."

There was laughter from those standing around them as he turned to look at Hanna, addressing her directly, "Fraulein Reitsch, you need no introduction as your extraordinary skills in the air are becoming legendary." He turned, speaking loudly to the room, "This young lady has already broken the world altitude and endurance record in a glider." There was a storm of applause as he continued, "She will be of great benefit to the Third Reich. We are honoured by your presence and I look forwards to your company at dinner." Von Greim then introduced Wernher to him and Göring shook his hand warmly. "You two represent the talents of the new Germany and we need your skills, Herr von Braun, to help us build new weapons, but," he paused, looking round as though he was worried who was there, "we must not tell anybody because the Versailles Treaty forbids it, so let it be our secret, eh?" More laughter ensued as he walked on down the line.

Seconds later, the Master of Ceremonies again drew attention, striking the floor with his staff, then, "Please welcome the Reich Leader of Propaganda, Gauleiter of Berlin, and Member of the Reichstag, Joseph Goebbels." More applause followed and the *Horst Wessel Song* was played again as the slightly diminutive figure appeared in an immaculate short-cut evening jacket over black trousers with a broad silk stripe running down the sides, over which he wore a white short waistcoat and matching bow tie worn with a winged collar. He stopped as he entered, raising his right arm stiffly in salute as the music played, whilst others gathered there followed suit. Unlike Göring, he did not socialise with those lining the room, but merely walked slowly down with a slight limping gait, smiling to right and left, acknowledging the applause he drew with an element of haughtiness. However, there was no denying the genuine admiration from those in the reception area. The music had changed to Strauss waltzes and the atmosphere was relaxed. Wernher was impressed with the sheer authority which seemed to exude from these two men whom he had read about but only seen in newspaper pictures and newsreel footage. There was no doubting their charisma and magnetism. *Perhaps,* he thought, *it is men like these that will inspire a genuine resurgence of national pride.*

There was a short period of time before dinner, during which von Greim directed to a brown uniformed assistant that Wernher should be taken to meet his guests. He followed the orderly to a small group where he was warmly welcomed by a tall, distinguished looking man with dark hair and a thin moustache who introduced himself as Hauptmann Walter Dornberger. "I have been briefed that you and I share the same interest. I hear that you are making quite a mark in your studies at the Berlin Technical Institute with research into liquid-fuelled rocketry." He then introduced him to four others, including his immediate superior, Oberstleutnant Karl Becker from the *Heereswaffenamt* (Army Ordnance Office HWA), heading research into new weapons, Otto Hahn, the renowned physicist, and Ernst Hanfstaengl, an American/German financier and businessman.

Hanna remained with von Greim, who informed her that, as guests of the top table, they would enter last. He then guided her over to a corner of the pillared reception area where Goebbels was talking to a group of attentive men. "Herr Goebbels, might I present one of the most daring and accomplished aviators in Germany, whom I have the pleasure of escorting to dinner." Goebbels immediately turned with a dazzling smile, his eyes seemingly devouring her as he dwelt on her appearance. Despite feeling a little intimidated, she realised there was no doubt of his charm and charisma as he kissed her hand, holding her fingers just a little longer than was the custom. "*Mein Fraulein,* the Fatherland is blessed by your beauty and your skills, about which I will be honoured to publicise, in order to make you famous when we assume power, telling the story of a true daughter of the Reich pioneering flight." His voice had risen as though already giving a speech, and despite her discomfort, she could not help experiencing a thrill from his words and his power.

4

'Shomer piv u'le'shono, shomer mitsarot nafsho'

(He who watches his mouth and his tongue guards his
soul from troubles) – Jewish proverb

Saturday 15th May 2021 3pm
Seasons Natanya Hotel, Natanya, Israel

They sat in the bar overlooking the Mediterranean, both enjoying a cool beer, which, as Mehedi stated, he felt a pang of guilt for, but he had long learned that a pragmatic approach to life was less restricting than always following the laws of Islam. "So, Mehedi, how many sheep and goats do you have?" David asked in a good-humoured way, as they sat in comfortable chairs, relaxing after the tension of their meeting. His question evoked the banter that Mehedi related to from his days in the army. He had grown up as a Bedouin Arab: his family had been proud of their roots, being of the Al-Azazma tribe. His grandparents often regaled him with stories of their days as nomadic Arabs freely roaming land between what was now border territory between Israel and Egypt. His grandfather had been an enthusiastic defender of the new state of Israel in the 1940's and had given proud service in the Israel Defense Force (IDF), joining in 1949. His father had turned away from any loyalty to Israel because of the way that Bedouin Arabs had been treated by the state. Despite this, he had moved to Rahat and become a successful lawyer fighting cases for human rights. Mehedi was proud of them both but drawn to the military as he saw that Arabs had an important role to play in modern Israel within which there was opportunity. He had studied at the University of Haifa, gaining a degree in mechanical engineering, before enrolling in the IDF in 2000 at the age of 22. He had suffered some discrimination but had also found a growing number of Jewish conscripts who, despite holding prejudices instilled in them from their upbringing, were open to building bridges of genuine understanding and friendship. There was suspicion on both sides and he, in his turn, had suffered from his father's disapproval which was uncompromising in his condemnation of the way the state had treated the Bedouin. Despite this, Mehedi had persevered, and had become an officer serving with distinction in combat within the elite *Sayeret Matkal* commando unit, gaining respect as both a courageous soldier, and an inspirational leader. After successfully carrying out some covert duties infiltrating militant Arabic groups, he left the IDF in 2015, having been recommended to Mossad as a highly capable operative.

He countered David's mockery with a grin, "Listen, *ahabal* (dumbass), when you have finished counting your shekels from money lending, or similar, just remember we were here first and you displaced us. Yet I was awarded the *Medal of Valour* for protecting you! What kind of justice is that?"

David laughed, – the tension had now evaporated completely. "You Bedouin Arabs discovered the Dead Sea Scrolls proving we were here and you use our Bible in your Islam. To think I was discriminated against protecting your homes by only being awarded the *Medal of Courage*. You men in the *Sayeret Matkal* are always favoured." Despite the exchange, David knew his counterpart must have been highly capable to have served in the special forces and, even more so, by the achievement of Israel's highest military decoration. He continued, "You know what, my friend, I think there is something big going on and your involvement proves it. They have roped me in and why? Because, I am less known and an outsider who is no longer officially connected to Mossad and I am being asked to investigate something quietly. Yet, someone has already heard, within the organisation, and they select you to tail me, not some minion, and that tells me we are both pawns here for something sensitive." On an impulse, he decided to take Mehedi into his confidence, relating to him the series of coincidental deaths of those formerly involved within Mossad.

"*Ya Allah,*" (my God) Mehedi responded, "I knew this was different from the outset as I am never tasked with just following someone without a wider briefing. By the way, you can add another name to your list, *Aluf Mishne* (Colonel) Joseph Abrams, but this one has been hushed up. You know why? Because rumour has it he was taken out by Kidon for selling information to the Iranians. I did not believe it as I knew him and he was a decent man. He was sixty-five years old and not only a good officer, but a physicist and headed up the inspection unit that I escorted into Iraq in 2003 after the mess the Americans left. Get this, two weeks ago, he was shot in the head as he got into his car by an unknown assassin, which was put down to be a rogue Palestinian attack, but we knew it wasn't because Mossad people went in to clean up his house and his office. Both buildings were absolutely ransacked then forensically cleared, with all his computers, papers, and research material removed whilst the police were instructed not to investigate the matter further. I am used to the filthy business of intelligence work but this alarmed me as I had mixed with him and met his family. After what you have told me, I am even more alarmed. Where do we go from here?"

David looked at him earnestly, "You know what, *chaver,* (friend) if those bastards in Kidon are involved, you needn't be.

They always cover their tracks and assassinate anyone who gets in their way, which the state will both authorise and cover up. I have a feeling we are into something very sensitive. Remember, the files that I have examined have information missing, which has been removed with the time for their secrecy extended under the recent instruction of Netanyahu no less. If you return and say you lost me, then that removes you from all this and takes you out of danger."

"Listen, *shakli b'tahat* (kiss my ass), I outrank you as *Sgan Aluf*, (Lieutenant Colonel) I'm right with you because you Jews only screw up unless you have Arabs backing you. So, what next? I'll take your orders…for now!" Mehedi extended his hand and David shook it firmly, sharing the warmth that the two men already felt.

Ten minutes later, they were speeding down Highway 2 in David's Jaguar, heading for Caesarea, with the ocean shimmering to their left. On the journey, David related how he had come to know the man they were going to see, Moshe Gellner. "When I first joined the IDF at the age of 21, I was already older than many of my fellow recruits. I was excused the draft because of my tennis when I began playing internationally. However, I sustained an injury which affected my play and, believe me, I hate losing." They both laughed as David continued, "During my military training, I became a crack shot and because of this, I was seconded to a unit specialising in sniping. I met Moshe at that point, who was my commanding officer but, my God, he led from the front. Everyone in the unit looked up to him as a ruthless, fair, and very courageous man. He was also highly intelligent, with a PhD in modern history, which was a passion of his outside his military service. He knew everything there was to know about presidents, prime ministers, and dictators; a fascinating man to talk to. I served under him during the Second Intifada when he led us forwards under fire to seize those who were leading the militants. That is when I got this." He raised his left arm, as they crawled to a junction, pulling the sleeve of his blazer and shirt back. There was a long scar down the forearm right back to the elbow. "An RPG (rocket-propelled grenade) nearly took me out but Moshe came back for me, carrying me on his back to safety." He grinned, "But, you know what, they stuck a metal piece in there and hey, I'm left-handed; my tennis serve is even stronger now."

Mehedi rolled up his shirt revealing a number of wounds on his side from his waist upwards. "*Ben kalbah* (son of a bitch) with an automatic weapon in the Lebanon in 2006, but, whatever, I shot back and I survived. He didn't!"

As they neared Caesarea, David related how he had become increasingly involved in covert operations after his injury, following Moshe into *Maglan Unit 212* specialising in commando and reconnaissance assignments. "We crossed borders of surrounding countries and often worked closely with Intelligence. Moshe left the IDF in 2008 and joined Mossad, whilst I did a period with Aman before Moshe invited me to join him in 2012. I served under him for five years until he retired. I left shortly afterwards to concentrate on developing my business but carried on doing some covert work, especially when travelling abroad. The pay is reasonable and allows me to count more shekels if needed eh?"

Mehedi responded, "You Jews, always talking about money whilst we simple Bedouin are happy with our sheep and goats." They had already built up a close rapport in the short time they had been together. David was quite surprised as, despite his sympathy with many Arabic issues, he had never formed any real friendship outside of his own Jewish community. He reflected that he had been brought up to be suspicious of anyone Arabic despite serving alongside many Arabs whilst serving with the military. '*Note to self,*' he thought, '*I must contact cousin Benjamin in Britain and say that, just maybe, I might be a recruit for Na'amod supporting Arab justice and equality.*'

David drove the Jaguar left off Route 2 onto a road signposted Caesarea National Park, taking another turn towards Caesarea Beach and then down a narrow road flanked with villas. They approached the entrance with iron gates opening onto a short drive to a white-painted villa surrounded by neatly trimmed palm trees. Both men alighted, donned their anti-viral face masks, and approached the panelled wooden door outside of which was an intercom. David pressed the button and after a few seconds there was a bleep followed by a message, "Please state your business". David merely said the words, "How is Galilee?" Seconds later there was the sound of locks clicking and the door was flung open to reveal a man dressed in a light flannel suit, with white, wavy swept-back hair, in his late sixties wearing dark glasses. He signalled dramatically to them both to remove their masks then his face broadened into a smile. "David, you old *nochel,* (crook) it is good to see you." They both hugged, then he turned to look at Mehedi, "You have a bodyguard now?" His bushy eyebrows were raised in mock enquiry.

"Forgive me," David replied, "may I present my colleague, Lieutenant Colonel Mehedi Saleh, this is Aluf (General) Moshe Gellner." The two men shook hands. "I can vouch for him despite him being an Arab." David added with a smile to which Moshe responded, patting Mehedi on the back, "I have spent most of my life fighting Arabs but now in Israel we are learning to integrate. The process is slow and we have to overcome our prejudices but look now in the Knesset, there are now many Arab members. Time for a drink." He led them inside then through the spacious hallway to a large lounge with an enormous panoramic window overlooking the ocean. Moshe slid back a door on one side to the terrace. "I think it is cool enough to enjoy a drink outside." He looked at Mehedi, "Are you permitted to share a bottle of Israel's finest Shiran unoaked Chardonnay?"

Mehedi responded, "General, I have a long career in the army which taught me how enjoyable it is to sin." Moshe laughed, then insisted that they all use first names as fellow soldiers. They sat in easy basket weave chairs around a low table with a view down a garden to the Mediterranean beyond. David began relating his story, covering the deaths of each of the five men who had died in the order of their age, including the shooting of Abrams, that Mehedi had informed him of, and the attempted murder of a sixth the week before. Moshe's eyes narrowed as each of the names was revealed, wincing occasionally as he heard of their service to Israel. At the mention of the last he exclaimed, "*Ya'boozdinak* (good grief), I know some of these men. I especially remember Joseph Abrams because he was involved in heading up a unit, indirectly part of my command, searching for WMD in Iraq after the Second Gulf War. Antoni Zielinski had quite a reputation, in the 1950's I think, working for Intelligence as a hunter of former Nazis. I did some research on him when I was working on a book. I recall that we covered up the fact that he had escaped from Treblinka so that any evidence he gave was not attacked as being prejudicial by defence teams. I came across him once or twice in the 1980's and recollect him as a very embittered man," he shrugged his shoulders as though dismissing the memory, "but who are we to judge after all people like him went through in the camps during the Holocaust? Yet, the extraordinary thing is, he still ended up working with the notorious former German SS commando, Otto Skorzeny. Simon Gerin was a fanatical Zionist but was a long-serving career soldier who was a general with the paratroopers. The others' names I seem to faintly recognise but, in any event, you were right to come and see me. These are dangerous times and there are sinister forces at work here in Israel, which is very sad to me because we should be coming together as a nation. As a result of my long service, I still have political and military contacts within many factions and on this one we must tread carefully. Once Kidon is involved, no prisoners will be taken." He sighed deeply – "To think we were a nation set up in the shadow of the greatest persecution in history under the Nazis and now we have to be wary of forces within our own country."

They finished the bottle of wine swapping stories and reminiscences of army life, all agreeing that within that period had been some of their greatest life experiences despite the stresses and dangers they had faced. The uniting factor had been the camaraderie they enjoyed being part of a team and reliant upon others in both surviving and accomplishing their missions. They moved inside the villa and Moshe led them to a spacious study lined with bookshelves from floor to ceiling. David noted how many books were biographies and autobiographies of political leaders from all over the world; his eyes were drawn to a who's who of the last century including Winston Churchill, Mahatma Gandhi, George W Bush, Henry Kissinger, Richard Nixon, Margaret Thatcher, Mikhail Gorbachev, Ronald Reagan, John F Kennedy, Charles de Gaulle, Pope John Paul II, Simon Wiesenthal, and Nelson Mandela. There were others that caused him some considerable surprise, including Hitler's *Mein Kampf*, together with biographies of Field Marshal Erwin Rommel, Rudolf Hess, Joseph Stalin, Chairman Mao, and even Saddam Hussein. Moshe noted his interest, saying, "I think it was Napoleon who said, "*The more you know about your enemies the easier it becomes to predict their mistakes*", and although not all of these people are my adversaries, they represent power. Learning about their motives, frailties, faults, desires, failures and triumphs has been a lifelong interest of mine, which has helped in my own life and work."

"Maybe you should go into politics." David remarked wryly.

"Perhaps making the decisions is more dangerous in many ways, than executing them," came the reply, with a chuckle, "although I have found that I often need to convince those in authority of the errors of their plans or of the infallibility of my own. However, when I persuade others to give me the orders or authority I seek, I take some comfort in that they take the responsibility."

"That confirms my thoughts," David countered, "You should be elected to the Knesset."

There were two desks in the room, on which were computers, each fronted by a captain's chair, and a table with an office chair against one wall. Moshe had stated that they needed to compile the commonalities with each victim from the information they held and anything that might link to a motive for their murder. They studied the physical files that David had brought with him and accessed the online data held on Mossad's system, splitting the task of analysing data between them, and sharing their findings. Mehedi began compiling the information they uncovered, cross-referencing the data with research he carried out on his tablet whilst also scribbling notes on a pad. After two hours, David and Moshe listened as Mehedi summarised, "So, the Prime Minister has not yet been consulted on this investigation, yet we know he has recently sealed access to data surrounding the activities of some of the victims for another eighty years; and data is missing from the files, hence we know it is highly sensitive. They all worked in intelligence and all but the most recent victim were militant Zionists, yet all were retired. Three had Eastern European origins and each of them had lost close family in the Holocaust. whilst one was actually incarcerated in the Treblinka Death camp. Four of them, the oldest, were all marksmen and assigned to what are described as 'deadly duties.' Those four have Unit 235 annotated, which I have never come across before nor is there any reference to that on the Mossad files."

Moshe cut in, "Perhaps I can help here, I still have access to the *Nistarot* (divine secret) database, which is a highly secret record of political intelligence. You will not have heard of this because only those who deal directly with politically sensitive areas are authorised to use it. Matters such as controversial decisions or agreements that are never admitted to, recorded, or released to anyone are kept there but, incredibly, it also covers ludicrously mundane issues; even marital indiscretions. As a historian, I am still retained to advise government occasionally and consulted on issues with a sensitive historical perspective. I am one of the few trusted persons with access to this data. I will need to access this through a special security office at Shin Bet HQ (Internal Security). Maybe that will shed some light on Unit 235."

"There is more we have here," added Mehedi, "I have been digging out information on that Nazi friend of Antoni Zielinski; he clearly was quite a character. Listen to this from the file, '*Otto Johann Anton Skorzeny, born in Vienna 12th June 1908 in Austria,* *but with Polish ancestry.'* First point of interest, Zielinski was from Poland! '*He was an adventurer with a reputation for daring and was highly skilled in fencing, fighting duels as a student which earned him a notable facial scar. Adult height 6' 4".* He joined the Nazi Party in 1931, and became a part of the elite SS bodyguard for Hitler known as the Leibstandarte SS Adolf Hitler. He distinguished himself on the Russian front participating in the push to take Moscow in 1941 and was known for his outstanding capabilities as a sniper.'* Link number two is here, because the oldest four of our victims were all marksmen."

David quipped, "Clearly, you have risen above just herding sheep and goats. I'm impressed" earning the retort,

"We Arabs can always be relied upon to get you money lenders out of the mire. If I may continue, "*'In 1942, after being wounded, he developed plans for unconventional commando-style warfare, sabotage, and targeted assassinations via highly trained units operating behind enemy lines. He was appointed commander of an elite special forces unit specialising in covert operations.'"* Link number three, as all four of the victims were involved in covert special operations.

"*'In September 1943, Skorzeny led part of an assault glider force in a daring mission which liberated the Italian dictator, Mussolini, from captivity on a remote, almost impassable mountain top location at Gran Sasso in the Apennines. Skorzeny flew back with Mussolini to Germany, delivering him personally to Hitler at his Wolf's Lair Headquarters two days later. This earned him the Knight's Cross of the Iron Cross with Oak Leaves presented to him by Hitler. In October 1943, Skorzeny headed up a team tasked with assassinating President Roosevelt, Prime Minister Churchill, and Soviet Premier Stalin at a conference being held in Tehran. The operation was aborted due to some advance agents being compromised.'* This last statement drew a whistle of astonishment from Moshe. "*HaShem yishmor,* (Oh my God), can you imagine if they had succeeded, the Nazis could have won the war with even more horrific consequences for the Jewish race.""

Mehedi continued reading. "'*Skorzeny took part in a number of other notable commando-style operations including the capture of the Hungarian leader, Admiral Horthy, taking him back to Germany. In the Battle of the Bulge in December 1944, he led German units dressed in American uniforms, causing disruption behind Allied lines. He remained a committed Nazi after the war, setting up escape routes for former SS comrades through a network known as Die Spinne. After escaping captivity from the Allies dressed in a stolen American uniform, the Spanish government helped him to travel to Spain where he set up a business funded by the Nazis. At this time, he travelled frequently to Argentina, developing influence, and was working on the formation of a Fourth Reich. Skorzeny ended up working directly for President Juan Peron training his forces and being part of his protection where he is rumoured to have had an affair with Eva Peron.*"

David interrupted, "So, where is the link with Zielinski?"

"I'm coming to that," replied Mehedi, "Get this: "'*In 1952, he began working for General Reinhard Gehlen, a former head of military intelligence for Germany in World War II who had been recruited by the CIA to work for them. He was building an intelligence network taking on former SS personnel in a network called the Gehlen Organisation. In 1952, Gehlen ordered that he go to Egypt to help train their military and protect German scientists who were there developing weapons. He assisted in military training of Egyptians and other Arab organisations in paramilitary activities, including one Yasser Arafat, the eventual leader of the Palestinians.*"

David exclaimed, "So we have this man to thank for the activities of that *kelev.* (dog). But, Mehedi, please, where does Zielinski fit in?"

Mehedi looked up, then raised a finger gesturing patience, before continuing, "Now the interesting bit, summarising what I have read. "'*In 1962, the Mossad Director, Isser Harel, sent two assassination squad agents to Spain with orders to either take out Skorzeny, or recruit him. They were Avraham Ahituv and Antoni Zielinski, who had a personal meeting with Skorzeny, persuading him*

45

not only to supply information on former Nazi scientists working for Egypt but to join Israeli Intelligence. The operation was co-ordinated by Rafi Eitan.'"

"I think we should all know Eitan," Moshe remarked – "He was the one who led the Mossad operation to snatch the renowned Nazi war criminal, Adolf Eichmann, from Argentina in 1960. He is quite a colourful character, who later became a terrorist advisor to both the Israeli and the British Government."

Mehedi continued, "I cross-referenced the data between Zielinski and Eitan. Guess what? Both agents were involved in paramilitary activities with Yitzhak Shamir and Menachem Begin, who were, as we know, to become Israeli prime ministers. So here we have links involving one of our victims with those at the pinnacle of power. Rafi Eitan and Antoni Zielinski were involved in a covert intelligence operation in 1968 to steal 200 pounds of highly enriched uranium from a US nuclear fuel plant, returning this to Israel. This was authorised and planned by none other than another future prime minister, Shimon Peres, who, at that time, was in charge of defense and co-ordinating the development of Israel's nuclear weapon capability. So now we have links to three prime ministers."

Then it was David who spoke, looking at his laptop screen in front of him. "I just checked out a little more on our friend, Eitan. In the 1980's he headed up a highly secret intelligence organisation, *Lekem*, originally set up by Shimon Peres in the late 1950's, which was an espionage operation tasked with obtaining scientific and technical intelligence abroad, especially that relating to nuclear development. It appears Eitan authorised many unofficial covert operations which eventually led to the demise of Lekem after an espionage scandal in the USA."

Moshe interjected, "We are really getting in very deep now. Can we go back a step to our oldest victim, this man Zielinski? Can you trace connections between him and the Nazi, Skorzeny, once he had been recruited?"

Minutes later, Mehedi announced, "I think we have it; Zielinski and Skorzeny worked together as a deadly assassination team. Skorzeny would identify former Nazi scientists and their location in Egypt; they would then either kill them or use terror tactics to frighten them. This was an official Israeli intelligence mission known as 'Operation Damocles', headed by Yitzhak Shamir, providing yet another link to our prime ministers."

Both David and Moshe gasped at the revelation together.

"However, this is not all, I have one final piece of intel that may provide the missing link that binds them together." Mehedi paused, looking up triumphantly, placing his notes back on the table with a gesture of finality. "The file confirms that in 1963," he paused for a moment, "Otto Skorzeny joined Unit 235."

5

The Edge of a Precipice

Tuesday 19th May 1931 – 1:30pm

Sportpalast, Potsdamer Strasse, Tempelhof-Schöneberg, Berlin

They approached slowly, down a long straight boulevard lined with armed men in brown uniforms, towards an enormous pillared building with huge red banners draped down the front, in each of which was a white circle containing a black swastika. Hanna's mind was in a turmoil after a whirlwind of events that had left her senses reeling. She was sitting next to Wernher von Braun in the back of a large Mercedes, who intermittently gripped her hand in his for a moment, glancing across to her with a smile. She would return his smile but she felt pangs of unease at her recklessness, and her rash failure to resist events without thinking through the consequences of all that had happened. In the front of the car, a brown-uniformed von Greim was sitting next to the driver, wearing a red armband displaying a swastika, with a military-style '*kepi*' cap.

The night before had been like a dream sequence from a fairy tale as Hanna had been escorted on the arm of von Greim into the dining room, some bowing as they passed, whilst others clicked their heels, raising the stiff right-armed Nazi salute. She felt wonderful as it all seemed so glamorous and nothing like she had ever experienced before. She was introduced to guests either side of where they were sitting at a table, at the end of which another crossed it forming a T. Opposite was a young flyer, Günther Lützow, whom, she was informed by von Greim, was excelling at flight training school. He looked debonair, she thought, and seemed quite charming with slick black hair, a fashionable pencil thin moustache in a stiff winged collar and bow tie. *'My goodness,'* she thought with a wicked giggle, *'there are so many handsome young men here. I think Wernher is going to have to work hard to keep my attention.'*

"Fraulein," Lützow said, taking her hand to kiss, "I have heard of your legendary skills as an aviator, but did not realise you would be so utterly beautiful. We live in a wonderful time and will be liberated by the Führer to live in a new Germany. I want to help in pushing the boundaries of aviation which excites me." He was round-faced with a smooth complexion and she instantly warmed to him. Next to him was an older man with thinning dark hair, and large blue eyes, who was immediately distinguishable as he, like von Greim, was wearing the 'Blue Max' medal at his neck, marking him out as a decorated aviator which immediately drew her interest. The young trainee pilot continued, "Fraulein Reitsch, may I have the honour of presenting one of Germany's greatest flying aces and a legend who has the unfortunate privilege of teaching me, Herr Ernst Udet." The older man smiled broadly, shaking her hand, but before he could say anything, von Greim cut in-

"This old dog had the temerity to score three times more victories than me in the air and still he is thinking of joining our movement!" They laughed and Hanna felt she was with people she could really relate to. On Udet's right was Joachim von Ribbentrop who, von Greim informed her, was a successful businessman. He

bowed stiffly, then took her hand and raised it to his face with a leer, which made her feel somewhat uncomfortable, before introducing his wife, Anna, who seemed more gracious. "I am considering joining the NSDAP," von Ribbentrop stated, "and I think they need me if they want Champagne at good prices," explaining he was in the wine business and that he could see commercial opportunities for Germany under the Nazis. To the other side of von Greim, there stood a thick-set dour man in a brown uniform with a swastika armband, who greeted her with a brief uneasy smile and a short bow, "I am pleased you could attend and I am hopeful you will join us," he managed, introducing himself before von Greim spoke. "I am Martin Bormann, and I look after Party finances so, maybe, we should buy you a proper aeroplane to fly in instead of a glider, *ja?*" He smiled at his attempt at humour and did not introduce his female companion who, Hanna found out later, was one of his mistresses.

At that moment the band, positioned on a stand at one corner of the room, dressed in white dinner-jackets, struck up with the national anthem *'Deutschlandlied'*. Everyone, standing at their tables, clapped as Hermann Göring walked in followed by Joseph Goebbels, both nodding their appreciation. Goebbels was raising his right arm at the elbow, with the palm of his hand bent backwards in a manner that imitated that which the Führer had initiated, being a more relaxed, informal version of the full Nazi salute. A short distance behind Goebbels, a beautiful woman followed with her blonde hair styled fashionably short yet wavy, wearing a diamond tiara, in a long light cream silk dress, gathered at the waist and worn off the shoulder, over which there was a slim white fur stole draped across her upper arms. "*Mein Gott*, she looks like a royal princess," Hanna remarked to von Greim. He whispered to her, "Many say she may well become the First Lady of the Reich. She is Magda Quandt, and is to be married to Goebbels later this year." The two guests of honour approached the top table and stood to one side, allowing Magda to take her seat between them. To Hanna's delight, mixed with some nervousness, the beaming Hermann Göring was immediately opposite her left side, less than two metres from where she was standing. Göring and Goebbels were joined by Heinrich Himmler, wearing his signature pince-nez glasses, in a double-breasted dinner jacket and swastika armband, with his somewhat unimposing wife, Margarete, together with Wilhelm Frick. He was introduced as a Reichstag Deputy who had, until recently, been Minister of the Interior, and who was there with his wife, Elisabetha.

As the meal was served, Göring monopolised the conversation and Hanna found his wit and charm engaging, with his ever-present dazzling smile, displaying his willingness to listen, and openly debate with others. Goebbels was a tad more reserved, although each time Hanna spoke, she felt his eyes upon her, with the same devouring look employed previously. He was, nevertheless, polite and well-mannered with an authoritative bearing which she found strangely attractive. His future wife, Magda, radiated graciousness and warmth, with dazzling, beautiful, wide eyes, taking great interest in hearing Hanna speak enthusiastically about her flying exploits. "Darling," she grasped Goebbels' arm, "Fraulein Hanna is so utterly charming, and courageous too; you simply must publish her stories."

"I would love to," Goebbels replied, "if, of course, she joins our great movement?" He finished his sentence as a question, raising his eyebrows and fixing Hanna with a deep look.

"Oh I am so very interested," Hanna replied, "Perhaps, after I hear Hitler speak tomorrow; if you will have me, of course."

"Fraulein Reitsch, after hearing the Führer, believe me, you will not only wish to join us, but you will implore us to accept you." His eyes had a twinkle as he nodded his head emphatically – "Then I will make you known as the greatest female aviator in Germany, I promise you."

Himmler and his wife remained aloof, passing odd comments between themselves, but apart from agreeing occasionally with

Göring's comments, the Reichsführer-SS seemed icy cold behind his thick, round wire-framed glasses. He rarely smiled and Hanna found him intimidating, especially when he did eventually speak to her – "So, Fraulein Reitsch, you live in Hirschberg, Lower Silesia, in what was wrongly ceded to Poland after the Great War?" Then, more chillingly, "I always do my research meticulously; tell me please, are your parents Aryan German, or are they interbred with Poles or Jews?" It was like a question from an interrogator and she felt his cold eyes bearing deeply into her.

Whilst she felt unnerved by his directness, she was never a person to be supplicant to anyone, with a streak of rebelliousness from her earliest years, fostering a fierce independence of spirit. As she grew up, this had been a source of exasperation to her father, who had called her wilful and wayward, declaring that she would undoubtedly be a highly talented achiever, but utterly ruin the life of any man she married. Frankly, she had no wish for marriage but was attracted to a life of adventure and daring, especially in her flying. She was both quick-witted and often judged to be outspoken, but that made her a strong woman who could hold her own in a man's world.

She found Himmler's question both ill-mannered and distasteful, but she was not going to be cowed by this rather insipid man. Her irritation strengthened the tone of her response – *"Mein Herr*, I shall treat your question with the disdain which it warrants. I hardly know you and, therefore, I shall overlook your impertinence just this once which is, hopefully, not indicative of either your morality or your manners." Himmler looked aghast, his lips pursed and his face whitening in anger whilst Göring bellowed with laughter, spluttering out his reaction.

"You see, Heinrich, you should never underestimate a flyer, especially this one who will be a high flyer with us, I hope. Even I have done my homework better than you and I know her father to be an extraordinary talented German doctor who has shown interest in joining our Party. Fraulein, please forgive his directness and accept that some of us know how to treat a lady." His humour diffused the tension as others joined in the laughter whilst Himmler grimaced and appeared furious. Göring then began asking Hanna about the aerobatics he had heard she was able to perform in a glider, comparing them with those he had used in powered flight to his advantage whilst in combat.

In the centre of the room, Wernher was surrounded by some of the most extraordinary men he had ever met, relishing the conversation about physics and the pushing of scientific research boundaries. He was completely absorbed by extraordinary possibilities that were being explored, not only in his own field of rocketry, but also in nuclear science. Karl Becker was dominating the conversation talking enthusiastically about the need for Germany to lead the world in weapons research. He was a well-built man, having a military bearing with a neat moustache. "I believe in National Socialism," he stated, "As a nation, we have lost our way and this movement promises strength of leadership, stability, and gives a direction for a new and more powerful Germany. Hitler has pledged that he will rip up the Treaty of Versailles, rebuild our strength, and regain our pride, demanding respect from the world. For this purpose, we will need new weapons to defend ourselves and take back territories stolen from us after the Great War. I have spoken to one of Germany's most eminent physicists, Werner Heisenberg, who is heading up research into quantum physics, and he says that atomic energy could potentially be harnessed to create a weapon of unimaginable power. I am gathering some of the leading scientists to work together in developing technology that will make us invincible."

Otto Hahn, who was in his fifties with dark but greying swept-back hair, interjected, "This is potentially the terrifying reality of what physics may deliver to us and an area I am working on. As a human being as well as a scientist, I am concerned that we are on the edge of a monumental new area of science with potentially horrifying implications in the hands of the wrong people." He appeared a little conspicuous and dishevelled in an ill-fitting dark lounge suit and spotted bow tie.

"My dear Otto," Becker responded, "this is exactly why we need this research, to protect Germany, and make us so powerful that our security cannot be threatened. The Führer desires peace with strength and when he becomes leader of Germany, we will need to bend our minds to his great purpose. Another war like the last one in which I fought, with appalling slaughter, is unthinkable. Science is our greatest ally in our endeavours to become invincible."

Walter Dornberger, a stocky man with receding hair and a genial disposition, added, "I was also in the last war and now I am pioneering research into weaponry to ensure we never suffer the humiliation of defeat again. My interest is in liquid-fuelled rockets, and one day, these will not only give us military strength but the ability to travel into space. Hitler is the only leader who is speaking out clearly for Germany to be strong. We must all unite and restore our national pride. This is why we need fresh new minds at the forefront of science, drawing on the talent and energy of young people like Wernher von Braun here, who has already made his mark in research at the Berlin Institute. I think there is no doubt that he could become a leading light in his field with the opportunities which will flow from the new Germany led by the Führer."

Wernher felt a surge of pride to receive such recognition, and was infected by the enthusiasm being displayed for the growing National Socialist movement. He had witnessed the extraordinary growth of the Nazi Party, which had come from being a minority Party of relative obscurity in the 1920's to hold the second largest number of seats in the Reichstag by 1930. Hitler's popularity was increasing and many felt that he was inevitably going to become Chancellor. "Herr Dornberger," he began, "I am passionate about rocketry and I have been since I was a child. The future destiny of mankind lies in space travel when we will visit other planets and herald the dawn of a new era of exploration. This is a dream of mine but I know I can make space flight a reality. Liquid fuel for rocket propulsion is the way ahead. Last year, I assisted a respected physicist, Dr Hermann Oberth, in developing a liquid-fuelled rocket engine which we successfully fired. The possibilities are endless and yes, you could have weapons too, or aeroplanes that travel at incredible speeds. We are on the verge of a new age." He laughed nervously, breaking off as he realised his voice had risen with his enthusiasm.

Sitting opposite Wernher, was Ernst Hanfstaengl, a stocky man with thick wavy black hair wearing a round Nazi Party lapel swastika badge. He stated, "Your passion is a credit to you and you are exactly what we seek for the new Germany. I am a business-man and investor. I admire your work, Wernher. This research could, perhaps, assist us in developing more powerful weapons which will be needed in a new and stronger Reich. I will consider investing money into your project. I am sure Herr Dornberger would welcome your input."

The dinner concluded with a speech by both Goebbels and Göring exalting the aims of National Socialism, the restoration of German pride, and the need to re-arm, backed by the strength, vision, and fortitude of the Führer whose whole life was dedicated to Germany. Göring had drawn much laughter in his speech although, Hanna noted, Himmler stayed stony-faced throughout. He had concluded his remarks by saying, "For those of you who are God-fearing Germans, I have good news for you. I have just returned from meeting the Pope and told him that we stand against the Bolshevik swine in Russia and the Jewish menace in Germany, and he said to me, '*Gott be with you.*' Ach so, we now have the Almighty on our side – With God and the Führer working together, we are unstoppable!" There was a roar of applause, and laughter echoed round the room.

Goebbels had spoken next, finishing with the words, "Tomorrow, in the Sportpalast, we will listen to one of the greatest leaders we have known in history. I urge all of you who have not yet heard the magnificent words of the Führer to be there. He is already a legend but soon he will be known as legendary and become immortalised for the glorious triumphs he plans for the Fatherland." His voice had risen, then he opened his arms in a dramatic welcome gesture. "The Führer, guided by Providence, and with his iron will, calls you to join our swelling numbers and become part of our titanic mission to make Germany invincible. *Sieg heil*." His arm shot out in the Nazi salute, which he held out stiffly as another storm of applause erupted, many rising to their feet also raising their right arms. Before they left the restaurant, Göring had leaned towards Hanna, holding his hand to his mouth as though sharing a secret, looking to right and left, before saying, "You must not say a word, but we recognise talent in the young and we will be calling upon you, Fraulein, to help us create and test new aircraft; our secret heh." He smiled, and she felt flushed and joyful that she should be so recognised.

An exuberant Hanna joined Wernher shortly after the dinner, escorted back to the cocktail lounge by a smiling von Greim. "I hope I may entrust this delightful lady to your good care as I must leave you." Then, he bowed to Hanna – "Would that you had a chaperone to protect you from this Romeo," he joked, before arranging to collect them the following day. They decided to have a final nightcap before retiring and both were exhilarated by their experiences of the evening. They sat in a corner booth and Hanna related to Wernher that Hermann Göring had promised she would be given a role in the new air force that would be created when the Nazis came to power. Wernher, in turn, informed her that he was to be invited to join a team under Walter Dornberger to carry out additional rocketry research. They were excited about seeing Hitler speak the following day and both agreed that the NSDAP seemed to offer wonderful opportunities both for Germany and their careers. Wernher, euphoric after the evening and emboldened by having consumed several glasses of wine, turned to her as she was talking animatedly about her hopes for the future. Looking directly into her eyes, he placed his fingers on her mouth, and as she stopped speaking, he leant forwards. Almost before she knew what she was doing, he kissed her, and she felt herself responding eagerly. His arms were strong as they went around her and she forgot their surroundings momentarily as she surrendered to the passion growing within. As he caressed her neck, he whispered, "I think we should finish our drinks somewhere less public," and she heard herself reply, instinctively, "Oh, Wernher, that would be divine." Seconds later, he led her from the bar, his arm linked in hers.

In the elevator, he embraced her once more, feeling her slim, athletic body pressed to him, responding to his passion, and desiring more. Once inside her suite, after he had placed their drinks on a table, she shied away from his open arms, giggled, then raised her glass in a mock toast, "Herr Greim warned me about you, calling you Valentino. Here's to you, Rudolf, and keep your distance or I may just succumb to your disgraceful attention." She downed her drink in one, before walking seductively towards him, allowing the strap of her dress to slide off her shoulder. "So come on, lover boy, live up to your reputation." This time it was Hanna who wrapped her arms around him, feeling his obvious arousal against her as she moved against him, her mouth seeking his. "*Gott*, Hanna," he breathed, "I cannot resist you." His hands were reaching around her undoing the back of her dress, until she wriggled free and her breasts were bared to him – "I want you," she had whispered as she reached for him, abandoning herself to her passion, "I think this day may be a beginning for us."

That had been the night before, and now she was disorientated, her mind in a whirlwind of contradictions, excited by the future, yet full of apprehension. As she gazed through the car window, seeing the swastika banners, the smartly paraded men in brown uniforms, she also felt that she was part of something new and momentous, yet, somehow, on the edge of a precipice.

6

Where There Is No Peace, Nothing Flourishes

(The Talmud)

Sunday 16ᵗʰ May 2021 – 4pm
Steele Tennis Club, Herzliya, Israel

"Deuce!" called the umpire as David walked slowly back to the baseline, clenching and unclenching his fist. He did not like losing but he knew his mind was not as focussed as it should have been, having been distracted by the revelations from the Mossad files they had studied the previous day. He knew he was dealing with an issue that clearly went to the highest levels of power in Israel, with sensitive implications. His next serve went wide, and his second was returned with force by his opponent, which David returned high, anticipating the inevitable smash that followed. "Advantage Benowitz!" came the stark voice of the umpire. A ripple of applause followed from the spectators and David was furious with himself. He was throwing away a winning point for a club title he had held for two years in front of a crowd because he could not concentrate. Then he recalled the words of his grandfather, Ehud, a proud man who had fled Hungary in 1944 as a teenager with his family when the Nazis invaded. "Never surrender your self-respect even when you lose, but, even better, never allow yourself to be in that position. You must be ruthless." When David was a young man, his grandfather, a former promising tennis player in Budapest, had never missed a match that David played in, giving him sound words of advice and motivation. He looked across the net, fixing his opponent with a steely look, then winding himself back, he sent a searing serve just off the centre line to score an ace. Raising his fist in the air, David was now resolute and this man facing him, although half his age, was not going to prevail. His next serve was returned fast but David already knew his opponent's weakness, correctly anticipating his aggressive over-confidence, running forwards to the net to be wrong-footed by a lob, then, as Benowitz desperately reached the ball, hitting a poor backhand, it was David's turn to hit a smash.

He heard the first shot just as the umpire uttered the words, "Game, set and match, David Stern," and the ground just by his feet echoed with a ricochet as he dived to the floor, rolled, and ran low towards his bag. There was a scream from the crowd and panic as another two shots rang out and he felt the sharp pain in his upper arm as the impact sent him sprawling. Dimly, he heard more shouts as a security man ran past him, drawing his weapon, heading towards the embankment adjacent to the court bordering the road above. Despite the pain, David's instincts kicked in and he rolled to one side then crouch ran the last few feet to his bag, extracting his trusty Glock 19 semi-automatic pistol. There were two further shots before he also reached the cover of the embankment, and threw himself down flat. His left arm began throbbing and blood was streaming down to his hand. Searching upwards towards the white building overlooking the court, he scanned each of the balconies on the upper floors, his military training drawing his eyes to where he would have positioned himself as a sniper. Within two seconds he saw a flash and ducked as the dirt and stones in front of him erupted with the impact. In a millisecond, he had raised his weapon in both hands despite the searing pain from his left arm, firing rapidly, the sound almost like an automatic weapon such was the rapidity of each shot. He was renowned for his skill as a deadly marksman, and he saw clouds of dust as his shots hit the balcony, and then the glass behind shattered as he loosed off fifteen rounds in quick succession. Then there was silence, apart from the cries of some of those who had not yet escaped the court area. He had four shots remaining in his magazine, and he waited unblinking as his eyes remained fixed on the building opposite. The security guard was about five metres to David's left, also pointing his weapon towards the building, but he had not yet identified the target. Then there was a brief flash of sunlight reflecting off his assailant's rifle; David's pistol was already trained and, after firing a further three shots, he saw an arm fly backwards. The sound of sirens could be heard. "Stay down!" he shouted back to the spectators remaining. His arm was dripping blood onto the floor, but his eyes remained fixed on the spot where he had last seen movement. Seconds later, he heard shouts behind him. "Armed police, no-one move!" He remained as he was until he felt the muzzle of a gun in his back. "Drop your weapon and identify yourself."

"I am with Mossad. My name is Major David Stern. My ID card is in my bag. I think I have hit the *mamzer* (bastard) on the 4th floor opposite." The helmeted policeman ordered a colleague to retrieve David's bag whilst two more trained their automatic weapons on the place where the gunman had been. Shortly thereafter, having seen his ID, the man who had first addressed him knelt down, shook his hand, and extracted a dressing from his uniform kit. "I think you need to put a tourniquet on that," David said calmly despite feeling the pain intensify. He was grateful for the shot of morphine he was given and then, as police continued to cover the building opposite, he was ushered from the tennis club to a waiting ambulance. Before he left, he turned to the young officer. "You may need to keep this quiet and not file a report. Get your commander to speak to the Director of Mossad. He must not talk to anyone else because I am under his direct orders. You will understand I can say no more." Thirty minutes later he was being whisked into an examination room at the Tel HaShomer Hospital in Tel Aviv.

After three hours, he discharged himself despite having been told he needed to rest after surgery under local anaesthetic to repair a deep flesh wound. His x-ray showed that part of his bone just above the elbow had also been damaged, and he was informed that further surgery may be required. He looked up at the military doctor with a grin; "I have had one attempt to ruin my left-arm serve with an RPG making a mess of the lower part, courtesy of the Second Intifada. Now, I will have another scar to make me look even more impressive on the tennis court." His arm was tightly bandaged and he asked for help in putting his shoulder holster on. His mind was now set on finding out why his investigation had resulted in him becoming the target, although he knew they were delving into sensitive areas. The police officer who first attended to him had come to the hospital and offered to give him a lift back, briefing him that when they had reached the balcony where the assassin had been, whoever had been there had left or been removed. However, there were blood stains confirming that David had hit the person, which gave some solace.

Back in his car, David made a call, "How is Galilee? Your office, tomorrow morning at 9am?" The response from Moshe was given with an unrestrained tone of excitement. "I have finally solved the crossword regarding 2 down and 35 across." David responded that he had suffered from an injury whilst playing tennis, and may need to escape for a few days, to which the reply was that a room would be booked. He then tapped a text to Mehedi inviting him for breakfast "where we first met at 7:30am." The response confirming was virtually immediate, with the quip that he had to attend to the sheep and goats first. David sent an emoticon of a camel in reply. He then made a call to the Director on his direct number, who answered immediately. "David, how are you? I am sorry to hear of the attack today and, of course, you can be relieved from the assignment." David replied he intended to continue and that he was making headway but that, in the light of what had occurred, he wanted to go to ground for a while. "After the assassination of Joseph Abrams, that takes the number of deaths to five, and including the attack on myself today, seven successful or attempted assassinations. I need to stay out of sight and act with some stealth."

"How did you find out about Abrams?" the Director asked with a surprised tone, barely hiding his irritation.

"I regret that my sources, for now, must remain confidential," David replied and, before the Director could ask further questions, he concluded the exchange by saying, "I will be in touch and brief you fully in due course." He then terminated the call but had a sense of unease in that the Director had clearly known about the murder of Joseph Abrams, yet had not communicated this to him. As he retired to bed, taking some additional painkillers, he double-checked his security system, which alerted him if there was any movement within five metres of the house, backed by lighting that came on illuminating any movement in his gardens. Despite all he had been through, he slept soundly and could not help but feel a thrill of anticipation tinged with foreboding from knowing he was on the edge of something very big indeed.

At 7:30 the following morning, Mehedi walked into the Hotel Seasons to join David, who was waiting in the reception dressed in a light beige safari-style jacket hung loosely over his left arm, which was in a sling. "*Ya'Boozdinak!* (Holy crap) What the hell happened to you, David?"

"An unexpected shot in a game of tennis." David responded with a sardonic smile. "Some *arsim* (low life) trying to take me out. I was nearly victim number six. I need to go underground and not be seen. You, my shepherd boy, are now unofficially invited to assist in protecting me. I only hope you can improve as I found you too easy to take down when we first met."

"Listen, you Jewish invader of my land, the only way I will help you is in return for a decent designer suit. You see, we Bedouin learn quickly how to behave like you. Do we have a deal?" Mehedi grinned at his friend with mock triumph, extending his hand. David shook it firmly, "You *lisanger* me. (Screw me over) OK, I will supply you with one *Dior* suit for you to wear on your camel." They laughed as they walked into the dining area and ordered breakfast. David had prepared a list of items they required, which included *IWI Tavor TAR-21* automatic assault rifles, a car with smoked glass windows, a false ID card for Aman military intelligence, and IDF uniforms, "Preferably allowing mine to outrank yours," David added with a smirk, stating that he also needed more ammunition for his Glock 19 pistol.

"You want your pound of flesh in return for my suit, then. I think you forget, I was a lieutenant colonel, so maybe I should give the orders huh?" Mehedi retorted. "I can get all these within twenty-four hours."

David suggested they use Moshe's house as an HQ, adding, "There is something major going on here and we are dealing with an issue that goes to the highest levels of power in our country. Someone, somewhere, does not want this looking into any further and clearly there is an attempt at some kind of massive cover-up." They finished their breakfast and David cleared it with the manager, showing his Mossad ID, that he could leave his car there under cover and out of sight.

At 9am, they were being welcomed by Moshe Gellner, who sat them down in his study, ordering coffees which were brought in by his housekeeper. After David had informed him of the shooting, Moshe immediately agreed that his house could become the covert HQ of operations. "There is some kind of sickness within this country, our homeland, for which former serving men have paid with their lives, and we must find it, and root it out," he stated with emotion in his voice; then, after a pause, "*Chaverim,* (my friends) I can tell you that Unit 235 is on the *Nistarot* intelligence database. It was originally known as 'Unit A', which had a remit to trace Jewish nuclear scientists towards the end of World War Two. This was set up by none other than our first Prime Minister, David Ben-Gurion, and was initially commanded in the war by one future Prime Minister, Yitzhak Rabin. I can reveal that it was a top-secret unit tasked with ensuring, by whatever means, that Israel acquired nuclear weapons. It was then named after the essential fissile ingredient for creating the atomic bomb known as Uranium 235. The man directing the unit after the war was Isser Harel, who subsequently became the head of Intelligence when the state of Israel was created. This was the unit involved in the mission referred to as *Operation Damocles* in 1962 to assassinate former Nazi scientists, which, by then, was being commanded by Yitzhak Shamir. Their operational remit shows they have the authority to carry out assassinations independently from Kidon, the normal unit assigned to such tasks. They had two further roles; first to ensure that our work on our own nuclear weapon was unimpeded and kept secret, and second, to spearhead any action against those posing a potential nuclear threat to Israel by any means necessary. Now the interesting bit; the database blocks any further access to Unit 235's activities after 1962 without the direct authority of the Prime Minister."

David whistled, then stated, "As I suspected, we are on the edge of something with huge ramifications here."

"There are three more points," Moshe added, "First, the limited information accessible confirms that some were recruited to the unit from the former nationalist para-military group, Irgun. Former Irgun agents were implicated in a plot to assassinate Chancellor Adenauer of Germany in 1952 and one of those agents was the oldest of our victims, Antoni Zielinski. Second, who do you think was controlling these Irgun agents? It was another future Prime Minister of Israel, Menachem Begin."

"Oh wow," David exclaimed, exhaling deeply and shaking his head, "We really are hitting the jackpot here."

Moshe continued, "Point number three is that the final and only reference to Unit 235 on the Nistarot database after 1963 is that it was brought under the control of Lekem by Rafi Eitan in the 1980's. Whilst Lekem no longer exists, there is confirmation that Unit 235 remained operational but no command structure is identified."

On the wall was a whiteboard and Moshe began making headings across it reminding David of the briefings he had sat through from him many years before. He had a brilliant analytical mind and would forensically examine information before putting in place military planning. As Moshe made notes on the board, he spoke, "So, we have six men who have been attacked, died mysteriously or disappeared, excluding you, David." He wrote their names on the left side of the board in a black marker pen. Then he wrote what he described as "uniting factors" across the top as headings. Intelligence – Eastern Europe – Zionist – Marksmen – Unit 235 – Political Connections. He turned to Mehedi. "We have concentrated on the information David dug out on the first four victims, and Berkowicz who fought them off, but we have not yet closely examined the file of Joseph Abrams. As you knew him, it is, perhaps, best that you access his file and see what you can find." Mehedi opened his tablet and began tapping as David and Moshe considered the key information to place on the board. David had his laptop open, which he kept referring to as they built up the intelligence they needed.

"Why would Unit 235 be such a closely guarded secret?" Moshe mused.

"Perhaps it is because we have never confirmed or denied Israel's possession of a nuclear weapon to the world." David suggested, adding, "I have never really fully understood our so-called '*policy of deliberate ambiguity*' on that one. We have nuclear weapons, so, for them to be a deterrent, why not admit it? Iran is attempting to obtain them; Libya tried, and Saddam Hussein was close to developing them in Iraq."

"Ah yes, my friend," Moshe responded, "and look what happened to Colonel Gaddafi of Libya and Saddam Hussein in Iraq. Now, perhaps I am beginning to overthink this but Egypt also had a nuclear weapons programme under President Abdel Nasser. He promised to cease development after Egypt's defeat in the Six Day War of 1967 but there were rumours the programme continued in secret. After his death in 1970, which some say was suspicious and not a heart attack, Anwar Sadat took over and was initially a hard-line opponent of Israel. However, his stance altered, and he signed the Camp David Accords with Menachem Begin. He angered the Arab world by pursuing his own policies without consultation or sufficient consideration for the Palestinians. Many in Israel were also angered because Begin ceded back the Sinai Peninsula to Egypt which we had occupied in the Six Day War in 1967. During and after this time, we know Sadat pursued continued nuclear arms development covertly; but remember, he was assassinated in 1981. Perhaps, a pattern is emerging here? Following his demise, Hosni Mubarak became president and took a surprisingly moderate stance against Israel whilst ceasing any nuclear weapons development. Coincidentally, he became fabulously rich during his tenure of office whilst pursuing a policy of peaceful relations with Israel. Is there a thread here linking the methods of assassination or intimidation carried out under Yitzhak Shamir against former Nazi scientists who were working for Egypt? There were rumours that Hitler had authorised a highly secret nuclear weapons programme although investigations after the war seemed to refute this."

"We should always doubt history." David remarked sardonically. Then, with a growing sense of anticipation that they were on the edge of a discovery, he added – "I'm going back to what you said about Unit 235 earlier. You stated a role of the unit was to prevent, by any means necessary, any nuclear threat against

Israel. Four of the men, who have, we presume, all been killed, were marksmen, whilst Otto Skorzeny was not only a trained assassin and a former commander of elite special forces, but also highly experienced in covert military operations. Clearly, someone is trying to cover something up and the nuclear connection could be the key factor here. However, that still leaves a question mark over the last victim."

Mehedi cut in, "Not anymore, my two *amoretz* (numbskulls), the file for Joseph Abrams is not annotated Unit 235. I checked the source access, and there is evidence the file may have been cleansed of data in the last week, so I have done some digging and it transpires that Joseph was working undercover in Iraq in 1980 posing as an English nuclear scientist. Abrams had been to Cambridge studying nuclear physics and was not only a gifted student but an ardent Zionist. He spoke out passionately, arguing against any halting of Jewish settlements of the occupied territories which he regarded as belonging to Israel by sacred right. He was recruited by Mossad as a student and underwent training in Israel. After passing out with a first-class honours degree, and completing a further year in atomic research, he was accepted to work on the Iraqi nuclear project in 1980 with a cover story that he had an Arabic background. He was assigned by the Iraqis to work at their Osirak Nuclear Reactor development near Baghdad. He identified an Egyptian scientist as the key player in developing the uranium enrichment programme with the aim of creating a bomb. Now, here is the first link; when cleaning the file, they carelessly missed the mention of Unit 235 which is spelt, rather than numbered, in the report, hence it would not have been picked up by a sloppy database search. The record states, as a result of intelligence reports generated by Abrams, and on the direct instruction of Prime Minister Menachem Begin, Unit Two Three Five (spelt) were instructed to eliminate the chief Iraqi scientist, Yahya El Mashad, in a Paris hotel on 14th June 1980. The operation was led by Colonel Tzadok Berkowicz, who was a military attaché at our Paris

Embassy, carried out under the auspices of Lekem and planned by our old friend, Rafi Eitan. You will recognise the name, Tzadok Berkowicz; he is our only surviving victim."

Moshe scribbled on the board and began circling certain words including Lekem, writing Eitan's name below Otto Skorzeny's. He then stated, with a long sigh, "We appear to be unearthing one hell of a Pandora's box here. Anything else?"

"I seem to dig up all the critical elements here," Mehedi replied, "Abrams was then recruited to work for Lekem by Rafi Eitan following the June 1980 assassination of the Egyptian scientist. Unit 235 was, therefore, operating under Rafi Eitan's direction at this time, and on the direct orders of Prime Minister Menachem Begin. On 29th May 1981, Abrams took some leave and travelled via the UK to Israel where he provided further intel on the Iraqi nuclear weapons programme. One week later, on 7th June 1981, the Israeli air force bombed the Osirak reactor complex, resulting in international condemnation. Incredibly, Abram's cover was not compromised and he actually returned to Iraq. He worked with them developing a secret nuclear fissile material production process alongside Dr Khidir Hamza, who later left Iraq to go to the USA. It was Hamza who gave evidence of Iraq's nuclear capability to the US government, giving a purported reason for the Second Gulf War. Here in Israel, we assisted in the deliberate rubbishing of Intelligence given by him after the invasion of Iraq to cover up the incredible reality, which I'm coming to. Abrams left Iraq in March 1991 to study for a PhD at Cambridge but had given invaluable information to Unit 81. This, as you may be aware, is a highly secret unit which gathers scientific data which may be useful to Israel. Abrams passed information to Unit 81 about the secret location of an Iraqi fissile material production facility. In March 2003, before the defeat of Saddam Hussein's forces in Iraq, he accompanied a Unit 81 mission to a secret location and Abram's file confirms they removed 50 kilos of plutonium. That is a sufficient quantity for the creation of several major nuclear bombs!"

"*Oy gevalt!*" (staggering) David declared, "The bastards were manufacturing WMD after all."

Mehedi added with quiet finality, "I was part of the protection squad at that time but none of us were aware of what was going on, other than we were escorting Abrams on a secret mission, not disclosed to the coalition forces, to find evidence of WMD. However, we were told there was nothing discovered although the scientific unit that we accompanied took containers away in trucks for what we were told was evaluation."

"Perhaps President Bush and Prime Minister Blair were right after all," Moshe remarked dryly, "but, with the curse of hindsight, maybe even they didn't know it!"

7

The Hammer or The Anvil

Tuesday 19th May 1931 – 1:50pm

Sportpalast, Potsdamer Strasse, Tempelhof-Schöneberg, Berlin

The wide podium in front of them had a long red banner spanning the front with a black swastika in a white circle below the centre. At either end there were side podia with round golden wreaths encircling more swastikas, whilst on the rear wall behind the dais mounted against a curtain backdrop was an enormous eagle clutching the Nazi emblem in another wreath. Armed guards, with handguns in holsters, lined the base of the podium, with *Kepi* caps and red swastika armbands, some holding neo classical-style Nazi banners with eagles above. The building was packed with people but they had front-seat positions. Von Greim, dressed in a smart brown uniform and jackboots, leant over to Hanna and Wernher, saying, "We are over-subscribed with over 15,000 having being admitted, despite the maximum capacity of 14,000. There are loudspeakers mounted outside and we expect thousands more, such is the appeal of the Führer." People were crowded onto upper seating areas too, which circled round the huge building.

The lower seating area was divided down the middle with a long, raised catwalk stretching from the rear. To von Greim's left, Ernst Udet sat with Günther Lützow, the dashing young flyer Hanna had met the evening before. He was wearing a dark double-breasted pinstripe suit and, Hanna noted, a Nazi Party lapel badge.

Hanna's concerns over her utter abandonment to passionate spontaneity the night before had now melted into anticipation as she sensed she was on the edge of an epic, historic moment. There was an incredible air of both awe and expectation as lines of brown-shirted men began forming on either side of the catwalk. Hanna observed younger boys in short trousers, with neckerchiefs and daggers, forming a line in front of the dais. Wernher, noting her interest, remarked, "They are the *Hitler-Jugend*, which is the youth arm of the NSDAP. They demonstrate extraordinary skills of organisation which I admire. We need leadership, direction, strength and efficiency at this time of political chaos."

"Oh Wernher, you sound like Herr Goebbels." Hanna giggled, "The next thing you will do is raise your right arm." He smiled at her, and her heart beat faster, sensing the knowledge of their shared intimacy that she could see reflected in the look he gave her. He patted his arm around her shoulders, then squeezed her hand.

Suddenly, the murmur of the crowd was interrupted by the thump of heavy drum beats; then lighter drums joined in with a roll then a beat, then a roll once more. Two men in uniform appeared, one in each of the side podia, lifting up brass horns; then, in unison, they played a short triumphal fanfare. This was followed by a military band at the rear of the building, which struck up the '*Horst Wessel Song*'. A sea of right arms was raised as the band marched two abreast down the central walkway above where they were seated. They split at the podium with the drummers remaining on one side, and the brass section on the other. As the music faded, the drums maintained a rhythm, and spotlights swung across the crowd, passing their beams overhead in a crazy circular fashion before concentrating at the rear. People stood in their seats peering backwards, desperate to see the entrance of the great, legendary, visionary. The drums came to an abrupt halt, and for a moment there was silence. There was a brief hiss from the speakers, then, a loud guttural voice, which Wernher instantly recognised as that of Joseph Goebbels. *"Mein Deutsches Volk, meine Damen und Herren, der Führer, Adolf Hitler! Sieg Heil!"* The last words were announced with a strong dramatic pitch, and the audience erupted with a huge cheer as the base drums began a beating rhythm, then the band played the *'Hitlernationale'*, a version of *'The Internationale'*, recently adopted by the NSDAP, which gave Nazi relevance and appeal to the working classes.

An even louder roar erupted as the solitary uniformed figure of Adolf Hitler mounted the steps to the walkway at the rear, standing solemnly for a moment, with his right arm stretched out stiffly. Then, he lowered his arm and turned to face another section of the audience, raising his arm again, repeating this until he had given a salute to all sectors of the massive auditorium. He began walking forwards, bending his arm at the elbow every few seconds with the flat palm of his hand facing back in the popular salute he had adopted as a gesture to crowds. The crowd began chanting, *"Sieg Heil!"*, adding to the spectacle, as Hitler, his black hair neatly parted, walked slowly but purposefully forwards followed by a number of others a few metres behind. Hanna recognised Hermann Göring, Heinrich Himmler, and Joseph Goebbels but asked von Greim to identify the others. "The man immediately behind the Führer is Rudolf Hess, Hitler's adjutant, who you have met. He is in front of Ernst Rohm, who is Chief of Staff of our protection force, the SA." Hitler had now reached the front but before he mounted the dais, he paused, turned and began shaking hands with, and talking to members of the *Hitler-Jugend* who were positioned alongside where he was walking. The music changed to the National Anthem, as the party finally climbed the steps, taking seats behind Hitler as he approached the microphones positioned in the centre of the long podium. *"Du Lieber Gott*, Wernher, he is magnificent," Hanna exclaimed breathlessly, "He exudes power and authority; I can feel it." Wernher felt it too and was surprised at how he was already now in awe of this man despite having previously wondered why others were so fanatical about him. Yet, there was no doubting that even before Hitler spoke, he just had an incredible charisma radiating from him which Wernher had never seen in anyone else before. His stance, his look, and the way he moved were somehow captivating, and the young scientist found his own reaction inexplicable as he, too, felt the undeniable urge to stretch out his right hand in the Nazi salute.

Adolf Hitler stood with a defiant look in his eyes, his arms folded, and a resolute expression on his face as he looked to right and left at the sea of cheering people, but did not speak. It was as if he was almost challenging them and the crowd loved him for it even before he had uttered a word. Then, he slowly raised his right arm, stretched it out, lifted his head to look upwards and outwards, before shouting, "*Sieg Heil!*" The audience exploded again, and his salute was returned with a huge cheer. He stood back with his hands on his hips, his chin thrust forwards, then moved to the microphones again. He waited, for a full minute, as if absorbing the moment, then raised his right hand, extending his finger, and the watching people were mesmerised. He began quietly, yet his guttural, gravelly voice was electrifying; "*Das deutsche Volk wurde verraten und dieser Verrat muss gerächt warden*" (The German people have been betrayed and that betrayal must be avenged.) His voice rolled the r's, pronouncing each syllable slowly, giving an emphasis to their meaning. He paused, yet again, then began waving his finger from side to side as his voice started to rise in pitch, stressing this would never happen again, not ever, because Germany would regain its strength and no-one would dare impose themselves against the iron will of the new Reich. The tempo of his words increased and people began rising from their seats as his speech roused their passion and admiration. He spoke of the betrayal of the Treaty of Versailles and that Germany would tear it up, revoke its terms, seizing back the territories plundered by other nations. "He is just incredible," Wernher gasped, placing his hand on Hanna's shoulder.

She turned to look at him, seeing his eyes fixed on Hitler, taking in every word. She, too, felt inspired, as though the years of Germany being the underdog in Europe were about to be swept away. This Führer seemed so confident, assured, and spoke out with such certainty about restoring Germany's pride.

"Wernher, he is intoxicating," she whispered back to him. "I have never heard anyone speak like this." By now, the atmosphere was at fever pitch, and Hitler was interrupted time and again with roars of approval from the audience. He assumed various postures, from standing with his hands on his hips, to dramatic arm gestures, emphasising his words with his fist time and again. He spoke of a "babbling democracy" lacking direction, crying out for strong leadership, which needed someone to assume authority.

"Providence has chosen this time and I will assume the role chosen for me and, when the time comes," he paused, and the crowd went silent, "there will be one will which commands, a will which has to be obeyed, beginning at the top and ending at the bottom." His voice rose again, becoming loud, commanding, insistent – "This will be the expression of an authoritarian state united behind that will; a state where the people are proud to obey." Then, after placing his hands on his chest, "I must obey the call of destiny and I will likewise be obeyed without question when I take command. *Ein Volk, ein Reich, ein Führer, ein Deutschland!*" His right arm shot out in the Nazi salute and, as one, the people rose from their seats, shouting their approval, their arms extended, with the chant, again and again, "*Sieg Heil!*" - As the crowd hushed once more, Hitler moved on to talk of the imperative need to re-arm, re-construct, and re-strengthen. "We will embrace new weapons, rebuild our pride, and because there will always be nations against nations, we will protect Germany and smash to pieces anyone who gets in our way. We will work with our scientists who lead the world and harness their efforts into one single mission, to create weapons that make us invincible. Our weapons will be ferocious, and, if tested, our armed forces will be victorious and destroy anyone who foolishly resists. We can either be the hammer or the anvil and I confess that we will be the hammer." He stood back as rapturous applause followed. Then he advanced to the microphones again, his arms outstretched. "Today, in this great moment, it is time to join us and seize our destiny. Now is the time, our time, a time for the true German *Volk*, with our pure Aryan blood, to triumph as the superior race." He began smashing his right fist into his left hand with each point. "Join us, *meine Kameraden*, fight for us, and with our iron will, we will forge a new Reich which will last for a thousand years. With our unshakeable resolve, a new Germany will rise from the mire of democracy which will annihilate all opposition. Germany will never be vanquished, but march, united to victory." The final words rang out to another roar as his head dropped in finality, then raised again, as his right arm extended. The crowd erupted, with Hanna and Wernher not only standing but, for the first time, both raising their arms to return the salute in utter reverence to the extraordinary magic that Hitler had wrought with his speech.

Two hours later, they were sitting back at their hotel, enjoying an afternoon drink of Pimm's No. 1 Cup on the bar terrace, awaiting von Greim, who was to escort them to the station. They were both enthused by their experience and spoke of their belief that National Socialism appeared to offer a better future for Germany, heralding wonderful career opportunities for them. "The Führer spoke of building new types of aircraft," Hanna said excitedly, "I will prove to the world that women can fly every bit as well as men; in fact, I will show them we can be better."

"I think the world is already finding out about you, Hanna," Wernher replied, "with you setting altitude and glider endurance records. That is why Göring wanted to spend time with you at the dinner and did he not say that they needed you? For my part, the

Führer clearly said that they wanted scientists to help create new weapons. This is fantastic because rockets will play a big part in the future of warfare and I am working at the forefront of that technology."

Von Greim, still in uniform, joined them smiling broadly. "I have news for you both, having spoken with Hermann Göring and Karl Becker. Göring believes that the NSDAP will be the largest Party in the Reichstag within a year, and there is little doubt that shortly thereafter, Adolf Hitler will become Führer of Germany. Göring already has major influence and he has arranged for a place to be made available to you, Hanna, within one of the secret air training schools for powered flight starting at the beginning of next year. I did warn you that we are creating the best opportunities for our youth under the NSDAP." He turned to Wernher, "You, my young Romeo, seem to have made quite an impression on your dinner guests. Ernst Hanfstaengl has even spoken of you to the Führer himself and you are to be financed in your research to develop rockets with military capability. All of these things will, of course, be dependent upon your commitment to, and membership of the Party."

Hanna quickly responded, "Robert, you scoundrel, I never accept pre-conditions, and my skills speak for themselves. If you want me, my terms are simple; you will respect my freedom of conscience and I will work with you. I think I will be an asset to you but only on my terms." She surprised herself with her audacity but she was headstrong, which had contributed to her single-minded drive to pursue her love of flying.

Von Greim laughed loudly- "*Mein Gott*, the Führer will love your spirit and I am happy to accept your terms." He kissed her hand then turned to Wernher – "I can only say your own path will be easier if you do join the Party because those without membership may be excluded from some positions when we come to power."

Wernher responded, "I think that Hanna's principles match my thoughts although I am attracted to all that National Socialism stands for. I want Germany to shrug off the outrageous conditions imposed by the Treaty of Versailles, assert ourselves internationally, and strengthen our economy. I am totally enthralled with what I have heard today and I think Hitler has the answers but I will wait until he assumes power before I commit to the Party. I am drawn to the Führer with all he represents and I will work with you. I am honoured if the offer of financial support for my research remains, and when our political future is more assured, I will join your Party."

"Bravo, Wernher," Hanna exclaimed, "You have spirit and I like that." She squeezed his arm and he looked back at her – his eyes held hers for a moment, and she felt the butterflies she had experienced the previous day. Von Greim sipped the beer he had ordered and appeared unperturbed by Wernher's response; then, after lighting a cigarette, he said calmly, "You are the youth of Germany representing our future and I admire your strength of will. We welcome your input and I totally understand your position, but let us unite in this great crusade to rebuild our divided country under strong leadership." He raised his glass and they did likewise, sensing a bond of purpose between them.

In March 1932, Hanna gave birth to a daughter. After their parting, she had not met Wernher again for three months. They initially exchanged letters once, but their correspondence concentrated on the new and exciting opportunities facing them, with a relaxed agreement to meet again at some future point, without a commitment to a date. Whilst she knew she had been enraptured by Wernher, she had no illusions; she was not in love with him. In late August 1931, however, Hanna decided she had to write to Wernher a second time:

"Mein Lieber Wernher,

    How wonderful our brief time was, about which I have often smiled recalling the prophetic words of von Greim when he warned me of your charms. I regret nothing as I have always been impulsive, or, as my parents would say, wilful!

However, sometimes there are consequences in life and before I reveal to you what I have to tell you, I want you to understand that I do not wish to become a burden to you nor do I seek anything from you. I am and always will be independent but, for once, I need to think of what is best for the future and, this time, not only for myself. I am with child and I have decided that I cannot assume the responsibility of the role of mother. It is not just the scandal, which concerns me little, although I have to think of my parents' position, but my heart is in my flying and I could never be a good mother. I take risks every day with my life and, in that, I only have myself to think of, which may appear selfish, but I could not do so if my feelings were compromised by the worry of a child.

I have told von Greim that I have gliding commitments in early 1932, and so he has arranged for me to attend the powered flying school later in the year. I do not wish my pregnancy to be known about nor to allow it to interfere with the incredible opportunities now opening to me. I trust you will respect the decision I am taking, which will protect your position from anything which may harm your career also."

As he read the letter in his Berlin apartment, Wernher felt a tinge of sadness, yet he knew that if he wished to pursue his passion in rocketry, he had to remain detached. He wanted to be seen as a person following the family values of National Socialism and this situation could jeopardise his prospects. If she could make the necessary arrangements, he made a commitment to himself that he would financially contribute secretly, albeit keeping his identity, as the father, hidden from the child.

In October 1931, Hanna sat down with her parents and faced them with the news in a business-like way. She was not overly maternal and knew, even before talking to her parents, that she could not dedicate herself to motherhood. Her father was furious, saying that she had brought the family into shame but, after calming a little, he drew solace from the fact that she did not intend keeping the child, agreeing that they should organise a secret adoption. She met Wernher at Grunau Flying Club that October where she informed him about the arrangements that had been made immediately after she gave birth. She was to disappear for a while after Christmas with an illness, which would account for her absence from flying. They both warmed to each other as soon as they met and, despite the seriousness of the reason for their meeting, it was not long before they were excitedly discussing their future hopes and dreams. They made a pledge to stay close and Wernher joked it may not be long before he had developed a rocket-powered aircraft and all they would need to find is someone foolish enough to fly it. Hanna had responded that all she needed was someone with sufficient imagination to design the aircraft, and she would fly higher, faster, and for longer than anyone else. Together, they agreed, they were part of the youth that represented the future of Germany with a new direction under the firm leadership of Adolf Hitler.

They discussed a name for the child and, on the birth of her baby, Hanna's wish was that her daughter be named Alicia Webber.

8

A State Turning on Itself

After two days' rest, David was feeling well enough to don the IDF uniform that Mehedi had brought for him the day before. Despite the pleas of his former commanding officer, Moshe Gellner, to rest for longer, his mind was set on this mission which he had not even informed the Director of Mossad about. A sixth sense was telling him that no-one could be trusted within his normal chain of command and that greater forces were at stake than those he had ever experienced before. They were all aware they were on the edge of something with massive implications beyond those they had uncovered to this point, and some answers must lie with Colonel Tzadok Berkowicz, the fifth victim, who had fought his attackers off.

They had re-visited his file and both the paper and the electronic record were clearly annotated U 235. There were entries about his service to Israel throughout his military career from 1974 until 1999, when there was a gap of three years, although the electronic file recorded that some content had been removed in 2015, under the orders of the office of the prime minister. Mehedi had the file up on his tablet, and Moshe requested that he look up the records of his service immediately prior to the missing period. Mehedi tapped for a second, then announced, "In 1998, he was working for Aman on a highly classified project dealing with UAV or drone development in conjunction with Lockheed Martin in the United States. He was attached to the Israeli Consulate in New York and was covertly stealing nuclear weapon information through a network of US Intelligence officers under the code name *Judas*. Most of his official work was carried out at the Lockheed facility in New York City where they were developing systems that could not only guide drones but which could interfere with aircraft and missile guidance systems in flight. The last entry was in June 1999 when he was recalled to Tel Aviv for a briefing. Then, nothing." Mehedi looked up, his hands in an open gesture.

"And the next entry after the gap?" Moshe asked

"There are no records until 2003 when he turns up, guess where? In Iraq working with a unit under the command of one Colonel Joseph Abrams, our victim number six."

"We need to pay this Colonel Berkowicz a visit." David stated tersely. "I have a feeling we may need to take the IWI Tavor assault weapons which our Arab friend here stole along with the car and uniform. I think plundering is in his blood, Moshe."

"Listen, you *schlemiel* (incompetent fool), if it wasn't for us inventing algebra, you Jews would never have learned to count your shekels. Fortunately for you, I also have my uniform with me, which means I outrank you, Major, and it seems natural to me that we Arabs give you Jews the orders. I need to protect you as you seem to have a habit of being shot." The growing banter reflected the deep respect which they already held for one another. They had agreed that they could not go through official channels to gain access to Berkowicz, as this may leak to those they now suspected were operating from inside Israeli Intelligence. Equally, they had decided that David should have no further contact with the Director of Mossad until they had uncovered more, as they already knew they were uncovering matters that even the Prime Minister of Israel had not wanted revealing. This whole business went right to the top and they did not know who was involved or to what extent. Clearly, they were operating in sensitive areas affecting the state of Israel itself and there were people out there who would stop at nothing to prevent their seeking further information. They also recognised that the home of Berkowicz must now be well protected, but they were experienced in overcoming such obstacles.

Two hours later, they were both in uniform and had travelled to Tel Aviv. David had parked their car, a black Kia Niro with heavily tinted windows, on Mizan Street, seventy-five metres from a house that they had identified as belonging to Berkowicz, surrounded by high walls with an upper outdoor patio area bordered by railings. As they had passed, they had noted curtains blowing around the upper doorway, which made their planned access easier. There was a police vehicle parked to the front for protection, which they knew was standard procedure after any attempted armed attack, especially if it involved any current or former senior military personnel. They had already studied the area on Google Maps before driving there. A house to the side had an adjoining garage from which Mehedi had stated he could gain access to the upper patio area, if David distracted the guards to the front. "You can't even hit a tennis ball with that arm wound, never mind climb a wall," he grinned at David in the dark. "We Bedouin are used to climbing in the hills after you lot stole our best land."

"Maybe you should be wearing a *shemagh* (Arab head dress) instead of a beret then." David responded; then, more seriously, "Once I have established he is home, I will buzz your mobile, and as soon as you have secured the place, buzz me." They had noticed a rear garden entrance set in the walls, which they knew would be locked but which they planned would be opened to allow David access. "*Shalom*, wish me luck." Mehedi shook David's hand before retrieving his assault rope gun from the rear seat, and strapping his Tavor weapon to his back. David sauntered down the centre of the street towards the police vehicle, deliberately ensuring that he would be noticed so as not to arouse suspicion. As he approached, he could see there were two men inside but before he was within ten metres of the car, the door opened and the police officer shouted, "Halt, place your hands on your head and state your business." The door opened on the other side and another policeman exited, raising his handgun and pointing it at David, who responded, "I am Major Rafa Talman with Aman and we are checking on the Lieutenant Colonel. He is one of ours and we look after our own." The first officer, who had shouted, climbed out of the vehicle and walked towards David. "No-one is allowed near this house nor are any visitors permitted. Where is your ID, Major?"

David informed him it was in the breast pocket of his tunic and kept his hands on his head whilst the officer retrieved the plastic ID card. "All I am ordered to do here is merely check the Colonel's security and ensure that he is safely inside." Having glanced over his ID, the policeman responded, "OK, drop your arms. He has not left here since the attack but I think, from what I hear, he can take care of himself."

David smiled, "Yes, he is a *totach*" (tough one), as he slipped his hand into his pocket, activating the buzz to Mehedi. "Keep your eyes open, or maybe he'll turn his automatic weapon on you." He kept them talking for a few minutes on the tedious side of carrying out "nurse-maid" guard duties, sympathising with their task.

As soon as he felt the vibration on his mobile, Mehedi climbed an olive tree that was next to the garage by the house, from where he could see the roof terrace. It was about twelve metres long with some loungers and chairs on it, but it was deserted. A security light lit the front but left the rear of the terrace in shadow. He climbed up a wall and onto the roof of the garage, which was about three metres from the slightly higher flat roof terrace. He took his assault rope gun and adjusted it for the distance; then, a brief hiss as he discharged it and the end of the rope curled around the rail, locking itself with a ring-catch device. He inched his way across the gap, noting that he could now see the police car and David talking to the officers in the street. Traversing the space in seconds, he hauled himself up, peering across the terrace; no-one there but the open doorway suggested that Berkowicz was still up. He hauled himself onto the rooftop and paused, listening. He could just hear the sound of a TV broadcast coming from the house and, as he edged closer, working his way through the shadows, he crouched low, pulling his Tavor from his back. This was the type of activity he had trained for and carried out many times whilst in the IDF, yet still the adrenalin flowed and his heart thumped, enhancing all his senses. He now lay flat, edging ever closer to the sliding door through which he could see the flickering images reflecting off the wall from a television. He heard a cough, then a curse, from a male voice, which was close by, just inside the doorway. He was now by the door and slowly raised himself up, placing his weapon at eye level. Moving with cat-like stealth, he strained his eyes, finally catching sight of an elbow just in view over the arm of a chair, tantalisingly close, yet far enough to enable his target to retrieve and fire a weapon. He was in the doorway now, and the curtains wafted in his face in the slight night breeze. There was a TV news bulletin underway, and the anchor woman was announcing a report from near Jerusalem where violence had broken out. As the sounds of shouting crowds and gunfire increased the volume, Mehedi seized his chance. He moved stealthily and a head came into view, he took two strides forwards, only then aware of a machine pistol being reached for by the man's side as he hissed out the words in a raised voice, "Mossad – Do not move! On the floor, now! Release the weapon or you will die!" He held the barrel of his gun against the man's neck and watched him slowly release his hold on his pistol. Mehedi spoke again in a harsh lowered voice, "Do not make any sound and move off the seat." The man moved forwards to the edge of the seat, as Mehedi kicked the machine pistol out of reach, barking, "I am with Mossad; you will survive...but only if you do as I say! Get on the floor. Are you Tzadok Berkowicz? Nod your head for yes." Berkowicz did so as he lowered himself to the floor. "Are you alone in this house?" The man nodded again as Mehedi made him lay flat, before frisking him. "I will say again, you will survive if you co-operate. I will kill you if you do not. I am here on a matter of national security. Now listen carefully. Your life is in grave danger and we can help you, but only if you help us. *Ata mevin*? (Understand) You may now speak."

The answer came with a question. "I hear you but who are you? Who do you work for?"

"I told you. I am with Mossad. That is all you need to know. You will do what we ask or you will die. I do not know you, so it is of no matter to me." Mehedi spoke the words with a merciless edge as was instinctive from his years of working on covert missions with the military, where he had learned to detach himself from any emotion.

Mehedi allowed Berkowicz to raise himself into a sitting position, then they had a brief exchange during which Berkowicz explained his wife had vacated the home because of the attempt on his life. Mehedi then bade him to obtain the key to the rear entrance to where he took him at gun point, buzzing David as he did so.

In the street outside, David had been chatting amiably with the two police officers, sharing some of his own genuine experiences of defending those he had looked after from attack, before bidding them good night and asking them to inform Tzadok, if they saw him, that old comrades were checking in on him. He sauntered slowly back down the street but as he disappeared into the darkness, he slipped down a side road and circled round to the rear wall of Berkowicz's house. As he approached, his mobile vibrated, and moments later, he was admitted, briefly grinning to Mehedi, who had his weapon trained on Berkowicz, before following him to the upper lounge. David then sat opposite a shocked-looking Berkowicz as Mehedi went to the window at one end of the room, holding his weapon against his body as he peered out. The police vehicle remained outside and all appeared quiet in the street below.

David leaned forwards, "Tzadok, we have no argument with you and can help protect you if you co-operate. The uniforms we wear show our true ranks in the IDF. I am a *Rav Seren*, genuinely, and now work for Israeli Intelligence. My colleague, like you, is a *Sgan Aluf* and the reason we are here is because the attack on you is one of several that have taken place recently against former intelligence operatives. You are unique because you are the only one who has survived."

Berkowicz looked up, now beginning to display some defiance, "You *kelevs* (dogs) break in here and expect me to co-operate. All my life I serve Israel and two *autists* (morons) disgracing our uniform threaten me. Listen, *ahabal doofus* (dumb ass), I was in the air force, flying F-4 Phantoms in the Yom Kippur War, whilst you two were in diapers. You do not frighten me. I have killed people in defence of my country and will do so again, if required. You better be well connected because my family were brought here from Poland protected by the great Menachem Begin long before he was prime minister. I have powerful friends inside government and you will regret threatening me."

"Then, Berkowicz, hear me out," David hissed back at him. "Why do you think you were targeted? It is because of who you are; and a few days ago, I was a target too." His voice had raised; he shrugged out of his military jacket, revealing one sleeve of his shirt pinned up, beneath which his arm was encased in a dressing which had blood showing through. "We are both decorated for our military service and, trust me, killing is not unique to you. I care about my country too, but some people have gone further than others in pursuing a more militant agenda. Assassinations come easy to them, but justification may not be so easy. Your Menachem Begin attempted to kill the German Chancellor, Konrad Adenauer, in 1952; that is the kind of action which endangers our country; when we no longer value life, but kill indiscriminately in pursuit of our goals. That was the policy adopted by the Nazis, and, Colonel, I will kill, if necessary, to prevent us becoming like them." He drew his Glock 19 from a holster inside his jacket, pointing it towards Berkowicz at eye level. "Do not screw around with me. I know what you have been part of and scum like you bring shame on our country as you assassinate anyone without conscience. For me, Israel would be better without you, so please do not give me a reason to pull the trigger. Now, we know you were part of Unit 235, let us start there."

Berkowicz looked up sharply, visibly surprised, pulled a face then sighed, all the defiance disappearing. "*Ya ilahi!* (Oh my God) I was waiting for this day to come. Is there no end to this nightmare?" He placed his head in his hands for a moment and David nodded a brief smile to Mehedi, who was standing near the window occasionally looking out to check the police vehicle below. Berkowicz raised his head, "You are wrong, more wrong than you know. Yes, I was a Zionist once, proud of the nationalist values we espoused. After my stint in the air force, I had no hesitation in joining Aman because I wanted to protect our country, which was constantly under threat. I took part on secret operations, which required the elimination of those who were endangering the security of Israel. Then, I began to realise we were going too far as more and more people were targeted, sometimes merely to cover up what we had done. We were guilty of state-sponsored killings but in our early days we had no choice. Look how the world stood by whilst we became the victims of the Nazis. However, it all began to go too far and what were exceptional cases of so-called justified assassinations in the early days became the norm. There have been more than 3,000 killings outside of any war, sanctioned by the state of Israel, with no court involvement or justice. There are strong opposing forces within this country today, quite apart from the Palestinian issue. We have the ultra-right wing who will stop at nothing to achieve their aims, and many other factions which take a more liberal approach, thank God. I fought for values that I fear we are losing, although I, too, have blood on my conscience." His eyes saddened as he spoke, "As I get older, I am wracked with guilt and then I try to address this with self-justification. I have watched, with dismay, the way we have behaved in our dealings with the Palestinians, who I, too, once thought of as enemies. But now, now... we seize land and property, plundering as we posture on the world stage. Despite my life in the military, which presents too many contradictions, I recognise we are failing our own nation, which not only comprises Jews but Arabic people, who make up more than twenty per cent of our population."

"Praise be to Allah!" interjected the sarcastic voice of Mehedi from by the window.

David's tone had softened as he lowered his weapon, "Forgive the interruption from my colleague, who, despite his uniform and rank, is a Bedouin Arab." He threw a sidelong glance at Mehedi, who raised his middle finger in a not unexpectedly rude gesture. David continued, a sixth sense telling him that Berkowicz could be trusted. "Perhaps, we should start again. My task is to uncover what is behind the attacks on Intelligence personnel and, like you, that now includes myself. My name is David and my instructions are from the highest level but I am now acting independently and covertly, as a result of what I have uncovered, until I investigate further. I would like to seek your help in tracing the cause of what I believe is a symptom of our state turning on itself." He placed his weapon on the floor beside him and extended his hand.

9

The Hand of Providence

The Mercedes turned slowly off Wilhelmstrasse, following two *Zündapp KS 750* motorcycle and sidecar armed escorts through huge iron gates, adorned with a golden eagle and swastika, into a long courtyard at the end of which was a grand entrance behind a towering portico supported by four round columns. On either side of the entrance stood two guards in black SS uniforms with silver epaulettes and white gloves, beside whom were two enormous bronze classical figures on plinths, one carrying a torch, and the other a sword. Hanna Reitsch gasped as they approached, "*Meine Güte*, Robert, it is awe inspiring, just magnificent." She now worried whether she had dressed appropriately, having selected a simple black jacket with white piping down each side, giving it a military style, over a matching skirt and shoes. She turned to von Greim, placing her hand on his,. "I owe all this to you. If you hadn't met me all those years ago at the Grunau Flying School, I would never have had all the incredible opportunities that have opened to me." He was attired in the mid-blue Luftwaffe uniform of a *General der Flieger* (air marshal), with gold patterned epaulettes, a white belt with an eagle in the centre, over trousers with white stripes down the side, and highly polished black boots; his blue *Pour le Mérite* medal was at his neck. He turned to her, smiling, squeezing her hand for a moment. "My dear Hanna, you have succeeded through your own dedication and extraordinary flying skills but the opportunities come as a result of our Führer, a visionary who has inspired our nation. Today is about you and you richly deserve this recognition." As the car drew to a halt, she looked up at him, shrugging her shoulders with a giggle, and, as she did so, she could not help but feel an attraction for this immaculately uniformed officer.

She had stayed the previous night at the *Hotel Kaiserhof*, recalling another occasion ten years before, when she had spent a passionate night in the arms of a man she had agreed to never see again after the birth of her child. Hanna seldom saw her daughter, who was being well looked after, but sometimes wished she could feel the bond of motherhood she had heard others talk of. Somehow that seemed to have passed her by as she was caught up in the whirlwind development of her flying career, now entrusted with testing some of Germany's most advanced high-performance aircraft. As she had arrived at the hotel, having been picked up from the station by von Greim, she had been presented with a bouquet of flowers and greeted by the manager, who bowed deeply. He informed them in an excited tone that he had just received confirmation that they would be joined for dinner by none other than Reichsmarschall Hermann Göring himself. She already knew that her immediate superior, Ernst Udet, would be there. He was now Luftwaffe *Generalluftzeugmeister* (minister for procurement and supply), but had more interest in aircraft development, working closely with Hanna at the Luftwaffe Research Centre at Rechlin. However, the prospect of dinner with the Reichsmarschall was completely overwhelming and she turned to von Greim to express her delight. He had smiled broadly then leant over to her, holding his hand over his mouth in a mock gesture of secrecy. "I can also announce that there are two more surprise guests; one is your old gliding friend Heini Dittmar, but the other will be revealed later." Hanna had known Dittmar well for a number of years as a fellow award-winning glider pilot. He had been the first to cross the Alps in a glider, and she had also shared a gliding expedition with him in South Africa. He was now, like her, working as a test pilot. She was bubbling with anticipation and grabbed von Greim by the arm- "Robert, how can you? I demand to know who else will be there or I shan't attend," she exclaimed in a display of exaggerated petulance, causing him to laugh loudly, before responding,

"If you stand up the Reichsmarschall, you will suffer the consequences. You will have Uncle Heine (nickname for Himmler) knocking at your door with his SS men and I'm not sure, after your last encounter, you will wish for his company."

"That man is utterly odious," she responded – "He looks like a frog, has no decorum, and flaunts himself like a pantomime peacock."

Von Greim looked at her sharply for a moment, then, in a low urgent voice, "Never, ever speak like that in public, Hanna; you are my friend but even I could not protect you if your words were reported. We must all be careful," after which he excused himself, saying he would return before the dinner to escort her. For the first time, she felt a moment of ice cold within, sensing real danger in his words, which haunted her.

That evening, she had worn a long, clinging, satin silver evening gown with a fur stole her mother had proudly given her, saying Hanna would have more use for it now that she mixed with the elite of German society. She felt ill at ease appearing so ostentatiously, which was not her way, but placated herself knowing that the Reichsmarschall too loved dressing flamboyantly. At 7pm, von Greim knocked at her door, which she opened to reveal him appearing unusually suave, standing in a smart dinner jacket, with his *Blue Max* medal at the neck beneath a winged collar. "You look breathtaking, Hanna," he exclaimed, and she felt the sincerity in his words. She put her black velvet evening bag over her shoulder, "OK, *Herr General*, take me down. I will surrender to your every whim to avoid Uncle Heine." In an unusually flirtatious and unexpected gesture, he patted her bottom in rebuke, guiding her from the room.

In the palatial restaurant, they were greeted by the maître d', who guided them to a table facing the band on the opposite side, taking their positions on the stage. They were in an alcove at the top of the room between two pillars in front of which a crimson rope hung from polished brass supports, cordoning them off from other guests. At the table, rising to greet them, was a smiling Ernst Udet, in the uniform of a Luftwaffe officer with a white sash, containing a gold line in the centre running diagonally from his shoulder over his tunic, adding panache to the look. "Hanna, I would not have recognised you," he exclaimed, bowing to kiss her hand.

"Why thank you, Ernst, just because you take no notice of me in my *Kampfanzüge* (fatigues). I am still a lady despite being able to outfly you." There was laughter as Champagne was ordered, and a growing anticipation could be felt in the room as news had travelled that Göring was to attend. As the glasses were being set, von Greim excused himself, saying he had to meet someone, winking at Hanna, who felt a ripple of trepidation. However, she could not have prepared herself for what followed. She turned as Udet muttered, "Ah, we have company," and watched von Greim weaving his way past tables, followed by two others. Then her heart leapt a beat as she saw the face that she had so often thought about, dreamed of, even yearned to reach out to, an impulse which she had resisted. Wernher von Braun stood out in a royal blue dinner suit with black silk lapels, smiling and waving to some who knew him, as he approached. He appeared utterly self-assured and despite having increased in weight since she had last seen him, he was still devastatingly attractive and she recognised the dangerous flutter within. Her head bowed in embarrassment as he approached the table, although she noticed he was wearing the small round swastika Nazi Party badge on his right lapel.

Von Greim spoke first, "May I introduce Untersturmführer SS (Lieutenant) Wernher von Braun."

His slightly quiffed hair and dancing blue eyes dazzled her as he took her right hand in his to kiss it, then squeezing, almost imperceptibly. "Hanna, it is good to see you again and your reputation as an incredible flyer has spread across all of Germany." His voice was deep, sultry, almost seductive as his deep eyes met hers, pausing for a moment before addressing von Greim, "Oh, and please, no need for ranks here; I am a scientist not a soldier." He turned to another, who was a young man in his late twenties, dressed a little untidily in a lounge suit, with thick unruly hair, who had followed him to the table. "May I present Carl Friedrich von Weizsäcker; he is a member of a prominent noble family and the son of the State Secretary to the Foreign Office, no less. More importantly," he said with a broad smile, "he is a fellow scientist, or should I say, physicist." Weizsäcker nodded to each guest in turn, as he shook their hands, appearing a little uncomfortable.

Hanna, despite initially feeling overwhelmed, could not contain her outspoken nature, for which she had something of a reputation. "I see you became a member of the Nazi Party, and to show your loyalty, you have joined the ranks of the SS run by that revolting little man, Himmler."

"Hanna!" interjected von Greim sharply in a reprimanding tone.

Wernher raised his hands in a surrendering gesture, "Sometimes, we have to recognise what we need to do in order to get things done."

At that moment, Heini Dittmar appeared in a black dinner jacket and red bow-tie. His hair was thick, slightly long and a little unruly. Hanna adored him as a friend, with his cheeky demeanour and lively, daring nature, which had driven them both to compete against each other in their gliding, each pushing the other to go higher, faster, or longer in terms of endurance. They had shared danger and built up an enormous respect for each other born out of mutual admiration. "Hanna, it is wonderful to see you and I am delighted you are getting recognition for your outstanding work. I think that you should be denied the accolade you are to receive, as a woman, but, clearly, we must accept the wishes of our Führer."

"Heine, you never could stay in the air as long as me," she retorted, "however, your hot air would make you more suited to ballooning perhaps!"

There was laughter as the band struck up the popular marching song, 'Erika', receiving a cheer in response from the diners, many of whom, including Hanna, joined in the words, encouraging the rest of the table to do the same. Many in the room raised their right arms in the Nazi salute and, as Hanna did likewise, Wernher, who was now sitting next to her, whispered in her ear, "I see you are a good and enthusiastic Nazi too," smiling at her mischievously, as she displayed a disparaging look.

"At least I never joined the Party," she responded, "but I do so admire the Führer." He patted her shoulder and in spite of herself, her body tingled. Years had passed, yet she had often thought of him and felt, even now, drawn to him, despite the passage of time.

Suddenly, the band stopped playing; the atmosphere was electric with anticipation and all eyes turned to the large double-door entrance to the dining room where the manager of the hotel had appeared. He raised one finger in the air then nodded to the band and immediately they began playing the 'Horst Wessel Song' and everyone rose from their seats. The manager stood to one side and a beaming Hermann Göring entered to a storm of applause. He was wearing a white dress uniform, with gold braid suspended across his chest, a blue-coloured sash, and a ceremonial sword hung at his waist. He too wore his *Blue Max* medal at his neck, whilst he carried a blue and gold baton in his right hand, which he raised, acknowledging his greeting. Hanna turned to Wernher, "*Alter Schwede*, he looks magnificent, like royalty."

"That, *meine Liebe* Hanna," he replied, "is because that is precisely what they have become." This was said with genuine admiration in his voice as he joined in the enthusiastic clapping. The Reichsmarschall smiled to right and left, gesticulating to some he recognised, stopping occasionally to kiss the hands of female guests who curtsied to him. As he approached the cordoned area, guided by the manager, he stopped, came to attention, then clicked his heels smartly, raising his right arm. The men at the table responded, and Göring walked to Hanna, bowing deeply, "Fraulein Reitsch, I am honoured to join you for dinner and, on behalf of the Fatherland and the Reich, I salute your courage and flying skill. You are an inspiration and your contribution to our great Luftwaffe has been outstanding."

Hanna glowed with pride, yet also felt overwhelmed, "I am proud to serve, *Herr Reichsmarschall*, and it is my honour to follow our great Führer, *Heil Hitler*." Göring turned to the manager – "I wish to order the finest Champagne in honour of my wonderful dinner companions. I trust you have stock of Dom Pérignon. This was the only reason we invaded France, to secure the best Champagne for the Reich," prompting laughter from all those at the table. Göring continued, "You know we now have appointed weinführers in each region to co-ordinate supplies. Sheer genius, don't you think? My friend, Otto Klaebisch, is weinführer for the Champagne region and his job is to keep my home wine cellar stocked at *Carinhall*." Dinner commenced with cream of lobster soup, whilst the orchestra was playing popular dance tunes. Göring sat at the head of the table flanked by Hanna, next to whom sat Wernher and von Weizsäcker. Opposite to them were Ernst Udet, von Greim, and Heini Dittmar. The conversation was lively and initially led with stories swapped by Udet and Göring of daring flying duels over the trenches in France during the Great War. Then the Reichsmarschall had asked Hanna about her work as a test pilot, showing real interest in her comments about the need to develop more tactically superior aircraft, which could make a real difference in the war. She spoke directly and critically about the vital need to achieve air superiority.

"We need faster aircraft with more powerful weapons which can out-perform the British Spitfires and Hurricanes. Planes like the Stuka are too slow and have limited capabilities. Sure, it is the best in the world for dive-bombing and accuracy, but it is vulnerable. The Me 109 is a wonderful fighter and a joy to fly but takes too long to turn. Speed and weapons are the keys to victory, *Herr Reichsmarschall*. I hear Goebbels giving fine speeches about our invincibility but where are the new weapons and aircraft we hear rumours about? I regret that hot air will not win the war."

Von Greim raised his arm, as if to interject, but Göring waved him away, laughing loudly, "I knew of your fearless reputation in the air, Fraulein Reitsch, but it appears you have no fear on the ground also, not even of me. I am delighted you are so direct because few people are, and it shows your honesty. This brings me to one of the reasons I wanted to meet with you all informally. Hanna Reitsch is correct that weapons will win the war, combined with our iron will, and our natural superiority as a pure Aryan race. You, *meine Herren*, and Fraulein Reitsch especially, have all proven yourselves in our great endeavour and made outstanding contributions to the Reich. However, there is one amongst you who has unlocked a secret of the universe; a secret which will unleash terrible and terrifying forces. This is found at the very edge of scientific research in a programme you will not have heard of. *Uranverein*" (literally Uranium Club). "Remember this, because we could have in our grasp the most powerful bomb ever known to mankind; a weapon which…" the Reichsmarschall paused, adding drama to the moment, "could annihilate whole cities, laying waste vast areas, in a single explosion of unimaginable ferocity. Imagine how wonderful this would be if we had such force. No-one would ever dare stand in our way and the war would be over. One man at this table holds the key. *Bitte*, Carl von Weizsäcker, tell our guests a little of this."

All eyes turned to Weizsäcker, who looked around a little nervously, but then seemed to regain his composure, sitting up and addressing them directly in a self-assured manner. "Here in Germany, we have been spearheading research into possibly the most exciting discovery ever in the field of physics. As the Reichsmarschall says, our programme has become known as *Uranverein.*" His eyes lit up as he spoke the last word, stressing each syllable with reverence, and gesturing with both hands. He paused as if to add more drama to the moment before continuing, "Uranium is a heavy metal discovered in 1789 and is a tiny component of most rocks. It was formed millions of years ago and is found in various forms known as isotopes. We know that when uranium decays, it produces enormous heat and this decay is the primary source of heat inside the earth. There are two main isotopes inside the earth's crust, Uranium-235, and Uranium-238. The latter makes up by far the largest portion inside the earth and decays very slowly, yet that is sufficient to heat the earth's crust. However, it is the incredible potential of Uranium-235 that excites the scientific community. The nucleus of the U-235 atom comprises protons and neutrons. When the nucleus of a U-235 atom is hit by a neutron it splits in two (fissions) and releases energy in the form of heat, with two or three additional neutrons resulting. These neutrons cause the nuclei of other U-235 atoms to split, releasing further neutrons. When this happens over and over again, many millions of times, an enormous heat is produced from a relatively small amount of uranium."

"*Herr* Weizsäcker, *bitte*," Göring cut in, "our guests are not interested in a physics lecture. Please get to the point more quickly, preferably before the end of dinner, so that I can still be awake to enjoy some fine Cognac." There was a chorus of laughter around the table whilst Weizsäcker winced and pushed a hand through his thick hair, attempting to hide his exasperation.

"Forgive me, *Herr Reichsmarschall*, I am a scientist and will attempt to be brief. In simple terms, when the atom of Uranium-235 is split, which we have found we can achieve by bombarding the nucleus with neutrons, it triggers a repeating reaction yielding an incredible energy which we call nuclear fission. More neutrons are generated during this process, which means the chain reaction self-perpetuates and grows in magnitude. The result, we believe, would enable us to create an explosion of a magnitude never before witnessed on the earth. I have been conducting experiments with Professor Hahn and Professor Heisenberg here in Berlin, and we have created the scientific model for a bomb hundreds of times more powerful than any explosive. One single bomb could wipe out a whole city." He stopped, aware that his voice had risen with excitement.

Hanna interjected enthusiastically, "This is what we need, not only to win the war, but also to ensure the glorious Reich is protected, whilst securing peace."

"That is precisely why," Weizsäcker continued, "I have just returned from visiting the renowned physicist in Denmark, Professor Niels Bohr, with the head of *Uranverein*, Professor Werner Heisenberg, in order to show him we have this capability, proving this through the results of our experiments. I told him that it was now inevitable that Germany would win the war, warning him we would develop this bomb and use it. Why? Because Niels Bohr is respected throughout the world and he can verify to his contacts in Britain that we have the means of developing this terrifying capability, having seen evidence of what we have already achieved." He turned to Göring, "This may serve to save many thousands of German lives and accelerate our victory."

The Reichsmarschall threw open his hands to the table, "Simple then, we need to examine how best we can deliver this weapon, once developed. This is where your skills in rocket development may come in, Herr von Braun. Perhaps, we may need new aircraft to drop the bomb, which the extraordinary test-pilot skills of Fraulein Reitsch and Herr Dittmar will give us. We will discuss this with the Führer tomorrow after Hanna Reitsch's award ceremony."

As she listened, Hanna sensed the danger and tried to prevent matters escalating, having been aware of him from the moment their eyes had met. Wernher had changed in that he was more confident and self-assured, with a commanding, poised, presence. He was full of smiles, and conversed easily with those at table, talking animatedly about his achievements in rocketry, which he said held the key to the future of mankind. Hanna was absorbed by him, despite the Reichsmarschall's attendance and, although she felt dazzled, Wernher's presence had eclipsed the occasion, but in a most delightful way. He had turned to her, placing his hand over hers with an almost imperceptible squeeze as he drew her to lead the conversation by inquiring about her latest highly dangerous assignment. This, she explained, involved attempting to cut the wires of barrage balloons with the wing of an aircraft. As she spoke, she shivered to his touch and throughout dinner she felt aware of his closeness. When he had asked her to dance to a Viennese waltz, she knew she should decline but could not. His soft, yet powerful voice was mesmerising, and he spoke easily to her, as if there had been no intervening years, as they danced. She felt herself melting as their bodies touched and she sensed that he too was aroused, yet neither spoke of their feelings nor alluded to their mutual attraction. They concealed their intimate awareness by sharing how their lives had changed and developed with their careers, which, they agreed, were due to the inspirational guidance and leadership of the Führer.

There was a certain inevitability in what followed after the dinner ended and the other guests parted. The Reichsmarschall had excused himself slightly before, saying he needed to prepare for the following day's meeting with the Führer. He had bowed deeply to Hanna, kissing her hand, and offered her an invitation to come for a weekend at *Carinhall*. Wernher asked Hanna to join him for a cocktail in *der Friedrich Keller* lounge as they had done so many years before. Little had changed except a portrait of Adolf Hitler adorned one wall surrounded by a red, black and white gathered banner. They moved to an alcove, sipping their cocktails, and he looked deeply at her, his blue eyes making her shiver, and before she could stop herself, she leant towards him and their mouths met. She surrendered, eagerly responding to his kiss, allowing herself to be pulled tightly to him. "I want you so much," he whispered urgently.

"And I you." She gasped, grasping his hand, and leading him to the elevator.

As soon as they were through the door of the bedroom, she dropped her bag on the floor, slipped out of her sheer dress, and turned to face him, delightfully exposing her nakedness. "Where have you been?" she said softly as he put his arms around her, his mouth tracing soft kisses to her neck. She wantonly responded as she felt his arousal against her thighs, and she pressed herself to him.

She had awoken feeling exhilarated, dimly aware of Wernher leaving in the early hours, after which she had glowed within, rejoicing in the deliciously decadent feeling of having no regrets, despite her rational thought, which was, so often, an adversary to her more daring nature. Now, she felt elated that she was to meet the Führer himself. Although she had seen him on a number of occasions and shaken his hand when he had visited the airfield at Rechlin, she had never had the honour of a personal audience. Embarrassingly, she had actually crash-landed her Dornier aircraft on the day of his last visit which was equipped with experimental cutting devices fitted to the wings designed to sever barrage balloon cables. The cables had parted but tore into the propellors of her aircraft, which she skilfully managed to bring to land without injury.

The Mercedes swept towards the steps of the Chancellery at the end of the Courtyard of Honour. Immediately they were approached by an officer in field grey uniform, although displaying the SS insignia on his lapel, who snapped to attention, clicked his heels, and raised his right arm, loudly proclaiming, "*Heil Hitler.*" He then opened the car door, this time giving a military salute – "*Herr Flugkapitän* Reitsch, and *Herr General der Flieger* von Greim, I am SS-Hauptsturmführer Hans Pfeiffer, personal adjutant to Adolf Hitler. It is my honour and privilege, on behalf of the Führer, to welcome you. Please follow me."

They were led up the steps, the guards either side presenting arms as they passed under the portico supported by four huge pillars into a reception room with marble floors lined with more classical columns. From here, they progressed through huge double doors into a large hall clad in mosaic. Hanna was awestruck, squeezing von Greim's arm – "Robert, it is like a royal palace," she gasped, "I have never seen such magnificence, such majesty!" They ascended several steps, passed through a round room with a domed ceiling, the walls adorned with classical paintings, and then, their guide stopped, stood back with a smile and gestured them through the tallest doors Hanna had ever seen. Before them was a gallery that caused both of them to stare in wonder, and even the normally implacable von Greim whistled in astonishment. The sheer length was incredible, with tall windows set in classical frames to the left, and walls to the right hung with tapestries, whilst occasional seating was arranged around tables positioned on rugs at intervals. The floors and walls were in polished marble in brown with hints of red. As they stared around them, Hans Pfeiffer, announced proudly, "This was built by Albert Speer from a visionary design concept created by the Führer. The Long Hall is 150 metres in length and eight metres wide; it is twice as long as the Hall of Mirrors at Versailles. The Führer says it is symbolic of the power and grandeur of the Third Reich. Now, please follow me as we proceed to the reception hall." They walked the full length of the gallery to another set of enormous imposing double doors, above which was a golden eagle clutching the swastika. There were two guards either side dressed in white uniforms who stiffened to attention as they approached. From the right, a young officer in a black SS uniform marched to the centre, and his voice echoed as he raised his arm – "*Heil Hitler.*" The party responded with the Nazi salute before Pfeiffer gestured them to halt. "The Führer always controls entry beyond these doors. Please wait to be announced." The SS officer then opened an ornate panelled door, and in a loud voice, like a Master of Ceremonies, announced, "*Mein Führer,* may I permit entry to Hauptsturmführer Hans Pfeiffer, Flugkapitän Hanna Reitsch, and General der Flieger Robert Ritter von Greim." He then bowed, backing away from the door, executing a smart about turn. "You may now approach the Führer, *Heil Hitler.*"

He stood back as they entered a room that, again, took Hanna's breath away. Two huge crystal chandeliers hung from a magnificent ceiling at least twelve metres high; on the far wall facing them, an enormous tapestry hung. A large ornately woven carpet covered the central area where a number of people were gathered with a large mahogany table beyond, behind which stood the unmistakeable figure of Adolf Hitler. Her heart leapt as he straightened up, his face beaming in an uncharacteristic smile. He was immaculately dressed in a grey military tunic, over black trousers, a red swastika armband on one sleeve, and an Iron Cross on the left breast below a small circular enamel NSDAP badge. Just below the knot of his tie was a gold eagle pin, which added to his imposing image. Also in the room were many Hanna recognised, including Hermann Göring, Joseph Goebbels, Ernst Udet, Albert Speer, Carl von Weizsäcker, and, making her heart flutter, in a smart black SS uniform, Wernher von Braun, who winked at her, causing her to avert her eyes. There were two camera men, one taking movie film and the other with a flash, who were being directed by Goebbels. The Führer walked towards them, raising his arm in salute from the elbow, then bowed to Hanna, who curtsied. She was utterly transfixed by the power of his presence, which had an aura of command and complete authority. He shook hands with von Greim, then placed both his hands over hers, and fixed her with his unflinching, penetratingly blue eyes, as though he could see within her, reaching to the depth of her soul. When he spoke, his familiar guttural voice held the rapt attention of everyone present, enthralled by every syllable. "*Flugkapitän* Hanna Reitsch, you are a true daughter of the Reich with a courageous unswerving dedication to purpose which exemplifies the principles of National Socialism. You represent the virtues of our superior Aryan blood which make us invincible." As he said the last words, his voice had risen. Hanna was almost overcome by the moment, as others clicked their heels, raising their right arms. Hitler continued, "Hanna Reitsch, Germany is proud of your extraordinary achievements which have contributed to the might of our glorious Luftwaffe and your deeds exemplify the spirit of a true patriot, signifying the indomitable strength of the Fatherland." He gestured and an orderly dressed in a white tunic stepped forwards holding a cushion on which was an Iron Cross surrounded by a white, red and black ribbon threaded through the top.

Hanna was spellbound by him, sensing his incredible presence, and felt that she was in the company of true greatness. He picked the medal up, and walked to her, raising his arm in his signature salute as he did so. "Hanna, I admire you, respect you, and honour you for epitomising the essence of the Reich." He placed the Iron Cross around her neck, clicked his heels, and shook her hand and in that moment, which she recognised was one of the proudest of her life, she knew she would always follow him with unquestioning loyalty. He turned to those gathered in the room, looking upwards as though gathering inspiration, his eyes gazing into a distant place. "*Meine Herren*, today we see the nucleus of our miraculous national community, which has become an incredible historical phenomenon started by unknown people and willing followers; we now unite as one invincible nation with millions and millions dedicating themselves with an iron will to our cause. The masses of the people are drawn to this indomitable and resolute will, the like of which history has never before witnessed. Today, I have made an historic decision, one which will secure the territory we have conquered and justify for eternity the sacrifices made by the people. I have called this *Unternehmen Armageddon*. We will consciously subordinate all considerations to a new scientific goal, shaping all interests according to it, and all our actions because the awesome power which science will gift to us, unleashing upon the world a weapon of such ferocity that no-one will dare oppose us again." He turned to von Weizsäcker, "*Herr Professor*, you will commit all your energies to the development of a bomb using your new atomic discovery, which shall be created in secrecy until the time comes for the world to tremble in fear at our power. The National Socialist world of thought must and will overcome individualism, and eliminate consideration of those who may fall victim to our use of this weapon for the greater good. The common interest is superior to individual life, liberty or even survival of the individual. This common interest regulates and orders, and, if necessary, curtails our lives and interests, but also commands that we are victorious in our struggle." He paused, the room was utterly silent as his voice lowered in tone – "I feel the hand of Providence is upon us, guiding and protecting our destiny. This formidable weapon will cause others to unite with us into a great common front; the front of Aryan mankind against the Bolshevik scum, international Jewish exploitation, and their destruction of nations. The banner of the Reich will daunt every nation that opposes the triumph of our will." His voice rose as he emphasised the final point by slamming his fist into the palm of his hand, his head moving with every syllable. He wiped a shock of his hair which had fallen forwards across his forehead with a dramatic gesture as he finished. As one, those in the room stood, extending their arms, crying out, "*Sieg Heil!*"

10

Divided Loyalties

Thursday 20th May 2021 – 12am
Mizan Street, Tel Aviv-Yafo

David related to Tzadok Berkowicz elements of what they had uncovered, being careful to omit some of the links to current and former prime ministers, nor referring to the Nistarot database. As this was only accessible to a limited number of people, he could not risk compromising the identity of Moshe Gellner. Berkowicz had listened with some incredulity, yet there were areas where he either confirmed information or nodded, saying he knew of connections or events. At one point, he had stopped David – "There is so much more, some of which even I will not reveal. I do not think you are yet aware of what you could eventually uncover nor whether it would serve Israel well to do so." He rose and went to a modern pine unit with glass doors in the corner. He extracted a bottle with a light orange-looking liquid inside. "Can I offer you both a *Tubi 60*? I think I could do with one after being held at gunpoint and having had my home invaded twice."

"What in the name of Allah is *Tubi 60?*" Mehedi asked, "Looks like orange juice to me."

"Where have you been?" Berkowicz replied, "This is a beautiful citrus liqueur made here in Israel. The young are drinking it and maybe they can teach us a thing or two. It is made from lemon and local herbs and spices. Just what we need when we are about to put ourselves on the target list. We will be hunted by some within our own intelligence agencies and others with vested interests not only here but globally. My apologies, I forget you are Bedouin; can I fix you a tea or coffee?"

"Listen, Colonel," Mehedi responded dryly, "you either pour me some of that *alquarf* (crap) or I'll be tempted to use my weapon after all." He grinned from his position still watching the police from the window.

David added, "Forgive him, Tzadok, he is an Arab and would prefer to be milking goats."

"You are so *dafook*" (such a moron) came the swift reply from Mehedi to which David responded with two fingers.

Berkowicz poured three generous measures before handing a glass to each of them and re-taking his position on the settee opposite David. He was a well-built man in his sixties, dressed in faun-coloured chinos and a cream short-sleeved open-neck shirt with military-style breast pockets. He had thick, short grey hair, unfashionably but smartly parted, and clearly kept himself fit. He raised his glass to Mehedi and clinked it to David's. "*L'chaim!*" Then he leant forwards, and looked at David directly, "You really do not realise how deep this goes. If you carry on pushing for too many answers, you will be in mortal danger, more so than you ever have been, because you are on the edge of something that no-one wants to be revealed. There are so many factions in this country and abroad who have a vested interest in preventing you from uncovering certain secrets which have potentially overwhelming implications. I strongly advise you to restrict your investigations to establishing who is orchestrating the murders and forget why." His voice had taken on an almost desperate tone. "There is something happening now which I fear may be part of a plot against government. You will recall the assassination of Prime Minister Yitzhak Rabin in 1995; that was when I first realised that matters were getting out of hand."

"I thought Rabin was taken out by a right-wing extremist" interrupted Mehedi, "What was his name? Ah, Yigal Amir, I think, and he's serving life for that."

Berkowicz sighed deeply, "There are so many events that we accept because of the way they are reported but then, sometimes, there is so much more that must never be allowed to become public. You know, I had ideals once of the highest order. Then I realised what a filthy business politics and power represent. I was a Zionist inspired by great fighters for our cause, such as Menachem Begin, Antoni Zielinski, Rafi Eitan, and Yitzhak Shamir. I met them all, and believed in what they stood for. My parents came here from Poland in 1939 to escape the Nazis and were helped by Begin to escape from Warsaw. When I was growing up, he was a regular visitor to our home and I came to admire him as a man of conviction."

Mehedi cut in, "One moment, you mention Zielinski; how did you meet him?"

"When I first saw Antoni, I thought he was incredible and I was initially dazzled by him." Berkowicz responded. "I joined the IDF in 1973 with a passionate desire to defend Israel and fight for our country, which I viewed as our sacred homeland. The threat against us had always been there throughout my childhood, and I wanted to join the armed forces from a young age. I had witnessed the constant fear in those around me of being attacked and overrun by the Arab states, like Syria, Egypt, and Jordan. I just missed out on the *Yom Kippur* War. I was eighteen and, as young conscripts, we witnessed the extraordinary achievements of our air force pilots who fought against superior numbers but triumphed. We destroyed over 400 Syrian and Egyptian aircraft with our losses being just over 100 and I was inspired to become a pilot. At that time, we were visited by Rafi Eitan at the Tze'elim military training base, who gave a speech on the need for Israel to adopt a policy of aggressive defense. He was an icon and we knew he was the legendary agent in Israeli Intelligence who had masterminded the capture of Adolf Eichmann. With him was Antoni Zielinski, who had escaped the German death camp at Treblinka. He was an inspirational figure who spoke with passion, and emotion about his life, stressing that our role was to ensure the Holocaust could never happen again. They were seeking volunteers to join an elite unit to protect the future of Israel through covert operations. He stressed that they would only consider the very best with qualities of initiative, drive and dedication to Israel. That appealed to me. Afterwards, along with many others, I put myself forwards and I was interviewed by them both. They told me I would need to be single-minded, never questioning, and prepared to obey any order for the good of Israel. They showed particular interest in my parents' friendship with Menachem Begin, who they described as a patriot. They impressed upon me that they would monitor my service and that any selection would be based upon my performance in the IDF, at which time I told them I wanted to join the air force. Three days later, I was selected to join the *Kheil HaAvir* (Air Corps), one of the first examples I experienced of influence being exerted which opened doors to me. I met with Zielinski for periodic reviews but did not see Eitan again until mid-1981 after I flew one of eight F-16s in the air-strike on the Iraqi nuclear reactor at Osirak in June 1981."

David intervened, "Ah, the first time that anyone had the guts to do anything to prevent Iraq gaining nuclear weapons."

"Well, I was subsequently again involved in preventing that becoming a reality on two separate operations." Berkowicz continued "However, returning to Zielinski and Eitan, I was summoned to a meeting with them at Etzion Airbase just after the Osirak raid. I met them in a private office but Rafi Eitan had a surprise, and presented me with the Medal of Distinguished Service. He then explained that he headed up a special unit which operated outside of the normal Intelligence agencies of Mossad or Shinbet, known as Lekem. The aim of the organisation was to obtain as much nuclear weapons material and intel as possible to increase the size and effectiveness of our nuclear arsenal which, as you know, Israel has always refused to acknowledge the existence of. However, the organisation was also involved in people-tracking through software which had been copied from an American format and which they were selling to other intelligence agencies. It was Zielinski who asked me directly if I would like to join the organisation and work undercover. I had been flying operational missions by then for over six years and I felt ready for a change. It was all agreed with a handshake and Antoni became my mentor and handler. He was charming on the surface, but I found him fanatical in his beliefs and ultra-right wing. We were given responsibility for covert operations against the United States."

"Hang on one moment," David interrupted, looking quizzical, "You say against the US, I thought we were on the same side."

Berkowicz gave a mocking laughter sound, "Rafi had a saying, 'Never trust a friend unless you have spied on them.' My commanding officer in the IDF AF (Israeli Air Force) at the time of the raid on the Iraqi reactor was Aviem Sella and I was shocked to find he, too, had been recruited by Rafi Eitan. Our job was to pursue contacts in the USA and turn them into Israeli spies. Aviem took a sabbatical to study computer science at New York University and was the funnel for information from those we turned. Those working for the US government who were Jewish had divided loyalties and we worked with two notable examples. You probably have heard of Johnathan Pollard and Richard Smyth. The former gave us a tsunami of intel in the 1980s on terrorist activities that the Americans were keeping close to their chest and the latter helped us obtain krytron switches which we used as triggers in nuclear weapons. So many were available to help us, including the respected Jewish film producer, Arnon Milchan. All of this was organised under Rafi Eitan's command. I have to say that he was even more right wing than Zielinski. Towards the end of his life, he openly supported the far-right AfD Party in Germany, which admired the Nazi regime."

Mehedi cut in, "*Ya Allah!* This guy Eitan comes up everywhere. Forgive me for interrupting, Tzadok, but we already have some of this information but how did you become involved in Unit 235?"

"That came immediately after this." Berkowicz stood, gathered their glasses, and refilled them as Mehedi continued to keep a wary eye on the street below. He continued, "Our two principal moles were discovered, which caused a hell of a stink and Rafi Eitan was the scape-goat as Prime Minister Begin pretended that he did not know of this rogue espionage activity. President Reagan went ballistic and we were pulled out double quick. Lekem was disbanded in 1987 as a sop to the Americans but Rafi continued to control the reformed part of it under the umbrella of the more secretive Unit 235, into which I was recruited by Antoni Zielinski. I was informed that our priority mission was to covertly ensure that Israel's defence and security was maintained by any means. This included the obtaining of nuclear weapons technology and covering up our work by elimination where necessary. You understand that elimination meant killing.

"During my time in America, I had come to learn that Zielinski was utterly ruthless in pursuit of the mission goal. His fierce loyalty to Israel was absolute but the means he adopted to achieve the end result were not always justifiable. He first demonstrated this to me when Richard Smyth was brokering the movement of krytron. Smyth claimed he needed more money from the Israeli government before he could finalise shipment. We were assigned as intermediaries and we went to see him at his business in Huntington Beach, California. After he invited us into his office, just as soon as the door closed, Antoni hit him with his fist, sending him sprawling to the floor, with his mouth bleeding.

He was shocked, then angry, saying he was working for people in high places. Antoni then grabbed him, held his head back, and forced his handgun into Smyth's mouth. He told him that he had made a mistake and that the price had been set, asking him if he agreed; if not, he would end his life right then, after which he would also shoot his wife. Smyth was choking, wide-eyed with fear. Zielinski asked him, as he knelt on him, if we had a deal. The terrified Smyth nodded, after which Antoni let him get up, and shook his hand thanking him for his co-operation, calmly saying, "If we are forced to revisit you on this issue, you will not be treated so leniently."

"After we had left, I had to say to him that I was shocked, especially by his threat to kill Smyth's wife. I asked him whether he would have carried this out. He just looked at me with his cold grey eyes and said it would have been unfortunate but loyalty to the Fatherland of Israel demanded sacrifices. I remember him quoting from 1 Samuel in the Bible, '*Thus says the Lord of hosts, 'I have noted what Amalek did to Israel…Now go and strike Amalek… Do not spare them, but kill both man and woman, child and infant, ox and sheep, camel and donkey.'*

"OK." David nodded as he scribbled notes on a pad, trying to place the information in context with what they already knew, "You stated there were two further occasions when you were involved on the Iraqi WMD issue, what were they?"

"I do not think it will be the Iraqi issue that lies behind what you are looking into; there is something much bigger but I suspect we are the victims of a far-right conspiracy." Berkowicz drained his glass, and walked over to pour himself another but David and Mehedi shook their heads as he proffered the bottle. He returned to his seat, sighed deeply, thought for a moment before continuing, "Well, the last of the two missions is easier to speak of, which was that in 2003, I commanded a unit in Iraq which, working alongside Unit 81, discovered the weapon-grade plutonium despite the Americans failing to find it. Why? Because we got there first and there was a decision taken that no-one in the Arab world should know how near another Arab state had come to creating a nuclear device."

"I was part of that, but without knowing the outcome," Mehedi remarked laconically, "and the other operation?"

Berkowicz looked downwards, pushing his hands through his silver hair, as though wrestling with his conscience, "There is only so much I can tell you because it is too big, and I dare not say more. What you are uncovering is beyond anything you might imagine." He paused again, then, "OK, I will go back to November 1995; I was operating under the direct orders of Rafi Eitan and often working with Zielinski in Unit 235 operations. They were both convinced that Israel needed a more right-wing authoritarian direction with a stronger leadership. They were appalled by the Oslo Accords, which, you may recall, established a self-governing Palestinian Authority, gave autonomy to the Palestinians over parts of the West Bank, and prevented expansion of Israeli settlements. Zielinski called it a betrayal, declaring that Prime Minister Rabin was acting like a Nazi in destroying the security of Israel with a policy which would lead to countless Israeli deaths. These were crazy times when there were street demonstrations for and against the Accords. Rafi Eitan declared that Rabin should be removed from office and, I have to say, I agreed with him. We were tasked with doing whatever we could to increase opposition to Rabin which would lead to his demise. We became involved, with some in Shin Bet internal intelligence, in organising street protests, making placards and even producing posters of Rabin in Nazi uniform. On a couple of occasions, Benjamin Netanyahu spoke at rallies we organised, where posters we produced proclaimed the words, 'Death to Rabin'." David whistled as he realised the implication of the involvement of Israeli Intelligence, especially in the light of what followed.

"Zielinski took it further…" Berkowicz shook his head as he recalled, "He hooked up with a Shin Bet agent, Avishai Raviv, who shared our views which he stated were held throughout their security network. In the summer of that year, my contacts near to the Prime Minister reported that Rabin was secretly arranging through King Hussain of Jordan to meet with Saddam Hussein of Iraq. He wanted to grant the Iraqi leader concessions, including the re-establishment of their nuclear programme in return for peace with Iraq and Syria. This was too much for Zielinski, who stated it could lead to the annihilation of Israel. A meeting was arranged, headed by Rafi Eitan, attended by Zielinski, Avishai Raviv, and myself. Raviv stated that he had a militant friend who was convinced the only way to avert disaster for Israel was to assassinate Rabin. He was a young law student whose name you will recognise, one Yigal Amir. I authorised, with Rafi's approval, that Raviv feed this guy with the intelligence I had gained about Rabin's plans to meet with Saddam Hussein. Within days, I had obtained more details about Rabin's developing peace strategy for the region which we all agreed would be catastrophic. As I obtained more intel, it was passed via Raviv to Yigal Amir, with his superior's knowledge in Shin Bet. Zielinski said that if Amir failed in his mission, he would also be there to pull the trigger. The rest, as they say, is history as Yitzhak Rabin was assassinated by Amir at a peace rally on November 4th 1995, with, surprise, surprise, lax security around the Prime Minister as he was shot."

"He was a good man," interjected Mehedi, "and I think you set back the opportunities for a lasting Palestinian settlement; and caused more deaths on both sides, quite apart from the effect on Arab-Israeli relations. This was a tragic loss to Israel."

David stood up, speaking decisively – "I think we could debate much of this throughout the night but that is the territory of politicians, not soldiers. We live in a democracy which is clearly under threat. We cannot change the past, and whatever imperfections exist, democracy gives us the right to disagree and exercise some control or restraint over government unlike many of our enemies. We must depart now, but I sense we have much more to share."

"Wait, please, before you go," Berkowicz also stood up, placing a hand on David's arm for a second. "My God, there is more, much more, which I will not reveal except to point you in the right direction. Please sit for a moment more. From 1997 I was involved in avionics and, in particular, worked on aircraft control systems for the UAV or unmanned aerial vehicle programme in the US whilst carrying out odd intelligence assignments. In 1999, Zielinski came to see me at the Lockheed facility in New York and asked how feasible it would be to jam the controls of an aircraft in flight without leaving a trace. I told him that we could achieve this via a transmitter many miles away from the aircraft, with no trace, unless an investigator knew what they were looking for. He told me we needed to disable a Piper Saratoga and I obtained diagrams of the controls, enabling me to develop a device for overriding the Automatic Flight Control System or AFCS. It was relatively easy to develop and, within a month, I passed over an electronic solution which was virtually undetectable. This was a simple method of interfering with the altitude hold mode and the vertical trim switch. On inspection, the AFCS would appear normal because the mechanics were not affected. Zielinski did not brief me on the intended target and it was not until a month later on July 17th 1999, when I saw the news on CBS, that I discovered, to my horror, what I may have been involved in." He stopped for a moment, putting his head in his hands, "I have already said too much." He sighed deeply, then, as if deciding he had to continue, he added, "I was summoned back to Israel for a debrief and was informed by Rafi Eitan that the aircraft control override development had not been authorised by the government nor was it known about by Mossad. I was ordered never to reveal my involvement to anyone and destroy any records relating to this. However, the reasons for such an operation, had it been authorised, were explained to me. I will leave it up to you to probe further but there you will find some answers about something I cannot, and will not, speak further about. As a result of being complicit in this, they had me under their thumb because, if my involvement became known, I would have either been killed by agents from Kidon, or suffered the death penalty in the US. All this because I thought I was carrying out loyal service to my country." He placed his head in his hands for a moment; unlocking areas he had tried to forget for years was not easy. His instincts were to keep secret what he knew and was torn, yet there had already been an attempt on his life.

"You are probing into a very dirty and dangerous world and there are factions here on the far right that are very powerful. They operate outside government control and have links globally with extreme right-wing organisations in other countries, particularly Germany, hence Rafi's admiration for the AfD. What an irony when you think many of our families came here to escape such elements after the Nazis came to power. I was never the same after that time but I can say that I often carried out actions without knowing who had authorised them. When the attempt on my life occurred, it was what I had expected for years but I was ready for them." He hesitated, wrestling with his conscience about saying more, yet, there seemed little point in keeping some areas secret any more if his life was threatened. He spoke decisively:

"There is one person you may wish to investigate, who you have not mentioned, but understand I have not told you this. Zielinski had a protégé, who often worked with him, named Omer Ravid, who joined Unit 235 as a young militant Zionist in the 1960's and he worked directly under Rafi Eitan. He keeps a low profile and is highly secretive which enabled his involvement in some of the most sensitive undercover operations. He commanded Unit 235 from 1995 and maybe still does, even though it was officially disbanded after the Second Gulf War by Prime Minister Ariel Sharon in April 2003. Shortly afterwards, Sharon suffered a stroke from which he never recovered, and there was speculation about his hospital treatment contributing to this. Whilst I have no proof, I suspected Omer Ravid's involvement. I know Ravid was approaching those he trusted to become part of a new clandestine

Unit 235 which no-one would be aware of, except those who he and Rafi Eitan took into their confidence. When I was asked to join them, my decision was to thank them but decline their invitation as I had decided to leave the military and concentrate on a civilian career. I had come to know Ravid by this time and I can tell you that he ruthlessly authorised assassinations without hesitation, especially of Arabs. There has even been speculation that he was behind the death of the former Palestinian leader, Yasser Arafat in 2004. I know he was a member of the banned extreme-right *Kach Party*, a movement which supported removing the right of Arabs to hold Israeli citizenship. They promoted a one state solution, absorbing all occupied and Palestinian territories under Israeli rule. He joined the far-right, newly formed *Otzma Yehudit Party* in 2020. You will note, at that time, our Prime Minister, Benjamin Netanyahu, formed a political pact with them. There are rumours that Ravid had been involved in terrorist atrocities such as the grenade attack on the market in Jerusalem in 1992.

"What makes you think this man may be involved in the recent attacks?" David asked.

"The link you have uncovered, which seems that all victims are former Unit 235 operatives and Ravid played a leading role in that organisation, but there may be much more here." Berkowicz leaned forwards, his tone more earnest.

"Two weeks ago, I learned something very alarming. I was told by former colleagues that Ravid is advocating a pre-emptive nuclear strike on Iran and is prepared to use military force, if necessary, to execute this. There are whispers that he is plotting a coup here in Israel imminently; he has support from some senior officers in the military, and former personnel who have far-right sympathies. I thank God I feel able to share this with you as I have not known who I can trust. I know that anyone who has stood in his way previously has either been liquidated, or had their position compromised. I know they will try and kill me again; it is just a matter of time. I warn you…you are poking into incredibly dangerous areas involving people who will think nothing of killing you. We live in crazy times where there are those here in Israel whose fanaticism reminds me of the very people who tried to annihilate the Jewish race in the Holocaust. My complicity haunts the depths of my conscience."

It was back in the car when Mehedi let out a string of expletives in Arabic finishing with "*Aljahim aldamawiu* (bloody hell), looking up from his Google search on his mobile to David who was driving – "July 17th 1999; that was the date the press reported the disappearance of the Piper Saratoga aircraft being piloted by JFK Junior. They discovered the aircraft in the ocean off Cape Cod two days later. There were no survivors."

11

"I should have listened"

Saturday 8th July 1944 9:30am
The Berghof, Berchtesgaden, Obersalzberg, Bavaria, Germany

They were driven in open-topped Mercedes limousines the
4.5 kilometres from the Hotel Wittelsbach in the centre of
Berchtesgaden to Hitler's Alpine retreat at the *Berghof*. In front
of them was an escort of four motorcycles with armed SS guards
in side-cars. Hanna Reitsch felt elated, just as she had done many
years before, suffused with the thrill of her illicit passion the night
before, once again ignited by her long-term, yet absent secret lover,
Wernher von Braun. He had arrived just in time for dinner, having
flown via Berlin from the rocket development base at Peenemünde
with his immediate superior, Walter Dornberger. Other guests
included Hanna's former mentor, General Ritter von Greim,
Hitler's architect, now Minister of Armaments, Albert Speer, and
the physicist Carl Friedrich von Weizsäcker. There was another
there, who seemed somewhat aloof, who was introduced to her
as SS-Obergruppenführer Hans Kammler, wearing a black dress
uniform. All the others there were in civilian suits, whilst Hanna

had adopted to wear a grey jacket over a long black skirt. As they sipped cocktails before dinner, Speer announced that they were to be joined by Reich Minister Joseph Goebbels.

The meeting had been somewhat hastily convened only three days before at the behest of the Führer. No-one present, even Albert Speer, knew the reason, although Wernher said he had been requested to bring film of the latest launches of the new vengeance weapon, known as the V-2 rocket. Von Weizsäcker stated that he had been instructed to prepare a presentation, which was to be given to the Führer, on the work he was carrying out on nuclear fission and the weapon development. He informed those present that his research had progressed far more quickly than even he or his colleagues had expected and that he had even taken out a patent on the explosive process using plutonium and uranium. Albert Speer added that he was aware that all of the inner circle of government were to be at the *Berghof* the following day. He stated that although he was a senior minister himself, the Führer often surprised those close to him with initiatives, announcements, or decisions he had reached without any prior consultation. This, he said, was what made him such an extraordinary, inspirational leader.

As they awaited the arrival of Goebbels, there was an air of growing anticipation over the following day's meeting, not without some apprehension too in the light of recent events. Things were not going well on the Eastern Front, and the German army had suffered a number of serious setbacks, including the capture of Sevastopol by the Russians and surrender in the Crimea. On the Western Front, there had been an enormous Allied landing on the beaches in Normandy only a month before, whilst Italy was also under threat from the Allied advance; many felt that even the security of the Reich itself was threatened. As they debated the worsening military situation, Hans Kammler intervened, "*Meine kammeraden bitte*," he spoke loudly and icily, "I would remind you that defeatist talk is forbidden and I will not permit this. I will have

no hesitation in arresting anyone who talks further in this way."
He looked around at each of them with all present coming under
his piercing gaze. Then he smiled, "Tomorrow, our great Führer
will meet with you because he has the foresight and the vision to
address the challenges that lie ahead. Be assured, he will not be
cowed in his monumental purpose, but will develop a strategy that
will annihilate our enemies. Let us now enjoy the evening." His
benign look, as he finished speaking and summoned the waiter
for more drinks, made Hanna shudder. She looked up at Wernher,
who gave her arm a reassuring squeeze, before leaning over and
whispering to her, "No-one is safe, so be careful what you say.
I was imprisoned by these people for two weeks in February for
no reason because of Himmler's paranoia." He squeezed her arm
again but she felt uneasy and torn by her emotions. The Führer she
knew had always been kind to her, and she admired his leadership
and the iron will he had exerted for the benefit of Germany.

At that moment, there was a stir around the hotel lobby just
beyond the bar as staff formed a phalanx, beyond the entrance,
headed by the manager. Two guards entered in uniform, led by an
officer who briefly spoke to the manager, walked towards the bar,
and raised his right arm, announcing, "The Reichsminister sends
his compliments and will be with you imminently." He briefly
surveyed the room, then walked back to exit through the double
doors, leaving the two guards who stood to attention either side.
Moments later, a beaming Joseph Goebbels entered, in a double-
breasted lounge suit, his black hair swept back, accompanied by
his wife, Magda, who looked radiant in a maroon silk dress and
black evening jacket. He shook hands with the manager, who
bowed, before guiding him to the bar. Those in the room who
were not with the group awaiting him, immediately rose, giving
the outstretched Nazi salute, which he returned with the more
relaxed right arm, bent at the elbow. He advanced towards the
awaiting group and as some clicked their heels, saluting, he waved
both hands, "Please, we are all friends here; let us dispense with

formality. I promise, I will not report you to the Reichsführer." His joking words, referring to Himmler's reputation for cold, enforced formality, drew a laugh from those present, apart from Kammler, which broke the tension.

Hanna's attention was suddenly taken by Magda's hand on hers. "It seems we are outnumbered. It is an honour to meet you again, dearest Hanna Reitsch. You are our heroine of the Reich with your incredible flying skills. We have met once before, you might recall, more than ten years ago when General Greim was bringing you to hear the Führer speak." Hanna was initially overcome by Magda's grace and the self-assured way she presented herself. She must have been in her forties yet possessed the beauty of a much younger woman, with large eyes, and a dazzling smile. "We have often laughed, privately I hasten to add, recalling you standing up to Himmler, which few ever dare do, but shh, don't tell anyone I said so." They both laughed and Magda gripped her hand for a moment as Goebbels approached her. "My dear Hanna, it is always such a pleasure." He was looking up deeply into her eyes as he kissed her hand, holding it as previously, a little longer than was necessary, a mannerism for which he had a reputation.

They were led into a private dining room with huge portraits on one wall depicting cattle and horses set against mountain landscapes. An enormous crystal chandelier hung above the centre of the table at the head of which Goebbels and his wife took their seats. Hanna was seated nearest to him, Wernher to her side, with Walter Dornberger and von Weizsäcker beyond. Von Greim sat opposite, next to Hans Kammler and Albert Speer.

After Champagne was poured, and the wine waiter left the room, Goebbels raised his glass. "The Führer, Adolf Hitler!" This was immediately echoed around the table. He continued, "So, *meine lieben Freunde*, what are your thoughts on our position in the war at this point?"

There was an awkward silence, and some shuffling around in the seats. "Come, come," said Goebbels, "we are all Germans here dedicated to the Reich; you can speak freely!" He opened his arms to them, raising his eyebrows. It was Hanna who spoke first, despite restraining tugs on her arm by Wernher.

"*Herr Reichsminister*, we are warned we cannot speak freely or we might be arrested. As a loyal supporter of the Führer, and one who has put my life on the line for Germany, I will speak out and I will not be silenced." She looked, with derision, towards Hans Kammler, who fixed her with an expressionless, but cold stare.

Von Greim cut in quickly, giving Hanna a warning look – "Forgive the *Flugkapitän*, *Herr Reichsminister*, she is, perhaps, a little outspoken."

Goebbels stopped him with a gesture, waving him away, "Has it come to this? Have we all become like me, telling whopping great lies that everyone wants to hear? What are we becoming? Yes, we need the German *Volk* to believe in our final victory; but you are trusted, loyal servants of the Reich and I need hear the truth." He looked down the table at each of them in turn.

Finally, it was Wernher who spoke; "Earlier this year, I was arrested and held for two weeks without trial by the SS, yet I hold a professorship awarded to me last year by none other than the Führer for my work on rocket weapons. You ask for the truth, yet we are told we cannot speak about what is happening. Germany is under threat of invasion by the Russians; our Italian allies are capitulating, and Allied forces are attacking us in France. We are now seeing bombs fall on Berlin, and have suffered staggering losses of civilian life in war crime bombings of Cologne, Dresden, and Hamburg. I have heard that last year, in one night of bombing, it is estimated that over 42,000 people lost their lives in Hamburg alone," his voice had become emotional, "yet we are told by SS-Obergruppenführer Kammler here that we will be arrested if we talk of such things because he classes it as defeatist. The truth is, *Herr Reichsminister,* that we are frightened to speak because of threats from these *Schweine*." Hans Kammler jumped to his feet, and pulled out a Luger pistol from his holster, pointing it at von Braun.

"Hör jetzt auf!" (Stop now) Goebbels barked in a loud commanding voice. "Kammler, if you fire that weapon, you will be taken outside and immediately shot, following which you will be hung publicly." There was a metallic rasping noise as two guards, positioned by the door, cocked their weapons. "No-one is ever permitted to draw a weapon in my presence except in my defence. Now, leave this room!" No-one moved for a moment, as Kammler hesitated, then slowly lowered his weapon, replacing it in his holster as he flashed Wernher with a sneering, threatening look. He walked stiffly to the door but no-one looked directly at him, before he stiffened, raising his right arm, and exited the room. Goebbels stood, then looked earnestly at each of them in turn, dropping his voice. *"Meine Kameraden,* tomorrow we will speak of *'Unternehmen Armageddon'.* Tonight, you will sleep, but tomorrow, we will consider the final, and total, annihilation of any opposition to our will."

As the motorcade neared the drive to the *Berghof,* Hanna shivered, recalling the delights of the night before, whilst trying to retain her composure in light conversation with von Greim about some of her exploits test-flying new aircraft. After Goebbels had left, after dinner, Wernher had leaned over, whispering to her, "I have Cognac, and I will be at your room before midnight." She wanted to say *'no',* but one look into his deep blue eyes, his warm smiling expression, and his curly chestnut hair, dictated her acquiescence, which thrilled her with her brazen acceptance of what she knew would follow and which she craved. He covered her hand with his beneath the table, stroking her palm with his fingertip and she shuddered. They hardly saw one another and yet, when they did, it was always the same despite the reputation she knew he had as a ladies' man and something of a rake. He just oozed sex appeal, and now he enjoyed a senior, well-respected role in the scientific community and was admired by Adolf Hitler which, somehow, made him even more appealing. After he had stood up to Kammler the night before, she was drawn to him even more, exuding his authority despite being under threat. As Goebbels was being escorted from the cocktail lounge, he had turned and walked back to where Dornberger, Wernher, von Greim and Hanna were standing. He looked directly at Wernher – "We need people like Kammler in the Reich to give us strength to enforce the Führer's will, but they will never lead Germany. Kammler has literally moved mountains to build you the Mittelwerk underground factory for your rockets, completed in just three months, I think. *Ach*, so you must co-exist with people like him but, after tomorrow, your position will never be threatened again. We need you to help in the destruction of our enemies with this new science that will ensure the survival and triumph of the Reich. *Heil Hitler.*"

As he departed, Wernher turned to Hanna, "*Mein Gott*, there is something magnificent, yet frightening, about these people and their utter resolve." In the room, later that night, they had both stripped completely naked, tearing at each other's clothes wantonly. He made love to her with an almost animal-like passion, his body demanding her; his vigour, and hunger, she had welcomed and returned in equal measure as they abandoned themselves, sensing a terrible abyss into which they were being drawn, with a future that excited and daunted them in equal measure.

Wernher had left her room at around 4am and Hanna was shocked when she next saw him at breakfast the following morning. He was attired in the black dress uniform of an SS-Sturmbannführer. She had developed a wariness of that organisation, which she felt represented some of the less attractive qualities of National Socialism, although she admired their reputation for a total dedication to duty. She had little time to talk with him as he was discussing a presentation, which he was to give that morning, with General Dornberger. He had then travelled with him separately to the *Berghof*. She had accompanied von Greim, whilst Albert Speer had gone with von Weizsäcker. Wernher had thrown her a sidelong smile, however, and she felt her stomach give a tremor as her mind flashed back. Despite having visited the *Berghof* previously in February 1944, when Hitler had presented her with a second Iron Cross, she still felt excited at the prospect of meeting the Führer again, having remained utterly enthralled by him. The line of cars entered the final driveway, passing by a guarded gatehouse, with SS soldiers saluting, as they swept past and drew up to the steps leading to the entrance above. The alpine-style building had three floors, with a balcony looking out from the middle, at the edge of which there were flowers draped from boxes. Traditional shutters surrounded the many windows under a large apex roof supported by huge timbers. The view across the valley to the snow-capped mountains surrounding the Obersalzberg was breathtaking and Hanna felt awestruck by the location. An officer, in an immaculate SS uniform, approached the cars as they drew to a halt, followed by a number of men who lined up and stood to attention. Four marched up to the vehicles, opening the doors, raising their right arms. The officer snapped to attention, clicking his heels, and spoke. "I am SS Obersturmführer Otto Günsche, *persönlicher Adjutant* to the Führer. Welcome to the *Berghof.* You will follow me please." They ascended the steps to a series of arches that preceded the entrance, then through large doors into a hallway created in a typically grand Bavarian style with vaulted ceilings supported on pillars, and arched doorways with heavy timber doors. Then, down a corridor lined with classical-style landscape paintings and portraits giving an air of a palace, although the ceilings were relatively low. They approached another hallway, which was timber panelled and dominated by a huge round chandelier with mock candles. Tapestries lined the walls whilst the floor was covered with an enormous Persian rug. A large portrait of Hitler in uniform dominated the scene, painted against a landscape background, one hand on his hip, whilst his other rested on a rocky outcrop, his face set with a steely, determined look, portraying his absolute authority. The officer turned to Albert Speer, "*Herr Minister,* your colleagues have arrived, so we can enter. The rest of you will wait here please." He approached a tall doorway, accompanied by Speer, knocking briefly before entering.

"Not a bad little Alpine retreat." Wernher joked, although his voice betrayed the nervousness that they all felt, with a sense of anticipation and some foreboding about what may follow.

Moments later, the door in front of them opened wide and the adjutant beckoned to them to come forwards. "*Mein Führer*, may I present your guests?" He then proceeded to announce them one by one. The scene in front of them, as they entered, was overwhelming even though all of them except von Weizsäcker had visited previously. The room was large, ornate, with a red carpet, hung with sumptuous tapestries depicting classical scenes and a wood-panelled ceiling in which more round candle chandeliers were set. However, it was the huge, panoramic floor-to-ceiling window stretching across the entire wall that commanded the attention, with stunning views to the Untersberg mountains beyond. To the left of the window was a grand piano on which was a large globe and to the right, a circle of easy chairs set around a low table in front of which stood Adolf Hitler, one hand behind his back, and bent forwards slightly. The Führer was dressed in his customary field grey, double-breasted military tunic over black trousers, his Iron Cross on the left side of his chest. Behind him was a phalanx of well-known faces, which included Hermann Göring, Martin Bormann, Heinrich Himmler, Joseph Goebbels, Albert Speer, and *Grossadmiral* Karl Dönitz, who commanded the German Navy, and had overseen the U-boat campaign. Hans Kammler was also standing in the group, remaining expressionless even when Himmler attempted a smile of greeting.

The Führer walked forwards, his shoulders looking a little more stooped, Hanna thought, since their last meeting. Somehow he seemed to have aged, and, although his piercing blue eyes still seemed to penetrate, even transfix, they appeared tired. "Welcome to the *Grosze Halle*" (the Great Room). He gestured to the mountains through the vast window. "That is where the great King

Charlemagne sleeps in his cave of ice, awaiting his time to save the world, or, perhaps, I have been given his spirit which called me here." He greeted each one of them individually, shaking their hands, as they raised their arms in salute. Then he walked back towards Hanna. "*Mein tapferer Flieger* (my brave aviator), you may yet hold one of the keys to unlock our victory." He smiled briefly, tapping her on the shoulder before inviting all to take their seats. He began to speak in a low guttural voice.

"Providence has chosen the greatest nation on earth to seize upon the opportunity to fulfil our great purpose through the harnessing of science. We have been hampered in our task through betrayal; by forces which have been too sentimental in the execution of our mission to both remove the evil of the Zionists, and crush the Bolshevik curse which threatens the world with the vile poison of communism. The warmonger gangster, Churchill, has refused our many offers of peace and he is the cause of the continuation of this war, and the misery he has inflicted. History will judge his short-sightedness harshly and will uphold the purity of our principles. We needed an iron will to achieve our aims and for that reason, I have dedicated my life to the Fatherland and promised the German *Volk* that I shall give them deliverance. The time has come for vengeance against the British and the Americans." His voice had begun to rise and he emphasised each syllable of key words with dramatic gestures, throwing out his hands, then clutching them to his chest as he spoke about sacrifices both he and the German people had made. Those present listened intently to every word as he strode in front of the window in the great room. "I have been chosen to lead because I will not flinch or turn from the horrors we may have to face, or those we may inflict. I will make the decisions which will guide us to total victory and the complete annihilation of our enemies." He thumped his right fist into his left hand, and shook as he raised his head, looking above as if seeking divine inspiration. Himmler sprung from his seat, shouting, "*Sieg Heil,*" and all those present joined him, rising from their seats, echoing Himmler's words in a chorus whilst giving the Nazi salute in adulation of their great Führer. Hitler continued, "Only I have the will to lead this monumental final mission. I will strengthen our historic purpose, arming it with the ruthless decisions which I must take to deliver our rightful destiny. A task which the Almighty entrusts to me of seizing this moment to bring violent retribution on those who have dared to oppose us. A retribution so powerful, that never before could it have been imagined until Germany discovered the scientific key to unlock the wrath of nature."

Hanna, sitting next to Wernher, inadvertently grasped his hand as she became utterly transfixed with Hitler's presence and his inspiring strength of leadership. Wernher squeezed her back, nodding to her reassuringly, before removing her hand with a smile.

Hitler continued for some time, his voice alternately raising, then lowering again, interspersed with long pauses to add drama to a point, or ensure the gravity had been noted. Finally, he looked at each of them in turn, his eyes seeming to devour their thoughts, as though he could read them. Then, he raised one arm in the air, his finger extended, his other hand on his hip; his tone had dropped, adding an earnestness to what he was saying. "I have taken it upon myself to take an interest in the work of two great areas of scientific development, that of rocketry, and that of nuclear fission. Both have the power to alter the course of this war, and both have been developed by the superiority of our Aryan scientists. We will combine these new sciences to create a weapon of unimaginable ferocity." He paused, then walked purposely towards the area where his admiring entourage were gazing at him with rapt attention. Then, he folded his arms, leaning back, almost as if challenging them, his mouth set in a grim expression. He had lowered his voice – "Which of you would stand by whilst Germany succumbs to the Bolshevik scum? Which of you would wish to see atrocities continue to be inflicted upon our people such as the bombing raid on Hamburg, which cost the lives of nearly 40,000 Germans? Which of you would allow the collapse of the Reich when we could have within our grasp total victory? Now it is the time for vengeance against those who oppose us and retribution for those who have betrayed us."

Another long pause, before he raised both his fists and his eyes brightened. "I have failed to take the decisive lead, allowing others to make decisions when only I have the vision and the strength to do what destiny demands." His words began to ring out more loudly, "I will deliver victory; I will demand victory; I will commit this great Reich to a new and terrible purpose, but one which will give us deliverance. I will execute *Unternehmen Armageddon*, unleashing a power which will result in the complete destruction of London, New York, and Moscow." His fist thumped down on a table by him three times as he named each of the cities. "This will be part of my new commitment to '*Totaller Krieg*' (total war) which will bring a finality to this struggle through the complete destruction of our enemies and I dedicate myself to this. Which of you will join me?" As his voice rang out, those present stood in awe, their right arms outstretched in complete supplication to his will, interspersed with shouts of "*Sieg Heil!*"

Hitler then sat down, wiping his hair back, which had fallen across his forehead as he had uttered the final words of his speech. He pressed a bell on the wall, as those around him awaited in anticipation of what would follow.

In seconds, a smartly dressed, well-built woman in her mid-forties appeared, dressed in a suit, with her dark hair tied neatly back, whom many already knew as the Führer's secretary, Johanna Wolf. She smiled briefly at the gathering, then saluted Hitler who suddenly appeared more relaxed. "Ah, *meine Wölfin*, I think some tea for our guests with cakes and biscuits." He beamed at those around him. "*Meine Kameraden*, history will record this moment as truly colossal, yet civilised by our sharing tea." The resulting laughter broke the tension in the room. Light conversation ensued in a more relaxed atmosphere during which smartly attired orderlies, dressed in white, served tea. The Führer then requested that Dornberger and von Braun give their presentation. The curtains were closed over the huge picture window and a projection screen was set up by some SS orderlies. As the projector whirred, dramatic music played and they watched, in amazement, as they were shown rockets with a checked pattern livery blasting off in huge clouds of smoke then arcing into the sky majestically as a contrasting, somewhat harsh, recorded commentary announced the new wonder weapon that was to deliver destruction to enemies of the Reich. The commentary went on to inform them that this was a terror weapon, which was to be imminently launched on England, and which had been christened by *Reichsminister* Goebbels as *Vergeltungswaffe* 2, (vengeance weapon) or V-2, following on from the success of the V-1 campaign, which had been commenced in June 1944. The documentary stated that the V-1 had already caused devastation, lowering the morale of the British and breaking their spirit. Whilst the V-1 was built using a jet engine, which could be intercepted, the V-2 used rocket technology, which would enable it to fly into space, then hurtle back to earth on its target with a 1 ton explosive warhead at speeds approaching 6,500 kilometres per hour. There were exclamations of surprise from some of those present, whilst Hitler sat, enthralled, rubbing his hands together in glee as he watched. After the film, there was applause, led by the Führer, with Himmler remarking smugly, "You may note that SS-Sturmbannführer von Braun is an officer in the SS which represents the best and most dedicated talent in the Reich," causing *Reichsmarschall* Göring to make an exaggerated mocking cough indicating his disdain for the remark. General Dornberger gave a short summary of the V-2 project, stating that it was in the final test phases and that he was confident the first attacks could be carried out by the end of September 1944. Hitler interrupted him, *"Herr General,* you will ensure that this weapon will be ready by the beginning of September!" His tone was icy cold and said in a manner that would not permit any dissention.

"Jawohl, mein Führer" came the response as Dornberger clicked his heels. Von Braun concluded the presentation with scarcely hidden enthusiasm, proudly claiming that they had the weapon system of the future, which could turn the tide of the war. No aircraft was capable of intercepting the rocket and he stressed that they were carrying out research on a system which could deliver a far greater weapon payload on its target. This time, Hitler stood up, walked forwards and shook Dornberger's hand, saying in a solemn tone, "I have had to apologise only to two men in my whole life. The first was Field Marshal von Brauchitsch. I did not listen to him when he told me again and again how important your research was. The second man is yourself. I never believed that your work would be successful. I should have listened."

Next, von Weizsäcker was invited to speak. He shuffled to the front and announced in a hesitant but dramatic statement that he had mastered and patented a process that would change the fortunes of war. He began to become more animated as he spoke, "This process, called 'nuclear fission', has the power to destroy a whole city with one incredible explosion, the size of which mankind has never witnessed before." He wagged his finger to add emphasis and drama to what followed – "The largest bombs used in this war have delivered around three and a half tons of TNT. Imagine a weapon which is not ten times more powerful, not even one hundred times more powerful, but, *meine Kameraden*, one which is over five thousand times more powerful! That is what I am working on and that is what I know I can produce. I will have this ready within six months." He paused as there were gasps of astonishment from around the room.

12

"Fight the Germans...to bring liberation..."

Tuesday 1ˢᵗ August 1944 – 1pm
Warsaw, Poland

A year had passed since the breakout from Treblinka, and Antoni Zielinski now had the same icy desire for revenge, tinged with anticipation, he had felt on that hot summer's day the previous August. This time, however, there was no nervousness, just a desire to kill as many Germans as he could. He hated them for their depravity and the evil they represented through horrific atrocities so barbaric that his mind had become numbed, indifferent, yet boiled with the need to avenge. He had witnessed the shooting of Jews indiscriminately for pleasure; for no other reason than they were Jewish. The news he had dreaded came from a former *Kapo* (SS appointed prisoners given tasks in concentration camps) who had escaped from Auschwitz. He had known Antoni's parents from before the war and had seen them arrive there as he worked in the camp selection area. The *Kapo* had told them not to worry;

that everything would be alright because that was all he could say as they were being separated from one another into queues of men and women, and informed that they were being taken to shower blocks. He never saw them again, knowing the dreadful reality that they were walking to their deaths in the gas chambers.

Even though Antoni had long ago ceased feeling emotion, witnessing death and murder on a daily basis, he cried that night thinking about the sheer horror of his parents' last moments, not even being able to comfort each other as they stood in the selection lines. His nights were tormented by nightmares about their appalling experience of the end of life alone, confused, and brutally gassed by their barbaric captors. Now he felt nothing about killing these *szkopy* (scum), and even relished the satisfaction it gave him in claiming a life in reparation for the evil they represented.

Today was a different day as there was an expectation of deliverance from the Nazi occupation after many months of planning, combined with the prospect of revenge. Looking across at Jan Nowak-Jeziorański, a young, handsome-looking, smartly uniformed Polish officer, he grinned, pointing to the stick grenade, the base of which he had unscrewed to reveal the string he would pull to arm it. Jeziorański nodded, pointing, in his turn, to the bayonet he had fixed to his captured German *STG 44* automatic assault rifle.

Antoni had arrived in Warsaw early the previous September, having lain low for nearly a month with a Polish farmer and his family who had taken him in, almost starving to death, after he had been turned away by many others. The Germans were everywhere, searching for those who had escaped from Treblinka. Initially he had teamed up with four of the escapees after the uprising, running through the forest as they still heard the sounds of gunfire behind them. They had all crammed food into their pockets, which had been saved over previous days, stolen from the German barracks by Jewish kitchen orderlies. The first night, they had slept in a deeply wooded area, but were woken by the sound of dogs barking. They knew they would be pursued and stayed away from the roads, crossing fields, trying to put as much distance as they could between them and the camp, taking water from streams and rationing their food. Antoni still had a handgun from the escape, a *Walther P-38*, which had six rounds left in it, plus a clip containing eight more. The others had one hand grenade between them and so they decided to stay together, allowing Antoni to lead them, adopting to head for Warsaw in order to try and link up with the Polish resistance based there.

By early evening on the second night, they had travelled forty kilometres but they were weakened by the malnutrition they had suffered during their captivity. Antoni's leg was bandaged but it was painful and he began to falter. During a rest, they decided they needed to find somewhere to hide, cautiously approaching a road where a sign announced they were approaching the village of Ostrówek. Circling round, they peered through trees, noting some German lorries and a *Kübelwagen* (military field-car) parked by what appeared to be a small military compound bordering the crossroads. A few hundred metres beyond, they came across a large farm with sprawling outbuildings where Antoni stated they should find a place to conceal themselves, reasoning that it was safer to hide there from searching Germans because of its proximity to the barracks. As they approached the farm, they observed some labourers working near an animal shed and crouched low, making their way towards a barn positioned away from the main group of buildings. They slowly prised open a side door, peering in, but it was deserted, with old farm machinery scattered round, and an upper storey accessed via a ladder, which Antoni opted for. As he climbed, his leg began to give way and Yanek, one of his fellow escapees, had to pull him up the final steps, after which he collapsed. His bandage was blood-stained and he felt a throbbing pain. "You need a doctor or at least a clean dressing," Yanek said, to which Antoni responded, "Tomorrow; leave me here. I'll slow you down."

"No way, my friend," Yanek replied, then with a grin, "besides, you have the gun."

He looked round at the other faces, all looking gaunt, each of them indicating they wanted to stay together.

"If you give me the gun, I'll see if I can find someone who can help; after all, we are Polish too." Yanek held out his hand, and Antoni handed the weapon to him.

Yanek turned to the others, "Jacub, you and Szymon come with me, and we'll leave the grenade with you, Izaak, whilst you remain with Antoni."

They scrambled down the ladder and within thirty minutes they had returned with a woman who Yanek introduced as Felka, the farmer's wife, who had a background as a nurse. She was middle-aged, dressed in a loose-fitting pinafore and had a scarf around her head. She had brought a container with warm water and anti-septic in it with which she bathed his bullet wound.

"You are lucky, there is nothing remaining in your leg. The bullet has passed through but you need to keep the wound clean as it is very inflamed and your bone may be chipped." He winced as she probed, then, "You can stay one night only," she whispered urgently, "they are everywhere and Janak, my husband, does not like Jews. We will be shot if we are seen to be sheltering you. He has permitted me to come and assist you provided you go by the morning." Antoni nodded his acquiescence. She handed him a brown bottle, telling him it contained morphine tablets, and Antoni thanked her, assuring her again that they would be gone by dawn. After she had left, Antoni took a tablet and within minutes he felt waves of relief as the pain subsided. Yanek produced some beef from a cloth bag Felka had given him and half a loaf of bread, which they ate eagerly. She had also given them a flagon of beer, which Jacub had carried up the ladder triumphantly and which they eagerly shared as the night closed in.

Antoni fell into a restful sleep, assisted by the effects of the morphine, and was barely aware of his arm being tugged urgently.

"You must waken, the Germans are here; the farmer must have turned us in." Yanek spoke in a desperate whisper. Antoni was suddenly very awake. There were sounds of vehicle doors slamming and shouted commands. Yanek pressed the Walther handgun into Antoni's hand, saying that he should have it, "because you are much younger than me." Headlamps illuminated the front of the barn and shards of light penetrated the gaps in the large timber doors.

A voice with a heavy German accent shouted harshly in Polish, "Jews, you will come out with your hands on your head. *Schnell!* If you do not, we will burn you alive. Do as we ask; we will return you to your camp."

They looked at one another, their eyes wide and desperate. Jacub spoke quickly, "Better to live like rats than die in here."

"I am not returning, and will die fighting these bastards," Antoni responded, pulling the safety catch off his weapon.

"I will go with Jacub," muttered Szymon, "maybe, this will give you time to break free. *Shalom.*"

"I am not ready to die," Izaak whispered desperately, "I will come out with you two."

"Please give me the grenade," Yanek said to him, as they shook hands.

The harsh voice from outside echoed in the farm compound, and was now more immediate, "You have seconds to exit before we burn you alive." Then, in German, *"Komm sofort, raus!"* (Come out immediately)

The three men waved briefly before descending to the cobbled floor below then walked to the main doors of the barn, slowly opening one of them. As they did so, Antoni turned to Yanek pointing to a small square window to one side at the end of the loft space facing forwards, which was bathed in light but offered their only means of exit. "Their appearance will distract the Germans and so you need to throw the grenade to the opposite side. Then, we drop to the ground." They moved to the window and watched as their three companions walked into the bright lights with their hands clasped behind their heads. They heard a command, *"Halt. Niederknien!"* (Halt. Kneel down) It was a command they had heard before and they both prayed within. From where they were, they could see the three men kneeling, their heads bowed. They saw a German officer walk around the men, after which he kicked Jacub, sending him sprawling to the ground. As he tried to straighten himself up, the officer drew his Luger pistol, aimed it at his head, and fired. Then he moved to the other two, standing in front of them. They could hear Szymon sobbing before the German lifted his arm, and fired again.

"Now," Antoni whispered, and Yanek smashed the window. There were immediate shots from the front of the building as machine guns opened fire, raking the front side of the barn. There was a pause and Yanek leant out, hurling the stick grenade towards the direction of the lights, just as another burst caught him in the chest. He slumped forwards, then grunted, before falling to the ground below. There was the thump of an explosion and the headlamps, bathing the barn in light, died as Antoni dropped, hitting the floor and rolling sideways to break the fall, hearing screams from the direction of the parked trucks. Fortunately, the morphine shielded him from the pain he would otherwise have felt but, in any event, adrenalin was dictating his movements as he took advantage of the semi-darkness, running towards the trees. Gunfire erupted and he could hear the bullets thudding into the ground and whistling past him. Then he hit the welcome cover of the forest beyond, and fell headlong into a ditch, his breath coming in rasps.

He lay there, hearing shouts interspersed with more gunfire, but it was sporadic and aimed wildly in the general direction he had taken. He peered back and could see flames leaping skywards from the barn he had been in with four others, only minutes before, all of whom he presumed were now dead.

That had been a year ago, after which he had arrived in Warsaw,

finally assisted by some of the *Armia Krajowa* (Polish resistance
Home Army) he had been put in touch with by a farming couple.
They had looked after him for a week after he had turned up,
exhausted, begging for help, in the third week of August. They had
listened to the story of his escape and were horrified by the betrayal
he had suffered with his fellow escapees by the farmer at Ostrówek.
Unlike many, they detested antisemitism and treated him warmly,
giving him a new set of clothes. During that week, they fed him and
cleaned his wound, after which he began to recover his strength.
Their son, Filip, they had told him, was a member of the resistance
and often travelled to Warsaw to meet with commanders there.
He had been a journalist before the occupation with *Nowy Kurjer
Warszawski* (the New Warsaw Courier), which the Germans had
taken over for propaganda purposes. He was retained as a part-
time reporter, which had given him a perfect cover whilst working
for the resistance, and the opportunity to travel.

At the beginning of his second week with the farmer and his
wife, Filip arrived. He was a large man in his late twenties, with
thick black hair worn in a parting and a long drooping moustache.
At first, he treated Antoni with suspicion, displaying some
reluctance to become involved in helping him. "You are putting
my parents in great danger by being here. If the Germans find
out they have helped you, they will be shot or, worse, sent to your
camp at Treblinka. Tell me why I should help you." His grey eyes
stared at Antoni, who felt a surge of pent-up anger and defiance,
speaking in a raised voice -.

"You think you are the only ones fighting the Germans! I fought
them in the Ghetto in April this year, before being captured and
sent to Treblinka. I grew from boy to man very quickly, learning to
kill them. You know what, I am nineteen years old and I have killed
more Germans than I can count. During the fight in the Ghetto,
I held my gun against the temple of a man pleading for his life
and pulled the trigger. You think I felt anything? They are vermin
and I hate their stinking kind. Where were you, the resistance

then, as we were slaughtered fighting the Germans? They took my parents and gassed them in Auschwitz. I was in Treblinka and I have witnessed scenes you will never comprehend. I have seen piles of bodies of my fellow Jews being thrown into pits after being exterminated by the Nazis. The old, the sick, women clutching babies beside their children, young couples, all looking pleadingly for reassurance, terrified as they walk to their deaths, herded there by German guards who have told them they are being taken into shower units. At Treblinka, we rose up and killed Germans, losing hundreds of my fellow prisoners in the gunfire turned upon us, climbing over the bodies of our comrades to escape. You ask me why you should help me? Is there no humanity left in this world? What has happened to your Catholic values in Poland? I lost four friends only a week ago because the Germans were told where we were hiding by one of your people. In God's name, whether we are Jew or Christian can we not help each other? Is this what we have come to? I want to fight with you against the German swine. We Jews fought alone in the Ghetto but we must forget the past, abandon our cultural divide, and unite." His voice had risen even further, but now dropped. "I once regarded myself as Polish, and I took pride in that, but now, now I despair."

Filip looked, taken aback by the outburst, and then began nodding slowly. "Today, I am ashamed of my country. You speak from the heart. These are bad times when men are making bad decisions. We need good fighters, and, my Jewish friend, I will help you, but first, we must bridge the divide." He smiled, nodding again, then extended his hand, before putting his arms around Antoni and embracing him. "You know what, Jew, I am only glad you are on our side. I will introduce you to someone who will take you in. He is English, a journalist like me, and he will shield you from those amongst our ranks who would, I regret to say, as easily kill a Jew as a German."

A week later, Antoni was driven to Warsaw in the back of an old truck, buried under a pile of sacks and farming produce for the market, and taken to an address where he was to meet with an Englishman by the name of John Ward. He was led down an alleyway by Filip, whilst another man stood guard at the entrance with a Luger pistol under his coat. They entered a gate, down an overgrown path to a door with peeling black paint. Filip hammered on it and seconds later, a rather incongruous figure appeared dressed in a shirt and tie, with slicked back dark hair, neatly parted to one side. He extended his hand, and spoke in Polish but with a heavy accent. "Delighted to meet you 'old boy'; forgive my pronunciation, I regret I was born in Birmingham, England. I have heard much about you and it seems we both like escaping from German prison camps. I've been captured twice but the Jerries are pretty awful at looking after my needs, so I decided I had to find somewhere better to live." He welcomed them in, pulling out a bottle of *Soplica* vodka and pouring large glasses out for each of them. He explained to Antoni that he had been in the aircrew of an RAF aircraft shot down over France in 1940, after which he ended up being captured and moved to a labour camp in Poland. He had escaped and met a local underground newspaper editor, helping him translate BBC news bulletins for Polish readers. "Now I have three jobs," he explained with a grin. "I hold a junior rank in the Royal Air Force, I work as a journalist for '*The Times*' of London, and I am liaison officer between His Majesty's government and the Polish Home Army. I hear you are a fighter; well, we need all we can get and you can help us by bringing young Jewish fighters to join us. You will have a room here and my protection will ensure your safety."

That had been a year ago, and since that time Antoni had become involved in numerous sabotage raids on German military units with the resistance, building a fierce reputation as a ruthless fighter. Even hardened Polish fighters were shocked as Antoni calmly executed any Germans, even if they were unarmed or surrendering. He recruited others into a Jewish unit, which he headed despite being only twenty years of age. He had even been given a Polish Home Army uniform, which was kept for meetings held with senior officers, who would meet clandestinely at Ward's home. Ward introduced him to General Tadeusz Bór-Komorowski, the commander of the Home Army, who had warmly greeted him, despite having a reputation for being anti-Semitic. The General had given him the rank of *Por* (Lieutenant), "My God, this man now outranks me," Ward had remarked drily, as they celebrated Antoni's appointment with a bottle of *Chablis* relieved from a German barracks they had attacked.

In early January 1944, news came through that Russian troops had advanced into Poland, and there was a growing sense of excitement amongst the people in Warsaw that liberation was at hand. By May, the meetings had become more earnest as the Russians were making rapid advances, although fighting was reported to be fierce with the Germans offering stiff resistance. The Soviet air force dropped leaflets on Warsaw extolling the people to rise up. General Komorowski began organising a plan for a massive insurgency to co-ordinate with the expected Russian offensive into Warsaw. More urgent radio bulletins were being sent by Ward to London to ensure that supplies were airlifted to the resistance, if necessary, during the Polish attack. Radios were being made by Ward, who was a skilled electrical technician, and Antoni would distribute these to various command centres around the city. As the Russian advance continued, tension was rising and there was an air of anticipation amongst the resistance fighters. Orders were given to cease clandestine attacks against the Germans in order not to trigger reprisals which might prejudice the element of surprise, if hidden arms were discovered. On 25th July 1944, during a meeting of resistance commanders, an enormous row broke out between Colonel Antoni Chruściel, 'Monter', the commander of the resistance on the ground in Warsaw, and General Komorowski. This took place at a strategy meeting held at Ward's home attended by a number of commanders. Antoni was invited as the commander of the Jewish fighters, together with

John Ward and Jan Nowak-Jeziorański, a Polish officer who liaised between the government in exile and the resistance in Warsaw. Monter announced to the meeting that the Russians were close to the outer perimeter of the city and that the time had come to mobilise all Polish forces against the Germans. Jeziorański cautioned against this, saying that there were no plans yet in place that the Russians had agreed to. As such, he stated it was unlikely that the Allies would be able to deliver supplies without Russian co-operation. Komorowski had agreed, arguing that they had to have a co-ordinated strategy in place involving the Red Army and that they could not mobilise without the approval of the Commander in Chief, General Kazimierz Sosnkowski, in London.

Monter exploded, "You sit around whilst these Nazi pigs continue to murder our people daily in the streets, shooting women and children indiscriminately. The Russians will come as soon as they know we are liberating the city. In that way, we do it on our terms, for the good of Poland, not Russia. Remember, the Russians plundered our land and occupied it by agreement with Germany in 1939. You want a free Poland or one under the yoke of the Russians? I am the commander of all forces on the ground here in Warsaw, and I say we act now."

"Listen, *Frajer*" (insult meaning utterly naïve), Komorowski cut in sharply, "you will obey my orders and not compromise the lives of 40,000 men or you will be dealt with. We must work with the Russians, and not against them, if we are to free Warsaw. The British and the Americans must be on side, understand? I will not permit an ill-conceived, half-witted attack. You will carry out my orders or resign!" His voice rang out loudly, as a sharp military command.

Monter drew his pistol, "I am a Polish patriot, and we are ready and we will act. If you try to stop me, I will kill you."

"Wait!" Antoni jumped up. "What are we doing? We are fighting each other instead of the German *szkopy*. General, I am with Colonel Monter. We Jews fought in the ghetto when we had no hope; if we had waited, we all would have died. Now is the time, and my Jewish fighters will follow me. If you want to stop us, then you will be helping the Germans. I say act now." As if to emphasise his intent, he took up his *Schmeisser MP40* machine gun, sliding back the safety catch.

At that moment Ward intervened "Look, chaps, passions are running high. Might I suggest you allow me to radio London and impress upon them the need for an urgent approval for action supported by an assurance of military supplies. Let us wait twenty-four hours and evaluate the position." He looked at Monter with whom he enjoyed a warm relationship. There was a long pause, then the Colonel brought his fingers up in a Polish salute, before replacing his pistol, muttering "Twenty-four hours. Good night." and walking out of the door.

Ward turned to Antoni, "My friend, please accept I too want the best outcome, so let me and Jeziorański try to sort this out over the radio. If not, he has a reputation as a hell of a fighter; hopefully he is better at that than broadcasting!" Jeziorański had been broadcasting to resistance fighters and the joked reference to his ability drew a laugh, breaking the tension. "If all fails, he can join you and we can all unite behind this."

Two days later, despite repeated requests from John Ward, no clear orders had been received from London. On 27th July, Monter began mobilising his forces in the face of opposition from General Komorowski, who attempted to rescind his orders. Antoni was infuriated by what he perceived as a betrayal, and on 29th July, on hearing that the Soviet forces had reached the outskirts of Warsaw, he decided to commit his Jewish force behind Monter. He was joined by the young Jeziorański, who felt he could do no more, and their action was reinforced by a radio broadcast from Moscow to the citizens of Warsaw on that day.

'Fight The Germans! No doubt Warsaw already hears the guns of the battle which is soon to bring her liberation …

The Polish Army now entering Polish territory, trained in the Soviet Union, is now joined to the People's Army to form the Corps of the Polish Armed Forces, the armed arm of our nation in its struggle for independence. Its ranks will be joined tomorrow by the sons of Warsaw' —Moscow Radio Station Kosciuszko – 29ᵗʰ July 1944.

The confusion caused by order and counter-order delayed matters until 31ˢᵗ July, at which point, General Komorowski, realising that the already partially mobilised forces could not be stopped, agreed to give the order for 'W Hour' for 1ˢᵗ August 1944 at 5pm. His order only reached many sectors of the city in the morning of that day, giving insufficient time for fighters to proceed to arms collection points and be at their designated places. In any event, many, including Antoni's unit, had already decided to attack as Soviet T-34 tanks had broken through defence lines in the eastern suburb of Warsaw the day before.

Thus it was that Antoni was lying next to Jeziorański at 1pm on 1ˢᵗ August in an alleyway opening onto Okopowa Street beside the Jewish Cemetary in the centre of Warsaw. Behind them were fifty Jewish members of the resistance, armed with an assortment of weapons, from handguns, old hunting rifles, and shotguns. A lucky few were equipped with captured or stolen modern German weaponry. Antoni had assured them that further weapons would be air-dropped by the Allies once their offensive was underway, based on reassurances received the night before by John Ward from London. Opposite their position, they could see a number of German military vehicles parked outside the municipal building housing the Gestapo, and acting as officers' quarters for the SS. There were four guards, positioned either side of two entrances. Other soldiers were standing around the greenish grey vehicles, some smoking cigarettes, and oblivious to the danger facing them. Antoni looked across at Jeziorański, "OK, my gentile friend, it is time for us to retake Poland."

Although Jeziorański was senior in rank to Antoni, he had agreed to act as his second in command, allowing for Antoni's more immediate fighting experience. They inched slowly forwards, lying flat on the cobbles, waving more men to join them, forming a line across the entry to the alley. Antoni, his hand firmly gripping his stick grenade, nodded to another fighter, Gedeon, who had a belt holding more grenades and a pistol. "OK, pass the word, as the first grenade detonates. I want all to open fire." A radio set on one truck was playing music, which hid the sound of their weapons being cocked. The voice of Lale Andersen singing the words of the song, *"Lili Marlene"*, echoed eerily across the square as German soldiers relaxed in the warm sunshine. Seconds later, there was a flash and a detonation followed by the deafening sound of gunfire, and a number of men crumpled to the floor whilst others dived for cover behind the vehicles amidst the frantic shouting of orders. Then there were two explosions in quick succession and screams from some of those caught by the blasts. One truck was catching fire, with a black cloud of smoke billowing skywards but also spreading across the street, giving some cover to the attackers. Soldiers began pouring from the entrance to the building and automatic fire from the alleyway sent them scurrying back inside after a number were hit, falling by the doors. From the upper storeys, windows were flung open, and Antoni sprayed the building with a long burst from his machine gun.

The attackers then rose to their feet, but crouched as they advanced. Antoni nodded to Gedeon, "Two more into the trucks." A fighter to his left cried out and fell, triggering an almost relentless response from the advancing Jews as further explosions shook the street. Although returned fire from outside was now more sporadic, they were being targeted from inside the building. A *Kübelwagen* was now also on fire, as Antoni waved forwards one of the fighters who had a *Panzerfaust* anti-tank weapon. "Take out the walls, Aaron." The fighter knelt to the floor, aiming at where the shots were coming from only thirty metres away, and seconds later there was a whoosh, followed by a thunderous explosion. As the smoke cleared, they saw a gaping hole where the window had been. Aaron turned the *Panzerfaust* to the other wing of the building, shattering another wall around a window. The firing became less and there was only the odd intermittent shot, although they could hear the sound of gunfire in the streets around them and echoing into the distance as the resistance groups began uncoordinated attacks across the city. They were now reaching the burning vehicles and Jeziorański, despite having been continuously firing as they advanced, was shocked as Antoni began systematically shooting any wounded Germans he saw. Even those who had their hands behind their heads in surrender were shot dead. "Never again!" Antoni shouted. "Never, never, never!" The sound of an accordion, drifting from the still intact radio, echoed over the cobbled street, adding a dreadful, horrifying poignancy to the scene of destruction around them.

13

Revelation

David was woken by his mobile phone buzzing on the cabinet beside his bed and he automatically answered without a second thought. The Director was clearly not happy. "Where in the name of God have you been? You work for me; I give you a mission; you are involved in a fire-fight, and then you disappear. For all I know, you might have been eliminated. I want to know what is happening and don't give me *bubba meye-she.*" (a fairy tale). His voice was angry and David thought quickly. There seemed no reason why he should not assess the Director's reaction despite not knowing whether he could be linked to the plot they were uncovering. "Yossi, I am unable to reveal where I am, but I have discovered some viable evidence of a plot to take out those who have been involved in Unit 235." There was a long audible sigh from the Director. David addressed his superior more formally to stress the importance of what he was saying. "Sir, we also believe there may be a right-wing conspiracy underway which may be targeted at overthrowing the government."

"*Inal deenak!* (damn) David, this is Israel in the twenty-first century. How reliable is your intel and how the hell did you find out about Unit 235? That was disbanded after the Iraqi debacle in 2003 and the failure by Unit 235 to discover so-called WMD." At that point, David concluded that the Director, despite his position, was unaware of the ongoing activities of the unit. He also decided not to reveal the identity of Omer Ravid, or mention the assistance he was getting from both Mehedi and General Gellner. The enormity of what they were uncovering demanded that those involved were not compromised, especially as loyalties may be divided.

"Yossi, my intel is good, but I regret for operational reasons, which I know you will appreciate, I am unable to reveal the source at this point. It is imperative I remain undercover but I will ensure that you are fully briefed. I am preparing a complete report which will be shared with others who will copy you in should anything happen to me."

"And Unit 235?" The Director cut in sharply. "Only those who were members, the Prime Minister, and myself are authorised to even acknowledge it ever existed. Where is the leak?"

David thought quickly; he knew he could not give away the fact that his primary source was Moshe Gellner. "Carelessness in the clean-up of old files, Yossi," he responded, "All of the names you gave me were linked by one common denominator, the annotation of Unit 235." He then decided to lie directly. "We have no idea what was behind the Unit at this point but we believe it holds the key which may unlock much more."

"You will not delve too deeply into that area and that is an order, David," the Director stated firmly. "This is a matter which is highly sensitive affecting national security and even I am not permitted to know the complete story. All references to it should have been properly cleansed from the files back in 2003. I will have to brief the Prime Minister on this today."

This time it was David who was direct – "I regret that would be ill advised. Sir; this goes right to the top and we do not know who is involved but I can tell you that former prime ministers have played a part in what we are uncovering. For the good of Israel, I am asking you to trust me on this."

"You are asking me to conceal this from the leader of our country?" The Director's voice was incredulous. "If I fail to inform him and this gets out, I lose my job and could stand trial for treason."

"Sir," David's voice was calm and unwavering, "if this gets out too quickly and we are not prepared, I fear for the state of Israel and the security of our democracy. I am asking that you hold back because the very future of our country is at stake. Give me one week and then I give you my word, I will fully brief you and then we may either go to the Prime Minister together with the information, or we may arrest him for the very same charge you fear."

"*Dreck!* (Shit) I must be crazy, but OK, you get your ass into my office next Thursday at 9am." The phone went dead and David reflected whether he had done the right thing. If, as he hoped, the Director was not involved, then he had bought himself time but if not, at least he had not given too much away.

He went to the kitchen to get a coffee and a glass of orange juice as he tried to piece together the additional pieces of the complex jigsaw emerging. Where to start? He needed to share his thoughts and consult with Moshe Gellner, but there was a note on the table that he had gone to do some digging which David knew meant that he was going to access the Nistarot secret national security database in Tel Aviv. Mehedi had returned to his apartment and was not due until the afternoon. He wandered into Moshe's study and peered absently along the shelves of books containing the names of so many political leaders and contemporary historical events until his eye was drawn to one title, '*The Kennedy Conspiracy*', which stood out to him. '*That family have suffered so much tragedy,*' he thought, but why would someone from within his own country want to see the demise of JFK Junior? He reached up and pulled the book down, then settled into a large green leather armchair, staring at the cover for a moment, reflecting on the familiar youthful smiling face of John F Kennedy, standing in front of a microphone, his right hand stretched out, a finger pointed in a dramatic pose. He leafed through the pages covering the familiar story of the assassination of the President on November 22nd 1963 in an open-topped limousine whilst visiting Dallas, Texas. The book was thick and examined various conspiracy theories surrounding the reasons for, and who was behind, the shooting. There were photographs of the main characters from the story, including the purported gunman, Lee Harvey Oswald, under a big heading, '*Did Oswald Kill the President?*' Inconsistences were explored, including those in the discredited *Warren Commission* report, which was set up to investigate the assassination. David shook his head as he read about witnesses with vital evidence who were never called because their narrative did not fit the story expounded by the authorities, and others who had died in mysterious circumstances either before their testimony was given, or as their stories were investigated. The testimony of many witnesses had changed after the investigation, with some retracting their statements in later years, including Oswald's Russian wife, Marina. The slowing down of the motorcade at the time of the shooting, and eye witnesses seeing muzzle flashes from other locations, with reports of more than three shots being fired, made the conclusion of the Warren Commission somewhat bizarre. Then there was the extraordinary feat of one man loosing off three shots from the Book Depository building, which purportedly were fired by Oswald using a *Mannlicher-Carcano* rifle, in just a few seconds that stretched credulity. The weapon had a reputation for jamming and inaccuracy, which would hardly justify its selection for such a high-profile target. As he read, he noted that there were also issues with the way the rifle sights had been set up for accuracy at the range and angle required to hit the President from the sixth floor of the Book Depository building where Oswald was stated to have been positioned. David also knew from his own military training as a marksman, that when on an operation, it was extremely difficult to achieve the same accuracy that may be obtained in ideal circumstances on a shooting range. The enormity of what Oswald was facing that day, shooting from an unfamiliar location at a moving target, notwithstanding the adrenalin pumping within him, made it extremely unlikely that he was the sole perpetrator. It was well known in Intelligence circles that the entire episode together with the conspiracy theory had been 'fogged', a tactic David was very familiar with, and which he had sanctioned on occasion. This was a process where conspiracy theories were spread or 'leaked', containing elements which could easily be ridiculed or disproved leading to distrust in any aspects of the events reported. Theories close to the truth would be hijacked by Intelligence and 'embroidered' with ludicrous additions. The truth behind what actually occurred would be discredited along with the propaganda disseminated, creating a fog of mis-information wherein the public would not know what to believe and become tired of looking into. The Kennedy assassination was cited as a classic case in Intelligence training of how to prevent too much unwelcome scrutiny and deflect those seeking from the reality of what may have taken place. As he scanned the pages, David felt some unease at his own complicity in such tactics, which he justified as being for the greater good of Israel.

He read a section which covered an extraordinary confrontation at Parkland Hospital, where the President had been taken after the shooting, between Dallas Coroner, Dr Earl Rose, who insisted on performing an autopsy, and secret service agents who stated they were removing the body of the President forthwith. During the altercation which followed, Federal officers had drawn their weapons, announcing that they would shoot anyone who got in their way, before removing the body in a casket. David shook his head as he read on, with incredulity at the drama described, which alternated with sub paragraphs highlighting areas of subsequent conjecture. His eyes were drawn to a section highlighted *Assassin*

Escape' and as he looked at the speculation over those who had been identified as possible suspects, one italicised heading suddenly jumped out at him, '*German Hit Squad*'. He read the section beneath with growing astonishment.

'*Two police officers, Lawrence Matherne and Jim Peterson, stopped a red Ford Galaxie Sedan on Cedar Springs Road at 1:15pm on November 22nd 1963, driven by one Giano Rivera, who was a well-known hoodlum working for Chicago Mafia boss, Sam Giancana. In the back of the car was a German who claimed to be an electronics salesman working for Siemens – he gave his name as Hans Kirchner. The officers searched them both, disarming Rivera in the process, who did not attempt to hide his identity. Recognising his Mafia connection, they became suspicious and then decided to search the trunk of the vehicle, where they found a German passport showing Kirchner's photo but bearing the name Otto Skorzeny. The German explained he worked for military intelligence but he was placed under arrest whilst Matherne called in on his radio. Minutes later, the police officers were surprised when they were contacted by none other than the Dallas Police Chief, Jesse Curry, who informed them they had apprehended a known Nazi war criminal. They were instructed to take Skorzeny to Dallas Love Field Airport and hand him over to Israeli intelligence officers. He ordered them to release Giano Rivera, and told them not to speak to anyone about what they had seen or reveal any aspect of this to subsequent investigations as it was a matter of national security.*

'*However, Lawrence Matherne felt uneasy about the episode and volunteered what had occurred to the Warren Commission investigation. The matter was looked into by the FBI, but even though Skorzeny was a former Nazi and a well-known trained assassin, he was ruled out of all enquiries on the direct orders of FBI Director J. Edgar Hoover. Neither Matherne or Peterson were ever called to testify, nor was Rivera despite rumours in the Dallas underworld that a professional German-led hit squad was responsible for the President's death. Six months later Matherne was shot whilst on duty by an unknown killer with no apparent motive. His colleague, Jim Peterson, died after falling from a multi-story parking garage in January 1965 with no witnesses present.'*

David leant back for a moment, uttering a deep exclamation, hardly able to take in the enormous significance of what he was uncovering, then continued reading.

'The Dallas Times Herald later did some investigation into some of the conspiracy theories and covered this story in early 1964. They reported that on Saturday November 23rd 1963, Otto Skorzeny was flown out of Dallas Love Field Airport on a private jet en route for Israel accompanied by five members of Mossad. Travelling on a separate aircraft with the same security clearance were unidentified officers from the BND (German Foreign Intelligence Service) whose names had been removed from the record and which have never been released. The newspaper obtained the flight manifest of the aircraft carrying Skorzeny, which was still held by the Dallas Police Department, having been seized along with all other flight records after the assassination. The manifest named the Israeli agents as Antoni Zielinski, Moshe Levi, Ben Herzl, Simon Gerin, Rafi Eitan and Omer Ravid. Information about these agents and their backgrounds was classified by Israeli Intelligence.' Looking at the names, especially the last one, David felt a wave of adrenalin flow over him and his heart thumped at the realisation of what he was uncovering. He read on:

'A subsequent investigation revealed that the plane carrying the BND personnel was piloted by Hans Baur, who

was later also identified as a former Nazi. In August 1964, one month before the publication of the Warren Commission report, J. Edgar Hoover shut down this investigation, the findings of which were then classified. Rumours persisted and it appears that some intel was subsequently deliberately leaked in order to add confusion to the theories emerging. There was speculation that Kennedy's death was linked to a Nazi plot to forge closer links with organised crime. Former Nazis were involved in efforts to infiltrate Government and embed those they approved into positions of power and influence. They were working with the Mafia, many members of which had far-right sympathies. The President had introduced legislation to combat racketeering and organised crime, together with his brother, Robert Kennedy, who was Attorney General. However, as there were so many other conspiracy theories circulating at the time that seemed more credible, and because Lee Harvey Oswald had been apprehended, this story did not achieve much attention.' There was a footnote at the end of this section of the book.

'In April 1999, John F. Kennedy Jnr announced he was unhappy with aspects of the Warren Commission findings on his father's assassination, and that he was funding a new investigation. This would complete a re-analysis of all credible evidence, including that omitted from the original enquiry. A report in the New York Times claimed Kennedy had stated that he was "not satisfied that the conclusions of the Warren Commission had been reached after examining all of the available evidence, but that evidence had," in his opinion, "been selected or gathered in such a manner that it met the needs of the conclusions already reached."'

' The investigation was never completed because John Kennedy Jnr was killed in a tragic air accident on July 16th 1999.'

He was interrupted by Moshe entering the house and his old commanding officer was animated as he strode into the study. "The intel you got from Berkowicz is priceless, David, because when I looked up the death of JFK Jnr, there was a classification of *'Unauthorised 235'* logged against it with no further data; but there is something far more extraordinary. I tried looking up President Kennedy and there is a wealth of information. However, all entries relating to his assassination outside the standard historical records are either inaccessible or heavily censored, other than the conclusions of the Warren Commission report. As we now know, much of that report, commissioned to investigate the assassination of the President, has been dismissed as an attempted whitewash and cover-up of the truth." David raised his hands to interrupt, but Moshe waived him back.

"David, please, what I have got to tell you is incredible. Get this, there is a record of a security meeting in April 1963 chaired by our first Prime Minister, David Ben-Gurion, which is attended by our old friend Rafi Eitan amongst other senior military, intelligence and political figures. Four of those there would subsequently become prime ministers of Israel, including Shimon Peres, Yitzhak Rabin, Ariel Sharon, and Yitzhak Shamir. A discussion took place regarding the threat of possible military action against Israel by the USA." As David expressed a gasp of astonishment, Moshe continued, pulling out his tablet and glancing down at the screen as a prompt. "It appears Kennedy was furious that Israel might be developing nuclear weapons and denying US verification inspections. Peres was a defense minister determined to ensure Israel had the bomb. Shamir was involved in Mossad and had organised hit squads working with people like Rafi Eitan. Yitzhak Rabin was a general with a reputation for effectiveness and efficiency who was to become Chief of Staff of the IDF, and Ariel Sharon was a resourceful but uncompromising senior military officer accused of controversially aggressive tactics. The meeting recorded that there was a split in the White House.

Vice President Johnson had privately stated to our ambassador that he was amenable, given the right arguments backed up by incentives, to support Israel's nuclear weapons development, or, at very least, turn a blind eye to it. Kennedy was rocking too many boats and many of Johnson's powerful friends were uneasy. Johnson let it be known discreetly that he believed Kennedy was a threat to national security because of his immaturity and his confrontational stance against the Soviets over nuclear weapons. Various documents are accessible recording growing tension at this time between America and Israel, because of their concerns that we were developing a nuclear weapon and covering this up. Of course, they were correct because we were doing just that on the site of the Dimona Nuclear Facility in the Negev Desert. A scientist was at the meeting, by the name of Yehudi Krimmer, who confirmed to all present that Israel now had a credible nuclear weapon capability; this had been in development for nearly ten years and he also stated that a detailed inspection of Dimona by US inspectors would confirm this. There was no way it could be concealed as they had done during the cursory inspections they had previously allowed." Moshe leant forwards in his seat, grasping David's arm to reinforce what he was saying, his voice dropping to almost a whisper, "What I then discovered as I did a little more digging, you will not believe as it is just incredible. This Krimmer was a young genius with an obsession for physics, but had been imprisoned as a Jew by the Nazis. Although a prisoner, his abilities were recognised by a brilliant German nuclear physicist, Carl Friedrich von Weizsäcker, who was one of the scientists heading up the Nazi nuclear programme. Von Weizsäcker found Krimmer in the Mittelbrau-Dora concentration camp whilst he was liaising with the rocket scientist working on the V-2 weapon, Wernher von Braun. David, the file reveals Krimmer confirmed, that in March 1945, just before the end of World War Two, he witnessed the Germans successfully detonating a nuclear weapon. They had the bomb!"

"Keebineemat!" (Damn) David exclaimed in shocked surprise, "They were that close? That would have changed the outcome of the war if the Germans had managed to resist a little longer."

Moshe continued, "Frustratingly, the files available do not reveal what decisions were taken at this meeting attended by Ben-Gurion, Krimmer, and our former prime ministers. There are no entries on the Nistarot relating to this area until 1964 when the relaxation is noted, under President Lyndon Johnson, of the US policy regarding Israel's weapons programme. So, I decided to find out more about the scientist, Krimmer. In May 1945, he was smuggled into Palestine by, wait for it, Rafi Eitan, who had snatched him from under the noses of the British. Eitan was at that time operating within an elite *Palmach* commando unit, attached to British forces for covert operations, commanded by Yitzhak Rabin. They arranged to bring Krimmer and another scientist to Palestine because of the highly secret information they were privy to on nuclear weapons development being carried out by Nazi Germany."

David could wait no longer and cut in to reveal what he had discovered whilst his old commander intermittently uttered expressions of surprise and expletives, especially when he was shown the article on JFK in the book that had sat on his shelf for years. Moshe's eyes widened in utter disbelief as he read the names of those flown out of Dallas Love Field, all of whom had fallen under their spotlight in recent days. "Moshe, we are on the brink of uncovering something we could never have imagined, and combined with what you have just told me, a nightmare is unfolding of unimaginable proportions."

Both men were silent for a moment, trying to absorb the enormity of what they could scarcely comprehend, nor wished to believe. David broke the silence first, "Moshe, you went to dig out information on Omer Ravid?"

The older man chuckled sardonically. "Where do I start in all this mess? There are so many terrifying links between all the players. I hardly even need to refer to my notes." He stood up, and paced as he spoke, briefly glancing at his tablet from time to time. "Ravid had a reputation as a harsh but outstanding military commander in the IDF. However, he shocked many of those who served with him because of his utter disregard for human life. There was speculation he was involved in clandestine shootings of prisoners who refused to co-operate with his interrogations. His mother, Gilana, had worked as a Jewish concentration camp prisoner servant for the scientist, von Weizsäcker, which is where she met Krimmer, who, you will recall, ended up here in Israel, working on our bomb. Gilana had been raped by an SS officer and fallen pregnant, which would have guaranteed certain death had Weizsäcker not taken her in. The Nazis did not like fraternisation of guards with Jews, especially if a child might result. Krimmer had moved into Weizsäcker's home near Mittelbau-Dora concentration camp, where Gilana was a housekeeper. At that time, the Nazis were desperate to develop an atomic bomb and were seeking out any physicists who might assist, even if they were Jewish. Yitzhak Rabin, who was serving as a British army officer, masterminded a snatch operation behind enemy lines with Rafi Eitan, in the last months of the war, to rescue Krimmer, who refused to leave unless they took Gilana and her baby son with them. They took Krimmer with another Jewish scientist, together with Gilana and her baby back to Palestine. The whole thing caused a terrible row, which was hushed up after the war. In the eyes of the British, a number of serving Jewish soldiers in the British Army had deserted, taking with them two valuable Jewish scientists from Germany who had worked on the Nazi *Uranverein* programme. The British demanded that they all be handed over for interrogation but von Weizsäcker intervened to protect them after he was captured. When Germany surrendered, he had been taken to England and imprisoned with a number of other nuclear scientists. He exerted his influence, as a result of his not inconsiderable bargaining powers, having substantive knowledge of Germany's nuclear weapons development, to allow the scientists to remain in Palestine. Krimmer did go to England after the war, studying nuclear physics at Cambridge, but returned to complete his studies in Israel, obtaining a PhD in 1953, and became a professor. He joined the Israeli nuclear research team, eventually moving to the secret Dimona reactor facility in the late 1950's, and was appointed nuclear advisor to the Government. He is still alive but retired to England some years ago. The entry for him is also annotated *Unit 235*.

"Gilana had suffered terrible deprivations in Mittelbau-Dora, before being taken out of the camp by von Weizsäcker, and had recurrent attacks of pneumonia which eventually took her life in 1955. Omer Ravid was just eleven years old and he was taken into the care of Yehudi Krimmer, who by then had married. The file records Ravid was a problem child, aggressive to others, and he was expelled from school for violent bullying at the age of fifteen. However, because of Krimmer's emerging position as an influential scientist, he was taken into a special training unit of the IDF for young problem teenagers run by, guess who? Rafi Eitan.

"In the training unit, he excelled himself, taking to military discipline, and established a reputation as a marksman. Rafi Eitan took a shine to him and began taking him on operations despite him being under eighteen. In 1960, Ravid accompanied the team, commanded by Eitan, that snatched Adolf Eichmann from Buenos Aires in Argentina. You may guess what is coming next; he was appointed to join Unit 235 in 1962 and then there is no mention of him until 1964. At that point he was given command of a special forces unit at the age of only 21, operating behind Egyptian borders, tasked with snatching military prisoners for interrogation. He served with distinction in the Six-Day War where he impressed the Chief of Staff, one Yitzhak Shamir, with his audaciousness. By 1973, he was a young *sgan aluf*, but was suspended after an operation in the Yom Kippur War under the overall command of none other than Ariel Sharon. It seems a number of Egyptian prisoners died in captivity. One hundred Egyptian commandos had been dropped behind Israeli lines in the Sinai, against whom Ravid led a night-time assault with a small unit of highly trained special forces. Some say that around seventy Egyptians died in the firefight which ensued, with no Israeli casualties; the surviving Egyptians being taken captive. However, in the morning when Ravid's unit returned, he claimed that there had been no Egyptian survivors. Rumours spread that he had walked down a line of prisoners shooting each one. This was too much even for Sharon and he had him suspended pending a military enquiry. However, because there were atrocities on both sides, it was all eventually swept under the carpet."

David walked to the antique Queen Anne drinks cabinet in one corner of the study, pouring them both large measures of Arak, into which he added a splash of lemonade, handing one to Moshe. "*Ya Allah* (Oh my God), we have one bastard on our hands with this guy. So, where did he end up and, more importantly, where is he now?"

Moshe touched his glass to David's, then took a generous drink. "*L'chaim.* my friend; this one has form. Apparently, he urged Sharon to use nuclear missiles during the Yom Kippur War, stating that he and many others would support a military coup to oust Prime Minister Golda Meir, if necessary. There were others who agreed with him about using nuclear weapons, including the defense minister, General Moshe Dayan, and Shimon Peres, who was also a minister in the Meir cabinet. Eventually, Golda Meir agreed to use nuclear as a last resort and authorised the arming of both aircraft and missile systems. We were that close to the first use of nuclear weapons since Hiroshima and Nagasaki in World War Two!" His arms gestured dramatically and his voice became more excited with the momentous nature of what he was saying. He downed his glass as David did the same.

"*Walla!* (Wow) David exclaimed in a loud whisper, shaking his head in shocked disbelief, taking Moshe's glass and refilling it as the older man continued.

"That night, Golda Meir cleverly placated both the hawks and doves in her cabinet by announcing that she would inform the American Secretary of State, Henry Kissinger, that unless the Americans agreed to supply immediate and substantive military aid, she would launch a nuclear attack on Egypt. The policy worked and equipment was flown to Israel the following day. This was the first time that Israel had admitted to having nuclear weapons, something that was still hidden from the rest of the world as it is to this day.

"Ravid joined the internal intelligence service, Shin Bet, in 1976, but he continued to work for Rafi Eitan in partnership with Antoni Zielinski. Both names were linked to the shady activities of Lekem in the eighties, operating clandestinely and almost independently from Mossad, which often claimed, perhaps conveniently, that Lekem had acted in various missions without proper authorisation. After Lekem was disbanded, Ravid joined Kiddon and was involved in numerous missions to take out those who were perceived a threat to Israel. He was married in 1980, but divorced ten years later, his wife citing cruelty. He has a forty-year-old daughter, Shira Ahava, who changed her surname and is now estranged from him, although she lived with him for some years. However, it appears he pulled some strings and got her a job working for the military intelligence unit, Aman, in Tel Aviv. Now, the interesting bit, the Nistarot database has not been cleaned as effectively as other files appear to have been and this confirms that Ravid was appointed head of Unit 235 in 1995, which corroborates the story given to you by our friend, Berkowicz. This means, I think, at least he can be trusted."

At that moment, the buzz sounded from the doorway, and they both glanced to the security monitor where they could see Mehedi. Moments later as he joined them, David remarked, "You are a little late, my Bedouin friend; might I suggest the internal combustion engine as an alternative to the camel."

The response was not entirely unexpected, "Listen you *arsim* (pimp), you are going to need us Arabs to deal with your total *fashla,* (screw up) ruining our beautiful country, and prevent you lot all killing each other. What news? Did I miss much?"

"Not a lot," David replied dryly, "Just that Germany had a nuclear bomb in 1945 and we may be on the edge of discovering the truth about who was behind the assassination of President John F Kennedy. Oh, and for good measure, we have established that Israel came close to launching a nuclear strike against Egypt in 1973."

14

"When will it end?"

The sound of gunfire was constant, intermingled with explosions, some distant, and some shaking the buildings around them. There were thirty of them, having emerged from the cellar of a large ruined house nearby where they had spent the night, awaiting word that their reinforcements from the *Zośka* battalion of the Home Army were in position. They had lain low after their attack on the Gestapo headquarters two days before but were impatient to re-join the uprising, which was gaining momentum across the city. Their spirits had been lifted when an excited Wacław Micuta, one of the commanders from *Zośka*, had arrived the night before to inform them, with a large grin, that they had "liberated" two German Panther tanks. One of those had been allocated to him, which he had named Magda. Their target was the Gęsiówka concentration camp as they had heard that systematic execution of Jewish inmates was taking place there. The plan was, he told Antoni Zielinski, for a frontal assault led by the tanks, followed immediately by his Jewish fighters, who could rally support from the inmates of the concentration camp.

As they emerged from the cellar, Antoni checked his weapon and felt the adrenalin pumping, combined with the thrill of what he knew would follow. He had removed an *MP40* Schmeisser machine gun and a box with spare ammunition clips from the back of a German vehicle when they had carried out the raid on the Gestapo headquarters. The weapon had a dual magazine giving him a rapid-fire capability of up to sixty-four rounds and he felt both a sense of anticipation and an impatience to take more German lives. His desire to kill had become embedded within him and he no longer had any thought for his victims other than pure hatred for the evil they inflicted upon his race and the Polish people. When he thought about his parents in quieter moments, he felt almost uncontrollable anger and a need to exact vengeance in whatever way he could. He looked across at Gedeon, his fellow fighter to the left, and they nodded with a grim smile of acknowledgement. On his other side was the man with whom he had been sharing accommodation, John Ward, who had insisted on joining him for the mission, stating that he could not broadcast on the BBC unless he had experienced real action. Ward spoke Polish but with some difficulty, adding English idioms at the end of sentences, which those who knew him well had gradually learned to understand. Hence, it was no surprise when Ward said to him in Polish, "I think this is going to be a picnic" but adding, "old chap" to the end of his words in English. He held a handgun in one hand with a German stick grenade in the other, and was wearing the uniform of a Polish officer, having been awarded with a commissioned rank by General Bór-Komorowski. They paused at the end of the street and waited, their signal to move being the arrival of the Panther tank.

They were only 100 metres from their previous target but now there were no Germans relaxing on the streets outside Gestapo HQ, only occasional passing armoured vehicles travelling at high speed to avoid attack. Their morale was high as news had come in of vast areas of the city falling under Polish control. They knew that the Russian forces had reached the Eastern bank of the Vistula, together with the Soviet-controlled Polish First Army. The Polish commander had made contact with the resistance fighters, assuring them that a river crossing would be made to support the uprising. John Ward remarked dryly, "Today, we have real broadcasting strength, old boy, with my friend here." Zdzisław Jeziorański had joined them the night before, saying he could not leave Ward to get the scoop of "live" reporting on the action, whilst he was confined to a studio. Both of them had been broadcasting daily bulletins and forwarding these to the BBC in London but they were setting up a studio in Warsaw with the aim of transmitting directly to the citizens as the uprising progressed. They had taken over the *Pocztowa Kasa Oszczędności* (postal savings bank) on Jasna Street and were establishing what was to be known as *Błyskawica* (lightning) radio station, from which they planned to commence transmitting imminently. Jeziorański was carrying a German *Schiessbecher* rifle grenade launcher and grinned as Antoni looked over at him. At that moment, they heard the squeaking and rumbling of an approaching tank. Antoni edged around the end of the building in which they had been sheltering. Wacław Micuta had his head stuck out of the turret, complete with a German military side cap, and was rather foolishly raising his arm in a mock Hitler salute, before lowering himself back inside the tank, behind which men in German uniform were marching. Antoni signalled those behind to move forwards. They crawled towards the open square beyond and looked at their target, an old prison with the main block viewable above three-metre-high grim walls stretching right and left, in which were set large square watchtowers. The noise of the approaching Panther grew louder, and, on Antoni's order, those of his men who were dressed in German uniforms marched to join the others behind the tank. His heart was pounding as they walked across the open square wondering whether they would be challenged or fired upon. However, other than seeing some Germans in the nearest watchtower idly watching, there was nothing other than the clank and noise of the tank as it rumbled forwards.

Antoni signalled to the fifteen remaining men behind him and the ratcheting of weapons being cocked could be heard. The tank continued on its course, now approaching the outer gates of the camp in front of which some guards appeared, one raising his hand up in a gesture to halt whilst others knelt behind him, their weapons held to the shoulder. The Panther slowed to a stop, the engine being lightly revved rhythmically, then the turret doors opened and Micuta's head and shoulders emerged. He waved a greeting at the German guards, then reached inside and in an almost nonchalant manner threw two stick grenades towards them. At the same time, there was a dramatic flash and roar as the tank's 75mm forward gun fired and the front gates to the compound disappeared in a huge explosion, followed rapidly by two crashes as the grenades detonated. The tank moved forwards, the men behind crouching as they followed, whilst from the watchtowers machine guns began firing towards them. Jeziorański knelt on the floor beside the *Schiessbecher* grenade launcher, which he held against the ground at an angle before taking aim. There was a loud, thunderous report and a puff of smoke, followed a second later by a flash as the nearest watchtower was hit, the machine gun falling silent. Now Antoni turned to Aaron Zapowski, who was already in position knelt on one knee with his *Panzerfaust* weapon wedged tightly against his shoulder, the bulbous head of its projectile poised. A moment later, a crashing roar was followed by a massive explosion as the highly explosive warhead hit the next watchtower, the roof of which was blown off.

The tank moved through the gates with the Jewish forward line shouting to the prisoners within in Yiddish to re-assure them, and, telling them, if possible, to disarm the guards. Inside, German troops were forming a defensive line in front of their barracks behind three parked armoured *Kübelwagen* vehicles. Others were firing from the old prison walls but the tank raised the long barrel of its forward gun and began systematically firing, gradually reducing the resistance. Antoni moved forwards firing his Schmeisser machine gun from the hip, with John Ward at his side, who was armed with a Luger pistol, which was his weapon of choice. "Every *kelev* (dog) I see will die this day," Antoni muttered through gritted teeth after he shot three German SS guards who had held their hands to the back of their heads, attempting to surrender. Smoke filled the air and, in front of them, barrack hut buildings were on fire. Suddenly, there were shouts and screams above them and two guards were pushed off the wall to their deaths by their former captives. As they advanced deep into the concentration camp, both male and female Jewish inmates began emerging in their blue striped attire, bearing the yellow Star of David with the term *Jude* printed in the centre. As they moved forwards by the side of a wall, trying to avoid the increasingly sporadic shots coming from the barrack building ahead, a stick grenade landed close by them. Antoni grabbed Ward, pulling him roughly away and to the ground, just as the device exploded and Ward felt a searing burning pain in his thigh. He looked down at the rip in his Polish uniform trousers from where blood began pouring. "By Jove, old chap," he said crisply and calmly, "I appear to have a slight problem with my leg." Antoni shouted to one of his men to find their medic, then turned back to Ward. "You must stay here, my friend, but first I have to save you so we can listen to more of your bullshit on the British news." Ward watched as the man, who minutes before had cold-bloodedly executed three men, reached into his tunic, from which he pulled a bottle of *Slivovitz* fruit brandy. He took a long swig, and then passed it to Ward, who welcomed the warmth flooding through him from the strong plum-flavoured spirit. "This will help ease the pain. I have no morphine to give you." Their brief respite was interrupted by a burst of machine gun fire, which hit the wall behind them, and Zielinski immediately identified the source from the flashes – a workshop building fifty metres to their right. "Excuse me, old boy," he briefly cried out in English, but with a thick Polish accent, before firing a long burst in return; then he crouched as he ran zig-zagging, towards the workshop from where bursts of fire erupted. Ward watched, feeling helpless, but with admiration for the courage of his comrade in arms. He saw Zielinski lob a grenade, then throw himself to the floor as it exploded. Then, he was up again, shooting from the hip as he stood, the loud staccato rhythm of his weapon echoing off the square despite the noise of battle raging ahead. Ward watched, virtually oblivious to the throbbing pain in his thigh, horrifically mesmerised by what he now witnessed as Zielinski walked the last few paces, lifting his Schmeisser to head height. He emptied his magazine in one long deadly burst, spraying to right and left to ensure he had killed all of the guards.

Zielinski now had a reputation for never taking prisoners he gained from killing and did not hide the satisfaction he gained from killing, a trait Ward found both unpalatable and disturbing. He tried not to think of his combat experience and hated the necessity for the grim task of fighting, although he never questioned the justice of doing so. He could not bear to allow his thoughts to dwell upon the fact that those opposing them had family and loved ones. They were the aggressors and many of them were, he knew, guilty of heinous crimes. However, but he also recognised that the evil of the Nazi regime had spread a culture of barbaric cruelty, justified by a twisted philosophy where a cruel end justified all means.

The irony of what he witnessed that day was not lost on him as Zielinski, upon his return, wearing a broad grin, pulled a dressing from his tunic and carefully bound Ward's thigh wound to stem the flow of blood. "*Te dranie to szumowiny,* (Those bastards are scum) but now they are nothing!" He threw his hands up, dismissing his killing spree with a gesture, and displayed genuine compassion to Ward as he placed his arm around him, supporting and half carrying him until they found a medic from the *Zośka* battalion. They saved 348 Jewish prisoners that day with a loss of only two Polish fighters.

Ward continued to witness appalling scenes in the ensuing days and weeks as the Polish Home Army's initial successes were countered by elite German troops sent to quell the uprising. They waited, in vain, for the expected crossing of the Vistula by the Soviet Red Army, which they were assured would happen. Units of the Polish First Army crossed the river in mid-September, by which time the Polish resistance had been forced to withdraw from the Old Town and centre of Warsaw, captured from the Germans in the early days of the uprising. Zielinski, Ward, and Jeziorański, had all survived but Zielinski's Jewish force had suffered over fifty per cent casualties killed, wounded or missing. When they withdrew from the city centre, they took to the sewers as a means of escape but were anguished by the news of the desperate people they left behind. Vast numbers were systematically massacred in their homes as the SS indiscriminately shot anyone they found, including the elderly, women, and children who were not involved in the conflict. On 5th August, Hitler gave personal orders to "kill anything that moves" as a response to the uprising, which resulted in the massacre of 50,000 Poles in the Wola region of Warsaw. Himmler had also given orders for horrific measures of reprisal to be inflicted on the people of Warsaw, which he followed by ordering the eradication of the city itself. It was as if humanity had ceased to have any meaning, which gave a terrible direction to, and reason behind, the executions carried out by Zielinski and many others.

Both Ward and Jeziorański were now broadcasting every day, not only to the Polish in Warsaw, but also sending increasingly desperate bulletins to London describing their plight, without the expected relief from the Russian forces. The Polish First Army, which did cross the river to support the uprising, was not adequately supported by their Soviet commanders and suffered enormous losses before they were forced to withdraw back to the Eastern bank of the Vistula. Zielinski had become increasingly angry and bitter at what he perceived was an international betrayal of both the Polish and the Jewish race. He began to openly speak of his desire to escape Europe and join other Jewish people who were settling in greater numbers in the British Mandate for Palestine, a territory which the Jews regarded as their sacred homeland.

On 30th September 1944, Ward, Jeziorański, and Zielinski joined a group of commanders for a meeting with General Tadeusz Bór-Komorowski in a half bombed out building on Kredytowa-Królewska Street. Komorowski was dressed smartly in full uniform but looked very tired and drawn. They sat in an intact ornate room with a dining table and twelve chairs arranged around it, which, despite the devastation around the building, still retained classical oil paintings on the walls. The General stood to address them, "*Moi dzielni towarzysze,* (My brave comrades) I am today promoted to Commander-in-Chief of all Polish forces." He paused as there were mutters of appreciation and some applause from those around the table. He looked at each of them in turn. "We have sacrificed so much already in our valiant struggle but we cannot prevail against the overwhelming forces we face. I have appealed to the Russian commander Konstantin Rokossovsky, but he has told me he is under a directive from Soviet Premier Stalin himself. The Soviets will not commit their forces and, regrettably, believe we are reactionary enemies of their revolution. They are awaiting our capitulation and now is the sad time when we must surrender, but we will do so with honour. Our time is not yet nigh but we have proven to the world how Poland will not bow under the yoke of Nazi tyranny. We have fought like lions and, today, I have met with the German Wehrmacht commander, General Günther Rohr, who has agreed that all Polish fighters who surrender will be treated under the Geneva Convention as prisoners of war and afforded all their rights accordingly. We will be permitted to march in columns to our dispersal points. I regret…" The General paused, looking solemnly at Zielinski, then with a sigh, "I regret that he does not have authority over how Jewish fighters may be treated."

Zielinski exploded, banging his fist on the table, "So, once again, we Jews are sacrificed. They will slaughter us without question and the world will look the other way." His eyes were blazing, and his arm outstretched, "We fight for a Poland that will not care because we are disposable. I swear to all of you on my parents' lives that I will fight on but no longer for Poland, but for a new land which shall be called Zion, or Judea, and no-one will ever threaten us again, not ever.

"Nations ignored what the Nazis were doing to us and would not accept us as refugees. The world has turned a blind eye to the death camps, to the slaughter of our race, and now they will sacrifice Poland again, if not to the Germans, then to the Russians. Poland will be swallowed up by Stalin's Soviet Union if the Germans lose this war. The Russians joined in the plundering of this country with the Germans in 1939, and they now want it all. This is not liberation, it is betrayal." He slammed his fist on the table again, drew his pistol, and fired into the ceiling, causing dust and plaster to rain down.

There was a moment of silence before General Bór-Komorowski spoke softly, "Antoni, I need to speak with you but understand I have arranged for you to be given safe passage out of Poland with John Ward, and Zdzisław Jeziorański." Then, in the continuing uncomfortable silence, adding, "Although, since working for the BBC, Jeziorański, I believe you have now adopted the stage name Jan Nowak. All you need to do is learn to Brylcream your hair like John Ward, grow a little moustache, and you can be British." He laughed and the others joined in, breaking the tension.

After the meeting, Komorowski summoned Zielinski to another room where they sat on wooden chairs facing one another. "My dear Lieutenant Zielinski, you have done more than we could have asked and now it is our turn to help you. You are correct that if you remain here, you will either be murdered by the Germans, or sent to a concentration camp. Even if you survive, you might then fall victim to the whims of Stalin's Red Army who have already butchered many of our people. I have useful, influential contacts in England and I am arranging for you to be placed into the Palestine smuggling network, which is run by two Zionist fighters in the elite para-military force, *Haganah*, known as *Palmach*. They have fought for the British in the war but I think it likely it will not be long before they turn on them and fight for Jewish independence." The General offered Zielinski a cigarette from a slim silver case, which he declined, before lighting one himself. "I have misjudged the Jewish race and have had prejudices which come from my upbringing. It is too late for me now to try and atone for my shortcomings or seek forgiveness for my countrymen or myself. These are terrible, tragic times for Poland; but our tragedy pales against the horrors perpetrated against your race. I do not believe that either of our peoples will find freedom here after this war is over. I fear a Russian victory will result in us exchanging one evil for another. I want to thank you for what you have done here. Your fight has not been in vain as we have weakened the German forces and shown the world that freedom can fight back" He leant forwards, offering his hand to Zielinski, who shook it warmly.

"General, I thank you. My wish is to join my people and fight for the freedom that we have been denied for centuries. We have suffered terrible injustices, had our land and property stolen, and our families butchered." He looked directly at Komorowski, who felt a little unnerved by the cold, penetrating stare. "I will have no hesitation in killing anyone who threatens not just my people but even a single Jewish person. No-one will ever do to the Jews again what we have witnessed in our lifetimes nor stand in our way." His look softened again as he reached in his tunic for his flask, from which he took a generous drink of *Slivovitz*. Then both men stood, shaking hands again.

"You mentioned two Zionist fighters who will help smuggle me to Palestine. Do you know their names?" Zielinski asked.

"Ah yes," the General responded, "They are Yitzhak Rabin and Rafi Eitan."

Excerpts from reports filed by John Ward in Warsaw for the BBC

September 2ⁿᵈ 1944

Warsaw is for the second time during the past five years fighting for its freedom. Almost exactly five years ago Warsaw was besieged by the Germans. For a month they hammered the city with heavy artillery and air bombs. In 1939 before the German invaders succeeded in taking Warsaw they destroyed 15% of buildings and damaged 75%. Today it is a different story... There is not a single house in the whole of Warsaw that is not damaged. There is no question of surrender in this second battle for the Polish capital. During five years of bitter occupation the people of Poland have learnt that it is better to suffer death in battle than to surrender again to Nazi brutality and murder.

I myself have been in Warsaw for over three years and can be a witness to many acts of savagery which would scarcely be credited by any civilised people. Man-hunts in the streets of Warsaw were a daily occurrence. The usual method was for SS troops to block a street and take all men and women between the ages of 14 and 50 years to special concentration camps. Here they were sorted – People who showed any sign of intelligence were then sent to permanent concentration camps where mostly they died after a few months. The rest were sent to forced labour in Germany. Any people who tried to escape were shot in the street.

The situation in Warsaw is critical.

September 4ᵗʰ 1944

*Today is the 35th day of the battle for the Polish capital
– a city with a population of 1,300,000 people. During
those 35 days there has been no communication with the
provinces. Therefore no food has reached Warsaw. Rations
are already very short, in many places people are starving…
Warsaw during the first few days of the uprising received some
much-needed help in the form of ammunition dropped by the
RAF, but for the past two or three weeks has received no relief
whatever.*

*Poland is our oldest ally in this war. Despite all she
has suffered at the hands of the German invaders, she has
remained always an active power against the enemy. Polish
troops fought in France in 1940; later Polish pilots took part
in the Battle of Britain, her troops fought at Tobruk, and
are still fighting in Italy and France. The Home Army in
Poland itself has now risen and is also fighting openly as it has
fought under cover during the whole war. Poland is a country
which I, as an Englishman, am proud to call an ally. She
produced no government to co-operate with the Germans. The
only government she has acknowledged is the one in exile in
London. To end I would like to make an appeal to the British
nation. It is short: HELP FOR WARSAW*

September 12ᵗʰ 1944

*The enemy bombing of Warsaw is indiscriminate, mostly
the bombs drop on residential houses that are actually playing
no part in the fight for the city. The civil population is suffering
horribly from these bombardments. What little food they had
is buried in the ruins and they are turned out into bullet-
swept streets to seek some shelter, however meagre. Yesterday
I spoke to the survivors of a family who had been buried in
ruins three times. Three of them were wounded and none of
them had had any food for three days. Two of the family had*

been killed. This is only one case of the thousands in Warsaw today. The one question on all peoples' lips is: "My God, when will it end?""

15

The Will of History

Saturday 8th July 1944 – 12 noon
The Berghof, Berchtesgaden, Obersalzberg, Germany

They listened in abject admiration to the words of the Führer whom they held in awe as if he had been sent by God, which many believed was the case. Despite recent military setbacks, they believed in him implicitly. Hitler was animated as he spoke. "We shall unleash a power so great, so destructive, and with such ruthlessness that the world will marvel in the aftershock, recognising and fearing the power of Germany. This is our fate: this is the time that has been chosen for us. That drunken gangster, Churchill, and the cripple, Roosevelt, will experience a wrath so terrible that they will beg our forgiveness for bombing the Reich as we reach for what awaits us: *Uberwältigender Sieg.*" (overwhelming victory) The Führer, dressed in his double-breasted grey military-style tunic, had become animated, pacing as he had been speaking, beads of sweat now forming on his forehead as he clenched his hands together, looking upwards as if appealing to a greater power.

His inner circle were there as guardians of his master plan, including Martin Bormann, Hermann Göring, Albert Speer, Heinrich Himmler, Karl Dönitz, Joseph Goebbels, and Hans Kammler. Those visiting guests he had personally selected to be the architects of his strategy for *Uberwältigender Sieg* were spellbound as they listened, convinced he was going to deliver them the victory that was, most assuredly, the destiny for Germany. Hanna Reitsch, Wernher von Braun, Walter Dornberger, Friedrich von Weizsäcker, and Ritter von Greim were standing in a semi-circle facing the window with its vast view of the Untersberg mountain framing the Führer. He was standing with his senior trusted inner-circle, positioned to his immediate left, in front of some tables on which there were china cups and saucers from the tea that had been served earlier. Hitler's rasping, guttural voice now calmed – "I have, with my unshakeable resolve, formulated a master plan for the destruction of our enemies, combining the skills of those within this room, which forms the foundation for the ultimate act of the war, *Unternehmen Armageddon*. I intend to stay this course with ice-cold determination. I recognise that I am the executor of the will of history. What people think of me at present is all of no consequence, because I am chosen to execute the will of Providence. There are four of you in this room who will be the executioners of my great plan. You, *Herr Reichsminister*," he turned to Albert Speer, "have been the person to whom I entrusted the overseeing of my historic project, and you have already prepared the ground?"

Speer, dressed in a brown military uniform, clicked his heels raising his arm smartly, addressing Hitler, *"Mein Führer*, in June 1942, as part of my duties as Reich Minister of Armaments, I met with a leading German physicist by the name of Wernher Heisenberg, and asked to be briefed on the benefits of nuclear science, not for energy, but weapons. He informed me that if we had such a nuclear bomb, the outcome of the war was an assured victory for Germany. However, he stated that the development of such a weapon would take at least four years. You, *mein Führer*, demanded that we achieve this within three years. Under my direction, liaising through Herr von Weizsäcker, we have been secretly working on this project and our nuclear weapon is nearing completion. By early 1945, we will have this incredible bomb."

Hitler held his hands out, with a brief smile, gesturing that all was well. "*Wunderbar!* Now to the execution of my great plan." Hitler walked slowly towards the group of guests, bowed briefly and smiled at Hanna, who felt a little overwhelmed, "*Mein liebling der Reich*, Hanna, you have been test-flying a captured British Lancaster bomber, I believe, under the personal direction of General von Greim. I am personally giving you the honour of delivering our new Armageddon weapon to Mr Churchill in London." Hanna felt a tremor within, and a thrilling wave of emotion to be so selected. She executed a salute before Hitler kissed her hand. He then turned to von Weizsäcker – "You are the brains unlocking the power that German science has delivered to us. This will make the whole world tremble and force them to recognise the invincible strength of the Reich and the power of my unshakeable will." The room was stilled and silenced as his voice had raised, ensnaring their attention. Next, the Führer walked in front of Wernher. "Herr Professor, and now a Sturmbannführer in the SS too, I see. I might have known the Reichsführer would have his nose to the ground watching over me." There was a ripple of laughter as Heinrich Himmler snapped to attention uttering the words, "*Heil Hitler!*" Hitler had now relaxed and appeared almost genial as he spoke smilingly to Wernher. "Your rockets, Herr Professor von Braun, will secure the future and will be Germany's salvation. The new and larger rocket I requested from you a year ago will carry our new wonder weapon. This will bring Armageddon to Moscow and annihilate the vile communist vermin that pollute our world. I am advised that the under-sea trials of the A-4 or *Vergeltungswaffen-2* (vengeance weapon) have been a success?"

"*Jawohl, mein Führer.* The performance capabilities of the rocket are unaffected by being submerged. We will have two of the larger rockets capable of carrying a ten-ton warhead ready by February 1945."

"*Sehr gut,*" (very good) Hitler replied, patting him on the shoulder. "Ach so, this is where my fourth executioner comes into play." He spun round to his senior entourage behind him, "*Herr Grossadmiral,* I think you have something to tell us?" Karl Dönitz was a tall, slim man in his mid-fifties, with a commanding presence in his dark blue uniform with thick gold sleeve tresses (bandings) denoting his rank, and an Iron Cross at his neck. He clicked his heels, extended his right arm, before speaking.

"*Mein Führer,* as per your orders, I have been working with General Dornberger to test and develop underwater chambers that can be towed behind a submarine capable of launching the V-2 rocket. I can announce that we have succeeded in overcoming the obstacles associated with this project and that we plan to use our new type XXI *Elektroboot* submarine as the towing vehicle; this will be deployed from our base at St Nazaire. We will soon have the means to cross the Atlantic, taking the latest version of the V-2 rocket, which Herr von Braun has been developing at Nordhausen. *Meine Kameraden,* we will have the capability of delivering a nuclear attack on New York City with devastating effect." There were gasps around the room as Hitler clasped his hands together in a victorious gesture, smiling broadly as his entourage burst into spontaneous applause. Then, as he raised his hands in a gesture to stop, he spoke quietly, his eyes looking distantly, "I have had the necessary will to marshal the might of Germany to take back our land, demand respect for the Reich, and instil pride in the German *Volk.* Now, as our enemies wage an aggressive war against us, joining forces with the communist barbarians, Germany will strike back with unimagineable force and history will record they paid a terrible price for opposing us. They will be cowed by our overwhelming superiority and beg for peace in their terror. We must wreak our terrible vengeance but, in so doing, mankind will benefit. Millions of lives will be saved; moreover, the security for the Third Reich and the purity of our race will be assured for a thousand years." As he finished speaking, there were Nazi salutes and the vast room echoed with the words, "*Sieg Heil*". in utter awe of the Führer and his providential foresight.

6th August 1944 – 2pm
10, Downing Street, London

John Colville, the Assistant Private Secretary to the Prime Minister, paused a moment before knocking on the polished panelled door in the victory-style rhythm he had adopted, matching the morse code three dots and a dash used by the BBC in radio news broadcasts. "Come!" The growling voice of the Prime Minister gave no clue to his mood. As Colville entered, Churchill was poised, nodding in front of a large map of Europe on which were positioned various flags, including Swastikas, Union Jacks, Maple Leaves and the Stars and Stripes. His large frame was dressed in pin-striped trousers, over which he wore a waistcoat and chain, and his familiar spotted bow tie. He was leaning towards the map, examining it closely, a cigar in his mouth, and a glass of whisky in one hand. Gesturing towards the map, as he turned to Colville, his eyebrows set in a furrow above half-moon glasses. "You see, Jock, as the great bard said, '*Our doubts are traitors and make us lose the good we oft might win by fearing to attempt.*' Had I not seized the moment, just six weeks ago, to sanction our great crusade, despite the grave warnings about the weather, and worries that the Panzers had moved their position, we would not now be celebrating the triumph of our breakout from the Cotentin Peninsula. Nevertheless, our certainty of the inevitability of victory and the right of our cause must not overrule our prudence." He lifted his glass to Colville before swiftly downing the contents.

Colville gave a polite cough, enabling an interruption, "Major General Sir Stewart Menzies is in the ante room, sir, shall I show him in?"

"You may show him in and ask Elizabeth to join us as I will need, I think, to brief the King after our meeting."

That morning Churchill had received a call from Menzies which had been more than a little alarming. "Prime Minister, I have a matter of an urgent and concerning nature I must share with you about Germany's nuclear fission programme, which I must impart IP." The last letters were an acronym used between them for 'in person' when there was an issue of a major security threat demanding communication without any danger of interception.

Minutes later, Menzies arrived in a dark grey suit, ushered in by Colville and accompanied by Elizabeth Nel, Churchill's personal secretary. Churchill raised his right hand to Colville, who nodded, and bowed in deference as he left the room, closing the door behind him. The Prime Minister then put on his jacket, walking over to a drinks cabinet from which he extracted a decanter. "May I offer you a dram of whisky, my dear Menzies? Johnnie Walker Black Label, nothing better."

"The smallest measure, sir, thank you." Menzies responded, having recognised, over time, that Churchill appeared more accepting of difficult private briefings if they were held in an informal atmosphere, which sharing a drink engendered. He was a slim, diminutive figure, in his mid-fifties, with little hair and a small military-style moustache. His words were spoken in a clipped manner, carefully pronounced, reflecting his privileged background. Churchill squirted soda onto the measures of whisky in two cut-glass tumblers, one of which he handed to Menzies, raising his; they touched their glasses together. Colville looked from Churchill to his secretary, raising his eyebrows, to which the Prime Minister responded, "I think I need your report recording, and I can assure you that, after many years of suffering my impossible demands, and my insufferable outbursts, which Miss Nel endures with remarkable restraint, I can vouch for her and have come to trust her implicitly. You may speak freely."

Elizabeth Nel smiled briefly in acknowledgement at "the boss" as she called him. After four years in her position since becoming his secretary at age twenty-three, she had come to both adore and respect this giant of a man for his clarity of thought and dedication to duty backed by dogged determination. He was demanding and impossible sometimes, yet he had the grace to acknowledge privately his indiscretions, often making her smile as he ridiculed himself to her in apology. She never objected nor criticised but would be supportive of him when she knew he needed a word of reassurance. She sat in a Regency-style chair, dressed in a three-quarter-length mid-grey skirt and a black jacket with military-style buttons. She held a pad in her lap, her pen poised to take shorthand notes.

Stewart Menzies began, "As you are aware, sir, we are, or were, in communication with the former head of the German *Abwehr* (military intelligence), Admiral Wilhelm Canaris. As the war progressed, he has become increasingly disillusioned with Hitler and finally agreed to pass over certain information which might assist in his overthrow. I have met with this man personally and I can vouch that he is a gentleman, and one who can be trusted. He was dismissed from his post last February when Himmler took over, briefly held under house arrest, then reinstated to the office responsible for securing supplies to the Reich in June. Last month, sir, as you know, there was an attempt on Hitler's life when a bomb was detonated at his Wolf's Lair Headquarters at Rastenburg. Following the failure to kill him, the plotters and those suspected to have had involvement are being rounded up."

"Ah yes," Churchill growled, lighting another cigar, puffing large clouds of smoke, "as Napoleon said, '*Treason is a matter of dates*', and those who are hounded now as traitors by the Nazis will, in time, be hailed as heroes by the victor or, indeed, as Alexandre Dumas more fully said in *The Count of Monte Cristo*, echoing those words, '*The difference between patriotism and treason is only a matter of dates...*' Do please continue, Sir Stewart."

"Sir, on July 23rd, Canaris was arrested but managed to smuggle a message out, which we have only just received and decoded. Communication with those inside Germany with whom we have contact has been virtually impossible since the 20th July plot. I think I should read the message in full to you, Prime Minister, as it has grave consequences for the Allies." He reached into his briefcase, from which he extracted a file, placing it on the small antique table beside his chair. He took out the top piece of paper and began reading:

"'*To: Major General Sir Stewart Menzies, SIS – London,*

Today, I am informed that my name is on a list of suspects for being involved in the plot to kill Hitler. I believe my survival is unlikely, which is merely a matter of time. I have done, in all conscience, what I believe to be right for my country and yet I shall doubtless be judged to be a traitor for which I will be executed. Humanity would not judge me well if I did not reveal the dreadful information which has come into my hands. However, no one person, and least of all the dictator under whose terrible will my people have succumbed, should be empowered to unleash the destruction which I regret to say is now a terrifying reality.

Our scientists have succeeded in developing the technology for a nuclear bomb which will have devastating explosive potential beyond anything previously seen or even imagined by the world. The nuclear research unit is based in Hechingen and Haigerloch with uranium production taking place at the Auergesellschaft plant in Oranienburg. I have attached a list of the scientists I know are involved. I am informed they are gathering fissile material which takes time to create and develop for the required number of devices. One single bomb may wipe out an entire city and they are planning on launching an attack with three such weapons; on New York by submarine, on Moscow via a rocket, and from a captured British Lancaster bomber on London. The operation has been named by Hitler as 'Armageddon' and if it were not playing on the conscience of my friend, Grand Admiral Dönitz, who shared this with me, I might not have believed it. The Führer has ordered these attacks to be co-ordinated and the target date is set for February 1945. I pray to God that this message gets through for we cannot let this madman succeed in his diabolical plan.

My life, I think, is over and I ask that, perhaps, one day, a prayer may be said for me. I hope I be not judged as a traitor, but as one who placed mankind before the dark will of the Nazi cause. God forgive me for the part I have played.

Wilhelm Franz Canaris – Admiral
July 22nd 1944

Churchill had his head bowed in his hands for a moment, his brows furrowed, before sighing then looking up with determination, his jaw set, reflecting his purpose and command. "I want to convene a meeting tomorrow at 10am with the Chief of the Imperial General Staff, General Sir Alan Brooke, the Director General of MI5, Sir David Petrie, Michael Perrin, the scientific head of the '*Tube Alloys* programme' (a secret British/Canadian project to develop nuclear weapons in WW2), and our dear Head of Bomber Command, Air Chief Marshall Sir Arthur Harris, with you in attendance, Sir Stewart. Our strategy will be based upon four principal elements.

"First, we must create a special forces unit whose sole purpose will be to snatch or despatch any German scientists involved in this dastardly project, preferably taking them alive. Whilst our primary objective will be to avoid this catastrophic event taking place, our second priority will be to get the scientists to the UK before the Americans get their hands on them. We will, on the surface, work with our American allies, of course, but our overall aim will be to obtain whatever knowledge these people have, with our loyalty being, above all, to the British Crown.

"Secondly, we must increase our bombing campaign targeting any part of their nuclear infrastructure, especially any facility which may fall into the hands of the advancing Soviets. Mark my words, our Russian friends today will, assuredly, be our adversaries of tomorrow and, doubtless, will be desperate to grasp the awesome power that they will rightly perceive these accursed weapons will give them and which, of course, they will doubtless wish to exploit in post-war Europe." Churchill rose from his seat and walked to the window overlooking the garden at the rear of Downing Street. He clenched his right hand into a fist and beat it rhythmically into his left as he pondered deeply, before continuing. "The final result of this war will assuredly be victory if it is concluded with what might be termed conventional weaponry; however, a bomb with a destructive force of such calamitous magnitude could alter the outcome. Such a weapon is assuredly not conventional, nor, in my view, morally acceptable. Therefore, our third task is that we must make plans to move the entire cabinet away from London but, I regret, without giving them reason. The affection and, indeed, the natural instinct of the human species for self-preservation, notwithstanding, perhaps, the word 'love,' that one might even use, which mankind naturally has for spouse and offspring, would overrule loyalty to the government under the threat of such a cataclysmic event." He paused again to re-light his cigar, puffing clouds of smoke before sitting back at his desk, assuming a resolute, determined look.

"Finally, and I must stress the vital importance I attach to this, this threat must be kept absolutely secret, and, indeed, we must never acknowledge, nor even concede, the possibility that Germany ever possessed, nor came near to possessing, an atomic bomb. All of your various dark resources, Sir Stewart, for covering up the horrific reality of that which we face must now be mobilised. I deem this one of the greatest tasks I have set during this dastardly conflict. If it be perceived that Hitler, with his band of Nazi thugs, even came near to possessing or exercising such power, you might imagine how it may encourage others to continue the struggle, even after the evil dictator is deposed, which would doubtless extend the war, or even motivate others to come to Germany's aid. You might also understand that the Soviets would, at best, re-double their efforts to capture such weapon facilities intact, or even, at worst, to conclude a peace with the Nazis. Such a strategy could conceivably result in the terrifying prospect of a pact which may threaten the free world, giving Stalin and Hitler a terrifying lever to, once again, carve up the territory of Europe between them.

"I believe, Sir Stewart, you utilise the term 'fogging' to describe the hiding of the truth through the illusion of false rumours, preposterous conspiracies, and evidential flaws dosed with a mere soupcon of truth to discredit the hidden reality?"

"Prime Minister!" Menzies responded in a mock display of shock, but with a twinkle in his eye, "I am utterly horrified that you feel that we might execute such action, but now you mention it, it does seem a damned fine idea."

Churchill briefly smiled his acknowledgement. "Miss Nel, I trust you have recorded the four pillars of my strategy to combat this menace?"

She looked up, momentarily replying with a confident assertive tone, "Of course, sir. I presume you will require a draft of a briefing paper preparing for tomorrow's meeting?"

"Indeed, Miss Nel, your assumption, which some may judge as presumptuous, does, in fact, do you credit." Churchill looked distantly, for a moment, adding, "As Macduff succinctly reflects in Shakespeare's '*Macbeth*', '*Boundless intemperance in nature is a tyranny; it hath been the untimely emptying of the happy throne, and fall of many kings.*' Let us hope Hitler's intemperate nature shall rapidly lead to his timely demise."

Saturday 30th September 1944 – 9:30am
HQ T-Force, Place de l'Opéra, Paris

The two men in British army uniform with maroon berets entered the ornate building bearing the pock marks of bullets on its walls from the liberation of Paris, which had taken place only one month previously. Inside the baroque interior there were boxes of papers and files stacked in what passed for a reception area around which people bustled, sorting the contents into piles that were then carried away by orderlies. They were ushered by an American guard to a desk where they were ordered to state their business by a middle-aged officer with short cropped greying hair, a thin moustache, and thick-lensed glasses. The taller of the two men saluted, "Sir, I am Captain Yitzhak Rabin, and this is Lieutenant Rafael Eitan of 10 Commando; we are expected for a meeting with Major General Kenneth Strong."

The American officer checked his clipboard, on which were typed out names and times, then spoke with a Texan drawl, "I guess you are expected, boys. Hell, your unit is in *Number 3 Troop Commando* it says here. You part of those boys known as goddamned X Troops? You Jewish fighters have one crazy reputation for kickin' ass."

The reply from Rabin was spoken in a cool, measured tone. "Perhaps, if the world had not abandoned us, we might have done more in this war, instead of being thrown into Nazi death camps."

"Where you from, son?" The officer looked up with an expression of compassion.

"Oh, we were lucky because our parents took us to Palestine before the systematic attempt by the Nazis to wipe out our race. My family was from the Ukraine, and my comrade here, his were from Russia. We are now living in our historical homeland but those we left behind have been persecuted and murdered, not only by the Germans, but also the Russians. That is why we fight because we will not suffer any more. We fight today for freedom from persecution by the Nazis but tomorrow, we will fight for our independence as a proud Jewish nation. Trust me, my friend, we will be strong and we will never suffer again, nor ever bow our heads in shame."

The American looked at the zeal in the young man's eyes in front of him, sensing the passion in his words. He stood up and walked round the desk, extending his hand to Rabin, "Major Austin S. Coburn, US Counter Intelligence Corps, I'm mighty pleased to make your acquaintance. Hell, you speak from the heart and I wish you well. Back home in Texas, my family have many Jewish friends and I'm only sorry that our President, FDR, failed to step up and offer more protection to you guys. If you here seeing Strong, I guess there must be something big goin' off which will be all hush-hush." He looked round furtively, for a moment, adding, "Anything you guys need, like real-quick where no-one needs to know, you just call me. I'm known as Mr Fix It, boys; no questions asked, but maybe the odd favour when it's needed." He tapped his nose with his forefinger then put it to his lips, before dropping his voice. "We call it networking; one of the guys in my section is in the Mafia and no bull, man, we find networking gets us a lot of booze, a whole heap of cigarettes, a few extra dollars, a lot of broads, and with the last mentioned, a whole heap of trouble. Anything you guys need, from cars, weapons, to equipment, Mr Fix It can get it." Rafi Eitan burst out laughing as he, too, shook the Major's hand. "You sound like one of us. In my race, we call that doing business. You scratch my back, and just maybe, I'll scratch yours but before doing so, perhaps, I'll negotiate additional terms." They enjoyed the levity of the moment as he handed them both a card on which was printed, 'Samuel Coburn Supplies', under which was written, 'International Supplies – London – New York – Paris; and, in brackets, ('Berlin Office opening soon'). Coburn put his finger to his lips again. "The clue is in the name boys, don't tell anyone but I too am Jewish."

Major Coburn led them down an ornate corridor with gilt cornices, and some classical oil paintings, which Eitan and Rabin were surprised had not been looted. At the end were two large panelled doors on which the Major knocked, winking as he let the two men pass, on the command from within. Inside were standing three men, one dressed in uniform who stepped forwards, "Good afternoon," he said in a clipped military voice. He had dark hair, large eyes, and an amenable look despite the very formal greeting. "I am Major General Kenneth Strong. How do you do?" He shook their hands brusquely. He then gestured to the first of the others in the room, a slightly stooped slim man, with receding hair, wearing a sports jacket, ill-fitting tie and round, thick-lensed glasses. "This is Professor Michael Perrin; he is head of a British scientific programme looking into advanced weaponry." The man nodded to them and coughed uncomfortably. Strong turned to the third man, "You will be delighted to know that this gentleman hails from Palestine and was, until recently, known as Szymon Perski, but has just changed his name to Shimon Peres."

He was a young man, no more than around 20, Rabin thought, but was very well dressed in a dapper suit, with dark, slightly unruly hair, brushed back from a handsome smiling face. He walked straight up to Rabin and Eitan, shaking hands firmly. He spoke warmly, "I have heard much about you both from your exploits with *Haganah*" (Zionist military organisation), and your various missions with the British army. We make strange bedfellows, do we not, working for those controlling our land, who prevent us having our own state, and who block access to more Jewish settlement?"

Rabin responded quickly, "My loyalties and those of my colleague are dedicated to the creation of a Jewish state. Nothing and no-one will deter us from achieving our aims, not even the British."

"Then we are on the same side" came the relaxed reply, "and it may interest you to know that I am here today on the direct orders of the chairman of the world Zionist Organisation, or Jewish Agency, David Ben-Gurion."

Strong interrupted, "Gentlemen, when you have finished plotting the downfall of the British Mandate in Palestine, might I suggest we concentrate on what unites us." His tone was cordial but commanding. He motioned them to take a seat, one of several positioned in front of a large table on which papers were arranged in neat piles. He retrieved a file, removing some photographs, which he passed over to them, then spoke in a grave tone. "My position is Director General of military intelligence and my role involves analysing any risks to the Allies, and, of course, protecting Britain's position. Gentlemen, we are facing one of the greatest threats to the world; one that sees us on the edge of a catastrophe of unbelievable magnitude. This results from the German development of what is called an atom bomb. In front of you are photographs of places associated with a plutonium enrichment programme taking place in Germany right now. Plutonium is needed as the component which enables what is called nuclear fission, an essential element in the detonation of an atomic bomb. The round structures are nuclear-reactors in which controlled nuclear material can have a sustaining reaction with an enormous release in energy or atomic power. The use of such advanced technology has, I regret, been turned by the Germans into weapons development and it appears they are on the verge of producing a bomb. A single atomic bomb, using such technology, just one, could destroy an entire city, killing hundreds of thousands of people in a single giant explosion. I am currently co-ordinating the operational section of what is known as T-Force, which has a specific remit to target any areas of scientific or advanced industrial interest in Germany together with our American allies. However, we are, of course, concerned that we secure the technological expertise that will assist us in developing our own atomic bomb. You might imagine the insurance this will give to us in protecting our position in the world after the war. Dr Perrin, please." He sat down as the scientist shuffled to a large map of Europe.

"Gentlemen, I regret that we have conclusive evidence that Germany, through a programme termed *Uranverein,* have developed the capability of producing such a weapon." He lifted a pointer and highlighted three areas: Peenemünde, on the Baltic coast, where he described rockets had been developed carrying conventional explosive; Mittelbau-Dora near Nordhausen where a concentration camp supplied slave labour to a nearby underground rocket manufacturing facility; Hechingen and neighbouring Haigerloch, on the edge of the Black Forest, where nuclear research and development were taking place. "In conjunction with the Americans, we have launched *Operation Alsos,* which is a joint initiative geared at seizing as much nuclear plant or material as we can. In addition, under a further operation named *Epsilon,* we want to capture as many of their scientists as possible. The Soviets are advancing fast and our primary aim, apart from preventing Germany from using such a weapon, is to prevent this devilish technology from falling into Russian hands. I can tell you that the Germans are ahead of us and we need to be well ahead of the Russians in this field in order to prevent, what the PM has described as, "a catastrophic communist threat to the world emerging." I can inform you that I head up an operation, known as '*Tube Alloys*', involved in nuclear research. We are getting closer to having our own bomb but, if we can exploit the German advances made with this technology, it will massively accelerate our programme."

Rabin interjected, "Forgive me, but I am struggling to understand the relevance of this to our work. We are commandos not scientists or politicians and our training is in military skills. To put it bluntly, we specialise in covert operations and killing Nazis."

Shimon Peres then spoke in a quiet but authoritative tone, "Captain Rabin, we are Jews and that is why you are here. We want you to target the Jewish scientists who are working, or who have worked on the *Uranverein* project in Germany. Some are forced to work for the Nazis which they do to avoid virtual certain death in the concentration camps. Put simply, we want these people rescued and smuggled back to England rather than the United States."

"Gentlemen," Major General Strong cut in, leaning forwards at his desk, with a resolute look on his face. "Your mission is to establish a small unit, extract those scientists we seek, Jewish or Non-Jewish, and persuade them, by any means necessary, to travel to England, under armed escort of course."

"Ah, kidnapping, you mean, sir?" Rafi Eitan raised his head with a sardonic smile.

"I think, Lieutenant, the term 'by any means necessary' is self-explanatory but I know you X Troops from No *3 Commando* make up your own rules. However, I have another mission for you first, which is to pop over to Poland and rescue two chaps. One is a former British airman, who provides BBC reports and invaluable intelligence from behind enemy lines. He goes by the name of John Ward. The other is a man who has been leading the Jewish section of the resistance during the Warsaw Uprising. He has quite a reputation for, as you succinctly put it, killing Nazis."

Rabin cut in, "Forgive me, sir, but isn't Poland occupied by the Germans?"

"I believe it is, but don't worry, old chap, I won't tell them if you don't." Strong smiled with a mischievous look. "We need a plan to get them out and that's where you come in."

"And our Jewish friend's name?" Rabin opened his hands in a questioning gesture.

"Antoni Zielinski" came the reply as the Major General got up from his desk and went to a cabinet in one corner of the room. "I think a drink is called for, don't you? Jerry left us with quite a selection."

16

Apocalypse...The End of Days

This time, David and Mehedi were admitted, together with General Moshe Gellner, through the rear gated entrance to the home of Lieutenant Colonel Tzadok Berkowicz. They were all armed heavily and were wearing their uniforms to avoid suspicion in case they were observed. Berkowicz peered around the gate, peering briefly to right and left, checking the street before closing it, an *Uzi* sub-machine gun cradled in his arms. They had risked calling him on his mobile to arrange a meeting at short notice.

The previous day, Moshe had sat down with David and Mehedi drawing together a plan of action. The General, with his customary flair for foresight and analysis, led the discussion mapping out their objectives on the chart in his office. He had identified four principal elements that needed addressing, to which he gave titles. These were:

Omer Ravid and Unit 235

State protection

Military intervention

National Security and secrecy

Moshe Gellner had assumed overall command, not by agreement but through an instinctive acceptance by David and Mehedi of his rank, status, and planning capabilities. They were sitting in armchairs in his library/study, looking up at Moshe as he addressed them. "I think we are agreed that the immediate and over-riding priority must be the threat to Israel emanating from Ravid and unknown associates. We can surmise that he or his organisation, probably still known as Unit 235, are chief suspects behind the assassinations and disappearances of former intelligence agents. That, David, would appear to complete your mission." He smiled, despite the gravity of their analysis, as he added, "Therefore, if you wish to leave now, Mehedi and I can tidy up matters." Over the years they had served in the IDF, they all recognised the importance of humour despite the severest of circumstances, which had served well in maintaining morale when each of them was faced with active service.

David was holding his middle finger up in a gesture to Moshe, as he responded, "I think you need to keep me in there, General, to protect your back from this *ahabal* (dumbass) and his goats."

The come back from Mehedi was swift, "Listen, you shekel-sucking *yatzur* (weirdo), you owe me a *Dior* suit, and, guess what, I now require this to be made of wool, cashmere, and silk. We Arabs learned how to trade before you people learned how to lend money."

The General continued, "I'm delighted we have a unified team. We need to investigate Omer Ravid, scout his home or HQ, check any additional intelligence, look for any weaknesses, and establish allegiances to him from those of influence. This especially includes those at the top, including our prime minister. No-one is above suspicion here, and God knows, there have been enough prime ministers involved in this comedy of errors already. David, you check out intel, and I think we should look into Ravid's background; start at the very beginning. We need to be in possession of all the links that have motivated him. I think, perhaps, we need to investigate the nuclear scientist, Yehudi Krimmer, who brought him up. We know he is alive and resides in England, so worth following up."

David interjected, "I may just be able to help there. My cousin, Benjamin, works for MI6 and he can be trusted. You would love him, Mehedi; he is a member of *Na'amod* and seems to think you lot bring much-needed culture to Israel."

Mehedi just lifted two derisory fingers, *"Rakuv!"* (Decomposed matter)

"Your bond is uplifting," the General remarked dryly, "Mehedi, you check out Ravid's strength, his HQ, known supporters etc. David, you dig out what you can on his background; a visit to his estranged daughter, Shira, might assist.

"State protection requires that we look at securing bases where we have nuclear weapons once we know who we can trust. We can scarcely imagine the disastrous consequences of a pre-emptive nuclear strike from Israel against Iran. This would destabilise the entire region and the repercussions would be unthinkable. Further Russian aggression in the region could be triggered, isolation from the US, notwithstanding an Arab backlash that could put the Middle East back into a war footing like we have not seen for fifty years. Nuclear retaliation might result, triggering a global catastrophe. Critically, we also need to put in place forces to protect our political institutions from a coup attempt."

This time it was Mehedi who cut in, "General, I think we need to establish which senior officers we can trust in the military and my suggestion is that we involve our friend, Lieutenant Colonel Tzadok Berkowicz. I have no doubts about his loyalties and his honesty after our visit. Whatever his past, he has useful connections, and which of us can look at ourselves and not question what we have done during our service?" David endorsed the point saying that, in his view, they should convene an urgent meeting with him.

Moshe had accepted the proposal and moved on. "In my view, we will need to attempt to arrest Ravid and that will probably require military involvement. We must assemble a force of crack assault troops whose loyalties are unquestionable. I can assist here, I think, with my contacts in *Sayeret Matkal* (elite commando unit). I know a number of their commanding officers well and many served under me.

"Finally, my friends, our entire operation must be carried out without anyone knowing the reason, without any sanction from above, and without any records being made. What we are facing may go to the very top and threatens the survival of Israel itself. No-one must know what is behind this, nor what we have already unearthed. Our national security trumps all other considerations and we must take the many secrets we are aware of to the grave. The errors and miscalculations of our forefathers may, ironically, have contributed to our strength today but the damage some of the revelations, we have uncovered, would cause to Israel and our interests is incalculable. We can never be seen as a pariah state."

They were sitting on the upper open-air terrace of Berkowicz's house, sharing glasses of Tubi 60, the palm trees fringing the garden offering some shade from their branches although the temperature was a pleasant twenty-two degrees. The former lieutenant colonel was speaking; "Strange, but you know what, it kind of feels good to be round fellow officers again despite saying enough was enough when I finally fully retired from the military in 2005. Of course, as we all do, I retain many contacts whom I can vouch for and some of those have top ranks in the IDF. Some of them know Omer Ravid. Nothing would please me more than to hit back at these bastards. I compromised my ideals for people like him and any chance to rid Israel from the evil he could bring, not least, the threat of Armageddon, I will embrace. Scriptures may refer to a dark period, calling it, "*The End of Days*" before the Messianic period, but I do not think we need Ravid to trigger the world war referred to in the Talmud, nor the ensuing Apocalypse."

The four men began compiling a list of trusted commanders and their key areas of expertise. By mid-evening they had an impressive list of senior officers together with a further list of those whose loyalties they were unsure of. It was not until after dark that they concluded their discussions with an action plan split into three core missions. Moshe and Berkowicz were to visit the home of retired *Tat Aluf* (Brigadier General) Malachai Rosen. He was a former commander of the elite special forces unit, *Sayeret Matkal.* Aprt from being a personal friend of Moshe, he had served under Benjamin Netanyahu within the same unit in the 1970's. He had retained connections within the IDF, from which he had only retired four years before, but, importantly, despite retaining a friendship with the prime minister, he had no obvious political persuasions. Mehedi was to investigate any intel on Omer Ravid within Mossad and establish his life pattern including his workplace(s), residence, and any known weaknesses. David was tasked with investigating Ravid's background, which needed to include the activities of his former guardian, the scientist Yehudi Krimmer. Berkowicz reinforced Moshe's suggestion from the previous day, that David should visit and seek any information he might gain from Ravid's estranged daughter, who he knew lived in Tel Aviv. After they had agreed a way forwards, they sipped their second long glasses of Tubi 60, glad of a brief moment to relax in the warm evening air under a brilliant starlit sky, but very aware of the enormity of the task ahead. Mehedi, returning from a look over the front of the house, remarked that the police clearly thought the threat on Berkowicz had reduced, as they were no longer watching the outside of the building. "The usual," Berkowicz replied dryly, "they do enough to be seen initially, then when all the fuss dies down. Paf!" He threw his hands up in a derisory gesture. "Unless, of course, they know something we don't."

The first shots hit the row of bottles on the shelves behind Berkówicz, the glass exploding and the mirror behind shattering. "Down!" David shouted, diving to the floor and rolling over, grasping his handgun from his holster just as he heard an agonised shout from Berkowicz, who was thrown against the table, before slumping to the floor. He gasped, "Kill the bastards!", as David looked towards the flashes coming from the roof of a building fifty metres away. The sound of automatic fire echoed off the surrounding buildings, and bullets smashed into the walls and furniture, sending shards of debris across the terrace. David set his Glock 19 to auto and within seconds he had loosed off twenty-five rounds, holding his arms outstretched, gripping the weapon in both hands as the cartridge cases flew from the top. Mehedi and Moshe were now crouched under the wall, each having retrieved their Tavor assault weapons. Moshe motioned with his hands for them to assume distanced firing positions, which meant separating to make them more difficult targets for their assailants. He then sighted his gun firing a long burst at where the shots had come from, then shouting at Mehedi to commence covering fire, using single shots in order to prolong the cover. David had now retrieved his own rifle and had moved to a bedroom on the floor above the terrace with a window that afforded a better view towards the taller building behind them. Keeping the light off, he could clearly see two points from which shots were being fired. Just as he was lining his sight on the source of one of the flashes, a security light from a terrace on an adjacent building was turned on, illuminating the source of their attackers. He glimpsed the silhouette of two figures crouched on a balcony and he had the red dot of his sights instantly trained on one. His reactions were swift and instinctive from his years in the military backed by his training as a sniper. Using the single shot setting, he knew, as he squeezed the trigger, his shot would count. His weapon's recoil was minimal and he clearly saw a figure thrown back with his arms flailing upwards. The terrace light on the adjacent building went out just as more shots hit the area where Moshe and Mehedi were positioned. David then slipped a drum magazine onto his rifle, which he rarely favoured as it meant his weapon was bulky and less easy to aim. However, he needed the fire power and aimed in the direction of where the last shots had come from, loosing off a long automatic burst of 100 rounds in seconds, spraying the target area of the building opposite. He heard the cries of someone wounded and then there was quiet as he turned and ran back down the stairs.

"I think the bastards have had enough." he said through gritted teeth as he ran, crouching, to where Berkowicz was lying. His breath was coming in short gasps and David knew there was little he could do. "Mehedi, find a blanket, anything warm," he commanded, taking control over a situation he had seen too many times before during his service. He turned to Moshe, "General, please keep us covered." His former superior waved back, already knowing what was required. David turned back to Berkowicz, who was trying to speak, but beginning to cough.

"They have done for me," he gasped, "tell Rebeka I love her and to say *Yizkor* (prayers) for me." David cradled his head as he shut his eyes, then he looked up again, his voice faint, "Get Ravid before he attacks Tirosh. Shira was..." He coughed again, blood trickling from his mouth, then his head slumped back. Mehedi appeared with a blanket, which David took from him, placing it over Berkowicz's lifeless body.

Sirens could be heard and this time the General barked out the orders – "Time to go now! Whoever gets here could be with them. We exit with five-second intervals between each of us. Mehedi, cover David and I, as we will when you follow. We will use the front entrance now the police have gone, as it is shielded from our attacker's view."

"I never thought I could trust an Arab with a gun behind me." David remarked dryly, bringing a grim brief smile to Mehedi's face, despite the trauma of the situation.

Moshe and David descended the stairs to the front exit of the building. Within seconds, David had reached their vehicle parked on a side street fifty metres away. Keeping his weapon in his lap, he gunned the engine into life, reversing towards a gateway where Moshe was crouched, holding his weapon at shoulder height, pointed in the direction of the Berkowicz house. The General backed towards the car as Mehedi appeared in the house doorway, looking quickly right and left before running towards them. Just as Moshe reached the car, some shots rang out, hitting the road beside them. He wrenched the door open, throwing himself in as David slammed it into gear, shrieking the tyres as he spun round and sped towards Mehedi, who was zig-zagging the last few metres before falling into the rear of the vehicle. The engine raced as David shot down the one-way system the wrong way, narrowly avoiding an oncoming vehicle just as the rear window shattered. As they approached the junction, two police vehicles turned into the street with blue lights flashing and blocked the way. David stopped the car with a jolt, reversed a little way, then shouted, "Brace yourselves my *chaverim;* (comrades) sorry about your car, Mehedi!"

Another shot hit the car with a loud metallic bang as Mehedi ducked down in the rear seats. Police officers were exiting the vehicles and crouching behind the open doors with handguns raised. David revved the engine, and the black Kia leapt forwards towards the rear of one of the police cars, which he hit, with a loud metallic crunch, knocking it back with the sickening impact, as he scraped past with more shots slamming into the car. At that point, Moshe fired his assault rifle, sending the police officers diving for cover as rapid shots hit the ground at the rear of the vehicles, exploding two tyres on one of them. They executed a right turn, then another, then left into a side road where they slowed down in order to attract less attention. They could hear more sirens and opted to navigate their way to a quiet area where they could dump the car. They twisted and turned from one side street to another, gradually making their way to an area of open land bordering Route 5 on the south side of the Ramat HaSharon area, north of Tel Aviv, where they parked to consider their options and formulate a plan.

"OK", said Moshe, maintaining command, "We are dressed in IDF uniforms and once we have left the car, we will not attract any undue attention as no-one knows who we are, although it is possible our assailants may have seen our uniforms at the home of Berkowicz. The difficulty facing us is that we have no idea who we can trust, but equally, the difficulty facing them is that they have no idea who we are, except for you, David."

"Trust me to get landed with a prima donna tennis player to look after. Still, I guess it beats sheep and goats." Mehedi remarked, drawing an expected curse from David.

The General continued, ignoring his remark, "Mehedi, you were sent to check on what David is up to. I suggest you report in to your head of section in Mossad in the next hour, saying you have been under covert instructions to trace David, but you are concerned because you know he has been involved in some kind of shoot-out with security forces in Tel Aviv. Say you think you know where he may be going, but as this has become messy, you need his advice. See if you can find out who is pulling the strings here and whether they work for Ravid or even if your own superior is involved. I think we need to begin finding out who is with us and for that, we need to split up. I will go see Malachai Rosen, who I know I can trust; he lives not far away. If I am stopped, my connections at the highest level will ensure my safety. I think you should both stick together for protection as David is a target, and I suggest paying a visit to Shira Ravid, or Ahava as she now is. What is the ancient saying, *'your enemy's enemy is your friend'*? However, she is Ravid's daughter, so we need to tread carefully and check out just how estranged she is, although the file does say he was violent towards her mother. If you have to go to ground, let's meet for a briefing tomorrow; say 1400 hours at my place."

Mehedi remarked dryly, "Knowing Ravid's reputation, if Shira has remained estranged, I somehow doubt he will see himself as '*a poor old man, as full of grief as age; wretched in both*'" He turned to David, "Shakespeare's King Lear, old chap, mourning his daughter's actions."

"Now you shock me," David responded, "I never judged you as a cultured man!"

The single word response, "*Mitoomtam!*" (moron) was predictable.

Thirty minutes later, David and Mehedi arrived by taxi at Shira's apartment address in the smart Neve Tzedek area of Tel Aviv, which they had obtained via the Mossad database. Before approaching the building, they went into a deserted alleyway where Mehedi called in to his superior, *Aluf* Mordecai Haddad, at Mossad HQ. He informed him that he had received secret orders to trace David Stern, and was following up on a lead given to him by one of David's former IDF friends but felt matters were spiralling out of control. He said he had established that David had asked his friend for a safe house until matters quietened down, after being involved in a gun battle in the middle of Tel Aviv. There had been a pause, then Haddad said, "Have you spoken to anyone else about this?" Mehedi realised with a jolt that his section head may be involved from both his lack of surprise and the question he had asked. He responded, "No-one apart from David's friend who has given him the keys to a rental house he owns." He then added for more authenticity, "This friend thinks I am on a covert mission with Stern, so he sang like a canary." He winked at David, who rolled his eyes upwards in mock derision. Haddad then gave him strict orders not to share information with anyone but himself, stressing that this was an issue of national security, telling him to proceed to the 'safe house' and to confirm whether Stern was there. Mehedi then decided to test the reaction of his superior by asking a question as though seeking clarification on what he had been told. "Mordecai, have you heard of Unit 235?"

The reply, when it came, confirmed what he suspected, "*Elohim yishmor!* (my God!) Mehedi, where did you hear about this?"

"Apparently, when Stern contacted his friend, he stated that he had uncovered some information about a clandestine unit called 235 which meant his life was in danger."

His superior then laughed. "That unit disbanded decades ago. It was dissolved by that old rogue Rafi Eitan when he got caught with his pants down in two spying scandals in the US. You may have heard of the Jonathan Pollard affair when Eitan turned a US naval intelligence officer who then passed defence secrets to us. That was followed by another scandal involving an American business man, Richard Kelly Smyth, who was caught illegally shipping atomic weapon components to Israel. Unit 235 was disbanded by Prime Minister Yitzhak Shamir along with Lekem, Rafi's pet covert unit." The words had flowed too easily from Haddad, and Mehedi recognised a well-rehearsed cover story. His superior added, "I think all that is still classified so best not mention it in any report. This David Stern character is involved in some kind of extremist militant left-wing movement who are attempting to destabilise and discredit Netanyahu's government. They have terrorist connections with Hamas and Hezbollah. This man Stern is dangerous and needs taking down; tread carefully, and use lethal force if necessary. Report to me immediately you have confirmation that he is at the house." The line went dead, and Mehedi looked wryly at David.

"Apparently, you are a dangerous leftie, my little *chalavi* (weakling). "Could have fooled me; you can't even play tennis without getting the bullet."

"You are one devious *chapper* (layabout). OK, at least we now know General Haddad is with them."

They approached the smart cream frontage of the apartment building on Rishonim Street, mounting some steps to where a row of illuminated names faced them. David selected the single printed 'Ahava' – an automated voice asked for a name and reason for the visit. He thought quickly, responding with "Mossad – on secondment to *Shabak*," (internal security) which was not quite the case, but he hoped it may, at least, guarantee a response. The reply, still automated, asked for a security code, a system set up to offer additional protection for those working within the Israeli security services. As Shira worked for the military branch of Intelligence, Aman, this came as little surprise. He looked at Mehedi; "Shall we try the method you used on Haddad?" drawing a nod in response.

"I think it is gloves off, David. Tonight, a patriot lost his life bringing the murderous toll of this man to at least six, and with you, it could have been seven."

David pressed the intercom button again, and said just two words, "Unit 235." There was a long pause and they both warily listened out for the sound of sirens or approaching vehicles. Then there was crackle before a female voice spoke. "Identify yourselves." David breathed a sigh of relief, recognising that the mention of the Unit and the reply meant that their visit was worthwhile. As an operative within Aman, David reasoned it was pointless hiding his identity as he was, in any event, already a target. "I am *Rav Seren* David Stern and I am accompanied by a single colleague but for security reasons, you will understand, I cannot give his name."

Another pause, then the voice returned, "I can see you are armed, please keep your hands away from your weapons. I have activated my call system; you have ten minutes to brief me before this place will be crawling with IDF and police; 1st Floor, Apartment 3. No need for covid masks." The door buzzed and they entered into a modern foyer with gold spotlights set into a panelled ceiling. There were plants positioned around the marble floor with a lift at one end. Their training took them to the stairs as their preferred access, affording less vulnerability than using a lift. As they reached the first floor, David went through a connecting door from the stairs first, looking rapidly to right and left, before Mehedi followed. They were both aware of the risks they were taking with this visit and adrenalin was running high. David approached a black door with a brass square plaque set in it with the number 3. Mehedi stood back, watching the lift and stairwell door, his hand poised by his *SIG Sauer P226* semi-automatic pistol, which was in the holster of his uniform.

David knocked on the door and, seconds later, it was opened but then he was not prepared for his own reaction. She was tall, imposing, and utterly beautiful; her long dark shiny hair was almost to the waist, with dusky looks; her wide, deep turquoise eyes and pouting lips accentuated by her make-up. Tight blue jeans were tucked into calf boots; a belt with a thick buckle emphasised her waistline, above which she wore a maroon silk shirt, with the top buttons undone, teasingly revealing a hint of her body, which he tried to ignore. Despite his normal self-assurance, his voice wavered as he spoke, extending his hand. "Thank you for agreeing to see us," he managed, feeling suddenly rather foolish, "I am David..."

"I know who you are," she smiled disarmingly, "and your friend?"

"This is Ali," David replied, which was followed by an expressed mock cough from Mehedi. "He is Arab."

The reply was direct and swift. "Then he is welcome, for we are all Israelis and if we all thought more that way, there would be less conflict in this region."

"Music to my ears," Mehedi responded cheerfully, "nice to meet you and, as a parched Arab, I would welcome a beer."

She laughed and beckoned them into a surprisingly spacious hallway leading to a living room area with easy chairs, a sofa, and a large window with external lights over a balcony. She motioned them to sit, after telling them to leave their bags by the door, which, she stated, she was well aware contained their automatic weapons. Then, as she sat in a simple timber-framed arm chair, she spoke firmly, "Clearly, this is not a social visit?" She looked over sharply at David, adding, "Regrettably for you, Major, I outrank you as an *aluf mishne* (colonel) and I am a combat veteran, so let us be straight with one another." Then, her look softened again, and David felt his heart jump as she continued, "Please state your business and, if I like what I hear, I will give your poor Arab friend here a beer and disarm the call security system."

David was dazzled by her eyes, and her exquisite looks, yet he knew, by her rank, that she clearly was an officer of outstanding ability and should be respected as such. His focus came back as he recalled the events of the night. He decided to be direct, "Shira, we are here because we have uncovered a plot to overthrow the democratic government of Israel, led by a man on the ultra-right wing of politics, who will stop at nothing to achieve his aims. He heads up an organisation that has a dark, sinister, and very secretive past. This has links to assassinations, and plots at the heart of power, not only in Israel but all over the world." He hesitated before adding, "That man…is your father."

She arose from her seat, moving towards the window. "I was expecting this day to come." Then, sighing, she continued in a manner without displaying emotion as though reading from a prepared script. "I loved my father once, not adoringly, but out of fear and I knew no different way other than to try and please him. He is nothing to me now other than a regret that I have carried with me all my life. So, tell me your interest before I continue?" She moved back to stand with her hands placed on the back of the seat opposite, looking directly into David's eyes, and he felt another jolt within him as her deep eyes sought his.

"I too am a combat veteran." David decided he would be completely open with her, sensing a growing trust between them despite this being their first meeting. "I have fought in innumerable campaigns including the Second Intifada, Lebanon, then back in Gaza. I was involved in covert operations with *Maglan Unit 212* until I joined Mossad, and, although I am semi-retired, I still carry out assignments for them. This is one of them which is becoming increasingly unofficial the more we uncover. I served with the IDF way beyond my national service years because I liked the military lifestyle but, more importantly, because I believed in Israel, despite all the shortcomings we have. I have long recognised our failure to properly address the pressing issues with the Palestinians, or effectively deal with the historic differences with neighbouring countries, or even, for that matter, to live side by side with our own citizens. However, my loyalty to our country is unwavering.

"*Alhamdulillah.* (praise be to God) The response from Mehedi brought a scarcely concealed smile to both Shira and David's faces which broke the tension, prompting from David,

"Forgive him, he is Bedouin," resulting in a rude gesture.

Shira turned to Mehedi, "I think you have earned your beer putting up with this shameful Jew's manners."

Mehedi saluted her, adding, "You know the best part of it is, this *beezayone* (disgrace) clearly has no respect for his superiors. Allow me to introduce myself, I am *Sgan Aluf* Mehedi Saleh and we both outrank this *ben-zona."* Shira laughed as David shot him a questioning glance, to which Mehedi replied, "I think it is time to reveal my identity and go with my instincts if we are to confront this threat. I am rarely, if ever, wrong about giving my trust."

"Your language clearly shows you are one of us." remarked Shira as she took three bottles of beer from her fridge, passing them each one after flicking the lids off, and taking a long drink herself. David found himself taking another look at her well-proportioned figure, and her long hair cascading down her back as she moved to the window, pulling the blinds down. He was shocked at his actions. '*What is wrong with me?*' he thought to himself, as he felt like a young teenager on a first meeting with a girl. He immediately dismissed the thought concentrating his mind on their mission.

"Shira, we are in mortal danger of a right-wing coup led by your father, who is intent on launching a pre-emptive nuclear strike on Iran."

She looked at each of them earnestly, "OK Mehedi, David, for some crazy reason, we appear to trust each other, although

I checked you out on the Aman database before I allowed you in." She looked directly at David. "I know you are a highly decorated veteran and that means much to me as I, too, love my country. I think we need to base our unexpected meeting on a firm foundation of mutual trust which, right now, is worth a great deal, I think. So, what you want to find out is, where I fit in with my father and, perhaps, what I know about him. I will return to my days growing up. I learned, very early in life, that if everything was going his way, all would be OK, but, if not, he had a violent solution. He hit my mother regularly and, now I believe, he murdered her by shortening her life. I was ten when she divorced my father, which brought some peace and happiness into our lives. At last, we could live away from him but it was only to be for three years. She died of a brain haemorrhage when I was thirteen and I moved back in with my father but, even now, I have never forgiven him for his gross brutality. He hit me when I was younger, a lot, but stopped one day when I was sixteen. I recall looking straight into his eyes and saying, "If you ever lay a hand on me again, I will kill you." I hated him then and would have done just that. He took to reminding me that he was dedicated to Israel, as if it excused his ways and that if I knew what had happened to the Jewish people, including my grandmother, I would learn to understand. I was aware that my grandmother had been held in various concentration camps until she was liberated and smuggled out by Jewish commandos in 1945. I never met her but I knew she died in 1955."

David interjected, speaking slowly and softly, "We know about that and who was responsible for her liberation and smuggling to Palestine; a squad commanded by Yitzhak Rabin, which also included one Rafi Eitan."

Shira took in a deep intake of breath – "This is all incredible, not so much the story but that you should be uncovering areas I have already been made aware of because of an investigation I was involved in some years ago when I met Rafi Eitan. He told me some of this. Now you appear and it is as if some strange fate has drawn us together." She leant forwards and touched her glass to both his and Mehedi's before continuing, "I knew very little; everything about my father's past was never spoken about except that I knew my grandmother had been in concentration camps. My father used grandmother's past to justify everything, including the cruelty against my mother, who he derided constantly, hitting her if she stood up to him. On some occasions, he pinned her against the wall whilst he threatened her, squeezing her neck. I used to scream at him to stop when I realised at around the age of five or six that this must be wrong. I asked others in school if their fathers hit their mothers and I began, even as a child, to recognise something was not right." Her eyes filled with emotion, for a moment, which she choked back looking at the ceiling.

"I am so sorry, this must be a terrible burden to carry," David said gently, wanting to place his arms round her which was not normally his way but, for some reason, he felt an empathy that drew him to her. "I am afraid your father has been the cause of so much tragedy. So, were you aware of who brought your father up after his mother died?"

Shira's face lit up for a moment, "Ah yes, Yehudi Krimmer, but to me he was dearest *Zaydee*. (grandpa) Even though he wasn't my real grandfather, he acted like he was. He was wonderful and gentle spirited. I recall him telling me stories about my grandmother that made me smile. They shared living quarters working for a German physicist called von Weizsäcker. They were lucky as they had been prisoners at Mittelbau-Dora concentration camp but were selected by this scientist to live in his home whilst he was working on a secret project. My grandmother was taken on as a housekeeper and *Zaydee* was living there because of his scientific background. He told me that grandmother became adept at stealing extra food, taking mischievous pleasure in what could have been very dangerous. When she could, she would smuggle this to other Jewish prisoners. *Zaydee* said it was all about survival back then, and he would laugh when he spoke about them storing the dregs of wine, left by von Weizsäcker and his guests in bottles, which they would save until they had enough to get drunk. My father looked up to *Zaydee* and was careful not to display his darker side in front of him."

"Do you know what Krimmer did for Israel?" David asked, trying to ignore what he felt each time her large eyes looked at him directly.

"I knew he was a scientist working for the defense ministry in weapons research but, when I was young, he would say it was secret and did not speak of it until I visited him many years later, which is when I first heard of Unit 235. There was much he revealed to me at that time which I was eventually prevented from fully investigating. *Zaydee* did tell me that he hated his work which he felt had betrayed his sense of humanity. He taught me to cherish love and never lose sight of the need for mankind to learn deeper understanding and embrace differences. He is a gentle man and now lives in England, which he says is a haven from all he once faced, and we write to one another from time to time."

"I think he may be useful to us," David stated. "What he knows may just help us avoid a tragedy for this country. I fear that now they have acted more brazenly in tonight's attack, we are in a race against time."

17

"The Lord has a sword"

Tuesday 3rd October 1944 – 12:30pm
Fouquet's Restaurant
99, Avenue des Champs-Elysées, Paris

The three men sat outside, sipping *Corton-Charlemagne* white Burgundy, basking in the sunshine of an unusually warm October day. Yitzhak Rabin and Rafi Eitan were clad in British military uniforms whilst Shimon Peres was dressed in an impeccably tailored double-breasted suit. They were young men, enjoying the liberation mood that had made Paris a welcoming place for Allied servicemen who flocked to the French capital if given the opportunity on leave. All around them were men and women in uniform of various nationalities but mainly US, Canadian or British. Rabin and Eitan had been given leave but, in reality, had been planning their operation to give Zielinski and Ward safe passage out of Poland. Peres had invited, or, more realistically, summoned, Rabin and Eitan to join him for lunch at the expense of the Palestine authority. Their wine had been served by a waiter in a long apron, and it was when Peres topped their glasses up that he addressed them in a serious tone, looking around to ensure no-one was in earshot. "*Chaverim*, the chairman of the Jewish Agency, David Ben-Gurion, has put us all in *Yishuv* (Jewish people in Palestine) on notice that he believes we may have to fight the British to secure our independence as a Jewish nation in Palestine, despite promises made to us many years ago. He has stated that as the war comes to an end, our struggle must be intensified to secure a new Jewish state in *Eretz Yisrael* (sacred territory of ancient Israel). The British think I am here to co-ordinate the direction of Jewish forces in the war effort, and to help plan the strategy for the release of Jews from the concentration camps as they are liberated *B'ezrat HaShem.* (with God's help). Let us drink to that, *l'chaim.*" They all touched their glasses together.

"Why do I suddenly get the impression that we are shortly going to be invited to be part of some clandestine treacherous behaviour?" Rafi Eitan said with a grin, giving a sidelong glance to Rabin.

Peres smiled, and leaned forwards – "The reality of my mission is to arrange the transport of as many Jews as possible from Europe to Palestine under the noses of the British, who have forbidden this. In the occupied countries, as per your briefing with Major General Strong, are the Jewish scientists who have been assisting the Germans on their *Uranverein* atomic weapons programme. However, we are one step ahead of the British and the Americans. A brilliant German Jewish scientist, by the name of Lise Meitner, worked on the nuclear programme and was a major player in discovering nuclear fission. She escaped to Sweden from Nazi Germany just before the war and has given us a list of those scientists who could be most useful to us. The mission of your new unit is to find these scientists, especially Jewish ones, and ensure that they are not taken by the Americans or the British, but smuggled to Palestine with the promise of a new life which will be very rewarding for them."

"And if they do not wish to go to Palestine?" Rabin asked.

"You will assist and accompany them to the new welcoming homeland which awaits them using whatever persuasion is necessary." Peres raised his eyebrows, seeking their understanding of what was required, adding, "Ben-Gurion is adamant that our new state must possess the ultimate weapon to ensure its survival in the hostile region surrounding it. As you are aware, Major General Strong has authorised the formation of a new Jewish unit for the purpose of concealing these scientists from the Americans. Our role is less devious and more honourable, which is to give them a better home amongst their own people."

"I am deeply touched by your integrity, Shimon," Rabin remarked dryly, "So my role is to command a unit whose main role will be to hoodwink the British, under whose noses we are forming it. I feel this will be the end of my career in the British Army."

"Ah, but think what opportunities will be opening up for you in the new Jewish state." responded Peres. "Your new command will be known by the British as Unit X, but by us as Unit A. As soon as you have completed your mission in Poland, you will be attached to the British forward command with clearance for covert, behind enemy lines operations, capturing scientists before they themselves realise they are about to be, ahem, rescued. You will allow the British to have the benefit of less important scientists whilst reserving the cream for *Eretz Yisrael*."

"You are one devious man, Shimon," Eitan looked at him wryly, "but I like your style."

"I am merely a politician serving the will of my people," Peres replied, raising the palms of his hands with a mock display of modesty. Then he turned to Rabin, with a sigh, "We have a bit of a snag with the plan you submitted for the Polish operation. There are no long-range aircraft available at present or pilots who could undertake such a mission. RAF Transport Command are pulled out keeping our forces supplied, who are advancing far quicker through France than planned. Bomber Command are screaming for pilots and it is proving difficult convincing the powers that be that Zielinski and Ward are worth saving. The Germans want Zielinski caught, the Poles want him saved as he is a bit of a hero, and the Russians hate anyone associated with the Polish resistance who they see as a threat to their future plans for a communist Poland. We want him rescued as a symbol of Jewish resistance to the Nazis which may encourage others. If we can't get an aircraft, we may have to attempt an over-land mission despite the obvious danger." Peres gestured to the waiter that he wanted another bottle of Burgundy and that he was ready to order lunch.

"Maybe we should give the Texan Mafia a try," quipped Eitan, reaching into his breast pocket for the business card they had been presented with three days earlier. Minutes later, after a call made from the restaurant telephone, a beaming Eitan emerged with his thumbs up. He smoothed his hands through his thick dark hair in a triumphal gesture. "Our man from Texas has asked if we need a squadron or just the one aircraft!" he said, laughingly, before announcing that the deposit was required immediately in the form of a large brandy and a dessert consisting of crêpes Suzette and banana cake.

Forty-five minutes later, a horn giving three short blasts followed by a longer one in the well-known V for victory sound, prefaced the arrival of a large khaki-coloured *Buick* staff car with the stars and stripes flag fluttering on the right wing, which swept to the curb, making an abrupt halt in front of where they were sitting. A smartly uniformed driver jumped out and opened the rear door from which Major Austin S. Coburn alighted in dark glasses, with a cigar clenched in his teeth. He adjusted his side cap and slapped his driver on the back before sauntering over to where Peres, Rabin, and Eitan were sitting. "Goddamn war goin' to be over 'afore I get a chance to make a dime. I hear tell you limeys reached the Rhine boys, but things got a little sticky round Arnhem."

Rabin stood up and extended his hand, turning to Peres. "May I introduce Major Coburn of US Counter Intelligence

Corps. Regrettably, he has little grasp of geography by terming us 'limeys.'"

"I think, sir, you might be offended if we Jews called you a 'Yankee'," Peres added with a broad smile as they all shook hands. A waiter was summoned and two large brandies were ordered, one of which was taken out to Coburn's driver, who was leaning on the wing of the staff car, smoking a cigarette. The Major handed a business card to Peres, tapping his nose to indicate a need to be discreet before decrying the gesture by announcing loudly, "I can fix a perfect transport for you guys. I gotten you one hell of an aircraft. You gonna be flyin' Coburn Airways style in a beautiful *Douglas DC3 Dakota*, on lease loan, you understand, from the United States military. These mothers have a range of 1,500 miles and we can get it delivered to Bari, our air base in Italy which is goin' to be the best airfield we got without arisin' no suspicion. This baby is special, boys, with sliding doors on either side givin' y'all a little more fire-power potential. The deal will give you a pilot, navigator, and I'll throw in a couple of armed special forces GI's. Oh, and, boys, I can announce the whole caboose will carry the authority of General Omar Bradley commanding 12th Army Group. He may not know about this personally, but in Intelligence, we draft the orders; don't y'all worry your heads none about that. Asides, he's a little busy right now dealing with them pesky Krauts." He gave them a wink, lit another cigar, then downed his brandy, gesturing to a waiter for another. He then looked at them earnestly. "The problem we got, boys, is the darned distance to Poland. We got no safe airfields in North-East France; our offensive into Holland has stalled and England is just too damned far. I just spoken to a pal whose been flyin' B-17's on missions from Italy to Warsaw during the uprising. The distance is 1,200 miles each way and they had to land at a Ruskie airbase to get refuelled."

"Is there no way we can do the same?" Rabin asked as the waiter arrived with plates carrying the crêpe Suzette and banana cake.

"Hell no;" came the response, "not directly as Uncle Joe Stalin has forbidden any more US aircraft to fly out of Russian airspace to that area."

Coburn said he would look at options over the afternoon with his Intelligence strategic planning unit. He reassured them he would find a way and then told them quietly that payment of $65,000 US (equates to around $1,100,000 in 2022) would need to be made in cash, with fifty per cent on delivery of the aircraft, and fifty per cent on completion, which Peres stated was not a problem. Major Coburn stated that the money needed to be delivered to the US Interrogation Centre at 84, Avenue Foch, Paris, in a sealed ammunition crate and marked 'Top Secret'. He explained to them that the irony was that it was previously the headquarters of the SS Intelligence Branch during the German occupation. After a third brandy, he rose from the table, "I am deeply honoured to be of service to you guys, and hell, I mean that." He saluted before walking back to the staff car where his driver stiffened to attention, holding the door open for him. Then, he waved from the window like a visiting dignitary as the staff car was driven sedately away.

At 6pm, the phone rang in the room Shimon Peres was occupying on the second floor of the Hotel Meurice, where he had been studying maps of Poland with Rabin and Eitan, who were staying in the more down-market Hotel du Pont Neuf. Peres passed the phone to Rabin who listened as Major Coburn outlined his plan, "OK, Captain, I think we are in luck. Your men, Zielinski and Ward are heading for Kielce and we have found a place to refuel nearby, although there are a couple of minor issues. There is an airfield just come available around sixty miles south of there in Mielec but it may be a little tricky. It is a Luftwaffe airbase and fuel dump which is still technically situated in occupied Poland, but we have just heard it has been taken by the Ruskies."

"I thought you just said Stalin won't allow US aircraft to fly over Russian territory." Rabin responded.

"Sure!" came the reply, "in order to avoid an international incident, this ain't gonna be an official US or British operation. We gonna put Polish markings on the aircraft, and give you a Polish pilot and navigator. Uncle Joe Stalin only stipulated no US aircraft. In any event, boy," he puffed out a large cloud of cigar smoke and grinned as he spoke into the phone, "that ain't goddamned Russian airspace, it belongs to Poland."

Wednesday 4th October 1944 – 3pm

They were sitting on opposite sides of the carriage travelling to link up with the 4th Partisan Group in Częstochowa, 220 kilometres south west of Warsaw. Zielinski was dressed in a crumpled pinstripe suit with a trilby hat, carrying a briefcase in which were engineering drawings hastily collected as part of his 'cover story.' Ostensibly, he was a Slovenian consulting engineer travelling to Kraków to work on a structural project for the German *Todt* organisation creating additional reinforced defence structures, which were being rapidly constructed to impede the Russian advance. John Ward was in dirty overalls and his cover was that he was a Polish worker required for a water infrastructure development in Mielec. Two months had passed since he had been shot in the leg and although he still suffered from some pain, he could walk and the appearance of the wound could be passed off, if discovered, as an industrial injury.

Both of them had very mixed feelings as they thought of all they had left behind in Warsaw after two months of heavy fighting. John Ward felt he was still needed to provide a vital communication link between the Polish resistance and Allied command in London. However, General Bór-Komorowski had insisted he go to save himself from almost certain death at the hands of the Nazis. Zielinski felt a sullen and simmering rage of betrayal, believing that the Russians had deliberately held back from entering Warsaw, allowing the partisans and the occupants of the city to be slaughtered. The train had slowed and pulled into the station at Radom, which appeared busy, but what caught their eyes more was the heavy German military presence represented by a substantial number of SS uniforms.

Minutes later they heard guttural shouts from the carriage behind and the sound of heavy boots as the train was boarded. *"Ausweis, Ausweis* (ID) – *schnell!"* This was the first time there had been a German check since they had left Warsaw two days before, obtaining false papers and their cover from forgers working for the Polish resistance. Ward looked across at Zielinski and smiled reassuringly, "Good luck, old boy." The door to the carriage was kicked open and an SS officer entered with his Luger pistol drawn, followed by a number of grim-faced soldiers with machine guns. The occupants of the carriage turned away, many wide-eyed with fear. *"Ausweis jetzt!"* (ID now) – The words were shouted as orders to be obeyed without question. No-one turned round as seconds later, they heard the officer's raised harsh voice, *"Jüdischer Abschaum!"* (Jewish scum) and the sound of someone being thrown to the floor followed by the rasp of a machine gun being cocked. Zielinski gripped his bread loaf in which was concealed a grenade, as he had done eighteen months before on his way to Treblinka, but saw Ward look across and shake his head with a sharp look. They heard the officer bark orders for the Jew to be taken followed by an SS guard shouting *"Raus…Raus!"* – as the man was forcibly removed. Then the officer was by their side. He glanced briefly at Zielinski's papers then looked up with, "Ach, I see you work for *Organisation Todt.* The Fatherland needs you engineers, *Heil Hitler!"* He smartly raised his right arm, and as Zielinski returned the salute for the first time ever, he had an overwhelming urge to kill him.

The officer turned to Ward, sitting on the other side of the aisle, snatching his papers. "You are a filthy Polack from Warsaw and you people attacked my comrades whilst we were defending you against the communist vermin." Ward stammered a reply in atrocious Polish, which, fortunately, the German did not speak well enough to notice. "Please, I am needed for the waterworks in Mielec so we can transport water to the front."

"You will come with us for questioning," the officer responded, putting his pistol to Ward's head. *'If he dies now, we all die.'* Zielinski's fingers were burying into the loaf, seeking the grenade pin. As Ward was ushered to his feet, he managed a quick wink to Zielinski before he was gone. Minutes later, he could be viewed through the train window lined up with others on the platform who were being separated into two groups. One rank of men was being issued with yellow armbands with a black star of David in the centre on which was printed one word, *"Jude"*. Zielinski cursed his own tortured thoughts, feeling thankful that Ward was not Jewish, recognising that it would have meant almost certain death in a concentration camp. As the train drew away from the station, he vowed he would not be taken alive.

Saturday 7th October 1944 – 12-00 noon

The drone of the Dakota engines was incessant, as it had been for five hours. Rabin sat next to Eitan on the uncomfortable rudimentary seating that had been hurriedly added to the spartan interior, used to accommodating parachutists who would sit on benches positioned around the edges of the fuselage. Major Coburn had organised substantial food rations and a few bottles of Mosel wine, much of which had already been consumed, improving their spirits. Stacked on either side of the aircraft were some boxes containing *Camel* cigarettes and Cognac, which Coburn had described as "international currency to ease any local tensions". There were four of them in the rear including Rabin and Eitan. They had been joined by two members of the elite US and Canadian 1st Special Service Force, which, Major Coburn had informed them, were also known as 'the Devil's Brigade' with a reputation like the Jewish *No 3 Commando* X troops. "These guys shoot first and ask questions afterwards so keep them boys sweet or you may get your butts shot off." The two members of the elite force had arrived at the Gioia del Colle USAAF air base at Bari, in Italy, introducing themselves as Captain Eugene Dekker from Montana, USA, and Sergeant Pierre Mouchard from Ontario, Canada. They brought a number of bags with them containing an array of weapons, including two *Johnson M1941* machine guns, which they set up on tripods between the two aircraft exit doors, fed from a belt of ammunition in large boxes either side. Dekker announced drily as he suspended a parachute from a bracket in the aircraft, "We like insurance, boys." He patted the parachute, "We have these in case we get our asses kicked in the air and we have these," he patted the barrel of a machine gun, "so we can kick ass when we land. Personally, I prefer the latter." Both men carried *Colt M1911* sidearms, which Dekker stated was "a little extra insurance." During the flight, they swapped stories about their varying experiences of combat. Mouchard handed a card to Eitan and Rabin. "You don't want to be the recipient of one of these," he said in a pronounced French accent, with a grin. "We leave our business cards with each person we kill." On the front of the card was the logo of the SSF (Special Service Force), a red arrow head with USA in white letters horizontally across the top and Canada down the centre vertically. To the right was written, "*Das dicke Ende kommt noch!*" (the worst is yet to come) Mouchard drily remarked, "I used to have a whole heap of these but I only have ten left now. I call them death cards."

"And I thought we were hard bastards," remarked Eitan. "If you ever need a job, come see me in Palestine. We have some big fights ahead."

The pilot, sitting at the controls, introduced himself in halting English as Major Andrzej Ladrow, giving the two upright-fingered Polish salute. "I am from Kraków and I fight with RAF as flight lieutenant. I don't like Russians or Germans," he said, holding his hand like a gun and making three imitation shot noises with a wide smile. He introduced his co-pilot and navigator as Warrant Officer Ryszard Sadowski, who patted his sidearm in a holster, saying slowly, as he nodded his head to emphasise, "I kill Germans or Russians; it makes no difference to me."

Eitan turned to Rabin, speaking quietly, *"Oy vey* (good grief), we're with a bunch of cut-throat renegades. I get the impression this will not be a peaceful flight."

"Perhaps, they are just like us," Rabin responded with a smile. They were all dressed in mid-brown Polish uniforms, which had been organised by Major Coburn as "A li'l free gift to prevent you boys causing too much trouble with the goddamned commies." Early in the flight, Ladrow told them he was flying low over enemy territory to avoid detection, "so you may hear the sound of tree branches brushing the bottom of the aircraft." He carried a large hip flask from which he took the odd swig of *Krupnik,* which he explained was a vodka and honey drink from Poland. Rabin felt somehow reassured by their unconventional spirit as they bonded together with a mutual respect for each other's skills. The navigator called back cheerfully to them after around five hours, "We will shortly be approaching the Luftwaffe airbase of Mielec- Chorzelów but I am informed the Germans have left, so we just have the Russians to welcome us. Do not worry, I will not shoot them, unless they are difficult." Mouchard stood up and walked to one of the machine guns, pulling back loudly on the cocking ratchet, adding, "I am sure they will be very understanding."

Ladrow, who spoke Russian, attempted to call the base, saying in both English and Russian they were returning from Warsaw and needed urgent assistance, but there was no response. Peres was using a shortwave transmitter to alert the Polish resistance of their approach. Within seconds, there was a crackled response saying the freight was in the depot. After circling the airfield once, on which they could clearly see German aircraft parked, identifiable from the black crosses on the wings, the pilot shouted they were going in. There was a thump and the Dakota was rumbling and bumping over the grass-covered strip, whilst being slowed rapidly by the pilot. The aircraft came to a halt near the perimeter fence, but the engines remained idling as Peres and Eitan took their *Sten guns* off a rack, and both Mouchard and Dekker took up position behind their machine guns. The pilot and navigator both had pistols in their laps as they waited, unsure how long it would be before their passengers arrived.

"Here comes trouble on our port side," announced Ladrow. Dekker loosened the larger exit door near the rear of the aircraft, letting in light as he opened it slightly to obtain a view. Rabin lifted himself into the observation bubble behind the pilot seats. Approaching them slowly was a Russian armoured scout car with four armed soldiers in an olive shade of khaki riding on the running board each side, and another behind the machine gun mounted on the top. Ladrow opened the cockpit window, letting his arm relax, with his elbow in full view of the Russians, whilst Eitan stood behind Dekker, his Sten gun gripped tightly. The scout car slowed down and the four men on the running board jumped off and separated. "Ivan knows his stuff," remarked Dekker, "splitting up to make a tougher target, but these babies can fire 600 rounds per minute, and on the tripod, we can sweep up any opposition pretty easily." The vehicle stopped twenty yards away in front of the aircraft; a small heavy metal door opened, and an officer emerged in a peaked cap with a red band around the middle. He gestured to each of the propellers then crossed and uncrossed his arms rapidly to indicate they should cut the engines. "Do as he says." Dekker shouted to Ladrow, taking command now they were on the ground, "Let's try to avoid trouble."

The officer barked a command to the four Russian soldiers, who dropped to the floor, lying with their rifles pointed at the aircraft. "*Zdraste!*" Ladrow called from the cockpit window, "*rat vas vée-deet.*" (greetings, good to see you) The officer walked a few yards forwards, drawing his pistol. "I can see him." Dekker confirmed, his hand tightening on the grip of the machine gun.

"*Kakogo cherta ty zdes' delayesh'?*" (What the hell are you doing here) the officer called out.

Ladrow shouted back in Russian, "We are Polish and were on a trip over Warsaw to drop supplies to escaping resistance fighters. We have permission to land in Russia to refuel but our tanks were getting low. We were jumped by a German fighter, so we diverted here. We have some cigarettes and Cognac if you people can help us out?"

The officer waved his pistol, "I am Captain Stanislav Sergei Vasiliev of the Red Army and you Poles insult me by attempting to bribe me."

Ladrow replied in a placating voice, "No, no, no, this is a gift from Poland to our gallant Russian allies to thank you. We were going to Smolensk and our gift was for them, but if you help us, then you should have it."

The Russian hesitated for a moment then ordered one of his men to approach the Dakota. "You will give to him and maybe we do business."

Minutes later the door behind the pilot was opened by Sadowski, who appeared holding an armful of cigarette packets. He threw them out so they landed near the waiting soldier, whose face lit up when he realised what they were, shouldering his rifle and picking them up. American cigarettes were prized and sought after, and here were hundreds. He ran back to his officer, who replaced his pistol in his holster. Within minutes, the armoured vehicle had been loaded with fifty bottles of Cognac and 2,000 cigarettes. A fuel bowser appeared and approached the aircraft as a now smiling Vasiliev stated he would need to ensure all permissions were in place, before he could permit them to take off. He then departed in the armoured car, leaving four soldiers there as guards. The Russians looked relaxed, smoking, and chatting with their rifles slung over their shoulders as the aircraft was refuelled.

"We are going to have big trouble here," Rabin announced, "when our friend Vasiliev gets in touch with his superiors and they find out that Comrade Stalin has forbidden any aircraft to land at Russian airfields to refuel."

"I like a little trouble," Mouchard responded, "then I can give out my visiting card, no?" He grinned, holding up one of his SSF cards. Peres was in no doubt that the man enjoyed his work as he went to his radio set, calling up the resistance. The reply, when it came, made them all sit up, "I am *Por* (Lieutenant) Antoni Zielinski. Greetings! We have been watching you from the trees outside the perimeter. One minute after the fuel truck disconnects from you, we will enter the compound from behind you in a T-34 tank which my Russian friends have leant me. I will be your only passenger, as my friend, Flight Lieutenant Ward, has been taken by the Germans. *Shalom.*"

"We are going to have a little fun I think," Dekker remarked dryly. "You wouldn't think the Ruskies were our allies. Never trusted any goddamned commies anyways." He rasped back the mechanism on his machine gun, which he pivoted on the tripod, swinging it to right and left.

"I thought Yitzhak and I were crazy." Eitan remarked, retrieving a couple of grenades from the bag they had brought with them.

Seconds later, they watched as the fuel pipe was withdrawn from the Dakota and a smiling Ladrow thanked the crew of the truck, waving them off with a packet of cigarettes each. He pulled himself back up into the Dakota, announcing he was starting the engines, shouting to the guards he was testing them. "It will give our friend, Zielinski, more of the surprise element as these guys won't hear the tank." Each of the engines burst into life, and moments later, Rabin watched, from the observation bubble, the almost surreal scene of a tank smashing through the perimeter fence thirty yards from the aircraft with a large red Soviet star painted on the turret and the long barrel pointed ominously straight ahead. The Russian soldiers looked bewildered but levelled their weapons at the tank, which stopped to the right of the aircraft. A man appeared in the turret of the tank, wearing a *ushanka* fur hat and

Russian military tunic. He waved at the soldiers, one of whom beckoned that he should dismount. He lifted himself out, but dropped to the other side of the turret; emerging a second later, he walked towards the soldiers, holding his arm as if injured. Dekker slid the door open, and Eitan stood behind him as one of the Russians began walking towards the man who had alighted from the tank. Vehicles could now be seen approaching fast across the airfield at the front as, suddenly, the man fell to the floor, rolled to one side and fired twice. Two of the soldiers crumpled just as Dekker opened fire causing the earth to kick up in front of the remaining two, who immediately raised their hands in surrender. The man in the fur hat ran, crouching, to the aircraft door.

"Good afternoon," he shouted in a forced high-class English accent. "Antoni Zielinski, delighted to meet you."

There was a loud report and a puff of smoke as the tank fired a round, which exploded just short of the armoured vehicles racing towards them. A number of Polish resistance fighters were now assuming positions, crouching behind the tank. The engines roared as the tank fired again and a scout car ahead disappeared in a flashing explosion. "*Keebineemat!*" (damn) Rabin shouted, "we were under orders from Strong not to fire on the Russians, except in self-defence."

The Dakota lurched as the engines roared, swinging round, and headed towards a runway at right angles to the Russian vehicles. "I am under no orders," Zielinski shouted back to Rabin, "Please!" He pointed to the Sten Gun in the hands of Rabin who shrugged as he handed it over. "Never heard of this Strong guy myself," Dekker yelled, grinning widely, whilst Mouchard was waving his hands in the air shouting, "The SSF is kickin' ass." As the Dakota gathered speed, bumping along the grass onto the runway, both machine guns opened up, firing in long sweeps, and Russian troops could be seen taking cover. The fuel bowser had been abandoned and Dekker gave it a prolonged burst. There was a huge flash followed by a major flaming explosion sending a mushroom cloud skywards, drawing a loud Texan whoop from Dekker. Zielinski sat on the floor by the open doorway, emptying the Sten gun magazine, firing continuously without stopping, then demanding another magazine, then another… as the aircraft lifted, leaving behind huge palls of smoke drifting across the airfield. Mouchard tossed some death cards out of the opening, whilst Zielinski had dropped the Sten gun, drawn his pistol, and continued to fire until that, too, was empty.

The doors slid shut and Eitan yelled out to Zielinski, "I take it you are not keen on our Russian allies."

Zielinski's eyes were wild, "They invaded and plundered my country, sharing it with the Nazis. So, Russian or German, I do not discriminate. *'The Lord has a sword…for the day of retribution.'* I just wield it for him." He gave the thumbs up with both hands, then, "We got any drink on board this aircraft?"

18

An Operation for Unit 235

They had shared two bottles of Chablis after a few beers and the atmosphere had become more relaxed as they first listened to the information Shira shared with them about her father, and then moved on to David and Mehedi relating to her the findings of their investigation. She had told them that she had tried, after her mother died, to forge a better relationship with Ravid but that he seemed to transfer the anger he once took out on her mother to her, until the day she turned on him. Despite this, she had tried to build bridges as she wanted a father figure in her life, and to be cherished as his only daughter. For a while, she had accepted his bidding, even listening as he explained his extremist views on politics. She recalled his pride when she joined the IDF and his intervention to gain her a transfer into Aman where she had excelled. David watched her, mesmerised as she spoke, somehow drawn to her in a way he had never experienced before. Her voice was soft and she was expressive with gestures, her head tossing, as she explained her background, '*like an actor on stage,*' he thought, and there was such warmth in her wide turquoise eyes.

She had been pacing but now she sat, looking pensive as she spoke, "I specialised in research, helping to develop policy and a public image for our intelligence work, but I served with combat forces before that time. I wanted to prove myself back then, and try and gain the admiration of my father, despite the fact I hated him for what he had done to us. There was a contradiction within me between a deep sense of patriotism combined with an unswerving dedication to duty, and my more emotive, humane side. Bizarre, I know, for a career soldier, but whilst I was an effective officer on the front line, using lethal force if necessary, deep inside I sought the love I never had from my father. The only time my father displayed any emotion or showed any real interest was when I was presented with the *Medal of Distinguished Service* in 2001. I had fought off our attackers and helped my wounded commander to safety under fire, after we were ambushed by a Hamas unit on the Gaza Strip in the Second Intifada. I was only 21 and was shocked when my father turned up for the presentation, which was given by Prime Minister Ehud Barak, who was like a God to us, as we looked upon him as a military hero. After the ceremony, my father came to see me and said he had read my military file, which showed I possessed many of his characteristics. He confirmed to me that my paternal grandfather had been an SS officer, and infuriated me by saying that we had both inherited many of his qualities. We had a furious row during which he blamed my mother for causing the violence in the home when I was growing up. He also said he had a vision for a stronger Israel, freed from the chains of democratic government, and in that, I agreed with him that he had inherited the qualities of a Nazi. That night, I lost any need to seek paternal love as I saw him for what he was. After that, I changed my name to Ahava, because it represents that which he never gave – love. We rarely spoke again and I came to despise all he represented and everything I heard about him. I no longer think of him as my father and usually only refer to him as Ravid."

David spoke softly, "I am truly sorry to hear what you have been through." Her eyes looked deeply at him and he felt his stomach jump at the intensity of her look.

"There are others who are concerned about him," she continued, "but they have warned me recently that to speak out could mean death. Ten years ago, I was asked by Aman if I would assist in compiling a dossier on Ravid because of my obvious family link. As part of that process, I travelled to the UK to meet with *Zaydee,* who you know as Yehudi Krimmer, and that is where I heard about Unit 235. I am ashamed to say I pretended that it was a social visit in order to gain the most out of him. Right at the end of my stay, he threw his arms around me with tears of emotion running down his face. I will never forget him saying to me that he loved me as if I were his own child and that he knew I was seeking intelligence off him. I can still hear his words, "My dearest *cheifale* (lamb), I wish you had not been exposed to this, but I know, with God's help, you will make a difference. You have inherited your grandmother's beautiful spirit, which shone light on the darkest days." Shira stopped speaking for a moment, her voice choking. David crossed to her, placing his hand over hers, and said softly, "We can wait, if you wish, and, perhaps, discuss this tomorrow."

She gripped his hand for a moment, then looked straight into his eyes, "No, I must continue, I am sorry. This is why I try to keep my emotions hidden, and, maybe that is what makes me a good officer." She shook her head as if clearing her mind, sighed and continued as David returned to his seat. "*Zaydee* sat me down on the last night I was there and said he had decided to tell me things he had never shared with anyone."

FISSION

The rain had begun falling more heavily and the wind blew it against the latticed windows of the cottage, set back from the road. *'This really is a haven of tranquillity; no wonder he came here',* Shira thought, as she sat in a Lloyd Loom basket weave chair in front of the traditional open fire, in which logs were burning. There was a cosy feel to the low-ceilinged room with oak beams running across it. Shira watched the man she had adopted as her grandfather from early childhood pour them both a glass of Arak, mixing his with water and, with a sigh, pouring diet coke into hers, which she had insisted he do from the first drink she had shared with him, on her arrival three days before.

Yehudi Krimmer was eighty-seven years old but looked much younger, although he walked with a stoop. He had green eyes, which were keen and very alert, accentuated by his thick glasses, which he had always worn, and appeared a little dishevelled despite still wearing a shirt and tie on most days, as he had done all his life. His jacket was worn with leather patches on the elbow; despite being relatively well off, he did not like throwing clothes away He explained that, at one time, he possessed nothing apart from his own life, which was under threat daily from the SS guards in the camp. Some days, he had once told her, the guards would just shoot someone for no reason and the prisoners tried not to look at them as though it would give them a cloak of anonymity. On his left arm he still bore the tattoo of a number with a triangle, which he stated he would never have removed because, "We must never ever forget what they did to us." Yehudi had developed a fierce determination to survive and to remember. His wife, Sarah, was five years younger than he, and they had met when he was teaching physics at the Technion Institute of Technology in Haifa in 1953. She was away staying with friends, which gave Shira the opportunity to discuss his life with him more directly. He had welcomed Shira warmly, throwing his arms around her, then admonishing her with a twinkle in his eye for not marrying and having children, "like a good girl." She had arranged to spend four days with him after having visited the Israeli embassy in London. That much was true, as she had been studying his file there, preparing for her visit, and discussing what was known about Yehudi Krimmer with an Aman case officer attached to the embassy. However, she had not told Yehudi the real purpose of her visit until he had surprised her by telling her that he realised she was there to obtain information about him only minutes before. "You see, dearest *cheifale*, I could always see through you. Remember when we used to play truth or bluff when you were growing up. You never could fool your *Zaydee*." After they had embraced, he sat on the soft couch opposite. "I know you work for Aman, and from all your questions, I think you are seeking information about your father's part in the programme I was involved in, yes?"

Shira nodded, saying there were some in Israel who feared that he was forming an ultra-right-wing faction with sinister aims.

"I am afraid it is people like him who made it impossible for me to stay there. Ironic, isn't it, that he was rescued from Nazi Germany and brought to safety in Israel and yet now he is, I regret to say, becoming like one of them. When he was a boy, Omer was already difficult and he did not become the man I wanted him to be. After your dear grandmother, Gilana, passed away, Sarah and I tried to give him a good home but he became impossible. Dear Sarah did her best but he was unruly, rude, aggressive and sullen. He joined the IDF and I put in a word through an acquaintance. You may have heard of the legendary Rafi Eitan, who worked for Mossad, and abducted Adolf Eichmann from Argentina in 1961. Eitan had also helped many of us to reach Palestine at the end of the war and I knew him well. He agreed to take Omer under his wing in the army. Sarah and I rarely saw him after that as he became a career military officer and had no real time for us. Sometimes, he dropped by with Rafi, who was a bit of a rogue, but likeable enough. We went to Omer's wedding with your mother but from day one it was not good; he spent precious little time with her and even when they were together, it was not a happy union as you know.

"Now for matters that I have never discussed with anyone before and which you may choose not to share because it may make you a security risk. As you may know, I was rescued from Nazi Germany together with another brilliant scientist by the name of Professor Aaron Kaufman. You will not find any records of him because Prime Minister Winston Churchill wanted the records of anyone who had worked on the *Uranverein* programme to be removed and the Israeli government were equally keen to erase the fact that Jewish scientists may have been involved. Kaufman was incredibly talented and had originally worked for two brilliant German physicists, Lise Meitner and Otto Hahn, before the war. He did not try to flee Nazi Germany until too late and was arrested in November 1938 when the Nazis openly attacked Jews and their property on what became known as *Kristallnacht*. He was sent to Buchenwald concentration camp. He was then selected to join, with other Jewish scientists, in a secret move by the Nazis using Jews to help in the *Uranverein* programme because the war was going badly, and Hitler wanted a nuclear weapon. In 1944, I met him when three of us worked under a German physicist, von Weizsäcker, who, I must say, treated us well, but could not be seen to. I even stayed in his house, and life for all of us improved from what we had suffered in the camps."

"Who was the third scientist?" Shira asked, genuinely interested as she was already hearing more than he had ever spoken of before.

A sad look came into the old man's eyes and he shivered. "That was Dr Fritz Gottheiner, who had also worked at the Kaiser Wilhelm institute in Berlin before being arrested, ending up in Auschwitz. He was killed by the SS during our rescue from German captivity." He sighed deeply, "So many lives lost, and so much tragedy that, at one time, I became immune to it. Until many years later; I could not show emotion or even cry." He paused for a moment, his eyes looked distantly, with deep sadness, and then continued, "Initially, after my arrival in Palestine, I was encouraged by Professor Kaufman to undertake further studies and carry out research into nuclear physics, although he laughingly stated that I already understood more than he. I studied here in Cambridge and always loved the English countryside. Aaron followed my progress and involved me in his work which became focussed on, what was euphemistically termed, the nuclear energy programme. Our energies were really being directed towards the development of weapons technology. He introduced me to Professor Ernst Bergmann, who became 'Chief of Israel's Defense Forces Science' after the state of Israel came into being. Bergmann was extremely interested in the work I had undertaken under the Nazis on the *Uranverein* project. We all worked together on a research programme with other brilliant physicists but there were very few of us at that time. I completed my PhD in Israel at the Weizmann Institute of Science and began teaching. Regrettably, Aaron Kaufman died of a heart attack in 1952; I remain indebted to him for directing my studies and encouraging me in my work. In the early 1950's I was approached by a young physicist I knew, called Amos de-Shalit, who said he was working for the Director General of Defense for Israel, a man by the name of Shimon Peres, our future Prime Minister. I was asked by de-Shalit if I was prepared to join a secret team helping to develop nuclear weapons. At that time, I was co-signatory to a letter to Prime Minister David Ben-Gurion urging that Israel invested in the new technology. We saw this as our ultimate deterrent, and the guarantee we needed for our survival with our land surrounded by hostile neighbours. De-Shalit told me that Ben-Gurion had authorised him to gather together a team of leading scientists to work secretly on the programme, which would be kept deliberately hidden from the world. The United States had stated that nuclear weapons must not be allowed to proliferate under any circumstances. We saw, at that time, that the world had abandoned us during the Holocaust, and the imperative to us was a guarantee that nothing like that could ever happen again."

The old man sighed again, as he looked at Shira over the top of his glasses, which he customarily wore low down his nose. "I was naïve then, Shira, about the politics and corruption that motivates so much of those in power. I went along with them, not even thinking of the consequences and the terrifying concept of '*mutually assured destruction*', which has haunted me in more recent years." He emptied his glass, stood up, and walked slowly over to take Shira's and refilled them. "In those days, we were full of idealism; that was until we began to become mired in the murky world of Intelligence with which, I am sure, you are more than familiar, mmmm?" He looked at her, eyebrows raised, as he touched her glass with his own.

"*Zaydee*, I too have witnessed terrible things, but I often justify what I do by looking at the alternative if we did not act. You know Israel has been threatened many times but, as a result of our strength, the world now takes us more seriously, and we are more at peace with some neighbouring countries. We still have much work to do to secure internal unity, but there is still a hard line and, in some ways, that is why I accepted this assignment, because I know the dangers of a man like my father, who I now only refer to as Ravid"

"There were many like him back in those early days," Yehudi muttered, lowering himself back down, as Shira picked up some logs and placed them onto the open fire, which hissed and crackled for a moment. He went on, "I started work, under the direction of Professor Ernst Bergmann together with a number of French scientists, on setting up the nuclear facility at Dimona in the Negev. Construction started in 1958 and we were involved, not only in consultations, but also in liaising with scientists in France. We worked together planning the detonation of a French nuclear device in 1960 which gave us the foundation for our own weapon.

At that point, the French became less co-operative because of political constraints under President Charles de Gaulle. He did not want any additional nations to acquire nuclear weapons but agreed to more limited French involvement, subject to a declaration that this was for peaceful purposes.

"I first became concerned around 1960 when I attended a meeting, accompanied by Professor Bergmann, with David Ben-Gurion and Shimon Peres. Rafi Eitan was there as an Intelligence advisor together with a very secretive, quiet man called Benjamin Blumberg, who was introduced as the head of covert operations in an ultra-secret organisation called *Lekem*. We were told the remit of *Lekem* was to ensure that Israel acquired the latest scientific and technical intelligence, especially in weaponry. The organisation would obtain this through espionage against any country, friend or foe, and by any means whatsoever. I recall Blumberg being utterly cold, devoid of emotion, and ruthlessly dedicated to his task. I felt unnerved by him with his staring eyes and a demeanour which always seemed threatening. Peres told us that the nuclear weapons programme had the highest priority and that Israel would do whatever was necessary to obtain 'the bomb'. Anything that we needed would be procured, and it was made clear that Lekem was there to ensure we had a nuclear weapon. I recall Blumberg saying, chillingly, that nothing was off the agenda for obtaining what we needed, even if it meant lives being lost. It was emphasised to us that the programme was now ultra-secret and must not be discussed with anyone, not even our spouses.

"From that time on we had no problem getting all the elements we required, including heavy water, uranium-235, and plutonium which we were told came from Britain, Norway, Argentina, and South Africa. The irony here is that we were dealing with former Nazis, in some cases, to arrange supply. All of this was happening despite there being supposed restrictions in place. Then, at the end of Eisenhower's US presidency in 1960, there was a problem as the Americans got wind of what we were doing. Newly elected US

President John F Kennedy wanted full disclosure. Prime Minister Ben-Gurion told him the plant at Dimona had been built for generating electricity and was for entirely peaceful purposes. My immediate superior, Ernst Bergmann, informed Ben-Gurion he could hoodwink the inspection teams which the US were to send over. Inspections began in late 1961 and carried on periodically over the next year or so. Regrettably, they were not convinced, and reported to Kennedy that we were not allowing full access to the facility whilst being evasive on certain issues. Matters escalated and Kennedy demanded that Ben-Gurion gave US inspection teams unfettered access. By 1963, the issue had escalated to such an extent that Israel received an ultimatum. The US informed us that they would withdraw financial and security support for Israel unless full access was granted to Dimona. In early 1963, I attended a security meeting which alarmed me as Blumberg and the former Director of Mossad, Isser Harel, were openly saying that anyone that stood in Israel's way would be neutralised. Ben-Gurion warned Harel that he would not tolerate further covert killings after the activities were exposed of a unit sent to kill or intimidate German scientists who had gone to work for Egypt in an operation called *Damocles*. This was just before it came to light that Israeli agents had assassinated a German scientist, after kidnapping him in Munich, which caused Harel's resignation. At that time David Ben-Gurion had been given advanced warning of a threat by Kennedy of even more serious US action against Israel. He resigned in April, purportedly without seeing the last US ultimatum, giving the official reason that this was "'due to personal needs'". However. It appears that the US ambassador, Walworth Barbour, had confirmed to Kennedy that he had personally given Ben-Gurion the ultimatum. The contents were so secret and sensitive that the US could not go public on the issue.

"Ben-Gurion's replacement, Prime Minister Levi Eshkol played for time but Kennedy eventually issued yet another written ultimatum to him. An urgent security meeting was called in

June 1963 by the defense minister, Shimon Peres, to consider all options, which really unnerved me. Curiously, Isser Harel attended even though he had resigned. Rafi Eitan was there with Blumberg, the head of Lekem, together with a German whose name I cannot recall. If I had thought Blumberg was intimidating, this German was more so. All I can remember was that he had a large scar down his face and I thought he looked like a caricature of a Nazi out of a bad war movie. This has remained embedded in my mind all of my life since, because of what followed. I also recall a high-ranking IDF air force officer being there. Professor Bergmann and I explained the complex technical issues we would face de-commissioning the nuclear weapons development section at Dimona, and the impossibility of attempting to conceal it from a determined inspection team. We had both played a part in covering up what we were doing, even creating false sections of the facility, and avoiding awkward questions on previous US inspections which had been more cursory. The air force officer said that his counterpart in the US military had leaked to him that President Kennedy had been briefed on sending in airborne troops to take over Dimona and, if necessary, a mission to execute a temporary occupation of Israel. The Prime Minister had stated this was unthinkable and ordered that every option must now be considered to remove this threat, or prevent Kennedy from carrying out his threat. You will recall the date; this was 1963 and that year did not end well for the President."

Shira gasped with a dreadful foreboding, recoiling from her thoughts, "*Oy gevalt!* please do not say what I think you will." The old man looked at her, his eyes filling, expressing his emotion. She pointed at his glass but he shook his head. She walked to the cabinet, mixing her drink, her mind already in turmoil.

"Please..." his voice was shaking, "I have no proof, only conjecture, but I carry a terrible guilt which has never left me; a burden I shall take to the grave. After the Prime Minister left the meeting, some of us remained behind. I do remember Peres stating that it was a pity we were not dealing with Vice President Johnson, who was more easily persuaded, providing the price was right. Eitan concluded our discussions by saying all final options must be considered in the interests of the survival of Israel, which may no longer fall under the political sphere. His ominous words echo down the years, haunting me, "*We may be left with no choice but to consider a Unit 235 operation*". I recall the German clicking his heels." Yehudi sighed deeply, shaking his head, and there was a silence as he reflected; then he continued slowly, as if painfully recollecting the past. "That was the first time I had heard of Unit 235 and I wish I hadn't because whenever I did, it was only at the highest level and always because it was involved in the worst covert operations; those that no-one wanted to take responsibility for. These usually involved Lekem, into which I learned that Ravid had been recruited by Eitan.

"I can tell you that I headed up a development which benefited from the activities of this unit, enabling us to build up a modern nuclear arsenal right under the noses of allies we were deceiving and stealing information from. I never knew the details of what they did, nor did I wish to know, but I believe they were responsible for terrible things. That is where your father became most active and, perhaps, where your investigation might concentrate. Extreme factions became involved, and even those at the top of our political establishment were wary of them. Yes, they had their uses when Israel was under threat but by the mid-1980's they had become out of control and committed the cardinal error in the intelligence world, that of being caught. When the Americans discovered we had been spying on them and stealing nuclear materials, it gave Prime Minister Yitzhak Shamir the excuse he needed to disband Lekem. At that time, the commander was none other than Rafi Eitan, who seemed to be everywhere anything was happening in Israeli intelligence. Remember it was he who had tracked down and kidnapped one of the architects of the Holocaust, Adolf Eichmann, and he was something of a celebrity inside and outside of Mossad." He stopped again and looked deeply at Shira, "Oh, my *cheifale*, I know too much that I feel I do not wish to share. I have so much on my conscience; too much, especially when lives have been lost because of our desperate instinct to survive after all we suffered in the Holocaust." Tears were in his eyes as she placed her arms around him. His voice was weak yet she felt the strength of the conviction in his words,

"The imperative of survival should never replace the wisdom of love; the former is an instinct, the latter is from God."

Sunday 23rd May 2021 - 1am
Rishonim Street, Neve Tzedek, Tel Aviv

In the pause that followed Shira's revelations about Yehudi Krimmer, Mehedi rose from his seat, downing the remains of his wine, and placed the glass down on the table decisively. "You Jews, all was peaceful until you arrived!" he said in an attempt to lift the atmosphere, then more earnestly, "This is all very interesting but I think, David, tomorrow's meeting should be pivotal after the loss of Berkowicz tonight. It seems to me that if they are prepared to be so brazen, matters may be coming to a head and we need to act swiftly. I am returning home for now but I think, perhaps, that it may be better if I stay with you at General Gellner's house. I'll meet you there tomorrow at 1400 hours?"

David turned to Shira, "Could I impose on you tonight and I'll have Moshe pick me up tomorrow? Our transport was a little compromised and is currently peppered with bullet holes. May God help me, it may be the last night I can sleep without wondering whether I will have my throat cut by a Bedouin Arab in the dead of night."

"You are such an *alter noyef*" (pervert), Mehedi responded, with a tired smile, giving his, by now, customary extended middle finger gesture.

"My goodness," Shira exclaimed, "I was counting on you to be my protection, Mehedi, whatever shall I do?" She looked at David, her face and eyes giving just a hint of a wicked expression, before she hugged Mehedi, thanking him for assisting with the briefing. As David's heart was pounding, she escorted Mehedi to the door but not before he had looked back, giving an exaggerated wink.

They decided to have a nightcap of a *Lavie* coffee espresso liqueur, which, Shira proudly announced with a giggle, contained 20 percent alcohol and had been made with premium coffee beans. She lay back lazily and languorously on the couch opposite David and he was entranced by her hair cascading over the arm of the sofa, her legs carelessly crossed and her bare feet swinging as she spoke softly. "I'm so glad you came here tonight; investigating Ravid was an isolating task and, frustratingly, one which was curtailed just when I thought I was onto something interesting. I raised the reference that *Zaydee* had made to Unit 235 with my immediate superior on my return to Israel and, at first, he was keen we unearthed whatever we could find. I knew this was the unit in which Ravid had served yet I could not find anyone who would talk about it, although there was a rumour that after Lekem was disbanded, it had re-formed under another name. I decided to track down the last known commander of Unit 235 who Zaydee had identified as Rafi Eitan. If you behave yourself tonight, I might reveal to you tomorrow what happened." She flashed a wickedly mischievous look at him, with a smiling, then pouting look of innocence. David's heart quickened as he looked deeply into her eyes, feeling totally drawn to her, not sure whether she was merely teasing or being genuinely inviting. She drained her glass, abruptly stood up, and held her hand out to him. Her skin was cool and soft as her fingers closed on his, pulling him up and then leading him to what she described as the guest suite, which was a little overstated. The room had a large window with a balcony beyond and was sparsely furnished with a simple pine double bed and matching table on which there was an ornate bronze art deco lamp, the light held aloft by a naked dancer. He turned to her, "Thank you for this…" He said the words rather clumsily, very aware of her proximity. His eyes met hers, and there was a heavy silence as her arm reached around his neck, her fingers wafting softly over his hairline. "I feel it too…" she breathed. Then, abruptly, she tapped him on the nose. "You need your sleep and, as I outrank you, I am giving you the order to retire," pausing for a second, then adding, "alone!" The last word was emphasised as she flounced out of the room with a suppressed giggle.

19

"Strike down the nations"

Wednesday 20th December 1944 – 2pm
Malmedy, Ardennes, Belgium

The four drab, olive-green jeeps, with their complement of twenty US soldiers, rounded the bend of the snow-covered road outside Malmedy to be faced with a column of trucks blocking their way, in front of which a number of troops were standing, beating their arms against the cold. The jeeps stopped and a young officer jumped out. "Hi boys, I'm Captain Wilbur Donahue of 15th Corps of the Third US Army. We are the advance party checkin' out what the heck is goin' on around here before our main force joins us in Malmedy. The whole area is swarming with goddamn Krauts."

The officer in front of the trucks crunched over the fresh white covering to shake his hand. "Major Eugene F Grant of the 99th Infantry Battalion. I thought you guys were up north."

Donahue lit a cigarette offering one to the Major. "We got word, sir, two days since from General Bradley that this area had kicked off bad and were told to get our asses south. Our progress been held up by this damned snow; half the roads are blocked. Seems like these German bastards ain't givin' up without a fight."

Major Grant took a deep draw on his cigarette, "We got orders to take up position and form an outer defence perimeter but we picked up some concentrated artillery fire about an hour ago, so we taking it real slow."

"Hell, we just got here in the nick of time, then, to put your minds at rest. Trust the boys from 15 Corps to show you guys the way." He pointed to the small hill behind him, pulling his greatcoat in to shield him from the bitter cold, his breath emitting a misty cloud as he spoke. "My guys are over the other side of that ridge. We got over a hundred and fifty in our company, so you pretty safe. We hit some Krauts in Panzers about two miles back but they were headed away from here."

"I guess we'll get on up there and dig in," Major Grant replied. "Mighty nice to see you guys; I think we gonna need all the help we can get." He waved to the men on the road. "OK boys, let's get outta here. We'll drive up the hill here and dig in over the ridge." He stubbed out his cigarette, gave a salute to Captain Donahue, and walked to the truck, heaving himself in. Moments later, five truckloads of men, rolled forwards, the soldiers waving at the men in the jeeps as they departed. Donahue climbed back in the front of the lead vehicle and turned to the man next to him with a long scar down his face and a neat trimmed moustache. *"Ich glaube, diesen Amerikanern steht ein ziemlicher Schock bevor, Herr Oberst,"* (I think these Americans are in for quite a shock, Colonel) Otto Skorzeny nodded his head and lit a cigarette. *"Ja,* just what the Führer ordered when I had tea with him in Berlin a week ago. I can hear his words now, *'Think of the confusion you could cause…which will destroy morale.'"* I think, *Herr Hauptmann,* we are going to have some fun." He looked across at Danneberg (Donahue's real name) with a roguish grin. "This is the sort of work I really enjoy." They watched the convoy of trucks disappear over the hill.

It did not take long. Suddenly, there was the sound of the thump and crack of tank shells, followed by prolonged machine gun fire. Explosions followed in quick succession, and a pall of black smoke appeared over the ridge, rising in billowing clouds, signalling the carnage below as sporadic shots continued, witnessing the firefight taking place. They waited for another thirty minutes and then an assortment of armoured vehicles appeared, followed by a Sherman Tank, some trucks, and an M10 tank destroyer that was, in reality, a disguised Panther tank. Shortly thereafter, a smiling figure alighted from an American scout car at the head of the column, and approached Skorzeny's jeep. "Mission accomplished, Herr Oberst; you would not believe it, but they were waving at us as we opened fire."

"Now for Malmedy," Skorzeny responded, undoing the brass buttons of his heavy US military olive drab coat, under which he was wearing his field grey SS tunic, as the other men followed suit.

Tuesday 16th January 1945 – 4pm
Hotel Adlon, Wilhelmstrasse, Berlin

"I bid you welcome, Frau Reitsch," The manager bowed deeply, as Hanna entered to be faced with an inner block in the lobby that reminded her of the entrance to a military barracks. "You will, I hope, remember me from the Hotel Kaiserhof which you graced many times. That was badly damaged in 1943 by the bombs and now…" he shrugged his hands gesturing, "oh mein Gott, it is ruined completely. Forgive this rather strange construction, but we had to build it to shield guests from the criminal bombing being carried out by the Americans and the British. Once, I remember Hermann Göring saying that no enemy aircraft would ever fly over Berlin or we could call him 'Meyer' (call him a Dutchman) "I think, perhaps, he now has that name."

Hanna put her finger to her mouth, gesturing him to guard his words with a 'shush', *Bitte Herr Hoteldirektor,* do not speak so openly, it is dangerous." You are lucky I am not like the Gestapo, or you would be arrested for this."

The manager looked at her with tired eyes, and she could sense the strain he was working under. "I am deeply sorry but we are suffering; so many are dying, and our beautiful city is being destroyed more and more every day. I should not have spoken out. I am instructed to give you the best room here, which is now on the first floor because of the raids."

Hanna replied sharply, "Who has organised this? I made my own arrangements to come here."

At that moment, a booming, familiar voice rang out in the lobby, "Always outspoken, and making a scene; I think even Reichsführer Himmler himself is wary of you!" A smiling Wernher von Braun appeared, wearing a smartly-pressed pinstriped suit with a white top hanky, carrying a bouquet of flowers which he presented to her. He turned to the manager, requesting a bottle of the finest Champagne, to be delivered to her suite.

As soon as they had entered the room, once Wernher had tipped the porter and the door had closed behind him, they embraced. "Oh my God, Wernher," she gasped, "what is happening to Germany? The Russians have crossed our borders in the east whilst in the west we are in retreat from the Allies. Is this the time when we must unleash the *wunderwaffe?*" (wonder-weapons)

"I think all options are being considered," Wernher replied gently, stroking her hair as he tried to offer her some comfort.

"The world will regret not listening to the words of the Führer. We should all have united against the Bolshevik scum!" She hissed through gritted teeth. "I hope we launch one of those terrible rockets of yours with the atomic weapon inside it against Moscow." She stepped back for a moment, holding his hands in hers. "The only thing I am uneasy about is dropping one of these bombs on London. Mr Churchill is a warmonger, but I would not wish to be the cause of so many deaths in England; they are more like us. I think the threat would be sufficient to enable us to negotiate a treaty which prevents Russia from seizing our territory. I know there are many, like me, who agree we need to try and find a peace settlement with Britain and America. Some are saying we should unite against the greater threat from Russia."

"I am not sure the Führer is ready to countenance that quite yet," Wernher responded, "although rumour has it that he has authorised unofficial talks to take place. He has returned to Berlin today from the *Adlerhorst* military HQ and is preparing to move into the *Vorbunker*. (the Führerbunker) I think the Ardennes offensive is lost and we must now defend the Reich itself."

"I know our Führer is a visionary and only he has the strength at this time to secure Germany's future," Hanna said forcefully as she removed her jacket throwing it loosely over a chair. Wernher's eyes were drawn to the sheen of her silky cream blouse, which evoked thoughts he tried to bury of her firm body in his arms.

There was a knock on the door and the *Veuve Clicquot* Champagne arrived on a silver tray with two crystal glasses. The waiter uncorked the bottle, offering Wernher a taste but he declined, gesturing him to pour before slipping him a tip as he departed. Wernher guided Hanna to a chaise longue where they touched their glasses together. '*He is so divinely debonair and handsome still,*' she thought, with a delicious inner thrill as he proffered a toast, "May the future bring peace and better times for Germany." His deep blue eyes captivated her and before she could stop herself, she was in his arms, seeking, craving and desiring release in a wanton need that reflected her despair at the world collapsing all around them. His strong hands pulled her to him, and her breath came in short gasps as he undid the buttons of her blouse, seeking the softness of her naked skin beneath the silky covering over her breasts, her body arching upwards. Her mouth devoured his deep kisses, her needs matched by his hunger for her, then she thrilled as she sought him and he whispered to her, "Never forget this moment!"

At dinner that night, he took her hand in both of his, and spoke earnestly, "I will speak with the Führer tomorrow and say you are too precious to the Reich to send on the London mission. We are building more of the larger rockets capable of carrying the atomic bomb and my rockets are increasing in accuracy, hitting London daily; they are impossible to intercept." Shortly after that, the air-raid sirens wailed, and the maître d' announced that all guests should proceed to the underground air-raid lounge. This was a luxurious shelter beneath the hotel, complete with ornate furnishings and mock windows with curtains shielding the thick concrete walls surrounding the space. Hanna trembled, burying her head in Wernher's shoulder as the thump of explosions could be heard over the swing music, being played by a three-man band, some of the bombs close enough to make the ground shake. They remained there until after midnight, at which point Wernher left her, saying he needed to prepare for the following day's meeting with the Führer.

Wednesday 17th January 1945 – 10am
The Reich Chancellery, Wilhelmstrasse 77, Berlin

Hanna had met Robert Ritter von Greim for breakfast at the hotel two hours before. He had arrived looking impecable in a blue Luftwaffe dress uniform of a *General der Flieger*, complete with gold braid, and matching lanyards looped below the eagle and swastika badge. His shoulder epaulettes were also in gold as were the rank flashes on a white background on his shoulders. '*Very distinguished; I could easily have fallen for him were it not for Wernher*' she thought, suppressing a mischievous giggle. She had opted for a military-style black trouser suit, upon which she wore the Nazi party decorative brooch given to her by Hitler, and her Iron Cross decoration just below it on her chest, with a red, white and blue button hole ribbon. She asked von Greim about his view of the future as they finished breakfast, drinking coffee. His words were a stark contrast to his normal warmth, sending a chill through her. "I regret, my dearest Hanna, that if we do not reach a peace settlement with the western allies, Germany will be overrun by the Bolshevik pigs. The Führer has an unshakeable belief in the superiority and purity of the German race, but this is not enough when faced with the overwhelming numerical superiority of our enemies. Europe will suffer the consequences as the perverse values of Russian communism destroy civilisation, contaminating and infecting as it spreads. The war of the future will be caused by the Russians because their vile race will attempt to impose the poison of its filthy creed on every nation."

Hanna had put her hands over her face – "Oh my God, Robert, stop, please stop. This is all so terrible. What of our wonderful Führer? Germany needs him."

He reached across the table for her hand, kissing it. "Forgive me; I am so sorry but I am seeing wonderful men I know dying every day. I think we need to rescue the Führer, not just from the Russians but from himself, otherwise I fear the consequences. Who will face up to the Russians if Hitler does not? He was the only leader in the world who had the courage to stand against the evil Stalin and his disgusting, depraved regime. One day the world will regret what is happening now to Germany and, if we lose this war, a dark shadow will fall across civilisation. I do not think I will wish to continue living unless I am in service of the Führer. There is talk of creating an impregnable mountain fortress in Bavaria and fighting on until the inevitable takes place; a conflict between Russia and the western allies with whom we can form a new alliance. Our priority, if the war is lost, is to ensure the safety of the Führer."

Hanna squeezed his hand. "We will never let him be taken. I will give my life for him but, surely, the *wunderwaffe* can save us? The new developments in our superior military technology will help, such as the incredible new jet and rocket aircraft that I am testing. They will give us unrivalled mastery of the skies."

He looked gently at her, sensing her desperation, which mirrored that of the nation. "That, of course, is why we have been summoned here; to look at the remaining options open to us. For that great purpose, we must rely on the Führer." As they stood up from the table, Hanna turned to von Greim, clicked her heels and raised her right arm, *"Heil Hitler,"* she said with vigour, to which his own salute was returned with equal enthusiasm.

They were told that the normal route from the hotel up to the Reich Chancery was impassable because of the bombing. Hanna stared bleakly from the windows of the large Mercedes at the devastation, which she could scarcely comprehend, here in the centre of Berlin that Hitler had taken such pride in improving, assisted by his loyal architect, Albert Speer. There were piles of rubble where buildings had once stood, doors hanging off at crazy angles, curtains blowing from windows in which there was no longer any glass, and even churches with their spires missing or shattered. She watched people scavenging for their belongings or, an even worse thought crossed her mind, seeking buried loved ones. She turned back, trying not to look, as they drove up Hermann-Göring-Strasse, turning left into Vorstrasse and then into the courtyard adjacent to the Reich Chancellery. There were SS guards there busy clearing up fallen masonry but, she observed, appearances were being maintained as more guards with white gloves stood either side of the main entrance, its pillars now showing signs of damage from shrapnel.

Inside the Reich Chancellery, the building was surprisingly intact, although, as von Greim informed her, most of the pictures and other works of art had been removed to keep them safe from the bombing. They walked through the corridor busy with staff packing or removing boxes and soldiers carrying out furniture. There was an atmosphere of impending forboding change as the once imposing testament of this monument to the strength of the Reich was being stripped. They walked down the 150-metre marble gallery, which showed signs of bomb damage with some rubble below crumbled masonry from the outer wall. Their footsteps echoed as they traversed the monumental dimensions of this edifice, now emptied of all furnishings, which seemed to dramatically emphasise the cataclysmic nature of all that Germany now faced. Hanna felt a strange and unusual pang of fear, being faced with such dramatic and terrifying evidence of the challenges threatening the survival of the Reich. At the far end of the gallery, as they entered the Reception Hall, with its huge crystal chandeliers suspended from the lofty ceiling some twelve metres high, they were met by Hitler's adjutant, SS-Obergruppenführer Julius Schaub, who jumped to his feet as they entered. *"Heil Hitler!"* he barked, clicking his heels and raising his arm in his normally, over-dramatic manner, which Hanna had observed previously. She had long ago dismissed him in her mind as one of the Führer's sycophants, full of his own self-importance, and had shared in joking about him with *Reichsmarschall Hermann Göring.* He had given Schaub the nickname (as he did for most members of the Führer's entourage) of *'Reisemarschal'* (Travel Marshal), mocking him as having the status of Hitler's porter.

"Today, the Führer has charged me with the honour of escorting you both to meet with him. Please be advised that he is experiencing some hearing loss after the divine miracle which spared his life from the traitor's bomb plot last July. He does not like to be reminded of this, so, if possible, speak a little louder and be mindful that he hears better on his left side. Please follow me." He clicked his heels again and executed a smart about turn. They followed him through the hall and finally reached Hitler's study, outside which two guards were standing dressed in black uniforms, who snapped to attention as Schaub walked towards the door upon which he knocked, but opened without awaiting a response.

"Mein Führer," he boomed loudly, "may I present *Herr General der Flieger Ritter von Greim,* accompanied by *Flugkapitän Hanna Reitsch."* Von Greim gave Hanna's hand a quick squeeze before guiding her through the entrance to the huge thirty by twenty metre room beyond. The vast study had red marble walls down

one side, upon which were brass lights with classical shades matching the marble colour, whilst on the other, large floor to ceiling windows normally gave a view of the Reich Chancellery gardens; however, all but one of these had external shutters closed to protect them. There was a single tapestry but the classical oil paintings that had previously adorned the walls had all been removed apart from the stark portrait of Bismarck; this remained above the fireplace, dominating the furthest wall facing the Führer's desk. Hanna was always impressed with the grandiose architectural style adopted by Albert Speer under the Führer's direction, yet, despite the size of this spectacular room, it retained an element of comfortable warmth. The rosewood square-panelled ceiling matched the magnificent polished doors, giving access from either end, and above one entrance there was a huge gold eagle clutching a swastika in a circle beneath, whilst in one corner stood an enormous world atlas globe. There were many in the study she recognised who stood up as she entered, Hermann Göring nodding to her approvingly, Joseph Goebbels raising his arm from the elbow in the short-style Nazi salute with a broad grin; Albert Speer bowed alongside Martin Bormann, who followed suit, and, as expected, an expressionless Heinrich Himmler scanned her with cold eyes through his thick, round glasses. She walked across the huge rug covering the floor towards the familiar smiling figure of Adolf Hitler, who rose slowly from behind his red leather-topped desk to greet her.

"*Mein Reich Engel!*" His familiar guttural voice was spoken with less force than she had ever heard, even detecting a tremor in his words, but it was his appearance which gave her the greatest shock.

She had last seen him the previous July when she had been at *The Berghof,* but now he appeared so different. She still felt the piercing, alert blue eyes that seemed to be seeing inside her mind, but he was not as she remembered. He looked exhausted, bent and drawn, with the skin around his face sagging, and grey streaks in his hair above the ears. She knew he was fifty-four yet he appeared twenty years older. She noticed that one of his hands appeared to be shaking, which he quickly covered with his other to hide the tremor. Even as he stood to greet her, his body was stooped and his demeanour displayed the kind of fatigue she had seen in others returning from the front after prolonged combat. His double-breasted military-style field grey tunic seemed to hang off him, yet he was, as always, smartly dressed with black trousers and a matching tie on which was an eagle tie-pin. On his left breast he wore his favoured World War 1 wound decoration, above which was his Iron Cross and a round gold-edged Nazi Party badge. On his left upper arm was the gold emblem of the eagle and swastika. He reached out to kiss her outstretched hand, and bowed, which had been his customary manner of greeting her, adopted many years before. Despite his appearance, she was mesmerised by his presence and smiled coyly, looking round catching the sneer of disapproval from Himmler. The Führer spoke, after briefly shaking hands with von Greim, raising his arm in salute from the elbow. "This incredible lady epitomises the indomitable strength and will of our race in which I have invested and to which I have dedicated my life. The German *Volk* needed leadership in their hour of need and Providence selected me for this great endeavour. I regret, *meine Kameraden*, that we have been betrayed in Germany's historic purpose and, as a result, the filthy communist vermin threaten to contaminate our land. They will never vanquish the German spirit, never!" His voice rang out with the final word, "*niemals!*" His hand crashed down on his desk. "Now is the moment of our destiny when we will not shrink from striking the terrible, yet magnificent blow which will deliver victory to the Reich! *Heil!*" Again, his voice had risen to a crescendo as all in the room raised their right arms in deference to this god amongst men who would deliver them in Germany's hour of need.

"*Mein Führer,*" Joseph Goebbels exclaimed proudly, "we believe in you because only your indomitable will could have led

Germany at this time and given to us the means of our deliverance in our mission of '*Totalen Krieg*' (total war), as decreed by you two years ago. Now, our hour of our deliverance is almost nigh and, tonight, *mein Führer*, with your permission, I shall announce this to the German people."

Hitler stated that the Minister of Armaments, Albert Speer, should make the announcement, as his broadcast would carry more authority if it did not come from the propaganda ministry. He then looked at each of those in the room in turn, the pause adding more drama to what was to follow. "Last July, I gave *Reich Minister Goebbels* the title of Reich Plenipotentiary for Total War. He, together with the Reich Minister of Armaments, Albert Speer, galvanised the *Unternehmen Armageddon* mission, injecting this with new energy." He walked forwards to where three men stood, dressed in suits, the only ones not in uniform, one of whom Hanna recognised as von Weizsäcker. Hitler shook hands with each of them, as they briefly bowed before raising their arms. "The Reich owes these three scientists a huge debt. They told me it would take four or five years to develop an atom bomb but I demanded they cut this time by half, and now the great moment we have been waiting for is almost upon us." He placed his right hand on the shoulder of each man as he named them. "These men dedicated themselves to the momentous task of creating the bomb. Von Weizsäcker pioneered the weapon programme, under the inspired direction of *Herr Professor Doktor* Erich Schuman, backed by the research of Professor Werner Heisenberg. They accelerated the programme and achieved results driven by the dedicated spirit of National Socialism." He walked slowly and deliberately with a slight limp to where Wernher von Braun was standing in his SS uniform, who clicked his heels smartly as Hitler shook his hand, patting him on the shoulder as he had the others. "This man is a genius and he has also worked miracles to construct a rocket capable of carrying the weight required for the bomb. Today, he has assured me that there is no need for an aircraft to carry this, because he has constructed more of the new heavy capacity rockets which are accurate enough to hit London. Therefore, my *Reich Engel*," he turned to Hanna, "I have decided that your work on test-flying our new rocket and jet aircraft is far too valuable for you to risk carrying the bomb." She nodded her head and raised her arm, smiling, yet, despite her relief, she could not help but feel an inner tinge of disappointment that she would not now be part of the Führer's plan. As Hitler turned back towards his desk, she glanced across at Wernher, who winked at her, a gesture not missed by Himmler, who noted to himself that she needed to be watched and, when the time was right, removed.

Hitler then turned to face the room, opening his arms wide – "Today, I feel the hand of history dictating our final move. All of you have played a part in building the new Germany under my leadership and we will not permit anyone to destroy the monumental achievements of the Third Reich. Our plans are not for ten years, not even a hundred years, but for a thousand. My destiny may fulfil the prophecy of Armageddon contained in the book of Revelation, '*From his mouth comes a sharp sword with which to strike down the nations, and he will rule them with a rod of iron.*' They tried last July to curb the mission chosen for me, but my will is iron and my resolve unshakeable in the task that lies ahead to make the Reich invincible." His words were delivered with passion, as he pronounced and emphasised every syllable and the room echoed with the cries of "*Zieg Heil!*"

That night, Albert Speer gave a speech to the German people over the radio announcing that rockets would soon fall upon New York City, sending an already nervous US Navy into a frenzied state of high alert.

20

"Someone will die for this..."

Sleep had welcomed him into a world away from the troubles of recent days and he was playing in a tennis tournament many years before, rejoicing in the challenge facing him as his parents watched him proudly. Although he was not immediately aware of her presence, the scent of perfume he had breathed in only a short time before began to interrupt his dream, and he sensed her before he opened his eyes. Then a hand gently stroking his forehead raised his awareness and she was there standing in front of him, clad in just a white chemise, the light from the lamp silhouetting her naked body beneath. Her long well-formed legs, now revealed under the short silky garment, drew his gaze which then travelled upwards, drinking her image, as his hands reached out to her softness, his eyes lifting to meet hers in the half light. Her beauty was intoxicating, overwhelming all thoughts of any rationality as he drew her to him. "We both sensed this…" she breathed as she leant downwards, her arms encircling his bare shoulders, kissing his mouth gently before their lips moved more ardently together. Then, she stopped, and stood before him, lifting her chemise over her head, revealing herself totally as he took in the vision of loveliness before him. Her body was so perfectly beautiful, toned, yet full, her breasts proud as she tossed her head provocatively backwards, then back down again so that her long hair with its ringlets was half covering her face. She reached for his hands, and his body pounded with desire for her. "You know it's rude to keep a girl waiting. Did they not teach you manners in *Maglan Unit 212*?" Then, with a petulant, mischievous look, she slid in beside him, reaching for him and he shuddered as he felt her cool fingers encircling, caressing softly but yet with urgency as they kissed deeply. His hands pulled her body to him, both rejoicing in their arousal as they arched, pressing their bodies together, each feeling the shivers of delight from their anticipation and need. Their sharing flowed in gentle, yet powerful waves as they each sought to give, to seek, and to sense each other's desire without taking. As their eyes met in the sheer joy of their passion, reaching a peak as one, they both knew that there was so much more in their union than either of them could comprehend and, within that moment, they became bound together.

At 8am, he awoke to the sound of her voice singing a song that was semi-familiar to him but he could not recall why. She flounced in wearing her chemise from the night before, cheekily swaying her hips to shove the door closed behind her, then adopted a provocative walk across the room despite carrying two cups of coffee, which she placed on a table by the bed. Her hair was dishevelled but her eyes danced as she threw a pillow at him saying, "Get your lazy ass out of that bed; you boys in *Unit 212* are all the same, good on missions but lazy in between."

David grasped her, and pulled her to him, the pain from his arm wound hardly noticeable in the moment, despite it throbbing at other times. He playfully slapped her bottom, delighting in her nakedness beneath the chemise, which rose as she pressed her warm soft body to his. His mouth searched for hers as she eagerly responded but, despite his arousal, he pulled back, as a thought from the night before hit him. "How do you know my former unit?" he asked, his old instincts of survival through constant awareness or suspicion of those around him, had suddenly been aroused.

She reached for one of the cups of coffee and passed it to him. "Last night, when you arrived, I already knew of you because, *neshama sheli* (my dearest soul), you have been noted within military intelligence as a danger to be arrested on sight. Last Monday, I was at my office in Aman and was tasked with preparing a report on you and on those with whom you associate. I was also made aware that you had been identified as a militant left-wing radical, and that you were involved in a plot against the government, with the potential to organise subversion, using your business as cover. You were identified as extremely dangerous because of your military background. I did not know what to think when you arrived last night but my instinct was to trust you within minutes. Once you informed me about your investigation, I knew you were the victim and no perpetrator. I studied your background in the military and even watched recordings of you playing tennis. I have to say you are no Rafael Nadal, nor as good looking, but you have great legs." She giggled as his face softened, "So, Major, have I said enough to convince you? After all, you have seduced me and forced me to betray my country. If not, I surrender to you and you can take me again." Any concerns disappeared as he leant forwards and kissed her softly, yet briefly, with a depth of genuine affection that shocked him, realising that he had never before felt so drawn to another in this way. "You are utterly beautiful, my *bubbeleh* (baby doll)," an intimate term he had never used before came easily as he ran his hands through her long, soft hair, "despite being a siren leading me astray." Then, struck with a feeling of guilt, as he abruptly recalled the traumatic events of the night before, seeing Berkowicz die in front of him, he sat up straight. "Something terrible is taking place, Shira, and we need to move. Not only our country is in danger but peace is threatened across the entire world and I fear we have little time."

They drank their coffee quickly, then dressed after agreeing to operate jointly, both recognising the contribution they could each make. After discussing the key elements of the threat, they recognised that in order to mobilise forces, they needed the most intelligence they could gather in order to convince influential military figures, and those with political power, of the need to act. As they discussed the revelations Shira had uncovered from Yehudi Krimmer, David suggested that they might attempt to secure any last details he may be able to provide, which could add to the jigsaw of pieces they needed to assemble. He informed her that his cousin, Benjamin Weiss, was based in London having been recruited to work for MI6 in the Jewish/Arab department, and that he could arrange for him to visit Yehudi. He stated that it may be an idea to prepare the way by briefing her adopted grandfather and obtaining his consent for a visit.

Minutes later Shira was on the landline exchanging pleasantries in which she praised the ninety-seven-year-old for his independence, although admonishing him for not giving credit to his long-suffering wife. Her voice then assumed a more immediate tone, "*Zaydee*, our beloved Israel is under threat from extreme elements within and I need to call on your help. You remember all you revealed to me when we discussed these terrible people that caused you to lose faith in the government. I need records from the past which back-up what you revealed to me. We are trying to stop them but I need any information you may still have. I have a dear friend, David Stern, who is helping me, with other good Jewish people. His cousin lives in London. Can you put together any documents or records you may have, and we will have him collect it, maybe later today?" She took in a sharp intake of breath and exclaimed emphatically, "No, I told you, no marriages for me!" then giggled in her hand, blushing as David pulled a wry smile. After a few more minutes as she gave a rolling motion with her hand to indicate that Yehudi was rambling, she finished with, "Yes, darling *Zaydee,* if I do, I will bring him to England and introduce you." As she put the phone down, she looked at David sharply, "Don't get ideas, Major, I am now on duty." David executed a mock salute before picking up the receiver and dialling a UK number.

"Benjamin, it is David, I need your urgent help." His cousin took the call in his office at MI6 Headquarters, at Vauxhall Cross, London, where he customarily worked at weekends. The discussion was business-like and brief, as David briefly stated there may be rogue elements of Israeli military defense threatening national security. Benjamin instantly recognised the gravity of the situation and what was required, taking note as David passing on Yehudi's address. After the call, he turned to Shira, recalling the meeting arranged at Moshe Gellner's house at 2pm, stating that she should attend and that they could travel there together. After he had called General Gellner to confirm, Shira re-entered the room with a laptop. "Despite the fact you were not a good boy, I have decided to grant you a reprieve and relate my report of my meeting with Rafi Eitan. I think you may find it interesting."

As they sat around the table in the lounge/kitchen, David asked, "What was that song you were singing this morning as you made coffee? I knew it but I couldn't place it."

She put her hands on her hips as she stood before him, with a shocked expression on her face. "Where were you last night? Israel was in the final of the *Eurovision,* which I had been enjoying until you barged in, having caused an outbreak of street warfare in Tel Aviv. The song was 'Set Me Free' which Eden Alene was singing. There is a line in it, 'Yalla balaganim' (Get on with it), which is exactly what we need to do."

"You are incorrigible," he responded as she leant across to give him a peck on the mouth.

As she opened the laptop, she explained, "After I returned from my trip to visit *Zaydee,* I was trying everything I could to unearth anything about Unit 235. In March 2013, I sent an email to Rafi Eitan saying I was doing research into the Mossad operation of 1960 to abduct Adolf Eichmann. A couple of days later, I was surprised to receive a call from him personally. He was put through on a high security passcode, reserved only for the most secure calls of the highest priority, usually used by top-ranking officers, cabinet ministers, or for the sharing of highly sensitive intelligence. I remember it like yesterday and especially his opening words, "'*Shalom*, (M/s) Ahava, this is Rafi Eitan. Before we speak, I shall deny ever having made this call, and you shall forget this ever took place unless, of course, I give you permission to reveal what we discuss. Do we have a deal?'" When I said 'yes', he laughed, saying, "'Never make a commitment unless you have contributed to the terms.'" I met him at the Jaffa Hotel where he had organised a suite purely to have the benefit of a luxurious lounge. The meeting was fascinating and I can say he was an extraordinary man who had an incredible charisma. He put me totally at my ease but then began what I might describe as a duel of words with which he was a master."

As she spoke, a mile away at Park Hayarkon, the headquarters of Israeli Internal Security, Shin Bet, there was a knock on the door of the communications director. The intelligence officer entered holding a tablet in his hand, which he flipped open as the director gestured him to a seat. The younger man spoke succinctly, used to giving military briefings. "This morning we monitored two calls from the same address here in Tel Aviv which may be of interest, sir, made to the United Kingdom. I can confirm that one was to one of our former nuclear physicists on our high security list, Yehudi Krimmer, who lives in England. The other was to an Israeli citizen who works for MI6, requesting that he picks up some evidence." The young officer paused for a moment before adding, "That may be significant enough, but there is something more important which is why I sought to report this personally.

The initial call requested that Krimmer collected together as much written evidence as he could about security issues they had previously discussed. Sir, the person who made this call and from whose home we tracked both calls was Colonel Shira Ahava, aka Shira Ravid, the daughter of Omer Ravid." The director leaned forwards, "You have transcripts of the calls? *Toda la'el* (Thank the Lord) that we implemented the foreign call monitoring system for IDF staff."

10am
Kdoshei Hashoa Street, Herzliya Pituach, Tel Aviv-Yafo

The phone buzzed on the highly polished desk behind which sat a thick-set man in darkened glasses with white hair worn slightly longer than was fashionable, in a light fawn flannel suit, wearing a crisp white shirt open at the neck. He glanced down at the display, recognising it was a call from an Israeli Intelligence source. "Ravid!" His voice, in one word, carried uncompromising authority. He listened, his eyes narrowing as the information was communicated to him. "Any mention of names during either call apart from the *alte kaker?*" (old fart) He listened intently for a few seconds before reaching for the cut crystal glass in front of him, on a gold coaster in which ice cubes bounced, floating on his favourite, locally produced, *Milk & Honey* classic malt whisky. He picked it up, swirling the contents for a moment, then, after taking a drink, he said emphatically, "Contact our Lekem man in London and have him eliminated immediately."

His brows furrowed for a brief moment as he ran his right hand through his hair, smoothing it down. He glanced at his gleaming Rolex watch, checking whether he was running late for a meeting he had arranged with an old friend with a seat in the Knesset, then pressed a button on his phone to book lunch for them both in the Mariposa Restaurant at the Caesarea Golf Club.

6pm
The Avenue, Bletsoe, Bedfordshire, England

As Benjamin Weiss had driven his prized Jaguar XK8 down the wide A6, five miles from his destination, four police cars in their blue, yellow and white livery had shot past him at high speed with their sirens blaring, and then, minutes later, an unmarked car had also overtaken with flashing blue lights. Up to this point, the drive had been uneventful and had taken him just over one hour twenty minutes from his office at MI6 HQ by the Thames at Vauxhall, in the centre of London. Traffic had been relatively light as he gunned the powerful 4.0 litre V8 engine, joyfully feeling the power of the acceleration, then onto the M1 where he pushed the speed up to 100mph. Although intelligence officers were normally instructed not to take advantage of their status with the police, he was now on a mission, which he told himself, would justify the speed, something in which he had always thrilled. He was proud to be working with his older cousin, David, who he had looked up to as a younger man. Benjamin was ten years his junior and had watched his cousin win trophy after trophy at tennis, which he envied and attempted not to resent. He too could play tennis to a moderate standard but found the training boring and longed for more excitement. He excelled at school, entering the IDF at the age of 18, where his quick analytical mind was recognised, ending up working for Mossad. Benjamin was an idealist, identifying with the Arab struggle, which caused some friction with fellow officers, if not suspicion. He joined *Na'amod,* which was a Jewish organisation committed to Arab equality, and when British Intelligence was seeking Israeli-trained agents for secondment to MI6, his superiors urged him to take a post with them. He was tall, always well dressed, blonde haired and well-built with deep blue eyes and was considered highly attractive by those females he worked with. He was seen as 'a catch', being single and owning a penthouse apartment in Wimbledon. He had developed a keen interest in motorsports, which had become a passion, especially after experiencing the performance of a Formula 1 car in his first event in 2013, driving at speed round the edge of Jerusalem's Old City, adding to his playboy image. Despite having a substantive income from his shareholding in his parents' textile business based in Haifa, he had opted to remain working for Intelligence which provided an element of excitement.

The visit he was to make today intrigued him. David had briefed him that he was to meet a physicist who had played a major role in the development of Israel's nuclear programme. He was to obtain any information about the scientist's connection with Israeli Intelligence operations, including his role in the development of a nuclear weapon in Germany during the Second World War. The news of this had utterly shocked him, having always believed that it was the Americans and the British who had got there first.

As he approached the junction where he was to turn off the A5, he noticed *The Falcon* pub and restaurant on his left, taking a mental note that he might have a meal there before returning to London. The village was picturesque, with a delightful church on his left and some thatched cottages lining a lane meandering into the countryside beyond. He passed the last of the houses as the way ahead narrowed into a single-track road with passing places. Moments later, he was shocked to find a police barrier erected, blocking access. Two armed police officers approached his vehicle, one speaking into a radio before gesturing for him to open his window as the other went behind his car.

"Exit your vehicle now!" the officer said in a raised voice. "Lay on the floor, do not move and do not speak!"

Benjamin attempted to talk but was met with a harsh, "Now! Do it now!"

As he did so, he could hear the voice of a female colleague on the radio. "B-bravo, W-whisky 1; Echo India Sierra. Stand by."

His number plate was being checked and he waited, deciding that discretion was required. Seconds later, after one of the officers took a message that he could not make out, there were some whispered comments, before he was kicked softly by the officer, "Christ, it's the bloody secret service – I might have known you bastards would be involved. Get your arse up, I won't shoot you."

Benjamin did so, dusting off his *Armani* jacket, as he retorted, "God help me if you had frisked me, Sergeant, because I am armed. What the hell is going on?"

"VIP murder. Professional job it seems but I don't know any more. See the guv'nor down there. Ask for DCI Russell but the Deputy Chief Con has also just arrived with someone from the Home Office, so God knows what's happening."

They moved the barrier and he drove fifty yards towards a gate, outside which a number of police cars were parked including the unmarked car that had passed him previously. He pulled in by the grass verge and took his Intelligence ID from his wallet, flashing it at the first police officer who approached him. He was shown into the cottage where he could see a body, draped over by a cover, slumped in an armchair. A woman in a smart suit was talking to a middle-aged man in a slightly untidy jacket and tie, who was approached by the officer to whom he had shown his ID.

"Excuse me, boss, but this geezer is from the hush-hush brigade."

The man turned to study Benjamin, "DCI Russell. Bit of a mess, I'm afraid." Benjamin shook his hand and, in turn, was introduced to the woman; M/s Georgia Armstrong from the Home Office. She looked at him suspiciously – "I am briefed directly by the Home Secretary, and she did not inform me that you lot would be involved. Have you official security clearance for this?" she asked coldly.

Benjamin had no time for bureaucratic officialdom and responded with, "I am Benjamin Weiss and I am here on the direct orders of the Israeli Prime Minister with clearance via the British Prime Minister. I trust that will suffice?" He had met her type before and turned to the DCI, flashing his MI6 identity. "What happened here?"

"Professional job. Bullet straight in the head and another to the heart about three hours ago. Looks like he let his assailant in. No signs of a break-in. His wife called us. She has been taken away under sedation but is not making much sense. There was no attempt to take anything. He has a file in his hands which, bizarrely, has the Nazi Party insignia on it. Forensic have not let us touch it yet."

Benjamin was moving to the body as a voice cut in, "Who the hell are you?" He turned around to face a tall, ginger-haired man in a smart business suit. "Trevor, this man is from MI6," DCI Russell offered, "and he is working in conjunction with the PM and the Israeli PM."

"Oh yeah," came the reply, "and my name is Micky Mouse and I'm here from Disney." The Deputy Chief Constable of Bedfordshire Police had a reputation for thoroughness and today would be no exception. "You, my son, will do nothing until I clear this. You know the drill, George, call the Israeli Embassy."

Seconds later, the phone rang inside the large Georgian embassy building in Palace Green, Kensington, and, after the code word was given, Detective Chief Inspector George Russell was put through to the Head of Security. He immediately confirmed security clearance from the list on his screen but as soon as he was alerted that the agent was claiming he was working under authority from the Prime Minister, he put the call through to the ambassador. Her Excellency, Mrs Tzipi Hotovely, took the call in her office. On hearing the name, Benjamin Weiss, she accessed the top-level security database and spoke briefly, using words with which she had been trained. "Mr Weiss has the confidence and authority given to him directly by the Government of Israel under the personal direction of our prime minister."

George turned to the Deputy Chief Constable, nodding his head, at which point Trevor walked forwards with a smile of greeting. "Good to meet you; sorry about the red tape but that's why I'm here and not walking the beat. This is causing one hell of a stink. He is, or was, one of your top boffins, I think."

"Yes, he was forced to work for the Nazis in the War on some of their secret weapon projects," replied Benjamin, as he removed the cover from the body and looked at what was, in fact, a large document box still gripped in the dead man's hands. It was reddish brown in colour with reinforced corners, displaying a black eagle clutching a swastika emblem. He prized it slowly from the man's arms, which still encircled the box, noticing the words '*Streng Geheime Dokumente*' (highly classified documents) written in faded German gothic script. He looked up at the Deputy Chief Constable. "After the war, he worked for the Israeli government and the nature of his work is still highly classified, and, therefore, you will please have this aspect of your evidence removed from the reports of your enquiry. Excuse me for a moment." He walked to a table on which he placed the document box and began to undo the buckled retaining strap securing the lid. He looked inside and his eyes were immediately drawn to the large title on the front of the first sheaf of papers '*Scientific Report on The German Nuclear Device Test at Thüringia.*' However, it was the date that caught his attention: '*14th March 1945*'. There was a small, light blue envelope resting at the base of the document on the front of which was written in unsteady handwriting, '*For The Attention of Colonel Shira Ahava, Aman, Tel Aviv-Yafo.*' Underneath these papers was another report entitled '*Thüringia Element 94 (Plutonium) Findings for Dimona – Codename Project Isaiah*' Beneath this was a file with a label saying '*Ministerial Meetings*' written in Hebrew. He shut the box and re-fastened the strap around it. Then, looking across at the officious-looking woman from the Home Office, he added, "I will clear this directly with the Home Secretary but, for national security reasons, I need to remove this file and its contents and report directly to the Prime Minister." He picked up the box and began walking to the door, then turning round, he addressed the Deputy Chief Constable. "Trevor, our belief is that the perpetrator of this murder is, regrettably, likely to be an Israeli citizen, probably claiming to be working for one of our Intelligence agencies. I would get your airport security division to check the passenger manifest for all flights to Tel Aviv over the next twenty-four hours and delay departures if necessary. I am sure it would not be too difficult to track the movements of these people and whether any were in this vicinity today."

As he left the village, he immediately called David, telling him to scramble the call on his device. "David, either your call earlier was intercepted, or someone you are with is not to be trusted. I regret I have bad news."

8:30pm
Brosh Street, Caesarea, Israel

David re-joined the meeting where General Gellner was analysing strategic options with Shira and Mehedi. He raised his hands as he entered. "We have a tragic development," he announced, painfully aware that his words would be devastating to Shira. "My cousin, Benjamin, has reported we have another death to record in this escalating situation. I am very sorry, Shira, but I have to inform you that your beloved *Zaydee*, Yehudi Krimmer, has been assassinated. Your grandmother, Sarah, is OK and is being looked after by the British police." He moved towards her but she held her hand up to stop him.

She choked for a moment then slowly rose from her seat, her eyes fixed in a cold expression, her voice devoid of emotion as she spoke – "Someone will die for this."

That night Benjamin flew out of London Heathrow on a British Airways flight bound for Tel Aviv. He knew the removal of the documents would cause a diplomatic stink but, he reminded himself, he had not told the police which prime minister he was briefing. On the aircraft, he had kept the document holder with him as hand luggage and he began shaking his head in disbelief as he read.

21

The Altar of Democracy

Shira was escorted down the ornate corridor under majestic white arches, with ceilings in blue, or burgundy, some edged with golden decoration, blending historic architecture with the glitz of an imposing modern building. She was nervous, which seemed crazy, she thought, unable to justify her feelings as she had experience of commanding hardened combat units, running sections of people within Aman, and having prepared and delivered briefings to the most senior commanding officers and Israeli ministers. The feeling in the pit of her stomach she likened to memories of being hauled to meet the headmistress at school for her somewhat customary wayward behaviour as one who was not easily compliant, a trait that had stood her well in her military career. However, he was an iconic figure with a fearsome reputation in intelligence, held up as an example for his daring, outstanding leadership, and resourcefulness, combined with being known as something of a maverick figure. Their footsteps echoed on the floor replete with classical tiling, giving way to marble. Her smartly dressed guide, the undermanager, ushered her into an escalator, which whooshed them silently up two floors, and then down a long corridor with thick maroon carpeting over a rich light polished wood surface. The impression was palatial, spacious, historic and grandiose. Finally, they reached an arched double doorway, and her escort pressed an external wall-mounted intercom, then spoke briefly. Within seconds, a green light flashed and he led the way into a sizeable open area with comfortable chairs, that had magnificent views through large windows over a long boulevard stretching to trees, giving way to the ocean beyond. The ceiling was vaulted, with a mottled, traditional-style white and blue pattern in the stone facings.

Standing by a marble bar was her smiling host, with his signature large black-framed glasses and thick grey hair, dressed in a dark suit, with a mid-grey waistcoat and burgundy tie on which was a gold star of David. The undermanager spoke; "*Tzaharayim Tovim* (Good afternoon) Mr Eitan, may I present..."

He was interrupted, "Please, Noam, I know who she is. Thank you for escorting my guest." He waved him off, displaying a natural authority, command, if not brusque manner. As the door closed, she walked forwards, "*Ma shlomcha?*" (How are you) her hand outstretched. His demeanour immediately changed, beaming and bowing to her, before shaking her hand warmly. "*Shalom aleichem,* Shira. (peace be with you) I have heard much about you and of your outstanding service to Israel for which we are grateful." She noted the word "'we'" which seemed, perhaps, to distance himself from the state. He gestured with his hands as though chatting to an old friend, "Is not this place wonderful, demonstrating our internationally renowned skills as a nation of investment mastery? Here in the ancient quarter of *Yafo* (Jaffa), we preserve and respect an historic area sacred to our biblical faith, built after the flood by the son of Noah; sacred to the Christians also, where Saint Peter came to preach. Alexander the Great stood here, as did

Richard the Lionheart of England in the Crusades, and even the Emperor Napoleon conquered this place. Now…" he clapped his hands together, "in my lifetime, the realisation of a dream as it is a part of Israel, becoming this, my favourite hotel, which embodies our traditions and culture." He stopped, holding his hands up, displaying a shocked look – "Please, this is remiss of me, you must join me in an aperitif. Let us savour a fine long drink of Arak with lemonade and mint unless, of course, you are uncomfortable with such decadent hospitality?"

Shira sensed he was already playing with her by giving her little choice but to accept. "A long one, *tov toda.*" (OK thanks)

Rafi motioned her to sit in one of the velvet-covered armchairs around a glass-topped table, in front of one of the large arched windows, then he walked to the impressive marble bar set against the wall under an image of Alexander the Great, and began mixing drinks in two tall glasses. "You see, Shira, we have created this state from a dream, from a past of relentless persecution culminating in the greatest genocide in history, which I also witnessed in my lifetime… *The Holocaust.* Our race has suffered more than any other from recorded history, through biblical times down to the present and it still happens today. We have come home from all over the world and unite as a nation irrespective of our country of birth. In this, we are unique and you are part of this incredible phenomenon. Your grandmother worked for a German scientist at Mittelbau-Dora concentration camp in the Second World War, and was rescued and brought here to Israel in 1945 by an Israeli Intelligence team led by our former Prime Minister, Yitzhak Rabin. She had a boy named Ravid, fathered by an SS guard, who was your father. Tragically, your grandmother died too young at the age of twenty-seven in 1955 and Ravid was brought up by Yehudi Krimmer, a Jewish physicist who had known your grandmother. Am I right so far?" He smiled at her with a disarming look, like a kindly grandfather, as he handed her a glass. Again, she knew he was toying with her but was also surprised by the level of detail he had gathered on her for an interview she was supposed to be carrying out with him. She knew he had a wily reputation and so she answered without comment in the affirmative, taking a drink of the Arak, which was quite strong and she welcomed the warm glow within. "You will be wondering how I know all this detail and thinking I have done my research well no doubt?"

She nodded, feeling helpless, blurting out, "Your reputation precedes you and so nothing surprises me." Her voice was slightly terse because she knew he had the upper hand.

Rafi, who was standing by the window, gazing out, now turned back to look directly at her, walked over, and patted her shoulder before sitting down and looking at her with warmth in his eyes. "The reason I know all this is that I took an interest in your welfare…because I accompanied Yitzhak Rabin, as his second in command. I took part in the rescue of your grandmother, Gilana and her infant child, your father, together with your adopted grandfather, Yehudi Krimmer, in April 1945." He stopped speaking, taking a drink, and then looked up over his glasses at her for a reaction.

She let out a breath, feeling dazed. "What can I say? I never knew and, of course, I can only be grateful for what you did. Sha paused for moment, then, gathering herself, she spoke more emphatically, "but you know that I no longer communicate with my father."

"That, I think, is because of the unfortunate relationship he had with your mother."

Shira cut in, her cheeks flushed with anger. "Unfortunate you call it? Unfortunate that he was violent, assaulted her, and nearly killed her on more than one occasion! Unfortunate that he abused her, constantly belittling her in front of me! Unfortunate that she died because of the injuries he inflicted on her! Is that how you describe it, Mr Eitan? Unfortunate!" Her voice had risen and, somehow, she no longer cared who this man was or what he represented. His reaction surprised her.

"Forgive me please, Shira, I know some of the tragic events which occurred. Let us have a snack and take advantage of the exorbitant rates they charge here." He looked at her, putting his finger to his lips with a wicked smile. "Shhh, you must not breathe a word, but they actually give me this room for nothing because of my influence with people in high places, or, maybe, out of respect, huh? Much money is spent here out of the coffers of the state of Israel but, please, perhaps better not put that in your report." His words were spoken warmly and she felt disarmed by his charm and some surprise that he mentioned a 'report'. He picked up an intercom handset. "Ah, Noam, please serve my guest and I with some *bourekas*" (thin dough snack with cheese/potato/pizza filling) and, maybe some *bamba* (peanut puffs) to help wash the drinks down." As he put the handset down, he smiled again. "I find placing my orders with those managing this place achieves a better service. This was a habit I learned as an officer in the IDF and which served me well in politics also. You will already know from your research that I am a combat veteran, having served with the *Yiftach Brigade* before transferring to Shin Bet internal Intelligence?" He raised his eyebrows as he sat down, indicating this was a question. Shira knew he had total control of the situation and she was trying to think how she could engineer the direction of the one-sided conversation. She decided to be direct and not be led by his question.

"What makes you think I am here to file a report when I requested an interview for our historical archive research files?"

His face gave nothing away as he waved a finger. "Ah, I expected nothing less from your training; answer a question with a question. I should know this as I wrote the manual." He leant back in his chair and closed his eyes for a moment then sighed before speaking. "There is no retiring for me, even now at the age of 86, which is OK because I have always enjoyed my work because it is not work. This place, this country, this Israel is in my blood and I have witnessed blood being shed for it, including my own. On the day we achieved independence I was wounded fighting Arabs who were attacking us. My parents came here from Russia as so many did in the 1920's and 1930's to escape persecution. It was not just the Nazis who persecuted us. They came late to the party but we Jews have been the victims of persecution for thousands of years. Israel was the point where we said, 'no more, never again!'" He spoke the last two words strongly with a ruthlessness breaking into his genial disposition. Then he added, "Shira, I have ears and eyes everywhere and I know you are probing into extremely sensitive matters, the incredible importance of which you may be unaware. These are areas of national security and you may speak with me directly, but, under the same conditions I made about speaking with you on the phone. I shall deny ever having had this conversation, and you shall forget this meeting ever took place unless, of course, I give you permission to reveal what we discuss." His face had assumed a more serious expression and his eyes looked very directly at her.

At that moment there was a bleep, and he picked up the handset, pressing a button as the undermanager ushered in a waiter in a crisp white jacket carrying two trays, which he placed on the table between them, bowing as he did so. As he left, another waiter in a maroon jacket entered with a bottle of Champagne in a silver ice bucket on a trolley with crystal flute wine glasses. "A little gift, sir." The undermanager gave an open arms gesture before nodding to the waiter to open the bottle of *Dom Pérignon* Champagne. "Thank you, Noam, I will speak as highly as ever about you at the next event I attend with ministers. Please give my personal regards to Aby Rosen when you speak with him and tell him that dinner is on him when I'm next in New York City because of all I do to promote his hotel here." After he had left, Rafi cleared the nearly full glasses of Arak off the table, depositing them on the nearby bar before returning and handing a glass of Champagne to Shira, touching it with his own.

"You see how humble I am," he said warmly, "I could be a waiter, no? Sacrilege, I think, to attempt a fine Champagne after the flavour of Arak, but a gift is a gift." She could not help but smile at his humour and, despite her earlier anger, she felt very at ease with him. However, she wanted to gain answers and knew that she must not miss her opportunity, by being blinded by his charm and his hijacking of the conversation.

Shira placed her glass firmly down on the table. "OK Rafi, I will cut to the chase. You are correct in that I did not wish to talk with you about Adolf Eichmann, fascinating though that may be. I want to know about Unit 235; whether it still exists, and, if so, who is in charge? Also, was Unit 235 involved with a certain mission in the United States in November 1963?" This time her expression was focussed and she delivered her questions as more of a military command.

His reaction was to lean forwards shaking his head; then – "*Oy, gevalt!* You have no idea what you are into. Shira, I hope you have not shared this with anyone and, if you have, you must tell me their identity. I think I know where you will have got this from and I can tell you now that if Yehudi talks openly, his life will be in danger, and even I could not stop that." He now assumed a more business-like, even military bearing. "Please understand that I exert influence right to the top of the state of Israel, including current and former prime ministers. One of the reasons I hold such power is because I know things that cannot ever be shared and which protect the security of our country." He stood up and walked to the large oval window and stared out as he spoke. "I have carried what I know for fifty years and there are only a handful of people alive who are party to this information. Our knowledge, and not speaking of it, ensures our survival. I am afraid, Shira, democracy is not all it seems and there are greater powers out there that dictate actions which are not governed by the rule of law nor judged by any court." He walked slowly across the windows, continuing to talk, but stopping to deliberate as though wrestling with how to express what he was saying.

"Perhaps you are not interested in politics but here in Israel, because we all have links back to our service in the military, you

275

might understand that there are factions at play which sometimes compete. Agreements and coalitions are made in a military style which most of us agree need not be inconvenienced by elections or public voting."

Shira interrupted, "Is that not a form of totalitarianism? I thought Israel was built on a firm foundation of democracy."

Rafi held his hand up, walking back and facing her – "Ah, that is where we have a problem, because more and more are coming into politics who call themselves democrats, and who are destroying the strength of government that we need to protect our future, and our race. This is not new; these tensions are everywhere in every country. Great leaders, thinkers, scientists, politicians, and former heads of state whose talents the world needs are failed by the whims of democracy. Power is too precious to leave to the people to decide. Democracy is just not working for the greater good. This is an international problem and, as a result, a global organisation called the Bilderbergers was set up. This is where major issues are secretly debated by leading minds, and solutions found which are then translated into policy. Of course, the electorates are duped into thinking their governments are originating direction but, often, this is not the case. This is no different to science where scientists make advances or discoveries which are then adopted by the world, partnered with the business resources we select." He re-assumed his eat, leant across, and picked up Shira's glass, handing it to her with a smile, which despite her concern at his words, she accepted as he took a generous drink."

"May I speak bluntly please?" she looked at him earnestly, feeling a rising passion within. He gestured with an affirmative wave of the hand. "Rafi, I am astounded that you, who lived through the Nazi era and, as you say, witnessed the Holocaust in your lifetime, can endorse such a process. You are, in effect, governing through deception. This is not 'government by the people for the people' but government despite the people. Who is in charge of this?" Her voice reflected her incredulity.

"Ah, the voice of idealism, which I too once held," He leant across and touched her glass with his, "however, I saw that idealism sacrificed on the cynically corrupt altar of democracy. Democracy produces fools who prostrate themselves for votes, making promises they can never fulfil, and always leaving the voters feeling disillusioned and betrayed. You mention the Nazis with their perverse culture. Yes, of course I agree with you; but we must also recognise that Hitler achieved a miracle of recovery, transforming Germany. Had it not been for his abhorrent antisemitic views, the evil of the camps, and intolerance of any opposition, combined with his obsession with his own status, he might have been judged differently by history. The lesson he failed to learn is that opposition needs to both be seen, and also controlled. I now have sympathies with many far-right wing views but that does not mean that I embrace National Socialism. However, neither am I close-minded enough not to acknowledge what could be achieved through a less perverse version. We need to open our minds and not accept the blind propaganda labelled 'democracy.'"

Shira knew that argument was pointless with a man whose views had been formed out of a lifetime at the top of politics and military intelligence, which had given him an intransigence, based upon his perception of his own wisdom. She spoke without any emotion, "You did not answer either of my questions concerning Unit 235 and who is in charge?"

He looked up sharply again, his eyes betraying a harshness that he otherwise had covered up. "First, I cannot talk of Unit 235 and neither can you. I regret that if you do so, I will not be able to protect you. After today you must never speak of this again. However, I will deal with the second part of your question without confirming the answer. I am reminded of the words of the great writer and literary wit, Oscar Wilde, who once said, "*He has no enemies but many friends who dislike him intensely*" This is where your father comes in. I may tolerate the man on a personal level because he has strength and purpose, with a single-minded drive to ensure the protection of Israel. However, he operates in a clandestine manner that is not without worry to me, and was involved after I stepped back, but from what, I will not say. He proposes decisive actions where others vacillate, and he leads a faction that he claims will make our nation invincible, secure our territories, and suppress the violent dissension that threatens us all. Does that seem so bad? A question I ponder." He stood, and it was clear the meeting was over."

Despite the contradiction with his earlier statement on tolerating opposition, she did not argue. After that day, she never saw Rafi Eitan again. Six years later, when he died, she could not help but feel that Israel had lost a great patriot whose extraordinary achievements should not be eclipsed by the views he held in later life.

22

A Tragic Irony

After alighting from the 'gooney bird', as the Douglas C47 transport aircraft was known, the three men in combat uniform were picked up by a driver in a jeep, which was driven towards a Nissen hut at the edge of the airfield. A German *Junkers JU 88* bomber was parked on a grass area off the runway, peppered with bullet holes. The driver of the jeep announced, "We took this goddamned place off the Krauts six months back. Some poor bastards tried to fly out as we attacked and this baby here is what's left of their attempt. You limeys here for long?"

The officer in British uniform looked at him sharply, "You may call us Jews or Yids if you prefer; we have heard much worse but never call us limeys." Then he smiled as he saw the young American's face redden with embarrassment. "Hey, it's OK, son, I am Captain Yitzhak Rabin, this is Lieutenant Rafael Eitan, and the ruffian next to him is Lieutenant Antoni Zielinski, who, you may note, has a Polish arm badge but do not call him a Polack or he may kill you." Zielinski gave a wide grin, which the driver was not quite sure how to take.

They swerved onto a tarmac area in front of the Nissen hut. A sign outside had written on it '*Flugplatz A213/XI*' with a line painted diagonally across in white, underneath which was written, 'No longer resident'. A much larger sign adorned the double entrance door with USAAF over the top of white wings surrounding a large red number 9 denoting that it was a Ninth Air Force base. As they alighted, Zielinski turned to the driver. "Do not worry, I only enjoy killing Germans, sometimes with my bare hands and especially if they have SS on their uniforms." He grinned again, his unruly dark hair protruding under his beret, and the driver was in no doubt that he meant it.

Inside the door was a reception desk at which a smartly dressed American sergeant was sitting. After announcing that they were expected by Major General Kenneth Strong, they were escorted between rows of desks staffed by women in olive-drab uniforms tapping on typewriters; the smell of tobacco hung in the air. There were some green-painted doors at the far end and the sergeant approached one on the left and knocked. He opened the door before announcing them, then saluted and left. "As they entered, Strong was seated at a desk, puffing smoke from a pipe as he shuffled some papers to one side. He placed the top back on his fountain pen in a precise movement then stood up, his arm extended. "Frightfully nice to see you again, Captain Rabin, and you too, Lieutenant Eitan. Ah, and this must be the legendary Antoni Zielinski about whom we have heard so much. I hear you have become one of the X Troops by joining Rabin's unit in 3 Commando. You are most welcome." He shook Antoni's hand warmly. "Glad you could make it, old boy, but I'm afraid the Ruskies were not too happy about the show you put on."

"They invaded my country, sir, and split it with the Germans, so, it is simple, I kill them."

"Yes, I see; I quite understand, Lieutenant." Strong looked a little uncomfortable then gestured to seats by the desk. "Please sit down, gentlemen." He reached forwards, retrieving a buff file from a filing tray. "Following our previous meeting, Captain Rabin, I am delighted you have had some success in capturing some of the more useful German scientists, delivering them to us rather than to our American…ahem…allies. Some time ago, Lise Meitner, the brilliant German Jewish nuclear physicist, gave us the list which we have been using to prioritise those scientists we particularly wish to, er, rescue. That was added to by a list which the former head of their Intelligence service, the *Abwehr*, Admiral Canaris smuggled to us. Today that priority list has been trumped completely as a result of shocking intelligence we received two days ago, from a member of the *Weisse Rose* (White Rose) German resistance group."

Eitan cut in – "I never heard of this movement. You mean they are fighting the Nazis?"

"I'm afraid not, old chap," Strong replied, "they are a group of mainly young student intellectuals committed to non-violent passive resistance. They distribute leaflets against Hitler's regime and that sort of thing."

"Paf, this achieves nothing!" Zielinski exclaimed.

Strong grunted and continued, "However, despite most of their leading members being executed, the movement continues and they smuggle out information to us which may help shorten the war. In return, we commit to this not being used to cause military or civilian deaths. Two days ago, one of their principal members, Willi Bollinger, made contact with us, passing information with potentially staggering consequences for the Allies. A week ago, the Germans successfully detonated a nuclear device in Thüringia, which effectively means they are on the verge of having an atomic bomb. From your previous briefing, you will understand the gravity of the situation, with such weapons having a destructive capability beyond anything mankind has previously witnessed. The explosion's size even caught them off-guard and I regret, gentlemen, many Jews were tragically killed amongst hundreds of other prisoners on the day. This weapon could alter the course of the war, notwithstanding which, Churchill has made it clear that we must do all we can to prevent its use whilst ensuring we have the scientific know-how to make our development of this weapon possible. We are engaged in an operation which has been labelled *Alsos,* with the objective of discovering German scientific developments, and which also requires that we capture their boffins. To that end, a number of scientists and their whereabouts have been identified as key targets. Clearly, those involved in the nuclear area become the priority." He pushed five photographs across the table and identified them. "These men are part of a team working on nuclear development at Hechingen and Haigerloch in the Black Forest area of Germany. They moved there to escape the advancing Russians. We are also aware that they have forced a number of imprisoned Jewish scientists to work with them but regrettably we do not have photographs of them. The Yanks are putting together a strike unit to snatch them, which is where you come in."

"Here we go again," muttered Eitan, shaking his head. "In the cause of Allied unity, we are to deceive the Americans. You know what, I like this."

"Lieutenant, we should harbour no guilt as the Yanks stole a number of V-2 rockets from under our noses and shipped them back to America. This brings me to the next little difficulty we have. The French 1ˢᵗ Army is advancing and have been designated a section of occupation in Germany in which the two towns of Hechingen and Haigerloch are situated. *Operation Harborage* has been launched under which a joint British and American task force will go behind enemy lines to ensure we get there first. The remit will be to capture German scientists, secure any research documents or material, and destroy facilities as appropriate. In this way no atomic weapons information or weapons grade material falls into the wrong hands."

"I assume we are describing our French allies as 'the wrong hands'," muttered Eitan dryly, adding, '*There's no trust, no faith, no honesty in men*.'"

"Ah, you know your Shakespeare," replied Strong, nodding his head as he thought; "'*Romeo and Juliet*', I believe. We digress but the Prime Minister has decided that we need to remove certain scientists before the task force gets there, giving them, shall we say, safe haven in England. Their knowledge will be critical in assisting us in the development of our own atom bomb. Lise Meitner has stated that these five scientists should be targeted because they possess the know-how to create a bomb." He pointed at each photograph in turn. "They are Erich Schuman, a committed Nazi who oversees their nuclear project, Carl von Weizsäcker, a brilliant physicist who patented his atomic weapon research findings, Werner Heisenberg, a leading pioneer in this field, Otto Hahn who assisted in the discovery of nuclear fission, and Kurt Diebner who is a director of the programme. On the list I am giving you are the names of the three Jewish scientists we want, Aaron Kaufman, Fritz Gottheiner, and a young chap who apparently is some kind of genius, Yehudi Krimmer.

"You will form a unit of ten of your best men, dress in German uniforms, and sneak behind enemy lines near Strasbourg in vehicles you will be provided with. Your job is to seize as many scientists as you can and deliver them back here. We will, of course, deny we have taken them and invent a spoof capture in a few weeks to cover our tracks. This time there will be air transport because your mission has been given the highest priority by Winston Churchill himself." He stood up. "Good luck, gentlemen and, um, don't get caught because in the uniforms you wear, Jerry will execute you immediately as spies. Right, a drink, I think; we have some rather nice *Chablis* which the Luftwaffe left for us. Frightfully decent of them. I believe it is a 1938, which apparently was a damned fine vintage." He went to a cupboard, retrieving a bottle and some glasses.

Two days later, Rabin received the message he had been waiting for from Shimon Peres, 'At the earliest opportunity, dispense with the German scientists. Your orders are to remove the Jewish scientists only. As soon as the operation is concluded, you are needed back here in the *Palmach*, (elite force in Palestine), as we are expecting trouble with the British securing our homeland. Return to *Yishuv*. (Jewish land in Palestine) with your guests or captives by any transport available. Your service with the British Army is over. *B'chatzlacha!* (Good luck!) *Bivrakha!* (Blessing) Peres.'

Thursday 15th March 1945 - 3pm
Field HQ *SS-Fallschirmjägerbataillon 600* (Parachute Batallion),
Ludendorff Railroad Bridge, Remagen, Germany

Acting *Generalmajor* Otto Skorzeny stared through his binoculars at the bridge from his vantage point 300 metres away. He could see the column of US military vehicles crossing, behind which others were lined up waiting, and was tempted to bring Panzers forwards, attached to his unit, and open fire. There were bomb craters all around the bridge and the structure of the single upper suspension arch over the road showed signs of considerable damage, with the ironwork on the upper structure buckled and twisted. His orders had come directly from the Führer after he had withdrawn from Schwedt a few days before, where he had dug in harassing and repelling the Russian advance, forcing a change in their offensive plans. He had innovated a tactical initiative through mounting 88 mm anti-aircraft guns on trucks. These were fired on advancing Russian units, giving them the false impression of more heavily positioned artillery, buying the German defences additional time elsewhere. Recalled to meet Hitler at the Führerbunker in Berlin, he was ordered to Remagen Bridge, which had been taken by the Allies on 7th March. This had resulted in catastrophic strategic consequences allowing Allied forces to pour over the Rhine into Germany.

His orders were clear, given by a stooped and very tired looking Hitler as he fixed his piercing blue eyes on Skorzeny. His uncompromising authority, despite his appearance, was as commanding as ever and his guttural voice unwavering. "You will either retake the bridge or destroy it. The *Schweinhunds* defending it against the Americans failed the Reich and I have had them executed. Many brave Germans have died attempting to destroy the bridge, including Luftwaffe pilots, engineers, and frogmen saboteurs. I call on you and entrust you with this great mission upon which the destiny of the Fatherland may rest. You, *Herr Generalmajor,* may be judged by history to have seized this moment, turning the tide in our momentous struggle to save our glorious Reich from being plundered." The Führer had then patted him on the shoulder before looking at a large map adorning one wall. He turned, his eyes now having a distant look. "All my life, I have struggled for Germany, conscious that my task is a greater one chosen by Providence. The German *Volk* needed a steadfast will, and this I gave them; they needed a new and powerful Germany freed from the shackles of Versailles and this I gave them; they needed strong leadership and this I gave them." His voice had risen and he thumped his right fist into his left hand. "I dedicated my life to the Fatherland and I have been betrayed. The sacred purpose of National Socialism will never be vanquished but triumph over those who seek to destroy us. That drunkard, Mr Churchill, will live to regret not standing up to the filthy Bolshevik scum led by the mass murderer, Stalin, who slaughters his own people. We have a purpose chosen by a higher authority and I will rise to this great task." He wiped back a shock of his hair from his brow, now beaded with sweat, then waved his arm, half in salute, and half dismissing the meeting. Skorzeny clicked his heels smartly, his right arm stretched out, "*Heil Hitler.*" He said the words with a preciseness, emphasising the syllables, his loyalty to his Führer unswerving, unquestioning, before executing a clipped about turn and marching out of the briefing room.

Now, as he surveyed the bridge beneath him from the bank of the Rhine, he called the loyal Captain Hans Danneberg to his side. "Hauptmann, it is time we become Americans again. We need uniforms and a team of explosive engineers." As darkness fell, twelve men walked from the German positions down a winding track towards the bridge in the uniform of American GI's, carrying explosive charges and reels of wire. They were led by Otto Skorzeny, who was dressed as a colonel, and Hans Danneberg in the uniform of a captain, which he had previously worn in the Ardennes offensive. There were deep craters all around the approach to the bridge, which had been caused by bombs dropped in numerous Luftwaffe raids in the preceding days, some full of water, which they had to dodge. No-one challenged them as they neared the bridge over which numerous lorries, tanks and armoured vehicles were crossing. Danneberg took a clipboard from his tunic, wanting to pass himself off as an engineer, as Skorzeny pulled back the bolt on his *Thompson M1928* machine gun with a magazine that gave him 100 rounds of rapid-fire power. They sauntered nearer to the bridge and when they were twenty-five metres away, they came across a soldier with a cigarette hanging from his mouth, and a rifle slung from his shoulder. "Sorry, guys, but I have to ask you to stop right there. What's your business here?"

Danneberg stepped forwards speaking in a long drawl he had learned from the three years he had spent studying at Princeton University, New Jersey, where he had studied mechanical engineering. His father had been posted, before the war, to work in the German Embassy working under Ambassadors Hans Luther and then Hans-Heinrich Dieckhoff. His university course fees and expenses were paid by the Nazi government in exchange for Danneberg volunteering to work for the Abwehr Intelligence. He had infiltrated various student bodies, reporting back to the ambassador on their activities and identifying both students and teachers with pro-Nazi sympathies. "Well, howdy son, I'm Captain Wilbur Donahue of the US First Army, and this is Colonel Skorny and we've been seconded to 276th Engineer Combat Battalion to direct urgent repairs to this section of the bridge. These boys have been with me since we landed on Omaha Beach on D-Day and we are the finest damned unit of engineers in the US Army. Mighty pleased to make your acquaintance, Corporal. Where you from, son?" He extended his hand and the young soldier shook it, feeling a little overwhelmed by the friendly manner of the senior officer. "Middletown, Delaware, sir, but no-one told us you guys were coming."

"You don't worry your head none about that, boy." Danneberg responded, slapping him on the back. "We operate on a kind of hush-hush basis but don't tell anyone, huh. I want you to block access to where we working, you understand me. No-one is permitted beyond this point." He pulled out a full packet of Lucky Strike cigarettes, handing them to the soldier. "You take these Luckies with my blessing, and protect our backs, ya hear?" He turned to Skorzeny, who was standing fifteen metres behind him. "This guy is gonna watch our rear, sir, let's move on out." He beckoned to the others following then placed his hand on the young soldier's shoulder. "What's your name, boy? I'll make sure you get mentioned in my report for headquarters."

The soldier swelled with pride, answering, "Corporal Ronald B Dexter, sir, of the 164th Engineer Battalion."

"So long, soldier, you look after yourself." Danneberg walked away as Dexter pondered whether he should have checked the officer's ID but dismissed the thought from his mind as they were, after all, accompanied by a senior officer. In addition, as the small group of men passed him, he could see they were laden down with equipment. Skorzeny muttered, once they were out of earshot, "*Herr Hauptmann, sie sind ein besserer Schauspieler als Hans Albers,*" (you are a better actor than Hans Albers) drawing a broad grin from Danneberg. After a brief rest and discussion on the next phase, they walked to the base of the bridge in darkness, with flashes lighting the skyline, accompanied by sporadic gunfire, and the occasional whump of artillery shells, some hitting the water near the bridge, sending huge columns of spray into the air. The engineers discussed the state of the structure, which had suffered considerable damage from the bombardment and bombing of recent days. It was decided to place charges as near as possible to the half-collapsed support, near ordinance that had been left in a previous attempt to blow the bridge, in the hope that this might increase the force of the planned detonation. The eight engineers scrambled to the place where the bridge connected with the banks of the Rhine on the eastern side. From there they edged their way over the damaged pier, climbing up the structure, and began placing charges, stopping every time there was silence from the traffic crossing to prevent them being heard. On the shore, Skorzeny and Danneberg waited, covering their movements and watching for any evidence that they had been seen.

At 9pm just after Danneberg had remarked that things seemed to be becoming quieter, the sound of aircraft engines could be heard. The shoreline erupted with anti-aircraft fire, which was deafening in a continuous barrage, lighting the darkness in a flickering thunderous inferno. Numerous searchlights swung in arcs across the sky, seeking out the aircraft as targets. This was followed by huge explosions around the bridge with one direct hit near the centre and they watched in horror as four of their men were blown off the latticed ironwork structure into the freezing waters below. An aircraft with both wings on fire spiralled out of the sky into the trees on the far bank, followed by a thunderous explosion. Suddenly, it was over and a strange silence ensued for a short time, but one searchlight swept downwards towards the smouldering damage caused by the bomb, catching in its beam the engineers on the ironwork, passing them then sweeping back. *"Verdammt!"* Skorzeny grunted, gritting his teeth, "Now we're for it, especially if they speak to our friendly Corporal Dexter." The engineers, realising their plight, had disappeared from view and shortly afterwards clambered back across the bank to join

Skorzeny and Danneberg with their leader announcing that they had successfully planted most of the charges with two delayed fuses to detonation, the latter for thirty hours. This had been planned beforehand so that in the event of their discovery, the initial smaller explosion would convince their captors that they had been unsuccessful in blowing the bridge, thus ensuring that the second detonation would cause the most damage to men and equipment crossing the Rhine.

As they prepared to leave, they heard shouts on the track they had used to reach the bridge. A searchlight began playing along the bank towards their position. They ran into some nearby woodland, dumping their gear. There were more shouts behind them and they saw a large number of US troops approaching where they had been minutes before, at which point Skorzeny opened fire with a long burst from his machine gun, scattering the approaching men, who dropped to the ground. The Americans deployed a portable searchlight, which now lit up their position. From behind them, there was more gunfire and one of the engineers crumpled with a brief cry. Another went to his aid but quickly looked up at Skorzeny shaking his head. Danneberg pulled the pin from a grenade and tossed it towards the source of the dazzling light; then followed the thump of an explosion, and a scream as the light shattered. Moments later a heavy machine gun opened up and bullets were hitting the trees all around them, with branches flying, splintering, and disintegrating. Two more men were hit, falling to the floor, one with a wound to the shoulder and the other, more seriously hurt, had blood pouring from his stomach. There was a short, silent lull before a voice spoke through a loud speaker.

"You are surrounded on all sides. You will surrender immediately or you will all be killed. Lay down your arms. Your commanding officer will now approach with his hands up."

In the short pause that followed, Skorzeny turned to his men. "I think we have little choice but to surrender." He shouted, his voice echoing in the unnatural stillness, "I am SS- *Generalmajor*

Skorzeny. We will not resist further. I will approach your position. We need medics; I have two wounded men."

He stood up, removing the M1911 pistol from his belt, which he tossed to the floor, took his SS field cap from his pack, and placed it on his head. He raised his arms up and walked towards the American troops fifty metres in front of them. As he approached, a US soldier shouted, "Halt, get your ass on the floor now! Get down." The last words were yelled loudly. Then, "Arms out. Do not move!" He did as he was instructed and seconds later there were shuffles of feet around him and he felt the barrel of a weapon in the small of his back. They checked him for arms, roughly moving him, as they frisked him. He froze, closing his eyes, as he felt the cold metal of a pistol against his temple. Then he heard another voice as a portable arc-light lit up the scene, "OK boys, calm it down and leave the bastard to me." Skorzeny looked up to see a tall, well-built, American officer walking towards where he lay. "Major General, you may get up, I am Lieutenant Colonel Clayton A Rust, commanding US 276th Engineer's Battalion. I will not say you are a prisoner of war because you and your men are in violation of the rules of war. We have the right to execute you right here, right now."

"You tell him, sir," a sergeant behind him said to shouts of approval from other US soldiers positioned around them. Skorzeny stood up, dusting himself off, speaking in clipped English, with a deep German accent, his voice, commanding, cold, and self-assured.

"Colonel, I would suggest that we speak privately in order to avoid unnecessary loss of life. Believe me when I say we have laid explosive charges and with one word from me, they will be detonated. First, please, I ask that medics attend my wounded, then we should talk."

Rust was slightly taken aback by his adversary's demeanour, which bordered on the arrogant. He pondered for a moment, "OK Kraut, get your men out of cover and I'll authorise the medics. Any monkey business, I will kill you myself."

Skorzeny shouted back towards the trees, "*Hauptmann*, you will leave your weapons and walk to me with your hands held up."

Danneberg shouted back, "We have two wounded, one seriously, and need a stretcher." Lights were trained on their position as six men appeared, one carried, and another supported; all were wearing SS side caps. Rust barked out orders and moments later two medics ran towards where the Germans were standing. After Danneberg had been frisked, he was escorted to where Skorzeny was standing with Rust. They agreed to talk away from the other US troops, although Rust was accompanied by a burly sergeant who kept a pistol trained on them as they spoke.

"OK, Kraut," Rust spoke brusquely, "talk, because I can't see one damned reason why you guys should not be shot on the spot."

Danneberg, standing next to Skorzeny, was shocked as he listened to his commanding officer speak, contravening all they had rehearsed before the operation to blow up the bridge. "We have a situation here in which I think we hold, what you Americans might say, the ace card. We have laid explosive charges on the bridge and you will release my men and myself in exchange for information on when these charges will detonate. If you use the bridge, the charges may blow and you will then lose many men and vehicles. If you execute us, you can search for the explosives but then they may detonate, killing your engineers. If you accept my terms, you may continue to use the bridge until I tell you it is unsafe. So, Colonel, do we have your agreement?"

Rust was feeling very uneasy and not a little unnerved. He had already lost a number of men in the preceding days, either caught by enemy artillery or sniper fire, whilst working on the bridge, or during the incessant German bombing attacks.

He attempted to sound resolute and tough in his reply feeling anything but, intimidated by the sheer arrogant assertiveness of the man with the pencil moustache and deep scar to his cheek who now stared unblinking at him. "Even if I were to accept your terms, General, how do I know I can trust you, or, for that matter, whether you have successfully placed charges or not?" He was surprised by the response.

"That is easy, Colonel, this war will reach an inevitable conclusion soon and, like you, I do not wish to waste life; but I am under orders from the Führer to whom I am bound by an oath of loyalty until death. You are anxious to move supplies across the bridge, which you may safely do for some hours. At a given point, I will tell you to stop all traffic crossing. Shortly thereafter, there will be an explosion but not enough to destroy the bridge, not yet. After that, you will cease permitting traffic to cross because a further charge will detonate at a certain point. You will release my men and myself at that time. As you would say in America, 'Do we have a deal?'" He smiled at Colonel Rust, holding his hand out, and Danneberg watched in awe at Skorzeny's cool resolve and cunning. The Colonel held his finger up in warning, "You cross me, you bastard, and I will hunt you and your men down as war criminals and I will make sure every last one of you is executed." Then he briefly shook Skorzeny's outstretched hand before giving a gesture of bewilderment with both arms, shaking his head.

At 9am the following morning, Skorzeny was taken, from the guarded billet hut he had been allocated, to meet Colonel Rust. All traffic and personnel were ordered to cease crossing the bridge. They watched as a flash and a cloud of smoke erupted on the eastern side of the bridge, followed by a loud explosive report, which echoed off the banks of the Rhine. Rust turned to the German, sitting in a chair opposite his desk drinking coffee, muttering, "I could have done without this. We got guys here filming newsreels for the folks back home telling them we captured this goddamn bridge intact."

Skorzeny looked up with a wry smile, "I won't tell anyone if you don't, Colonel. It would not be good for my reputation to have surrendered. Perhaps, the structure was so damaged by all the collateral damage from the fighting and shells like the one that just hit...well, it just collapsed eh?" Despite them being adversaries, both men laughed, shook hands and laughed again. "Skorzeny then informed the Colonel that the bridge would be safe for six more hours, before re-joining his men. Shortly thereafter, five figures still dressed in American uniforms, one limping with a crutch, were escorted away from the encampment, leaving one of their seriously wounded as a prisoner of war.

No more men or vehicles were permitted to cross after this and two pontoon bridges were erected under enemy fire by US engineers to the north of the Ludendorff Railroad Bridge. However, Supreme Allied Command wanted the bridge saving and, in one final tragic irony, a decision was taken to search for and diffuse the devices left by the Germans in the time the Americans thought was remaining, whilst effecting emergency repairs to the severely weakened structure. Engineers swarmed over the bridge but at 3pm on 17th March 1945, there was a bang and the sound of tortured metal twisting as the centre portion of the bridge collapsed into the Rhine and the two end sections were wrenched off their piers. This was not as a result of explosive charges, but on account of the structure failing. Around 200 engineers and welders were working on the bridge at the time and many were tipped into the fast-flowing Rhine. Twenty-eight soldiers lost their lives, whilst a further sixty-three were injured. Lieutenant Colonel Clayton A Rust was thrown into the river and briefly pinned down by a piece of heavy metal before breaking free, struggling to stay afloat as he was swept away, to be pulled from the water downstream onto one of the pontoon bridges being erected.

Two days later, Otto Skorzeny was personally awarded the Oak Leaves to the Knight's Cross, one of Germany's highest military decorations, by Adolf Hitler in the Führerbunker where he was given his final orders. He was to command and train military units that would operate behind enemy lines under *Unternehmen Werwolf* (Operation Werewolf) and set up an escape network for loyal Nazis to a new Reich being established in Argentina. The network he created was to be named *'Die Spinne.'* (The Spider). He was also tasked with ensuring that scientists working on the new atomic weapons development were spirited away, before they were captured by Allied forces advancing on the facilities at Hechingen and Haigerloch. This was to be the last time Skorzeny would see Hitler during wartime.

23

'The heavens tremble'

Monday 24th May 2021 – 9:30am
Brosh Street, Caesarea, Israel

The day was calm and balmy as they sat round a glass-topped table on the terrace of General Moshe Gellner's villa, overlooking palm trees and the Mediterranean beyond; in front of them was a large jug of orange juice with ice. There were five of them, including Moshe, David, Mehedi, Shira and David's cousin, Benjamin Weiss, who had joined them at 8am that morning, having flown in from London the night before. He had spent the night at his parent's house in Nahsholim, a fifteen-minute drive north of Caesarea.

He had taken a call from 'C', the Chief of MI6, Richard Moore, at 7am (which was 5am UK time). The Chief was furious, having been called by the Foreign Secretary, Dominic Raab, who, in turn, had been contacted by the Home Secretary, Priti Patel. The Home Secretary had demanded a report on the incident at Bletsoe from the Chief Constable of Bedfordshire, Garry Forsythe, for two reasons. The first was that she had been alerted that this was a 'sensitive' murder because Yehudi Krimmer was one of Israel's former top nuclear physicists. He had a high security ranking because of his role working for the Israeli government in what was annotated on the file as '*Israel's Suspected Nuclear Weapons Arsenal*'. The second reason was that she had been alerted to a further related incident at London Heathrow airport. The Metropolitan Police had authorised armed police from the Aviation Policing Command (APC), operating in the Security Unit SO18, to board a British Airways flight about to leave for Tel Aviv, and they had taken two Israeli citizens into custody. The press had found out and the late-night news bulletins had already run a story that a mysterious aircraft arrest had taken place of suspected Israeli Mossad spies on an aircraft at Heathrow.

The Israeli ambassador had demanded an explanation and in a rather uncomfortable phone call with the Prime Minister, Boris Johnson, the Home Secretary had to admit that she had not been briefed on the arrests beforehand. To make matters worse, it appeared that sensitive evidence from the Bletsoe murder scene had been removed, without authorisation, by a Jewish agent working for MI6 who had since disappeared. The whole thing was a mess and becoming worse by the minute. The PM had not held back, "Christ, do you not think I've got enough on my damned plate? I'm trying to dig the bloody country out of the covid pandemic lockdown through the f'ing roadmap and being criticised for it. I didn't act soon enough at the start of the pandemic and I'm criticised for that and now they say I'm too slow raising restrictions. I've got a story breaking about the damned fool former P.M., David Cameron, writing directly to Rishi Sunak asking for money for his failed business interests, and now I've got a home secretary who doesn't know her arse from her elbow. For God's sake, Priti, stop buggering around and find out what the hell is going on by morning. Shall we say 10am at 10 Downing Street?" He had put the phone down and she was smarting with anger, and even more so when it was established that a certain Benjamin Weiss had left the country without being challenged on a later flight because he worked for MI6.

'C' had demanded a full explanation from Benjamin, who stated briefly that matters had arisen about Israeli national security about which he would brief his boss when he was able, before terminating the call.

A copy of the *Jerusalem Post* lay on the table, delivered to Moshe's house a half hour before. The front-page headline ran, ISRAEL 'SPY' ARRESTS AT UK AIRPORT. "There will be repercussions from this which could be good for us," remarked Moshe. Benjamin studied the story through his dark glasses, taking some comfort in the fact that the likely killers of the old man, Yehudi Krimmer, had been detained, at least for now. Details were sketchy in the report and it was clear that very little had been leaked to the press but enough to create a political storm.

Shira was noticeably quiet and withdrawn. She had retired early to a bedroom set aside for her in Moshe's large villa but in the middle of the night she had retreated to David's room. "Just hold me," she whispered, saying nothing more as she lay cradled in his arms until morning when she turned to him, briefly attempting a smile, squeezing his hand, and mouthing the words, "Thank you," before returning to her room. She felt like she had lost her father, or the man who she most closely associated with as a father figure. He had shown her nothing but warmth and kindness, contrasting with the cool aloofness and violence exhibited by the man whose biological connection with her meant nothing. Now she associated Ravid with the death of her beloved zaydee, even though she had no certainty. In the light of all the other murders and the links emerging between them, she sensed his involvement. Now she sat flicking through the pages of information in the file brought over by Benjamin. There were 'Top Secret' minutes of meetings Yehudi Krimmer had attended with David Ben-Gurion; a man who assumed an almost mythical status in her education at school as not only the first prime minister, but also the founding father of Israel. Various attendees at these meetings included the Director General of the Ministry of Defense then Deputy Minister of Defense, Shimon Peres, the Chief of Israel's Defense Forces, Moshe Dayan, the Chairman of the Israeli Atomic Energy Commission, Ernst David Bergmann, the Internal Security Chief, Benjamin Blumberg, and, inevitably, one Rafi Eitan. She knew that Blumberg headed Lekem and recalled Zaydee informing her, during her visit to see him in England in 2012, about his utter ruthlessness; she also knew that Eitan had taken over Lekem in 1981. She began looking at an extraordinary report, filed by a young Yehudi Krimmer, dated March 14th 1945, on the successful detonation of a German nuclear device in Thüringia. Another report was attached, but fronted by a thicker page yellowed with age, on the front of which was the Nazi eagle emblem clutching a swastika. The stark words appeared on the front in German gothic lettering:

Uranverein
STENG GEHELM ['TOP SECRET']
CHEF SACHE
Für den Führer
Unternehmen Armageddon

The report was virtually identical to one bearing Yehudi Krimmer's name and signature except it was signed by Friedrich Carl von Weizsäcker, with no reference to Krimmer, which Shira realised was because Krimmer was a Jew. She broke her silence. "We have an incredible amount of information, it seems, but we need to draw together reasons and motives for the assassinations that have taken place. It seems to me we are dealing with conjecture which, as an intelligence officer working for Aman, I know would hold no evidential value in a court of law, nor justify actions which we may need to take. Yes, we have a suspect, an alarming prospect, a potential threat to Israel, a catastrophic plan for a pre-emptive strike which could trigger World War III, but no proof.

Everything we have is circumstantial unless, of course, the British torture a confession out of the Mossad assassins they've arrested. My guess is they will be out of the UK within days, claiming diplomatic immunity. Remember what the Libyans did in the 1980's, murdering a British policewoman in broad daylight with an automatic weapon. The British government let the assassins go and that was during the premiership of the 'Iron Lady', Margaret Thatcher. Even worse, think of the murder of eleven of our own athletes at the 1972 Munich Olympics by Palestinian terrorists. Remember the name, Abu Daoud, who masterminded this atrocity. He was allowed to escape justice by West Germany, after being captured, and ended up living out the rest of his life in Libya and Syria. We tried to take him out but abandoned it because it was not politically expedient. What did the families of those young athletes feel? The British will release our men in order to spare Israel any embarrassment, and the whole thing will be covered up as a terrorist motivated killing, backed by a statement saying the real perpetrators fled the country.

"The difference here is that this is, of course, our own threat from within but trust me, I know my father. I hate to acknowledge who he is but he will wriggle out of any difficulty using his powerful friends. He has exemplary military service and there were operations he was involved in that those currently in power would not wish to be exposed or admit to." Her voice held a tone of steely authority betraying no emotion, which her training now removed from her direction and demeanour.

"So, *Aluf Mishne*, what do you suggest?" Moshe responded. "I think we have evidence enough to convince colleagues and take action."

Shira stood up as if to add authority to her words, first looking at Moshe and then to each of them in turn. "I stress again that we must be able to justify any action we take to overcome, or win over, any powerful factions in this country. The answer, General, in my view, is to look at what Benjamin has brought in this box, and, in particular, at *Project Isaiah*. This was launched by David Ben-Gurion in his drive to obtain the ultimate deterrent and protect the security of the Jewish race for all time. I recall from my studies that he was possessed by the horror and tragedy of the Holocaust. You may recall the phrase, often used both by our leaders and others of 'Never again' – referring to the horrors of what our people suffered under the Nazis whilst much of the world looked the other way. I studied politics at university and did a dissertation on Ben-Gurion. He was obsessed with obtaining the nuclear weapon, hence it was he who authorised the establishment of Lekem, under Benjamin Blumberg, on the behest of Shimon Peres in 1957."

"I met Ben-Gurion," Moshe interjected, "As a young officer trainee in 1970 when he visited our unit on the front. He was a legendary figure then and had previously been defense minister as well as prime minister. He was retired but as he was the founder of the IDF, he still took an active interest. We were stationed in positions by the Suez Canal during the War of Attrition." He grimaced, remembering his first taste of combat, fighting the Egyptian army, during which he had lost friends from his unit.

Shira continued, "Lekem and its activities provide the foundation for all that followed, and to a degree, link through to what we are seeing today. Looking at the evidence you have gathered, which is all shocking, we must consider what elements are the most damaging to anyone involved. Is it the fact we stole nuclear material from the United States or that we secretly set up a nuclear weapons development facility in Dimona?... No. Is it that we routinely assassinate people who pose a threat to the state of Israel?... No. Is it that we purchased nuclear weapon ingredients secretly off the French and the British, under the noses of the Americans? Or even that Saddam Hussein did possess, if not WMD, certainly WMD potential development materials? Equally, no. Sadly, because Colonel Berkowicz has been killed, we cannot use his evidence regarding the sabotage of John F Kennedy junior's aircraft in 1999 which would be dismissed as conspiracy hearsay. Regrettably, these are historic issues which may be shocking but insufficient on their own. However, we need to consider which areas of our evidence may cause the most potential for a backlash?"

"Clearly, you are referring to the Kennedy factor," Mehedi proffered. "If, as we now believe, a team of assassins were despatched from Israel, you may imagine what waves this would cause. No matter how long ago, no American president nor the American people would ever forgive those responsible for assassinating President John F Kennedy."

Moshe responded, "If we add into the equation that the operation was carried out in conjunction with a former prominent Nazi and member of the SS working for Mossad, the Israeli people too would not forgive anyone involved."

There were exclamations around the table as they suddenly thought through the ramifications.

David added, "If a leader were to seize power in Israel and was then found to have been complicit in the assassination of the president of the United States, he could not survive and would assuredly be removed by force, if not by us, then by the US. I wonder why they called it *Project Isaiah*."

"*Allah yakhthek ya hemar*" (God take your soul, you donkey), Mehedi responded in a mock derisory manner, "Did they not teach you Jews the scriptures in school? The first of the major prophets, I believe, in your Hebrew Bible says, '*Therefore I will make the heavens tremble; and the earth will shake from its place at the wrath of the Lord Almighty, in the day of his burning anger.*' If my memory serves me, this is Isaiah 13 in the Old Testament, which we examined, studying its relationship to the Quran. Thank goodness we Arabs are enriching your impoverished culture."

"*Ya Gazma,*" (You shoe [Arab insult]) replied David, "If it was not for us, you would still be living in tents."

Shira cut in, "Alright children, enough of your re-play of the Arab-Israeli conflict. Remember I outrank you both so pay attention please. We can, I think, deduce from our investigations that our key suspect and the mastermind is Omer Ravid." As she said the words, she took some comfort that she could not even think about him as her father. "However, we are still short of the proof that we need in order to persuade anybody who may have sympathies with his views or his agenda to reconsider. No-one would wish to be involved with anyone associated with the assassination of JFK and this is Ravid's Achilles heel, hence the killings. Critically, we will need to gather as much support as we can from those in the military and incontrovertible evidence is the key. I think we need to interview anyone associated with those who have been murdered, particularly close family."

"Bravo, Shira," Moshe cut in, "I am delighted we have you on the team. We need to check their files and start with any surviving spouses. In the interim, perhaps you and Benjamin could study all the documents in Krimmer's box and see if there is anything else of interest to us. David, Mehedi, and I will retreat to the study and pull together details of any persons we should visit."

Two hours later they reconvened on the terrace and Moshe brought out some bottles of white wine. "This is 'C' Blanc du Castel, one of my favourites produced at a fine winery in the Yad Hashmona village outside Jerusalem." He poured the wine into crystal glasses, which were passed around the table, before raising his drink in a toast, "*L'chaim* and our homeland, Israel," which they repeated back as he picked up a notepad. "We have looked at family connections of each of the victims from our list in relation to the JFK assassination. Joseph Abrams, the physicist, and our tragically deceased military friend, Tzadok Berkowicz, were both too young. Simon Gerren was predeceased by his wife and has no surviving family. Ben Herzl never got married and seems to have been a bit of a recluse. Moshe Levi's wife is in an old people's home in Ramat Gan suffering from severe Alzheimer's. They have two sons, who both live in the United States; one is a US Senator, and the other is a prominent lawyer. I doubt whether either would want to whisper a word about anything, even if they had any knowledge of what happened. That leaves Zielinski, whose wife, Rebekah, was fifteen years younger than Antoni and lives in Be'er Sheva. They have two daughters, one is employed here in Israel as a teacher, whilst the other is a senior steward with Emirates airline, currently living in Dubai. I think we need to pay Rebekah a visit and, perhaps, David, you and Shira might wish to do that. Of those who were also on the aircraft that day, departing from Dallas, Rafi Eitan died in March 2019, we think of natural causes. His whole life was shrouded in secrecy and I think it unlikely we would find anything from his connections. Otto Skorzeny died in Spain in July 1975 of cancer. He was married three times but his spouses have all died. He has a daughter, Waltraut, although her whereabouts is not on file. Hans Baur was the pilot that day whom we identified as a former Nazi, but, looking further, we have established that he was otherwise known as SS Gruppenführer and Police Generalleutnant Baur, who was none other than Adolf Hitler's personal pilot during the war." There were more expressions of shock around the table.

David vocalised his astonishment. "As the saying goes, 'You could not make all this up', that is just extraordinary."

Shira turned to him with a brief smile despite still reeling inside, emotionally raw. "I will add to your surprise with what Benjamin and I have uncovered in a moment."

Moshe continued, "We have all the motive we need, which I know, Shira, will be an essential element required as we expose this to others, but I concur, we still have no proof, which you correctly stated is critical. If nothing else, we need this to face down Omer Ravid and make him realise he cannot succeed."

"We can add to this, as I just alluded to," Shira replied. "The papers that Yehudi had compiled are a goldmine of intel. There are reports on the detonation of a nuclear device by the Nazis in 1945 plus a summary of technical data. Incredibly, there are also documents summarising or minuting meetings regarding the requirements for the Israeli nuclear weapons programme and clandestine operations to covertly obtain, by any means, materials from other countries. These implicate Shimon Peres and Yitzhak Shamir as major architects but also the former head of Mossad, Isser Harel. My grandfather, Yehudi Krimmer, was present at many of these meetings, taking notes meticulously, which he later had typed up. Harel apparently gave orders directly to Otto Skorzeny, in the early 1960's, to take out former German scientists who were assisting the Egyptian weapons programme. He was implicated in the use of letter bombs, and other assassination methods in which a number of innocent people, other than scientists, were killed or injured. David Ben-Gurion was increasingly unhappy with Harel's tactics, describing them as not unlike those of the Nazis, and there was a growing rift between them. Matters came to a head in late 1962 and early 1963. In September 1962, Skorzeny kidnapped a former Nazi scientist by the name of Heinz Krug, under orders from Harel. Yehudi's minutes record that one Antoni Zielinski was on Skorzeny's squad to capture Krug."

"Ah, this will be the *Operation Damocles* business we came across before," Moshe proffered. "Our intelligence services engaged in a policy to assassinate, justified by the need to protect the state."

"I think this is called politics." remarked Benjamin wryly. "After all, is it not a fact that most of those involved in organising these activities ended up in high office or even prime minister? I think I need another glass of wine."

Shira continued, reading from her notes, "Yes, you are right because *Operation Damocles* was headed by future Prime Minister Yitzhak Shamir. It was *Damocles* which was the undoing of Harel because, after Heinz Krug was kidnapped, he was purportedly interrogated in Israel for a considerable time and then executed. When Harel was challenged about his methods, he responded, "There are people who are marked to die". This was too much for Ben-Gurion, who was trying to build bridges with West Germany. Harel was forced to resign as Director of Mossad in March 1963, which, in turn, caused the resignation of Yitzhak Shamir in protest at his treatment."

Mehedi cut in laconically, '*To this I witness call the fools of Time, Which die for goodness, who have lived for crime.*' My goodness, you Jews certainly know how to conduct yourselves." He turned to David, speaking in a mock English accent, "Shakespeare's *Twelfth Night*, I believe, old chap."

David's Arabic expletive in response was not unexpected, "*Telhas Teeze.*" (Kiss my ass)

Shira looked at them with mock derision, "I will ignore the schoolboys. But here is the interesting bit; the incoming manifest of that flight on 24th November 1963 was recorded by Mossad and, somehow, Yehudi Krimmer obtained a copy. There were a number of Germans who had been presumed to be from the BND and, amongst them, was another notable name. One Rochus Misch and here I echo your words, David, 'you could not make this up'. This man served in the *Führerbegleitkommando*, which was the unit responsible for safeguarding Adolf Hitler. Rochus Misch was a trusted bodyguard to Hitler right up to the end of the war. His military record shows that he was an outstanding marksman. Other names included Germans about whom we know very little but they served during the war in *502nd SS Jäger Battalion*, a special forces unit commanded by Skorzeny."

Moshe Gellner's commanding voice cut in decisively, "Even though we still have no proof, which Shira pointed out, we must act now as time may not be on our side. This maniac, Ravid, is not only going to attempt a coup, but is intent on launching a pre-emptive nuclear strike on Iran. I have invited friends of influence here tomorrow afternoon when I think we need to hold a council of war. Shira and David, I think you both need to go and visit Rebekah Zielinski at Be'er Sheva now and see if you can dig anything up."

"Before we do that," Shira spoke her words brusquely in the manner of a military commander, "Benjamin and I have copied one set of documents that forms an essential part of this jigsaw, which we have printed off for each of you." She handed them out to Moshe, Yehudi, and David. He was overwhelmed with admiration for this woman he had held clinging to him for comfort the previous night. No other person had ever penetrated his personal shield, behind which he kept his private feelings; an inner self which was never exposed, and had not been since an early age when he had learned that winning in every part of life was the only way to be recognised

Now, as he glanced down at the papers in front of him, his incredulity increased as he read.

SOHD (Secret)
SECURITY BRIEFING
Project Isaiah
Wednesday 20ᵗʰ March 1963
Chaired by: The Prime Minister
In Attendance:
Foreign Minister – Golda Meir
Deputy Chief of Staff – Major General Yitzhak Rabin
Deputy Minister of Defense – Shimon Peres
Director of Mossad – Isser Harel
Head of The Atomic Energy Committee – Professor Ernst Bergmann
Deputy Head of the Atomic Energy Committee – Professor Yehudi Krimmer
Head of Lekem – Benjamin Blumberg
Minutes Recorded by: Liza Shvetz (Secretary to the PM)

1. *The PM requested a report from the Mossad Director about the location/fate of the Austrian scientist, Heinz Krug. The PM stated he had been informed that Krug had been kidnapped by Mossad agents in Munich on September 11th 1962.*
2. *Isser Harel stated he was unaware of Krug's fate but confirmed that he had been kidnapped as part of Operation Damocles by*

a unit under the command of a former German commando who now worked for Mossad, Otto Skorzeny. Mr Harel further confirmed he had been interrogated using methods that Krug may not have survived.

3. The PM expressed his distaste for both the recruitment of a former Nazi and the methods employed by an Israeli unit. He insisted that Mr Harel had more information than he was admitting to and that he believed Krug's body had been disposed of in the sea, dumped from an Israeli aircraft.

4. Mr Harel responded that he naturally had to maintain confidences to protect Mossad operatives.

5. The Foreign Secretary, Mrs Golda Meir, expressed her displeasure at Mr Harel's response, accusing Mossad of using deplorable tactics, likening them to those adopted by the Nazis against the Jewish people. She further appealed to the PM that she was attempting, under his instruction, to build ties with West Germany in order to secure Israel's status on the world stage.

6. Mr Harel demanded an apology, appealing to the PM, but Mrs Meir declined.

7. The PM asked for Mr Harel's resignation as a result of using tactics that had tarnished the standing and reputation of the State of Israel, after which Mr Harel was asked to leave.

8. The PM announced to those present that he was under pressure from the United States government to allow increased access to the nuclear facility at Dimona. Previous inspections had been cursory and, more recently, those on the inspection teams had reported that they were being impeded or prevented from entering certain areas. He stated that President Kennedy was involved personally and that he had indicated to the PM that the patience of the United States was wearing thin. The PM asked how long it might take to conceal or remove evidence of nuclear weapons development.

9. Professor Bergmann responded that this was impossible to achieve in the short term as it would involve removal of major sections of the plant, and that weapons grade materials stored there would

leave traces even if they could be removed. If parts of the plant were dismantled, the new US Corona satellites had the ability to detect this.

10. *Shimon Peres stated that he had been assured during meetings with Vice President Lyndon Johnson that political pressure was being brought to bear on the President not to interfere with Israel's sensitive defence strategy in the region. There was a growing belief in the USA that allowing Arab states to assume that Israel may possess the bomb may be in the interests of security in the region. Mr Peres concluded that a policy of ambiguity could be furthered if Israel never admitted possessing such weapons nor denied it. He further stated that the Vice President was acting in the interests of those involved in the armaments industry who were anxious not to impede Israel's need to obtain and maintain military superiority in the region.*

11. *Benjamin Blumberg informed the meeting that covert monies were being diverted to assist the Vice President in his co-operation and that he was also being supported financially by the armaments industry for the influence he could exert.*

12. *The Deputy Chief of Staff was adamant that nuclear weapons were essential for Israel's security in the face of an increasingly hostile Egyptian position supported by an alliance of other Arab states; the survival of Israel was threatened.*

13. *Shimon Peres echoed the position outlined by Major General Rabin, stressing that obtaining the ultimate deterrent had been the cornerstone of his strategy since his appointment and that Israel's defence could only be guaranteed by nuclear weapons capability.*

14. *Professor Bergmann endorsed the position by saying that he had to repeat again what he had said on many occasions publicly, that 'we shall never again be led as lambs to the slaughter.' All present concurred with this.*

15. *The PM concluded the meeting by saying that his position may become untenable if President Kennedy could not be dissuaded from his insistence on the inspection programme. He instructed*

those present to consider any and all options before the next meeting.

David looked around the table as each absorbed the magnitude of what they might deduce from the meeting minutes. "I think," he said slowly, "we have uncovered so much that we must all agree that none of this can ever be revealed. A move against Ravid is critical, but only fractional elements of our evidence can be shared and whoever we share any part of this with must understand that we cannot allow any of this into the public domain."

As Moshe arranged a late lunch with his housekeeper of an array of *salatim* (salad dishes) followed by grilled chicken, they sat in the easy chairs positioned around the terrace, chatting through key elements of their discoveries to date. Shira took the envelope addressed to her that had been in the box retrieved from Yehudi Krimmer and retreated to her room. She had wanted privacy before reading his last words to her. Her fingers wandered over the spidery handwriting on the front, as she reflected that only one day before, her beloved *zaydee* had been alive, holding this very envelope. She sat on the bed and carefully slid a comb neatly across the top, not wishing to damage any part of what had been in his hands. There were two sheets of paper neatly folded inside.

My dearest cheifale, I should have shared more with you when you came to see me years ago. The truth is that I have guarded so much all my life, it has been hard not to continue to do so. My life has been darkened by what I have heard and witnessed at the heart of power. Was it all for the greater good, as I tried to convince myself? Tokhnit (God's purpose) maybe. I hope what I have gathered will assist you, and maybe I can add just a little more.

We Jews are nothing if not practical and within a few years of the war, we were encouraging not just Jewish scientists to work for Israel, but those from Germany who we knew had the expertise or skills we needed, including known Nazis. I worked closely with a brilliant physicist, Wolfgang Gentner, who was genial, polite, and amusing, yet he had been a leading player in the Uranverein nuclear programme under the Nazis. You know what, dear Shira, he became a member of the board of governors at the Weizmann Institute of Science in Israel. Pragmatism makes strange bedfellows. Technicians and even former SS men were recruited; the latter we needed to carry out operations which we officially would not admit being part of. Lekem and Kidon were responsible for many operations where those who got in the way were killed. Blumberg and later Eitan from our Intelligence network would stop at nothing, although Eitan was more adept at achieving his ends. I was glad to get away from it all and no longer wished to be part of what I had allowed myself to be sucked into.

I can say to you that these organisations were acting in a clandestine manner in the 1960's and continued to do so until Yitzhak Shamir intervened in 1988. My belief is, if my worst fears are realised about the events of November 1963, that the action was not sanctioned by the government, although there were many who welcomed the outcome. There were mavericks like Eitan and Isser Harel who had operated for years on a pretty free rein. I hope the documents I gathered today assist you in making some sense of what was happening.

I still have my sources and know what is at stake with Ravid. Bless his poor mother, who was an angel of kindness when we were lucky enough to be taken out of Mittelbau-Dora concentration camp, despite the terrible suffering she had been through. She always only thought of others, putting their needs before her own. I know in my heart that you have inherited that from her. I am fading with the years, dear Shira, and hope I will have one last chance to say goodbye in person but if I do not, say Kaddish for me. I need to tell

*you that knowing you has been a joy. You are like the child I
never had. Forgive me for what I allowed myself to have been
part of.*
    Your Zaydee

Tears welled up, which this time she could not hold back and,
after a soft knock on the door, when David entered, she buried her
head in his shoulder.

Outside on the terrace, Mehedi was making notes on his
tablet in order that he could begin piecing together a file of all
the critical facts they had gathered. At some point, they knew
that they would need to present a report to the Prime Minister,
Benjamin Netanyahu, and probably the Defense Minister, Benny
Gantz. Moshe remarked, "We have to proceed on the basis that
we can, at least, trust our most senior politicians...don't we?"
He added the last two words as he saw Mehedi exaggeratedly
shaking his head with a groan. Benjamin was reeling with all the
information he had absorbed since the preceding day. He possessed
a deeply analytical mind but he found the entire story almost too
improbable to accept, yet in that improbability lay the shocking
reality of the revelations that had been uncovered. He paced the
length of the swimming pool below the terrace, tracing the events
in his mind from the earliest days, trying to ascertain how all this
had come to pass, and what lay at its roots. How could it be that
the country he loved so much had actually employed known Nazis
after all they had done in an attempt to wipe out the Jewish race?
How could a survivor of Treblinka become part of a team led by a
renowned leader in the SS? As he returned to the seating area, he
spoke out loud what he was thinking, "Why did the Germans not
use the weapon they had discovered? They were terrifyingly close
to changing the course of history..."

24

"Providence shows no mercy"

Tuesday 3rd April 1945 – 2pm
Schloss Haigerloch, Swabian Alb, South-Western Germany

The nineteenth century neo-gothic castle at Haigerloch loomed large, with its conical towers and spires on the skyline, as they drove in their small convoy towards the hill of the Zollernalb. There were twelve of them in two *Kübelwagen* followed by an *Opel Blitz* (truck) with a canopy over the rear. All the vehicles had been captured during the battle for Strasbourg in the preceding month and were clearly marked with the black cross insignia of the German forces on their dark grey paintwork. Yitzhak Rabin, Rafi Eitan, and Antoni Zielinski were in the leading *Kübelwagen* with a driver, dressed respectively in the uniforms of *SS-Oberführer* (colonel), *SS-Sturmbannführer* (major), and *SS-Hauptsturmführer* (captain) followed by four heavily armed and battle-hardened members of Number 3 Troop Commando in the second *Kübelwagen* and four more in the truck. They had not been challenged since driving over the pontoon bridge at Strasbourg at 5am, travelling through recently occupied Kehl in Germany, on the front line, and then adopting a route across country towards Haigerloch, ninety kilometres away. They approached up the drive to the bottom of a small incline leading to the castle entrance where two guards stood. Zielinski jumped down and barked in fluent German, "*Heil Hitler*, our orders come directly from Reichsführer Himmler. We are here to meet Professors Schuman, von Weizsäcker and Heisenberg. You will show us where they are located now, *schnell.*" His tone was cold, commanding, and the young guard was in no mood to argue with senior officers, especially from the SS, who, he had heard, even shot Germans who stood in their way. He stuttered back that they were in the laboratory basement research area, through the double arched doors in the external courtyard, and down some steps to a disused beer cellar beneath. Zielinski clicked his heels, raising his right arm in salute, then beckoned. Four soldiers from the second *Kübelwagen* alighted and followed Rabin, Eitan and Zielinski as they walked purposefully to the double doors, then into a well-lit cobbled area to some steps in the corner, hearing the hum of machinery as they approached. Zielinski and Eitan both loosened the holster fasteners on their Luger pistols in their belts, as they reached the top of the entrance leading down to the old beer cellar.

As they descended the steep steps to a half landing, they surveyed the scene below where they could see a number of people milling around a curious circular structure. Some were in white coats, whilst others, dragging and carrying components, appeared emaciated, many wearing the striped clothing issued to concentration camp prisoners. Zielinski winced as he looked, feeling tempted to wrench the Schmeisser machine gun out of the hands of one of his men behind, and open fire on the German guards below. The three SS officers then walked slowly and deliberately down to the floor towards two of those wearing white coats who were standing, looking at some paper drawings, by a smaller circular object on the floor, which looked like a turbine of sorts. Zielinski, who had the best command of German, approached and addressed them, once again, in a curt manner. "*Bitte*, we are instructed on direct orders of Reichsführer Himmler. He wishes to see the foremost German scientists working here. We have been informed that you have selected *Juden* to assist you. The Reichsführer wishes to see you now at his mobile HQ at Hechingen with your *Juden*. Do they need cleaning up before we take them?" A German guard leaning on the wall close by sniggered at the last question. Zielinski, fully assuming the role he was playing, shot the guard a look of derision, which was not feigned, causing the man to snap to attention as he saluted, muttering an apology. The taller of the two men responded, "I am Professor Carl Friedrich von Weizsäcker," he trembled with nervousness as he spoke. "There are only four senior scientists here but we have three Jews who are assisting us with scientific work. This was all approved by the *Organisation Todt* and authorised as necessary *Zwangsarbeit* (forced labour) by Armaments Minister, Albert Speer." The shorter man standing next to him with rounded glasses and silver hair nodded as his eyes blinked rapidly.

Zielinski snapped, "We will bring these Jews with us. Who are the German scientists here?"

"This is Professor Erich Schuman," Weizsäcker responded meekly, gesturing to his colleague, before pointing to two other men in white coats who were standing near the large circular structure, "and they are Professor Otto Hahn, and Professor Werner Heisenberg." Then having gathered his thoughts, his voice was stronger. "You need to know we are working on an urgent project and I report directly to the Führer."

"You need to know I report directly to Reichsführer Himmler and if you fail to come with us, you will be shot, Jew lover. It is of no concern to me. Your choice, Herr Professor," came the icy reply as Zielinski pulled his Luger pistol from its holster, holding it against Weizsäcker's temple. He turned to the guard who was watching, unsure of how he should react. "I want no interference, *du verstehst?* Gather your comrades, get up into the courtyard and wait for orders. We are now in command." As if to emphasise Zielinski's words, his fellow commandos on the half landing pulled back the bolts on their machine guns with a loud rasping movement. Eitan, in his uniform of SS-Hauptsturmführer, had also drawn his weapon, which he pointed menacingly at the soldier, who mumbled, *"Jawohl, Herr Hauptsturmführer,"* before waving and shouting to four other guards in the long cellar. *"Komm jetzt!"* (come now)

As the guards made their exit, Zielinski shouted, "All scientific personnel, including Jews, will come here now with their hands on their heads." Otto Hahn walked slowly forwards, who they recognised from the photograph they had been given. Behind him, also in white coats, came three others with yellow bands on their arms bearing the star of David in black and another star on their chests displaying the word, *'Jude'.* The remaining prisoners moved forwards behind them. Zielinski turned to Weizsäcker, gesturing at the three men, "Identify these Jews."

"These two are former Professor Aaron Kaufman, and former Doctor Fritz Gottheiner, and the young man is their protégé, Yehudi Krimmer."

Zielinski turned and shouted to the remaining twenty-five prisoners who shuffled forwards. "You will form up and exit this cellar in front of us and proceed to the wagon directly outside. You will line up behind the truck as we exit. Do as we order and no harm will come to you." The prisoners wore the disdainful look of acceptance to their fate that years of terrifying maltreatment had taught them but they knew better than to even flinch in front of an SS officer. The four commandos on the landing descended, holding their machine guns at waist height as they escorted the prisoners out, leaving Rabin, Eitan and Zielinski behind with the scientists. Now it was Rabin's turn to speak directly to the Jewish scientists in Hebrew, *"Shalom,* we are your brothers from Palestine come to bring you home." The three men looked utterly bewildered before Eitan shook hands with each of them, then briefly threw his arms around them as they struggled to understand. Rabin turned to the German scientists, speaking in German but with an accent. "You are prisoners of war but today, because we are wearing the uniforms of the SS, you will understand that if you make one sound, or one gesture as we leave here, you will be shot immediately. Your choice is whether you wish to live or die, which is not a choice you give Jews. Now, we move out and you will climb in the truck outside. Remember, we will kill you if you make one move to alert anyone. *Verstehst?*" He spat the last word out, angered by the sight of the emaciated prisoners in their striped clothing. All four of the scientists nodded, looking terrified.

As they exited the double doors into the courtyard, they joined the other commandos outside, who had shepherded the prisoners in a line behind the truck. There was no sign of any discovery from others occupying the castle. Zielinski ordered the four guards to return to the cellar and guard it until they returned. He then watched as the scientists climbed into the truck and gave orders quietly to the sergeant in charge of their guarding to shoot them in the event they may be recaptured. The three vehicles turned in the courtyard and then proceeded towards the gate slowly followed by the procession of prisoners walking wearily behind. As they aproached the exit gate, a tall SS officer walked slowly into view, holding his hand up, and, within seconds, a dozen more troops ran out with their weapons at shoulder height, pointing towards the advancing procession, which halted.

"*Zoobie!*" (screw it) muttered Rabin, "We may have a fight on our hands."

The officer walked slowly towards the first *Kübelwagen,* stopping around twenty yards away.

"This guy has balls," muttered Eitan as he slipped a grenade into his hand.

The officer shouted across to them. "I am *SS-Generalmajor*

Skorzeny, you are in a hopeless position. You will surrender and hand over the scientists. No-one needs to die here today."

Rabin turned to Eitan, "Time to do a business deal, I think. These *szkopy* need educating the Jewish way."

Rabin stood up, "Herr Generalmajor, I am Captain Yitzhak Rabin of X Troop. No-one does need to die this day if you listen to our terms."

Skorzeny laughed, then with some incredulity, "*Sie sind Juden? Mein Gott.*" He gestured with an exaggerated shrug back to his men, causing more laughter. "I think we have the upper hand here, Jew."

"I think not, Herr Generalmajor; we have four of your scientists, one who tells me he reports directly to Adolf Hitler. We are all prepared to die but if you open fire, we will execute our prisoners first. The war will soon be over and you may be judged harshly if this ends badly. We will release your German scientists in exchange for the freedom of the Jews and the three Jewish scientists who have been assisting them. Do we have a deal?"

Skorzeny held his hand up and walked back to where Captain Hans Danneberg was standing by the soldiers. A machine gun, mounted on a tripod, had now been positioned on the cobbles by the gatehouse, and was trained on the vehicles, behind which two more soldiers were lying, one opening a box of ammunition on a belt which was being loaded.

"Hans, shall we kill them? The opening fire would take out all those in the two *Kübelwagen.*"

Danneberg took in a deep breath as the soldier behind the machine gun cocked the weapon, the noise echoing off walls, his finger hovering over the trigger. "These scientists could be our saviours in stopping the Fatherland from being overrun. The *Schwein* has a point in that if we kill them, we may well be judged after the war is over, and also we risk suffering the wrath of the Führer. Look what happened to those poor bastards defending Remagen. We have all seen Field Marshal Kesselring's despatch.

Four of them executed on Hitler's orders and I've heard another shot himself. What is the point for the sake of a few Jews?"

Skorzeny looked back at the wagon, grimacing. He was not a man who ever liked being cornered. "'*Die Juden sind unser Unglück*'. (the Jews are our misfortune) Today, I get that slogan. I'll negotiate with the *Judensau.*" he muttered grimly, adding, "Put a sniper up in the gatehouse tower and open fire on my command." He walked slowly back towards the leading *Kübelwagen.*

Zielinski had his hands gripped to his Schmeisser, having watched the SS set up the heavy machine gun. He recalled, with a momentary shiver, the day at Treblinka when he had watched a similar weapon mow down so many prisoners as they climbed over each other, scrambling to escape the withering scythe of death. He was not afraid, having seen so many die, and having long lost count of the numbers he had killed. He had become cold and immune from emotion other than the need to survive; a need which meant that he too wished to ensure others of his race survive. He spoke tersely, "Why not kill that piece of scum now then lob a couple of grenades? We would, at least, have a chance plus the satisfaction of taking a few of these *Heinies* with us."

"I think," responded Rabin, "we may have succeeded in securing a deal, otherwise our Generalmajor would not be returning."

Skorzeny walked a little closer and Zielinski noticed the long scar down one side of his face as he struggled with his urge to kill him. Skorzeny spoke, "You may leave with your *Juden* but we will keep your scientists here as insurance that you release ours. You will drive 500 metres and then release two of the Germans. When we see them walking back to the *Schloss,* we will release one of your men so that they pass about half way on the bend in the road. You will then release the third scientist, and we will do the same. In this way, there is no danger of a deception, which protects us both. You then have a chance to make your escape. No-one need die here today if you accept my terms, Jew." His tone was slightly mocking but Rabin was a pragmatist, recognising that to an SS officer, a Jewish life meant nothing and to obtain even this chance was already more than they might have expected.

Minutes later, Aaron Kaufman, Fritz Gottheiner, and Yehudi Krimmer alighted from the truck whilst Eitan supervised as the Jewish prisoners climbed in. The SS soldiers in front of them moved away from the gate and the three vehicles moved slowly forwards. As they passed, Skorzeny raised his hand, imitating the shape of a handgun, and pointed it at Rabin, mimicking the sound of a gunshot. They travelled slowly away from the Schloss, reaching a right-hand bend where Rabin asked Zielinski to wait and cover the approach of their hostages. They pulled in on the downward incline 500 metres from the castle, which remained in sight higher up, although their view of the entrance was impeded by the bend. The four German scientists, Carl von Weizsäcker, Erich Schuman, Otto Hahn and Werner Heisenberg, climbed out of the truck and Eitan ordered Erich Schuman and Otto Hahn to walk back up to the schloss. Shortly thereafter, Zielinski appeared on the bend giving the thumbs up signal and it was not long before a nervous Yehudi Krimmer joined them, followed by Aaron Kaufman after Heisenberg had been released. It was then that Carl Weizsäcker addressed Rabin earnestly. "Please, this is important. I have a young Jewish mother and her child at my house only six kilometres from here. She has been my housekeeper but shared accommodation with Yehudi Krimmer. I tried to help her because she was with child after being raped in a concentration camp. Take her with you, I implore you. I know what these people in the SS are like. They will take her." He turned to Krimmer, "I wish you well and hope we can meet as equals after the war." He offered his hand to Krimmer, who hesitated, but then he smiled, and warmly shook his hand before von Weizsäcker walked away.

For the third time, Zielinski appeared, giving the sign that the last hostage, Fritz Gottheiner, was on his way. At the schloss, Skorzeny shouted a command to the sniper positioned in the tower. "When you are ready, *Feldwebel*, (Sergeant) let us kill at least one of the *Schweine*." He turned to Danneberg with a smile, "I said I would allow them to leave but gave no assurance that they would arrive. My oath is to the Führer, not to the Yids."

"Your honour does you credit, Herr Generalmajor," observed Danneberg. "Shall we pursue them or alert the garrison at Hechingen?"

"I think not, Herr Hauptmann, tempers are frayed and we cannot risk being judged, as you pointed out, like those at Remagen. Let them go and we are following our duty to the Fatherland by ridding our science from Jewish influence. We are doing our bit for '*Entjudung*'" (Jew removal policy)

The slightly stooping figure of Gottheiner had just rounded the bend when the first shot rang out, the second spinning him round as he fell. Zielinski screamed, "Reverse the truck," He ran to the corner and aimed his machine gun, firing until the magazine emptied, which he flung to one side before attaching another. His continuous bursts of staccato fire seemed longer than their five-second duration and echoed rhythmically off the hillside. He knew the range limitation of his weapon but his rage took over his senses and his one instinct was to kill. More shots rang out as the truck revved and reversed towards Gottheiner, who was struggling to get up. Rabin, from his kneeling position taking cover by the *Kübelwagen*, shouted, "No, stay down!" But Gottheiner struggled to his feet, staggering towards the truck as a further shot catapulted him forwards on his face where he lay unmoving. Zielinski fired again, then ran the few metres to Gottheiner, immediately realising by the severity of the man's headwound that he was dead. He tried to drag him as the sniper fired again, kicking the ground up just by his leg. Eitan was standing on the back of the truck shouting "Leave him, leave him; we have to go now!" The truck had begun moving forwards as Zielinski ran, being hauled in by Eitan and another commando. As he stood, holding on to the bar supporting the canopy, he looked at Eitan, his face perspiring, his eyes wild with fury, "One day, I will have that man in the sights of my weapon. *Yimakh shemo.*" (curse his name)

Friday 20th April 1945 – 10am
The Führerbunker, Reich Chancellery, Wilhelmstrasse 77, Berlin

The spring weather was unusually warm, once referred to as 'Führer Weather' by Berliners, but not anymore. The brightness and warmth outside contrasted with the plain stone walls of the bunker, fifty feet below ground level, which seemed oppressive, despite the forced jollity of the occasion. A number of guests were gathered in the waiting room ready to be summoned to greet the Führer on the occasion of his fifty-sixth birthday. There was a map of Germany on one wall and two classical-style country scene paintings on the other. The room was only twenty feet long and twelve feet wide, in marked contrast to the palatial-style rooms where they had formerly met in the Reich Chancellery, only a few weeks before. That was still standing but was damaged with chunks of the building lying in heaps around the adjacent garden and courtyard. The ground around was pitted with craters as were the streets in the surrounding areas, which had suffered greatly from Allied bombing raids on the city of Berlin. Those gathered included Reichsmarschall Hermann Göring, Minister of Propaganda Joseph Goebbels, Foreign Minister Joachim von Ribbentrop, Reich Chancellery head and personal secretary Martin Bormann, Gestapo chief and Reichsführer-SS Heinrich Himmler, Chief of the Navy, Grand Admiral Karl Dönitz, Chief of the High Command of the Armed Forces (OKW), Wilhelm Keitel, Chief of the Operations Staff of the Armed Forces High Command, Alfred Jodl, and Armaments Minister, Albert Speer. The conversation was subdued, depressed even further by the sound of artillery fire being clearly heard from the east for the first time from the the advancing Soviet Red Army. There was a sense of uncertain finality and even the normally jovial Göring had only managed a brief quip, hardly raising a smile, saying, "I hear that Traudl Junge and the girls are having Champagne whilst we will be having cups of tea. Secretaries have a better time than the elite now." Himmler shot him a derisory look, his personal distaste for the over-indulgent, corpulent figure of Göring, now scarcely hidden any more.

"You should try living down here," replied Goebbels, who had recently moved into the bunker with his wife and six children.

Albert Speer joined in, "I designed this place with the utmost comfort and security in mind when I built it. How long are you staying?"

"Until the…" Goebbels stopped himself, changing his intended words, "Until I am no longer needed. I will not leave the Führer's side." The words had the effect of uncomfortably silencing the room, which was not broken until ten minutes later when the door opened and Sturmbannführer Otto Günsche appeared, clicking his heels smartly before raising his arm, "*Heil Hitler, meine Herren*, the Führer and Fraulein Braun are ready to receive you."

There were some expressions of surprise around the room as it was unusual for Hitler to include Eva Braun in meetings with his elite. They filed through into another similar sized room with a long table. Biscuits and small cakes were positioned in the centre of the table, which added a sense of surreal unreality. This was followed by another surprise as Hitler's personal valet Obersturmbannführer Heinz Linge entered, followed by some orderlies bearing bottles of Champagne and glasses, which they set down in front of those present. Linge then uttered the words, "*Der Führer, Adolf Hitler!*"

They stiffened to attention as he entered slowly, in his customary field grey uniform, almost shuffling, his frame stooped and his complexion yellowed, one hand behind his back. His appearance was of a much older man, the lines deep around his face and his forehead furrowed. Then, he stopped, looking at them with the piercing blue eyes that seemed to penetrate, and they were instantly aware of his complete authority, his right arm now held up, bent from the elbow, the palm of his hand facing upwards in his familiar salute. All present responded by smartly extending their arms stiffly with a chorus of *"Heil Hitler!"* There was the briefest abrupt smile before he stood back and Eva Braun entered, wearing a polka dot dress and matching jacket. She smiled warmly around the table and was given a short bow by each of them.

Hermann Göring stepped forwards dressed immaculately in the light blue dress uniform of the Luftwaffe, his *Pour le Mérite* medal at his neck, *"Mein Führer*, as the most senior person present, it is my honour to say, *Herzlichen Glückwunsch zum Geburtstag und alles Gute für das kommende Jahr."* (Happy birthday and all the best for the coming year) The greeting was echoed around the table.

Hitler nodded in response, gesturing to the cakes and biscuits, his familiar guttural voice was still spellbinding to them and they listened with rapt attention as he spoke, "We are today facing the greatest, the most heroic and historic struggle of modern times, in which we must prevail against the barbarians from the East. My sacred duty, which Providence chose me for nearly a quarter of a century ago, was to harvest the soul of the German *Volk* and even now, throughout Germany, there is a unity of purpose behind the banners of National Socialism. The heart of the *Deutschen Volke* beats with my own as one." He gripped his right hand to his chest as they hung on his every word. "We have suffered betrayal from those who sought to gain from our struggle or who shrank from the providential purpose which I have striven for unceasingly. I will not flinch from my conviction now, even though thousands will die at my command, for my purpose must remain inviolable and my iron will must drive that purpose." His fist thumped down on the table. "We will avenge the betrayal that has allowed the Bolshevik scum to cross our borders with death and destruction of an unimaginable magnitude. My own life has only the value that it possesses for the destiny of the nation; now, I will unswervingly act to re-establish and strengthen our fronts for revenge and attack. Under my direction we have created weapons of proven capacity and staggering force. My destiny is to unleash upon mankind the awesome capacity of these *Wunderwaffen* (wonder-weapons) and re-establish the greater German Reich. I have hesitated to use this power out of a belief that I would not be failed by those I have entrusted with the defence of the Reich. Perhaps, even I sensed that the step I must take should be paused for the sake of humanity but now the time has come for me to act. We must annihilate and eliminate all those who oppose us. In one step there will not be 1,000 deaths, not even 10,000, but 100,000 or more. First with the Bolshevik filth, then, if the Allies do not pull back and join our crusade against Bolshevism, with one terrible strike, we shall destroy the American resolve, and, finally, we will make that gangster, Mr Churchill, cower, realising the foolishness of his resistance. Nothing will ever stop the destiny which Providence has chosen for Germany. *Deutschland über alles!*" His voice had risen as if delivering a speech to massed crowds as he raised his hands up in the dramatic pronunciation of the last words in an almost religious pose staring upwards.

Goebbels could not contain himself, shouting, "*Sieg Heil!*" The others raised their right arms as they recognised that their beloved leader was going to be the saviour of the Reich even at this late stage. Hitler then turned to Eva Braun, "Some tea, I think, although on this day, I have relaxed the rules and permitted alcohol." He sat down, appearing exhausted by his monologue but clearly resolved on the action he was setting in motion.

Sunday 22nd April 1945 – 3pm
Briefingkamer, Reich Chancellery, Berlin

The Führer had been in a better frame of mind for the last two days, and staff had remarked that matters must be taking a better turn at the front, despite the increasingly loud explosions that could now clearly be heard in the bunker. That morning, Hitler had even taken his pet dog, Blondi, a German Shepherd, for a walk around the Reich Chancellery garden, ignoring calls by his loyal bodyguard, Rochus Misch, that it was dangerous to venture outside.

After lunch, Hitler had been asked to convene a secret meeting by the Chief of Staff, General Hans Krebs, after the customary military briefing on the ongoing defence of Berlin in the conference room. Various staff officers and adjutants attended, together with Hitler's Party secretary, Martin Bormann, as the Führer pored over a map surrounded by General Krebs, Field Marshal Wilhelm Keitel, General Alfred Jodl, and General Wilhelm Burdorf. General Krebs had just informed Hitler that the position was grave, with the Russians gaining ground far quicker than anticipated. Hitler turned to him sharply, "Yesterday, you told me that the III SS Panzer Corps, under Obergruppenführer Felix Steiner, could attack from the north to support the IV Panzer Army, who are advancing from the south. Where is Army Detachment Steiner?" He hissed the last words with a suppressed anger which they had seen before."

Krebs was white-faced, "Mein Führer, forgive me, but Steiner reports his men are pinned down by superior numbers and are unable to move. He says he cannot mount an attack." There was an uneasy silence, then Hitler swept his arm across the map, violently sending pens and crayon markers across the room. He gripped his fists around the map, his eyes wide and his hands shaking, then, gathering the map up, he crumpled it and then began slamming it rhythmically down on the table, his face covered in sweat.

Bormann cut in, "Mein Führer, shall we retire?"

Hitler's voice shrieked, "Nein!" His eyes were glazed, then he clutched Bormann's arm, "We will triumph. Order all units to attack now!" he barked, then more quietly, in a shaking, restrained voice, "This conference is over. Krebs, Keitel, Jodl, and Burdorf only will remain and we will meet again in thirty minutes."

Bormann escorted a hunched Hitler from the room as the less senior attending officers nervously and warily felt a moment of relief that they were not required further.

General Krebs left the room to make a telephone call, returning ten minutes later, trembling and shaking his head, but no-one spoke. Field Marshal Wilhelm Keitel smoothed over the map and began studying it intently as General Jodl watched him with utter disdain, viewing officers like him as weak yes-men responsible for Germany's demise. They waited; General Krebs had removed the monocle he customarily wore and was rubbing his eyes. He had scarcely slept in days and fatigue was taking its toll. Report after report was coming in about the rapid advance of the Soviets, the speed of which had surprised and overwhelmed the German defences. Only three days before, the Red Army had broken through the Oder-Neisse Line, the last German position to the east of Berlin, and begun its encirclement of the capital. Most of the remaining German forces were outside the huge Russian gathering of one and a half million men poised for the final assault. Krebs had desperately tried to organise counter offensives but now he recognised the position was becoming hopeless. He knew that he could only muster around 50,000 regular soldiers together with around 40,000 old men and civilians in the *Volkssturm,* together with boys from the *Hitler-Jugend.* But there was worse news he now needed to impart to the Führer. There were sighs around the table in the small meeting room as the four most senior officers in the military faced the inevitability of the collapse of the German defences and defeat. The atmosphere was claustrophobic and oppressive as they all felt the impending doom of the Reich. Bormann strode in and they all stood as Hitler entered. He sat behind the table facing his generals as Bormann took a seat in the corner to his side. The Führer was visibly shaking, his eyes reddened with a grim expression on his face; then he spoke quietly but with a harsh tone. "My *Wunderwaffen* must be deployed immediately to destroy Moscow. Army Detachment Steiner will now attack the Russian barbarian vermin. They will obey my orders. Remind them they have taken an oath of loyalty to me." He emphasised his order by slamming his fist on the table, his voice rising in tone.

Krebs spoke hesitantly, "Mein Führer, I must inform you that today I received a signal from *Oberbefehlshaber West* (Supreme Command West) saying that our *Uranverein* centres at Haigerloch and Hechingen have been overrun and that the bombs have been seized. I have also contacted General Gotthard Heinrici of Army Group Vistula, who has spoken again to Obergruppenführer Steiner. Steiner states he will not attack because he is not in a position to do so."

Hitler's face reddened as he screamed, "*Ich bin verraten.* (I am betrayed) Any officer who betrays me betrays the Fatherland. This is treachery and it is not my will that has faltered, but others that have weakened in the face of adversity. I gave Germany pride, strength, and power but I have been failed by those around me, in a relentless series of betrayals bringing the Fatherland to the edge of catastrophe." He stood up, drawing his chest out as they had all witnessed him do at great rallies in previous years. Now his voice dropped but began building as he spoke. "History will judge my actions and nations that have opposed me will realise their folly, and regret they bowed in the face of the evil of communism, instead of joining with us in our great crusade. Only I stood and dared to speak out; only I had the courage and the foresight forged in German blood, now squandered because those that I relied on were too weak. I seized the moment, recognising the destiny of the Reich to exist not for a hundred years, but for a thousand. Now all this has been plundered by weaklings who were afraid of the strength of my will and purpose, epitomised by the great creed of National Socialism. Providence shows no mercy to weak nations, but recognises the right of existence only of sound and strong nations. I gave the SS the status of an elite force and even they betray me; and so…it is finished; we are finished…but I will remain here until the end. *Ich bin verraten!*" The last words were screamed furiously as he thumped his fist into his chest and collapsed into his chair.

Outside, staff could hear the voice of their leader rising and falling and they continued in their duties in the surreal world collapsing around them.

Thursday 26th April 1945 – 10am
Gatow Airfield, South West of Berlin

The thirteen *Focke-Wulf Fw 190* fighter aircraft began their approach with six either side of that piloted by von Greim. As they descended to 100 feet, he shouted, "Please brace yourself, we shall shortly be landing."

The voice of Hanna Reitsch from behind his seat shouted back, "With your flying skills, I am becoming worried." Their mission was highly secret but they had unexpectedly received orders to meet with the Führer at the Reich Chancellery earlier than had been planned. As no two-seater aircraft were immediately available where they were stationed, they had compromised. Hanna had climbed into the aircraft tail section through a small emergency hatch for the short flight from Rechlin–Lärz Airfield to Gatow, where a light *Fieseler Storch* aircraft awaited them. They both knew the war was going badly but Hanna's faith in the Führer was absolute and she felt pride that she had been selected to fulfil such a critical role.

As she alighted from the aircraft, extricating herself with some difficulty, they laughed at how ridiculous life had become. They laughed at so much now because it was a way of dealing with the impending tragedy they could see unfolding for Germany. As they climbed into the Fieseler Storch, she leant over and gripped von Greim's hand. "Please tell me everything will be alright."

He looked back at her with sadness in his eyes – "The vision we had and dreamed of for Germany is over. I see no future for our country afterwards. The Russians are my worst fear and they are at the gates of Berlin. That is what makes our role in this tragedy so important and the secret we share must die with us. The safety of the Führer is our only concern now and that is our sacred duty to the Fatherland." She leant across and kissed him lightly on the cheek.

One hour later, as they began their descent towards Berlin, they could see huge clouds of smoke arising from the city. Von Greim banked the aircraft, and, as he did so, they were rocked and buffeted by anti-aircraft fire. They were also hit by small arms fire, hearing the crack of some bullets striking the fuselage. The aircraft lurched as von Greim cried out, then shouted, "I'm hit...my leg!" Hanna forced herself into a position next to him, telling him to pull his legs off the rudder as he tipped his head back, wincing with pain. She grabbed the joystick and using that and the throttle managed to manoeuvre towards the Tiergarten, which was being used as a temporary airstrip. After a somewhat bumpy landing she turned to von Greim, who smiled at her, but winced with pain. "I think, as our Führer might say, Providence brought you to me all those years ago at Grunau Flying School."

Six days later at 9am on 2nd May 1945, Red Army soldiers entered the bunker. The bodies of Joseph Goebbels, his wife, Magda, and their six children were found. Those of Adolf Hitler and Eva Braun were never discovered.

25

'Love your enemies...hate your friends'

David was at the wheel of Mehedi's white Toyota Corolla and had been driving for over an hour on their journey to Be'er Sheva, around 160 kilometres from Caesarea. Shira had called Rebekah Zielinski that afternoon to inform her that she was part of an ongoing investigation into her husband's death, which, she justified to herself, was partially true. The information they had unearthed on Zielinski confirmed he had married Rebekah, who was then studying law, in March 1963, and that they had remained together, having two daughters when she was in her thirties. One bonus was that she had once worked for Mossad, which they thought would make her more open to their visit.

Shira had fallen asleep not long after they had left Moshe's house. David looked across at her lying back on the seat, her long dark hair slightly covering her face, her gently pronounced cheekbones with a slightly upturned nose and pouty lips giving her a provocative beauty. Her appearance to him, ridiculously belied her accomplished military career, and that made her even more desirable to him. He wished they could have met in different circumstances, yet, somehow, he felt comforted that they were sharing what they were facing together. He was captivated by her, despite the seriousness of the situation, and he dismissed the thoughts that threatened to flood his mind as he ran the tips of his fingers across her temple, drawing a half smile in response. Her head moved and then she opened her eyes and sat up. Her thoughts instantly focussed and, like David, she forced herself to concentrate on the mission despite sensing the overwhelming connection she felt with him. "I think, David, we should take Rebekah into our confidence, to a degree, in order to let her feel she is helping us to uncover those who may have been responsible for Zielinski's death. You might be best placed to come across as the professional investigator whilst I play the role of the more empathetic caring one offering support."

"Ah the old good cop, bad cop routine," David laughed, "We used to use that very effectively when interrogating our Arab prisoners. I was always the softer one, of course." He recalled grimly techniques they had been taught in the IDF where one would take their handgun out, before cocking it and holding it against a prisoner's head whilst the other would say, "You cannot do this; please do not kill him." The holder of the gun would argue, shout and storm out, leaving the 'softer' one to talk to the prisoner, offering to protect him in exchange for information, yet the whole charade was pre-planned.

Shira opened her tablet and pulled up the little available intel on his wife in Zielinski's file on his wife. "OK, Rebekah studied International law at the Buchmann Faculty in Tel Aviv, otherwise known as TAU Law, passing out with a first class degree. She was recruited as a student by Mossad and ended up working in the political department of the Ministry of Foreign Affairs, but seems to have kept a pretty low profile, leaving after the birth of their second daughter."

"Is there no-one we come across that does not have some connection to Mossad?" David remarked drily. "I used to be an idealist but increasingly, I think I am becoming cynical as I see the hypocrisy of power and the institutions that purport to protect us. The worst of it is that I am part of that."

"Hey, lover boy," Shira replied, laughing, "we both are; but what do we have without that?" Then, more seriously, "Look back at our history and what has happened to our race just in the last hundred years. Is it any wonder that we are immersed in our own security measures?" She paused, scanning the notes on screen. "Hey, this is interesting. It seems Rebekah had some involvement with advising government on the implications of Eitan's 'purported' theft of 200 pounds of enriched uranium from the US in the *Apollo Affair*. Apparently, he posed as a chemist and visited the US Nuclear Materials and Equipment Corporation, or NUMEC, before removing material which ended up in Israel."

"This investigation has more links in it than chain mail," said David, shaking his head. "This guy, Eitan, seems to be implicated right down the line. Quite a character by all accounts, especially that which you give of your meeting with him." He glanced at the satnav announcing that they were very close to their destination. They swept past impressive tall modern buildings interspersed with apartment blocks and surprising open spaces, which prevented the claustrophobic feelings of some cities. They turned off a small roundabout, into HaRav Tana Street, and then drove to a barrier. After giving their assumed names to security, which Shira had used in her earlier call to Rebekah, they drove into the carpark of a small apartment block and walked to the entrance at the rear. The building was set back from the others, behind which was a courtyard with palm trees set amongst planters, containing various exotic shrubs with a grassed-over area around which seats were placed. Some steps led down to a small swimming pool surrounded by pillars giving it a neo-classical touch. They entered through glass doors into the cool air-conditioned interior set on light grey marble flooring. From there, after the receptionist made a call, they were directed to a corridor at the end of which was the apartment entrance. Seconds later the entrance signal lit green, then the door clicked open to reveal a surprisingly tall, upright woman, with long grey hair tied back, dressed in a kaftan and wearing darkened glasses.

Shira outstretched her hand, "*Shalom*, I am Colonel Shira Levy and this is Major David Efron. We are with Shin Bet."

Rebekah smiled; she looked far younger than her years, Shira thought, as they shook hands. "Ah, your motto, *Magen veLo Yera'e;* (Shield and not be seen) very apt for those who may be looking into my husband's affairs. Come, please."

She led the way into a spacious living room looking out onto a paved exterior area on which was set a table and chairs, with a low wall beyond overlooking the palm trees of the courtyard. She gestured to two comfortable arm-chairs before taking a seat on a large sofa, sighing as she began, "I was wondering how long it would take you, after my request for a full post mortem was rejected. I worked in security for far too long not to smell a cover-up. The saddest part of this is that my Antoni survived so much, the horrors of Treblinka, two uprisings in Warsaw, combat in the Second World War; then fighting the British, followed by the Arabs. He never stopped fighting for Israel up to the day he died." She shivered for a moment then tried to suppress the emotion within her but choked, placing her head in her hands.

Shira went across to her taking her hand. "We know," she said softly, "Genuinely we are here to help and root out an evil within our society that we believe is behind your husband's death, together with others. If you could tell us more of him and what you know about his work, it may assist us." She patted Rebekah's shoulder then returned to her seat.

"Thank you," Rebekah whispered, "You know, he could not forget his past yet rarely mentioned it. Antoni was a troubled man haunted by his experiences but motivated by one terrible principle, that Israel must never be vulnerable nor should our people ever again suffer whilst the world ignores us. I call it terrible because it motivated and justified his involvement in terrible things. He dedicated himself to his work and I know he had a reputation for ruthlessness. I saw a different Antoni; a man who cared for me and who provided a secure home for us and our daughters. Sure, he could not show love, however important it is to demonstrate that;" she shrugged, "but he showed his affection in different ways." She stopped, realising she had given a monologue without considering her visitors.

Shira took the opportunity from the pause, "I am so very sorry for your loss, Rebekah. We know he fought for Israel, for the Jewish people, and that he had suffered from exposure to terrible, unspeakable atrocities and tragedies in his formative years. Both David and I have been in combat and so we know a little of how this can brutalise a person. I recently lost a dear grandfather at the behest of a greater evil gripping this country and I fear that may have been behind the fate of your husband. That is why we are here."

Rebekah's eyes sharpened and Shira knew she had already gained credence and empathy from what followed as the older woman spoke with utter clarity. "I am eighty-one years of age but you know, I do not feel it. Sadly, I am too old now to practise law but I would love to. You know why I left it? My skills were being hijacked to justify the misdeeds of others, and allow Israel to blatantly breach international law. Antoni had a friend, Rafi Eitan; you know, the one who kidnapped Eichmann and worked for Mossad. They were thick as thieves and took pride in carrying out missions of dubious legality, or total illegality, which they joked that it was my job to cover up. They were so brazen. Their attitude was that the end always justified the means and even boasted about it. Later, there were others like the shadowy Omer Ravid, who was an odious individual, who I think worked for Kidon, and the former head of Mossad, Isser Harel, who Antoni said still wielded huge power after he left." She shook her head, sighed and stood up, "I am sorry, I have not been a good host. Will you join me in an Arak and grapefruit juice? This is a weakness of mine."

David then intervened, "Mrs Zielinski, I have to impress on you that we are dealing with matters of national security here. We thank you for your offer which we must decline. I think we should concentrate on the substantive issues that we need to investigate and we have some serious questions we want to put to you."

Shira's retort was sharp, loud and abrupt, even taking David by surprise by its commanding tone, although he was playing their pre-agreed strategy. "Major, enough! Rebekah has been through a great deal and has invited us into her home. Please treat her with the respect that she deserves." She addressed her remarks directly at him and he felt her absolute authority, which would have made many junior officers wilt. She then turned to Rebekah, "Forgive my colleague's directness. We would be delighted to accept your hospitality and I, for one..." she shot David a withering look, "... would love a drink of Arak and my colleague will join me."

As Rebekah fixed the drinks, Shira looked over at David, giving him a large wink and an impish smirk, which he had to suppress laughing at; a skill he had honed over many years from his mischievous days at school right through his military career. Minutes later Shira had clinked her glass to Rebekah's and they both proclaimed, "*Mazel tov!*" (good luck). Then Shira turned to David, "*Mazel tov,* Major!" putting her glass to his, and he feigned a sullen but audible response. Shira then asked, "Were there any specific areas of his work you might recall from the 1950's and 1960's that were, perhaps, a little unusual?"

Rebekah was now more visibly relaxed as she responded, "I saw and witnessed so many things that astonished me but was staggered one day when Rafi and Antoni brought this man back to the apartment. They were drinking together until after midnight. He was German and I remember he had a deep facial scar running from his cheek up to his ear. I recall he was tall, gallant in an old-fashioned way, with a thin moustache like that film star, Clark Gable. He wore a monocle and had impeccable manners whilst being a touch flirtatious...yet I found him somehow menacing. They began joking and, to my horror, this man turned out to have been a prominent Nazi who was a leading member of the SS; and there he was in my home, being entertained by a former inmate of Treblinka. I was a young, freshly married girl of twenty-two but, even then, I wondered what kind of world we were in. The memories of the Holocaust haunt us today but back then it was fresh in the minds of us all, with more and more abhorrent stories emerging from that dark era. I was incredulous that this man was in our home, but Antoni laughed it off and I remember the phrase he used, '*Love your enemies means hate your friends*', which he said was a quote from Benjamin Franklin. I remember the meeting vividly because I was so shocked that this man was there. It was May 1963 and they were discussing a secret mission that they said was one of the greatest challenges they had ever faced, but did not mention what it was in front of me. I never knew until after Antoni died what he could never share with me."

Shira's heart leapt a beat in the brief pause that followed, "Perhaps you can help us with this information?" she ventured. David too recognised they were on the cusp of a revelation and was transfixed, the sense of anticipation overwhelming.

At first, Rebekah did not appear to react in response, but David and Shira began to realise she needed to balance the magnitude of what she may share with them with the loyalty she felt for her husband; "Antoni was a good man, in many ways misdirected but is that any wonder? He witnessed more horrors that most human beings would ever experience in a lifetime. I think they used him in many ways but he rarely had, or expressed any regrets. I think another Arak is needed." She stood and took their glasses and this time David said nothing. "You know he was a great chess player, my Antoni, and became well-respected, proving a challenge to some of the Grand Masters, many of whom live here. You know that Be'er Sheva is the home of Israel's national chess centre, and some say it is the chess capital of the world." She handed the glasses back to them as Shira and David nodded their thanks, yet were desperate to know more of what she could tell them. Shira spoke first, "We believe that your husband was killed because of what he knew and, if you can help us, we can take steps to avert a great threat to our nation from within. I met Rafi Eitan, and I know what these people are capable of. What they are attempting now, in the name of Israel, I do not think even he would have sanctioned."

Rebekah sighed, "All my adult life, I have been around those wielding power and seen what it can do to people. '*Power is a dangerous thing. Be careful that you don't abuse it or let it make a tyrant of you.*' Have you read *Jo's Boys*, by Louisa M Alcott? No matter, but maybe I have something for you. I think it is time." She walked to an ornate, colonial-style sandalwood cabinet, retrieving a polished wooden rectangular box with brass corners and an inlaid pattern on the top. She placed it in front of them and retrieved a key from a small drawer under the table. As she inserted the key she said, "Antoni wrote no letters to me in his lifetime despite being away a great deal and, of course, in those days there were no mobile phones or texts. He used to call me but invariably he could not tell me where he was or what he was doing. Such was life, but he provided for us generously. I knew this was his box of personal papers and when he died, I decided to open it and discovered an envelope addressed to me. No-one else has seen this and I will entrust it to you on the condition it is never made public."

This time it was David who responded but in a less officious tone than previously. "Rebekah, all of the information we have used to pursue our enquiries has been suppressed and it has been a herculean effort to reach the stage we have. Many lives have been lost already, taken by a group of fanatics who are acting with an extreme right-wing agenda. Two nights ago, we lost a valuable friend and patriot who was shot because of what we have unearthed. Only twenty-four hours ago, my colleague here, suffered the loss of her beloved step-grandfather, with whom she was very close. He was ninety-six years old, living quietly in an English village. That is a measure of the evil we face. I can assure you that whatever we unearth now will be hidden by the authorities after this is over, for state security reasons."

Rebekah's face softened as she turned to Shira, "I am very sorry for your loss; it seems we are all affected by what is going on. Please, I want you to copy this and use it for my Antoni, for all who have tragically died, and, not least, for humanity. That is why I ceased being a lawyer for them, because I despised the deadly games I saw being played out." She reached inside the box and pulled out a large cream envelope, which she handed to Shira, who examined the front as David crossed to her. On it was written 'S'lach na' (I beg forgiveness) then just the name Rebekah in long scrawling handwriting sloping to the right. Shira pulled a few A4 sheets of paper from the envelope, looking across at Rebekah, as though seeking reassurance, who nodded to her with a resigned smile of sadness. The sheets were type-written without double spacing, reflecting, David thought, the fact that Antoni was not a man used to paperwork or reports. As Shira unfolded the paper, Antoni leant over her and their eyes widened as they read.

Sunday May 26th 2019

Dearest Rebekah,

When you read this, I shall be gone for the last time, hopefully judged to be worthy of olam ha-ba (the world to come) where one day our souls may unite again.

I know I have not been a good or attentive husband but I have tried to provide for you and our wonderful daughters.

I have never lost sight of how fortunate I was that a young, talented, and beautiful woman with a bright future in law could accept the advances of an uneducated Jew from Poland. You have been my sanctuary, for which I rarely thanked you, nor demonstrated the love you deserved in a world which is more evil than I once could ever have imagined; an evil which has tainted my soul and corrupted my being.

I witnessed my parents being beaten by Nazis as they were led away; the last time I saw them before they died because, as you know, my family were all slaughtered in the Holocaust. I saw the horrors myself of the death camps, the barbarity, and the pointless bestial cruelty. My conscience tortured me as I was complicit in working for the Nazis or I would not have survived. I hated the perpetrators and, after Treblinka, I killed countless times without conscience or feeling, each victim grimly satisfying my need for vengeance, although I never felt I did. Survival has been my instinct which became an obsession; after a time, this was not for my survival, but for that of my race which subsequently became represented by Israel.

Somewhere, I lost all sense of humanity or justice, the end of protecting my race justifying any means necessary and now I must unburden my conscience which only surfaced some months ago after decades of cold indifference to the tasks or missions I carried out. I killed without thought for the victim or compassion because I had none. That was all left behind in the camps, in the sewers of Warsaw, and in the massacres. Then, just over two months ago, I experienced an epiphany; a realisation of my own horrific complicity in events which placed me in a category which was no better than the Nazis. I now need to unburden myself before I die and can only beg for your forgiveness and, if you choose to share this, that of my daughters.

In 2018, my very special friend, Rafi Eitan, and I nearly came to blows on a night that changed me. Imagine that, two ninety-odd-year-old men fighting in a restaurant in central Tel Aviv. Rafi had just returned from a trip to Germany where he endorsed the far-right AfD Party, stating that their movement was the answer to Europe's problems. The AfD epitomise Nazism openly which is no shock because but we all knew in Intelligence that former Nazis had spread their influence and infiltrated every part of society after the war, especially in the United States, Britain, and Europe. Nazis even had meetings in Spain, Argentina, and Chile where they wore their uniforms. We all knew, but no politician dare speak of it, hence those of us who had the courage of our convictions began hunting these people down. Simon Wiesenthal hunted them peacefully but here in Israel we took whatever steps were necessary to ensure our security and my boss, Isser Harel, recognised the need. My argument with Rafi was a turning point in my life but, alas, too late to change what I have done.

In the early days, in the shadow of the Holocaust, we were angry and would do anything to protect our homeland. In 1952, we attempted to assassinate the German President, Konrad Adenauer, because we believed our Prime Minister was pandering to the Germans who were failing to properly compensate us with reparations. Why? Because we wanted to do business with their armaments industry. You know who gave the orders at this time? Menachem Begin, the same man who became our Prime Minister. At least, he was not a weasel. When their scientists began working on Egyptian weapons development, we took them out, kidnapped them, or applied pressure, using their families to assist in persuading them of the errors of their ways, and I was proud of that. This was official covert policy sanctioned by our government and why not? Rafi and I worked well together but we also recognised that, sometimes, former enemies have their uses; hence I was part of an operation to recruit Otto Skorzeny, the Nazi commando leader, to Israeli Intelligence. Pragmatism sometimes overrules our principles, although I had little time for principles other than the protection of Israel. This guided my actions and was my motivation for my willing involvement in some events which have come to haunt me as the shadows fall upon my life.

When Rafi endorsed the AfD, I realised suddenly that I had been blinded by my experiences and I had lost sight of the humanity which we need. It had been brutalised out of me and I had become what I hated...I was a Nazi in all but name. I raged at Rafi and could have shot him on the spot in my anger but then I, too, realised that he was a victim. I had been recruited after the war for ultra-secret operations under the direction of those not always working for government. We were useful to them but operated in a clandestine manner. We were our own organisation operating under our own rules and Rafi had been my immediate boss. In the mid 1950's, our key priority became the obtaining of nuclear weapons by whatever means under the direction of Shimon Peres. Obtaining such weapons and material, then covering up our methods, was the key element of our work in which I regret I involved you. For this, I beg your forgiveness.

Our priorities were to ensure Israel would have the ultimate deterrent of nuclear weapons. I attended meetings with Eitan, Isser Harel, Shimon Peres, and the Prime Minister at which the constant mantra was 'materials and production'. David Ben-Gurion was determined that Israel would be a nuclear power in all but name. Uranium was the stumbling block as we possessed very little and so we mounted operations to steal or procure this from every source we could, including the US. I know Shimon Peres was directly involved in a successful covert move to obtain a huge amount, but the source was kept secret from us.

I now regret that the protection of my race became an obsession that caused a blindness. My blindness to humanity led me to do some terrible things that I can never share but there is one which I need to unburden. By 1962, our nuclear weapons development had made great strides. All of us close to power in the military believed these were the critical key to protect Israel and prevent anyone daring to ever again attack us, or attempt the annihilation of our race. Suddenly, there was a problem in the youthful US President John F. Kennedy. He demanded that there was no proliferation of nuclear weapons in the world, specifically informing Israel that he would not tolerate our nation developing such a capability. I attended meetings, some chaired by the Prime Minister, David Ben-Gurion, at which we explored all options.

As the situation became more critical, I was summoned to an ultra-secret meeting chaired by Isser Harel, at which time we were informed that Israel may suffer the unthinkable, US troops on our land and the destruction of our weapons. Vice President Lyndon Johnson was on our indirect payroll and he had made it clear that if he were president, the matter would no longer be a priority. The Nazi who I helped recruit to work for Israel, the monster I had once sworn to kill, offered to form a hit squad unit with one aim, the assassination of the president of the United States. This was to be an operation without any official sanction or knowledge, and those recruited to this unit would be either from former crack Nazi special forces or those who had emigrated to Palestine in more recent years with ties to Eastern Europe. This was to provide a confusing picture whereby Israel was completely distanced from the operation in the event of discovery. Skorzeny said he had links with organised crime in the US, specifically Sam Giancana, who was head of the Chicago Mob or Mafia, to whom he could turn for assistance.

My dearest, I regret I volunteered to be part of this operation together with a number of eager militant 'idealists'. Skorzeny selected those with the necessary organisational skills or, more importantly, those who were trained marksmen, including our youngest team member, a radical who I shall come back to, one Omer Ravid.

Before that fateful day, we rehearsed and rehearsed with split-second timing to obtain 'the perfect triangulation', as it was termed, and four shots were fired, not three as is always reported. There were two teams of snipers, one German and one Israeli with each of us having a reserve in case of unforeseen circumstances or discovery. Only one person fired a shot from the Texas Book Depository and it wasn't Oswald nor did we use the weapon which the subsequent story claimed he used. We had high-powered precision rifles and the bullets were removed or swapped in the cover-up.

The operation was huge, requiring the preparation of a major dis-information strategy plus follow-up hit squads after we left the US who would be provided by Giancana. Money was no object and we bought off or threatened officials, police officers, and even judges, together with witnesses. Lee Harvey Oswald had no part in what took place and truly was the 'patsy' he claimed to be. There was not one victim that day but many, many, more as people decided to volunteer information to the Warren Commission, inside which we had people working for us, many without even realising it. Witnesses were murdered or died in mysterious circumstances. There is much more I could tell you and more I cannot, because much of what went on in the immediate aftermath of the shooting was shared only on a 'need to know basis' to protect the identity of those involved and the secrecy of the operation.

Afterwards, those organising the operation did everything to conceal the truth under the direction of Werner Naumann, the former Reich Minister for Propaganda in Nazi Germany, who had succeeded Goebbels and was a personal friend of Skorzeny. He was a master of mis-information and falsified TV assassination recreations, spread crazy conspiracy theories, published contradicting marksmen and weapons expert opinions, and exaggerated witness evidence to confuse the public and create conspiracy theory fatigue. This has continued since, and the modern version of this operation swings into place every time something new brings the assassination back into the public eye.

Years later, people were still being murdered to cover up the evidence and one of Skorzeny's last operations in 1975 was to co-ordinate the murder of Mafia boss Sam Giancana, who had become a loose cannon and was due to give evidence to a committee on mob involvement in the Kennedy assassination. Giancana was trading information for freedom and his knowledge of what happened could have been catastrophic. He was shot dead at his home and no-one was ever convicted or even arrested in connection with the shooting. Ironically, Skorzeny died less than three weeks later from lung cancer."

Now, I look back at this and so much more and I feel horror at my actions. I am tortured with guilt for becoming part of a crazy policy where state-sponsored killing becomes the norm or a 'solution' when I know it lowers us to the status of Nazis. Oh, my dearest Rebekah, what have I done? Can you ever find it in yourself to forgive me?

When Rafi retired as head of our clandestine unit, officially, because those of us involved in our line of work seldom do, Omer Ravid took over and he would stop at nothing in the pursuit of his aims. This uncompromising drive was a trait I admired initially but later I came to distrust his motives and harboured a profound dislike of him. However, his single-minded strength of leadership made me and others want to follow him, including Rafi Eitan. Ravid is the one to watch and he represents a terrible style of leadership, inspiring blind loyalty in others, through a belief in his own will that I can only compare to Adolf Hitler. But, there is one essential difference; this man represents the deep state operating by stealth. I understand that he now seeks to break out of his secrecy and become a leader. If you have any influence after I am gone, you should warn others about him; perhaps my words might assist in discrediting him. At a recent meeting, he spoke about the need to use nuclear weapons against neighbours in a first-strike policy to protect Israel, starting with Iran. This is a crazy idea; he is a fanatic and he is a danger to Israel. I told him so myself recently, causing him to enter into a rage bordering on the hysterical, shouting that no-one should ever question his motives or his authority. He finished his tirade by saying that I had outlived my usefulness, which, I suppose, prompted me to write this as I took his words as a genuine threat.

Now I have unburdened myself to you, I can only thank you for the wonderful support you have given me throughout a long life during which I came to value you like no other, and regret not having told you so, but such spoken words do not come easily to me. I have rarely used or even understood the word 'love', but is it too late for me to say to you that I love you now as never before? If nothing else, I hope that you might embrace that thought.

Goodbye, my dearest, good night,
'S'lach na'
Antoni

Shira spoke first, "That was a man in the depths of contrition. I am truly deeply sorry. This must have been hard to read."

David added, after a pause, "This letter is the key to what we needed." His voice softened – "Thank you, Rebekah." The elderly woman embraced them both before they left and had tears in her eyes as she bade them good luck.

As they drove away, David turned to Shira, "I'm thinking back to those powerful prophetic words Rebekah said Antoni Zielinski used, "*Love your enemies means hate your friends.*" I wonder how a committed former SS officer like Skorzeny could have become so embedded in Israeli intelligence and, even more so, with Zielinski, who had a lifelong hatred of Nazis?"

26

Mutual Deterrent

Moshe Gellner had summoned them for a breakfast meeting, in advance of the 'council of war', by which he now referred to the meeting scheduled for 2pm. As they ate on the terrace, he marked up on a white-board some of the essential elements of evidence they had gathered. "The unifying factor behind virtually every aspect of what we have unearthed is the drive to obtain nuclear weapons and eliminate the threat of advanced weapons being developed in potentially hostile nations. On a more sinister note is a desire to cover up what happened in November 1963, and eliminate any reference to Omer Ravid's involvement in order to facilitate a coup d'état. Zielinski's letter gives us the critical missing evidence which Shira correctly identified we needed. David, your boss, the Mossad director, requires that you report this morning, I recall. I suggest you state you wish to arrange a security briefing with the Prime Minister."

"You mean we brief Netanyahu first?" David said uncertainly. "What if…the unthinkable?"

"Did I say 'first' David? I never have trusted politicians even though most of them are former military colleagues. However, after we have acted, we must immediately involve the political establishment otherwise we undermine the very democracy which, after all, is what we purport to protect. After reading Zielinski's letter, I am off to Tel Aviv to do some more research on the Nistarot database on our former PM, Mr Shimon Peres, who seems to be well entangled in this; especially in the obtaining of a large amount of uranium. Benjamin, as you have come with a fresh mind to this, can you start preparing the dossier and report which we will present to the PM. David and Shira, I think we need to prepare a separate presentation for our military colleagues, which omits the key sensitive issues, concentrating merely on the imminent threat to Israel. There must be no reference to the historical events we have unearthed." Shira looked across at David, smiling, and he shivered inside with a delightful awareness, evoking a brief thought of the intimacy they had shared the previous night.

Mehedi added, "I will do some research on our friend, Skorzeny, and see if we can dig out more as he keeps appearing and seems to have played a central role in the Kennedy plot and other assassinations."

At 9am, David called Mossad HQ and there followed a heated exchange when he refused to impart the intel that he was being asked for, or attend a meeting. "All I am asking for, Yossi, is a meeting with Benjamin Netanyahu on an urgent matter of national security, which I am sure he will permit you to attend. I need to collate a full report, so I suggest later this week. The issue is so sensitive, I regret I am unable to share it with you further." The director was furious and after threatening David that he could have him arrested, he realised that he was getting nowhere. Finally, he agreed to speak to the Prime Minister himself and attempt to organise a meeting for the following Friday.

At 12noon, Moshe returned and they gathered at his request on the terrace as his housekeeper served a lunch of *falafel* (chickpeas and broad beans fritter), wrapped in *taboon,* (flatbread) with salad. Wine was served; a Nana Winery Chenin Blanc, which Moshe claimed was another of the finest wines in Israel. As they ate, he briefed them on his findings. "As the saying goes, and we seem be using this more, 'you could not make this up'. A massive historical irony; our biggest haul of uranium in the 1950's was, in effect, an indirect gift from Nazi Germany." There were gasps around the table and a drawn out, "No way!" from Benjamin. Moshe continued, "Our friend, Shimon Peres, was fixated on obtaining nuclear weapons and was appointed by Prime Minister David Ben-Gurion as Director General of the Ministry of Defense at only twenty-nine years of age. Although Ben-Gurion was officially Minister of Defense, as well as Prime Minister, it was Peres who was effectively minister. The records on Nistarot were incredible reading and I was staggered as I followed a lead recording a request for a private meeting by a French former Deputy Prime Minister and Defence Minister, Jules Moch. As you hear what I tell you, you might also bear in mind he was a French representative at the Geneva disarmament conference throughout the 1950's."

Sunday 21st October 1956 – 1:45pm
Commune de Sèvres, South West Paris

The black Citroën DS swept down the newly surfaced D910 after a brief visit to The Palace of Versailles, which Shimon Peres had requested. Dressed in a tailored dark grey business suit, and wearing a blue and red striped tie, he was feeling singularly unprepared for a meeting about which security advisors were equally puzzled. The message from Jules Moch had been brief but Peres knew him and felt compelled to honour the request.

He had known Moch for many years as a prominent French politician who had served as a minister in various roles, including defence in 1950/51. He had earned the respect of Peres in building up and modernising the French army. He was a regular visitor to the new state of Israel, with which, as a Jew, he felt an affinity, and had built up a close relationship out of mutual respect of their similar roles. Moch recognised that Peres was creating a highly effective, well-trained and well-equipped defence force in Israel. Before moving to defence, Moch had served as deputy prime minister and, as current French delegate to the UN disarmament commission, he had gained enormous international recognition.

The message from Moch had been delivered to Peres personally by an emissary from the French Embassy in Israel and said simply,

'My friend, Shimon, as I become more advanced in years, I am increasingly sensitive to the needs of my second country of Israel. As you know, Israel is of huge importance to me and, as a result, its security is paramount. I need to see you, old friend, because I believe I can gift to you the key which will give access to a resource ensuring the survival and security of Israel for all time. I can say no more and trust that this message will be classified as Top Secret. No-one in France is aware I have sent anything but a request for a diplomatic meeting on disarmament.

As you are aware, there is a covert meeting to consider sensitive 'security issues' in the Middle East which will be held at Sèvres on 22nd October. Perhaps we could meet there without arousing undue interest.

Bivrakah (blessing)

Jules

Jules Salvador Moch

The conference taking place at Sèvres was shrouded in secrecy, but Peres knew that Moch would be in the know as a prominent political figure. The need was to ensure free access to the Suez Canal, which had been unilaterally nationalised in July 1956 on the orders of President Nasser of Egypt. The company that had controlled the Suez Canal had been under joint French and British control. The aim of the meeting at Sèvres was to co-ordinate the varying interests of Britain, France, and Israel. If Israel could be encouraged to attack Egypt, this would reduce Egypt's capability to resist a joint Anglo-French operation in a military action to retake the Suez Canal. All parties to the conference recognised the critical need to ensure secrecy in the negotiations and avoid a hostile reaction from other nations, including allies such as the United States.

The Citroën swept through the tall iron gates and down a short drive to a small two storey isolated house with brown louvred wooden shutters either side of the windows. As they drew up, two men in dark suits approached the car, one standing in front holding his hand up, whilst the other came over to check the occupants. On seeing Peres inside, he saluted, standing to attention, whilst the other man waved them forwards to a cobbled courtyard. Within seconds, Peres had been ushered through a heavy slatted door and down a corridor with a stone floor to a large room, outside which uniformed armed gendarmes were standing. Inside, sitting at the end of a simple farmhouse table, was a smiling Jules Moch. He was dressed in a black suit, his greying hair swept back, with his small moustache and thick-lensed rounded glasses adding to what Peres thought was an image of a pre-war political caricature. He rose and shook Peres's hand warmly, adding both hands to emphasise the gesture. "*Shalom*, my friend, come share some wine; we have much to discuss."

A bottle of Beaujolais was brought in by an orderly dressed in a maroon waistcoat, adding a bizarre, theatrical touch to their simple surroundings. After pouring them both a glass of wine, Moch began earnestly,

"*Mon ami*, what I tell you now must never be shared, other than with your most trusted and, even then, you must never reveal my identity in this."

He removed his glasses, blinking for a moment as though reflecting on whether to continue. Then lifting his glass, he touched it to Peres's. "*Lecháim.*" He emptied his drink, pouring another, then continued, "In the war, I was in the *Maquis* (resistance), and in 1942, I was informed that there was a stash of uranium being held in a warehouse under German guard in Toulouse. We had heard that uranium was critical to the production of an atomic bomb and that there were many competing factions trying to get hold of it. We were aware that the Germans were anxious to keep the location secret from the Allies because of the danger of Allied bombing and they thought it was safer in France than in Germany. My commander was a communist with ties to Russia and so I decided to organise a private raid using only those I could trust, and remove the uranium. In June 1944, just after D-Day, we conducted a covert operation and actually knocked through the wall of the warehouse from the adjoining building whilst staging a diversionary attack on a military vehicle compound which was opposite. We removed what we could and then covered the breach in the wall, which was not discovered. Shimon, my friend, it was incredible but we managed to steal forty-nine tons of uranium, and conceal it, before we were liberated in August. My commander never knew and those under my command never really understood the importance of the loot. It was placed in a barn on a farm near Verfeil and that, my friend, is where it has remained. I am one of two people left alive who knows its whereabouts and the other is my brother-in-law who owns the farm and who, incidentally, is also Jewish."

Peres had been listening to the story transfixed but now interjected, "Why was it not recovered after the war? Surely, when you were Minister of Defence, you should have secured it."

"France was in political turmoil and remains unstable under this Fourth Republic," came the reply. "There is little stability and all we see are collapses of government. In any event, part of me knew that this day would come as I witnessed the birth of Israel. I will give this to you but there will be a price. You are seeking to build a nuclear development complex and we, in France, have the expertise and experience; you also need uranium. Quid pro quo, I think. As a result of our discussions and as a gesture of goodwill resulting from this conference on Suez, you will award France the nuclear contract and I will ensure you get the uranium. Do we have a deal?"

Shimon Peres looked directly at Moch askance, then a broad smile crossed his face, "You old *nochel* (schemer), you are truly an Israeli but with a French heart." The two men stood up and embraced, forging an understanding based upon respect, genuine warmth and mutual need.

Three days after their meeting, the '*Protocol of Sèvres*' was agreed with the core aim of toppling President Nasser and regaining control of the Suez Canal. On 29th October 1956, Israeli forces invaded the Egyptian Sinai, followed days later by a British-led attack, triggering the Suez Crisis, which proved disastrous, triggering international condemnation. In less than two years, secret French construction was underway of the Nuclear Research Centre in Israel's Negev desert, later named after Shimon Peres. The existence of the agreement signed at Sèvres for the Israeli attack on Egypt was never admitted by any of those involved, and major attempts were made to cover it up for all time.

Friday 16th March 1962 – 6pm
Gran Hotel Inglés, Calle de Echegaray, Madrid

The atmosphere was tense as they sat in a secluded corner of a raised area of the enormous hotel lobby with columns down each side, dominated by an array of large gold chandeliers beneath which was a polished wooden floor covered with ornate rugs. There were standard lamps set by each seating area creating the illusion of a small 'room' above which fans rotated bringing a welcome cooling. Both men were united in their hatred of the man they were due to meet and all he represented, despite one of them never having met him before. Avraham Ahituv was slim, with dark curly hair, and a neat moustache; he was dressed smartly in a single-breasted lounge suit. He had been born in Germany and had been selected because of his fluency in German, which he spoke like a native. His parents had fled with him to Palestine after the rise to power of Adolf Hitler and the beginning of the Nazi persecution of Jews. He still had vivid memories, as a young boy, of the fear that had infected his family and their community, which had inbred in him feelings of suppressed anger towards former Nazis. Antoni Zielinski was also in a suit but he somehow appeared more dishevelled, with his tie not fastened to the neck, in a shirt which had seen better days.

Two days before, both men had been summoned to a briefing with Mossad Chief, Meir Amit and Rafi Eitan, who was now the Head of Mossad European Intelligence. They had been informed that there was a need to infiltrate the Egyptian weapons programme, which was being staffed by many Nazi scientists. They, in turn, enjoyed security protection afforded by an officer who used to be commanded by the legendary former German commando, Otto Skorzeny. From intel reports, Skorzeny was a freelance mercenary involved in assisting with the training of the Egyptian military and of more clandestine units of Arabs carrying out operations against the British. "He is number one on my list of men I will kill." Zielinski had spat out at the mention of the name.

"He is a powerful figure and may be of invaluable assistance to us." Meir Amit had responded. "We may not like those with whom we do business and, as my friend, the Director of the CIA, Allen Dulles said, *'There are few archbishops in espionage'.* You know who he was referring to? General Reinhard Gehlen, who was Adolf Hitler's Chief of Espionage on the Eastern Front, whom the Americans recruited after the war. We are behind and need to catch up here. Skorzeny works for *'the Gehlen Organisation'* and is, therefore, working for the CIA. Skorzeny's wife is a lady of somewhat loose morals by the name of Countess Ilse von Finckenstein. She is a socialite who likes the attention of prominent suitors. I recently despatched one of our people, the head of our Nazi-hunting unit, *Amal*, Rafi Meidan, to charm the lady. He succeeded…" the Mossad chief shrugged his shoulders dramatically, "and who am I to condemn the proclivities and indiscretions of others? She is under the impression that Meidan wishes to arrange a meeting between her husband, Skorzeny, and a senior representative of the Israeli Government for talks, which he has agreed to. This is where you come in. We want Skorzeny; he is well connected both with influential Nazis who have powerful connections and with those working for the Egyptians. He is also dangerous and he must be made an offer which, if he does not accept, will simply mean he no longer lives."

"Like the Eichmann operation," Zielinski interrupted animatedly. "We bring him here for trial and hang him."

"Sadly, not on this occasion," Rafi Eitan replied, "we are acting here in the best interests of our country. We need this man on our side. We have to recognise *Realpolitik* and the Nazis are still powerful and, in many ways, more powerful than before. They are infiltrating other countries and ideologies using political stealth, which, today, they recognise as more effective than *Blitzkrieg*. We need to work with them to counter those forces in this region who threaten us."

"Then maybe, I hope he does not agree to come over to us," Zielinski stated bitterly. "I swore I would hold a gun to that man, and I want to pull the trigger."

Now they were in Madrid and waiting, after Countess Ilse von Finckenstein had arranged for her husband to secretly meet with two representatives of the Israeli government. Zielinski reached inside his jacket and felt the reassuring and familiar shape of his Walther P38, which had become his sidearm of choice since seizing one from an SS officer he had shot in his days in the Warsaw Uprising. They had been alerted by Rafi Meidan that Skorzeny was staying at the hotel and had business engagements arranged in Madrid. He was due to return to the hotel at 6:30pm when he was expecting to find them in the lobby in an open area, which he had specified for personal security reasons. "Antoni, this is not the time...not yet! Not until we give him the chance." Ahituv looked sharply across at Zielinski, whose fingers were still gripped around his handgun. The large clock in the reception area crept towards the allotted time and at exactly 6:30, the revolving doors of the reception swirled and a large, very tall, bulky figure entered, filling the entrance, carrying a light trilby. He had swept-back fair hair, a neat moustache, and was expensively dressed in a dark tailored suit, complemented by a white top handkerchief. He stopped, glancing around as Ahituv stood, and walked briskly across to meet him. As he approached, Skorzeny smiled broadly, his alert blue eyes softening, "Ah you must be Mr Ahituv, from your foreign ministry, I am charmed and delighted." He spoke his words in English with a clipped accent.

Skorzeny's disarming bearing and ebullient demeanour surprised both Ahituv and Zielinski, who were unprepared, believing he would be arrogant, with a cold character. He was the opposite, full of good humour and bonhomie. Ahituv spoke to him in fluent German as he wanted to get a true feel of who they were dealing with and put Skorzeny at ease. As it was, he appeared completely relaxed and self-assured, snapping his fingers, as he sat down, to a waiter who immediately attended their table. "Ah, Pablo, how is your wife and son?" He placed a 5,000 peseta note in the waiter's hand as he ordered a large Cognac with lemonade, demanding that the others enjoy his hospitality. They both accepted a beer and then Ahituv leant forwards. "I want you to know, Mr Skorzeny, that we are here on orders but that my family fled Germany because of people like you. You know what my real surname name is? Gottfried. I was born in your Fatherland and many of my family died because of the ideals you followed. Today, we make you an offer but, frankly, I do not care whether you accept it or not. My colleague was in Treblinka and saw at first hand the Warsaw Uprising; he wishes to kill you. Just so you know."

To their surprise, Skorzeny laughed, "I am no politician, Mr Ahituv, I am just a soldier who sometimes obeys orders. Many on my side wanted to be rid of me and still do. Ach so, I am used to this and I take no offence. Yes, there were excesses which I played no part in under that *dummkopf*, Himmler, but you know what, I admired Hitler for bringing order and stability. What is wrong with racial policies? I believe you have them in Israel. You prefer Jews to Arabs I think." He raised his glass, then leant across to touch theirs with his. He sat back, pulling a gold lighter from his pocket, and took out a packet of Rothmans King-Size cigarettes. "Damned fine smoke these British chaps produce. Good fighters too. I think you people fought them after us. You see, *meine Kameraden*, we have much in common."

A tall imposing man with slicked back hair in a black bolero jacket approached the table, shaking Skorzeny by the hand, before clicking his heels giving the Nazi salute. "I am honoured to welcome one of the Führer's finest men. From this moment, you pay nothing this evening." They had a brief exchange before the man departed. "Don't look shocked, my Jewish friends," Skorzeny said acknowledging their surprised looks. "He is a friend of German patriots living here in Spain. Here, the Nazi salute is often used. This is normal; Spain is ruled by General Franco, who adopted the ways of other 1930's leaders they came to call fascist dictators. You see, our ideology survives." Ahituv, despite his revulsion at the Nazis, found that he warmed to Skorzeny, who was affable, well mannered, and relaxed whilst seemingly demonstrating a genuine interest in Israel and the ways of its people. It was Skorzeny who brokered the subject of the meeting, making their mission easier. "Gentlemen, I know why you are here; you came here 'not to bury Caesar' but perhaps not to 'praise him' either. I am a friend of President Nasser of Egypt, whilst assisting in military training and co-ordinating the security of their weapons programme. This is stupidly assisted by former scientists of the Reich. I have no loyalties here, but live under constant threat from people like

Simon Wiesenthal who seem bent on hunting any former Nazis, irrespective of their complicity or blame. If you can scratch my back, as they say, perhaps I can scratch yours, *ja?*"

After four hours, Skorzeny thanked Ahituv for his hospitality and excused himself. Zielinski had left them talking an hour before, saying he had business to attend to, when it had become clear that no deal was to be struck that evening. Sums of money had been floated but Skorzeny was more interested in obtaining guarantees for his safety from Jewish units carrying out acts of retribution against former Nazis.

The old-fashioned locks were easy and within seconds Zielinski was in Skorzeny's suite. A large entrance lounge led up two steps to a colonnaded semi-circular area with a bar. A swing door opened to a small kitchen used when the suite was hired out for functions. He went to the side of the kitchen and smiled as he saw a doorway leading back to the hotel corridor providing a staff entrance. In seconds, he had unlocked the door and tested the mechanism to check there was little sound. He took a small container from his pocket, containing light oil, which he applied to the hinges in order to ensure that they would not creak. To the rear of the upper area on one side were double doors, which gave access to an expansive bedroom. A quick search of a suitcase had revealed, amongst the clothing, a shoulder holster, a Luger handgun, a smaller silver Sauer pistol and a number of clips of ammunition for both. There was also a knife, which Zielinski had seen before, in a black and silver scabbard with a slender-shaped handle inlaid with an eagle and swastika. In one corner of the case was an oblong box, which caught his attention. He flicked open two gold clips on each side to reveal a black, white and red ribbon, which was carefully folded, in front of which was the Iron Cross with oak leaves, swords and diamonds. He knew from their research this had been personally awarded to Skorzeny by Adolf Hitler himself. He was tempted to steal the medal as a souvenir but decided that such a move would prompt a storm, if discovered, jeopardising any possible success for their mission.

Returning to the lobby, he saw Ahituv in conversation with a man he recognised as Rafi Meidan in a dinner jacket and white bow tie, together with a tall, striking lady in a long evening dress. "Ah, Antoni," Ahituv exclaimed, "May I present the Countess Ilse von Finckenstein." Zielinski bowed and kissed her right hand. She was slim with shoulder-length auburn hair and her dress was silk, hugging her body like a second skin. Her arm was linked to Meidan's, which Zielinski was surprised at considering her husband was in the vicinity. "I believe you are with your country's foreign ministry?" she asked politely, adding, "I hope you can help my husband, who is being accused of terrible things. The war has been over for seventeen years and we must all move on."

"I think tonight matters will be concluded," Zielinski responded as Ahituv shot him a quizzical look. "We all carry memories of those days, Countess, and, if we take proper steps as a result, we can ensure this never happens again."

"My husband tells me he has business interests to consider in Egypt which may affect his dealings with you."

Zielinski smiled as he replied, "I feel sure that we can overcome any concerns with the choices we can offer."

As Meidan led her away, saying that they were expected for after-dinner cocktails, Ahituv turned to Zielinski, "What was that all about? Nothing has been concluded or agreed yet."

"I will conclude negotiations tonight." Zielinski replied coldly.

"Antoni, I know how you feel but we are not here as assassins. You will not harm or kill Otto Skorzeny and that is an order."

Zielinski responded icily, "One thing this Nazi pig and I have in common is that we only sometimes obey orders. I bid you goodnight." As he walked away, Ahituv knew and understood. He felt the same but equally he recognised that nothing could compare to the real horrors that he knew Zielinski had experienced.

It was 3:30am when Zielinski entered through one of the service doors behind the hotel, rapidly mounting the stairs to the first floor where the suites were situated. He glanced round quickly then entered the deserted corridor he had left just six hours before. In seconds, he was at the small, plain doorway. He drew his gun from his shoulder holster, ensuring it was ready to fire, then slipped soundlessly into the darkened kitchen area beyond. He crept slowly past the units to the swing door, which he inched open without it making a sound. The upper area of the lounge was dimly lit and he could see one of the panelled doors to the bedroom was slightly ajar. He now held his handgun at arm's length at eye level as he inched forwards, his heart-beat quickening and his senses heightened. The room beyond was in darkness and as he attempted to accustom his eyes and edge inside, there was the slightest creak and he heard a movement from the direction of the bed. In an instant he flicked the light switch on shouting, *"Still sein oder stirben!"* (Be still or die) Skorzeny had his Luger pistol in his hand and was half out of bed but he instinctively knew his visitor had the advantage and dropped his weapon, holding his hands up. Despite having been sleeping seconds before, his focus was total and his demeanour calm. "Ach so, this is how you Jews conduct diplomacy? I trusted you and now you betray this."

Antoni moved forwards, keeping his weapon trained on Skorzeny's head; his mind was in a turmoil as part of him wanted to kill this person who represented everything he had suffered from and fought against. "Trust you say; that is rich coming from you." Zielinski hissed, "You cast your mind back, Nazi. Remember Schloss Haigerloch; I was there. You gave your word and opened fire, killing an unarmed scientist; a victim of your brutal regime who had survived Auschwitz and who was forced to work for you. Do you know his name? I will tell you; it was Fritz Gottheiner. His mother, father, sisters and brother all died in the camps. Tell me why I should not do what I want to do now?" He walked closer to Skorzeny, gripping his Walther-P38, his knuckles whitened, straightening his arms even more as if to fire.

Skorzeny was aware his life hung by a thread, but from experience he knew that if he became excited or passionate, it could tip the scales, causing his assailant to fire. His voice was calm as he responded quietly, "Mein Gott; you were one of those commandos?" He sighed deeply – "Yes, there were excesses at that time and I am not proud of what they did to those people in the camps, but I was not involved. I took an oath of loyalty to the Führer and I honoured that until the end. I told you; I was a soldier and I fought for my country. Please imagine, if you can, that your country is being invaded by the Russians, whose cruelty on the battlefield and off was shocking even to us. Imagine there is little hope left and you are desperate to do anything and everything to protect your family, your wife, your mother and your children. You arrived to destroy our last hope of survival, represented by the *Wunderwaffen*. You had the advantage that day but I was a soldier defending my country. It was not I who pulled the trigger but I regret to tell you I would have done. That is what war does to us. You fought in the war as a commando. Ask yourself if you have any memories of things you or those around you have done which others would condemn?" He saw the look soften slightly in Zielinski's face. He knew this was the time to offer what he knew he could deliver. "Please, sit. I have no weapon on me as you can see." He was sitting on the bed and kicked the Luger pistol away from him, gesturing to a nearby armchair. Zielinski sat down but kept his gun trained on Skorzeny. His instinct was still to pull the trigger. "OK Nazi, speak; it had better be good," he said harshly.

Skorzeny looked earnestly at him. "I have no quarrel with Jews or your country, which, incidentally, I admire, but I know it is under threat from Egypt. I believe you will be with the Israeli Intelligence group, Mossad. A former SS officer, Hermann Valentin, co-ordinates security for the Germans working on Egypt's advanced missile weapons programme. I was his commanding officer and he will obey my orders without question, even now. I can influence the situation through co-operation with him so that no German will wish to continue working there. I propose heading up a unit which will take out some of the scientists working in Egypt and persuade others that they should cease. I will use whatever means are necessary and I always achieve my aims." He uttered the last words with a steely look in his eyes, then raised his hand and made the gesture of firing a gun, whilst imitating the sound of a shot. "Trust me, Mr Zielinski, Egypt's rocket programme will cease and your country will no longer be threatened. I can give your country this, but I want your people to speak to the Nazi Hunter, Simon Wiesenthal, and call his people off my case. We both can deliver to the other something of value or should I say we have a mutual deterrent?"

One hour later, after a hurried meeting with Ahituv and some phone calls to Isser Harel in Tel Aviv, agreement was reached, including a budget requested by Skorzeny, "to cover my costs", as he put it. As the meeting concluded, Skorzeny extended his hand to both men, and to his own astonishment, Zielinski found himself shaking hands with the man he still wanted to hate.

27

Council of War

The first sign of what was to follow was the arrival of a sand camouflaged *Wolf* Armoured Vehicle with a small contingent of heavily armed soldiers from the elite General Staff Reconnaissance Unit or *Sayeret Matkal*. A young officer introduced himself to Moshe Gellner and announced that he was there under the direct orders of Lieutenant General Aviv Kochavi, the Chief of General Staff of the IDF. They had been tasked with ensuring the security of the house, which would now be under 24-hour guard. Mehedi proudly announced to the others that this was his former unit, drawing a response from David, *"Sociomat"* (Egoist), to which Medi responded with a two-fingered gesture. Shira intervened, "I think, little boys, we should adopt a little more decorum for our visitors." They began gathering in the large dining room of Moshe's home, which had tapestries depicting biblical scenes on one wall, with oil paintings of Israeli landscapes on another; a long modern sandalwood table on two chunky rectangular supports ran down the centre of the room, with eight matching chairs, beyond which was a long window hung with blinds overlooking the garden and palm trees beyond. A large monitor screen had been placed in front of the window. Suddenly, a rather excited looking Benjamin Weiss entered, running a hand through his blonde hair and shaking his head. "Listen to this, people. On a whim, I decided to pursue a slightly different angle and looked for evidence on record of any Germans snooping around President Kennedy or his security people prior to his assassination. There is a CIA report of a conversation between a group of ex-Nazis at a dinner in July 1963 during which one of those present stated that if Kennedy threatened the Eagle's Nest in Argentina, he would need to be dealt with. Apparently, there were reports at the time, being taken seriously, that Hitler had set up a base there. One of those present was Reinhard Gehlen, who you may recall was a former Nazi Head of Espionage on the Eastern Front. By this point he was working for the CIA and filed a report. Incredibly, the guy who masterminded the rockets which took men to the moon, Wernher von Braun, was also present. It seems that Kennedy had attended a meeting during a visit to Berlin in June of 1963, when he had given an assurance that any Nazi bases in Argentina would be eliminated."

"*Keebineemat!* This gets more and more insane," Moshe exclaimed. "More motives there to add to the crazy mix."

They were interrupted by the entrance buzzer and the IDF officer announced that their visitors were arriving. The Chief of Staff had made it known to Moshe, who trusted him implicitly, that he could not be seen to be involved as it compromised his position with the PM. It would need to be co-ordinated at a lower level and passed off as a Mossad operation. The cover story was that Moshe Gellner had reported that he had evidence, through contacts within Mossad, of a terrorist cell with sensitive connections to members of the Knesset operating out of Tel Aviv. He had requested military assistance, which, as a trusted relatively recently retired general, he was given without question. In the event the operation went wrong, the Chief of Staff's position was unaffected. It had been agreed that Brigadier General Malachai Rosen, the former head of special forces, would command the operation, which would enable it to be dubbed a somewhat clandestine affair, if required, minimising any collateral issues.

As three men were ushered in, Malachai Rosen stood out. He was well over six feet tall with a broad, well-built physique, earning the nickname 'the tank' when he was in command, four years earlier. He had retained a level of fitness from a disciplined daily regime and although aged sixty, he could have passed for someone ten years younger. He had donned his former uniform for the occasion, with his red beret, denoting his paratrooping experience, neatly folded in the epaulette of his jacket and, on entering the room, his sense of command was palpable. He carried a swagger stick, which he had been given by a British officer on joint NATO exercises, practising landings from ships off Haifa in 2008. He had a reputation for uncompromising discipline, balanced by a dedication to the welfare of those under his command, which earned him respect. He was accompanied by Major Yosef Peretz, who operated as a commander in Unit 217 *Mista'rvim,* an elite counter-terrorism undercover unit, and Captain Isaac Malkah of the 5135 Paratroopers Brigade, specialising in airborne and special operations assaults.

After brief introductions, they sat round the table, Moshe offering the seat at one end to Malachai Rosen signifying his position as commander. Moshe then spoke, "We are pleased you could join us as we are facing a grave security threat. This has been uncovered following an undercover investigation into a series of assassinations of former military personnel. For national security reasons, I cannot go into too much detail, but we do know there is a plan for a coup d'état to topple our government and take power by force. I cannot stress too highly how important it is that we act swiftly, and decisively. I can tell you that this is a serious and real threat from within and, as we do not know the identities of all involved, secrecy is essential. What we have unearthed must never be shared with anyone after this operation is over nor at any time in the future. The status, reputation, and security of Israel would be compromised, giving our enemies the opportunity they seek to undermine us. I will now pass you over to David, who served with me in Maglan Unit 212, distinguishing himself in combat."

David now stood up and walked towards the monitor screen, as Moshe pressed a button that closed the window blinds with a hum. Shira was operating a laptop containing the presentation they had both rapidly prepared that morning. David began, "Ten days ago, I was asked by the Director of Mossad to investigate the murder or assassination of a number of men who had all worked in intelligence or on sensitive covert operations. We discovered a common link between them, which was that they had all been involved in a secret unit; one you may have heard of, known as Lekem. This was set up to conduct highly sensitive espionage activities, which included spying on friendly countries and the stealing of weapons data or technologies which might be used as Israel developed our own deterrent. As we all know, our country has pursued a policy of 'deliberate ambiguity' on our possession of a credible nuclear weapon. Keeping our enemies guessing, whilst placating our allies by accepting the non-proliferation of nuclear weapons, has been our strategy since the 1960's. Lekem was officially disbanded in 1986 after the embarrassing exposure of our spying activities in the United States. We had an informant who worked for US Naval Intelligence, who you may have heard of, by the name of Johnathan Pollard."

"I remember the fuss about that bastard," grunted Malachai Rosen in a deep growling voice. "He was a wannabe guy seeking attention, who caused us a lot of trouble."

"You are correct in that," David responded. "We knew that his cover was about to be blown and we were trying to make arrangements for him to disappear, but the then Defense Minister,

Yitzhak Rabin, forbade this. He persuaded the PM, Shimon Peres, that we needed to admit little, claim it was a clandestine operation, not endorsed by government, and allow Pollard's arrest. On that day, Rabin made an implacable enemy of one of the more extreme Lekem operatives, one Omer Ravid." He turned towards the screen, in the centre of which was the word Lekem. Underneath were two names, which were in boxes, Rafi Eitan and Omer Ravid, beneath which were listed those who had been killed or assumed dead, with a brief resume, labelled 'Victim'. Each one had a number, but no name, and a date, followed by a word describing the method of their demise. David continued, "Lekem was disbanded officially, but continued covertly, occasionally under the guise of another name, initially under the control of the legendary spymaster, Rafi Eitan, and subsequently by Omer Ravid. The organisation is not sanctioned by the Israeli government and for many years has recruited more extreme members from our security agencies for the carrying out of assassinations with more of a 'political agenda'. Ravid still runs Lekem, which is more like a personally controlled paramilitary operation, but I will return to him shortly."

He turned back to the monitor, pointing at the victims. "As you can see, there have been seven victims; six were former special forces and died in Israel but one, a nuclear physicist, was killed in England. We now have overwhelming evidence linking all the deaths or disappearances to Omer Ravid."

Yosef Peretz, the young commander, with wiry black hair, from the undercover counter-terrorism unit, spoke, "Why haven't the security forces been involved or alerted before now? If we know who heads this clandestine operation, surely, we can just arrest him."

David raised both his hands in a gesture laying stress to the enormity of what he was to reveal. "If it was a normal situation, yes, but with what we began to uncover, we did not know who we could trust. As I began my investigation, I had no idea what I was unearthing. Records had been altered or deleted and, as a result of that, I knew I was on to something. The day I was tasked with investigating this by the Director of Mossad, I was followed by an agent who, after we met, I realised was a patriot, and one who I now count on as a valued friend." He gestured towards Mehedi, "This is Lieutenant Colonel Mehedi Saleh; he is an officer with a long, outstanding military career, completing this with Sayeret Matkal, and he is a trusted member of our team." He smiled at Mehedi, who responded with a single-fingered gesture delivered with a grin, drawing laughter from around the table. David continued, "I realised very quickly that my investigation was making waves because I nearly became the next victim. I was shot and wounded in an attempt to kill me only ten days ago." There were muttered expressions of surprise from the three military officers.

"I had involved my old friend and commanding officer, General Moshe Gellner, who massively assisted in co-ordinating our investigation and gaining access to deeply classified information. We became aware that a militant group led by Omer Ravid was intent on seizing power through a coup d'état. His ultimate aim is to launch a pre-emptive nuclear strike on Iran and, alarmingly, he is planning to take over our nuclear missile launch facilities at Tirosh. There are many current and former soldiers who would support his aims and we believe he can muster a strong force. We discovered that all the victims on this board had been involved in highly secret and sensitive covert operations which, if revealed, would compromise his standing, and make it impossible for him to assume a role as head of state or even as a dictator. We all know that our country is a coalition with political extremists itching to get hold of power, whether on the right or the left, requiring compromise at every level. Omer Ravid represents the extreme right, holding a belief that Israel needs to assert dominance and secure this region from any threat. Iran, he sees as the pariah state threatening our security through their own nuclear weapons development programme, which he has stated cannot be tolerated. In that, he shares the thoughts of many, but not in the means of dealing with the matter. If this man succeeds, not only is our credibility as a democracy destroyed, but we have the potential for a situation which could trigger World War 3. Iran and Russia are allies and, militarily, jointly involved in Syria. In recent weeks, we have seen Russian forces building up on the border with Ukraine, and it is clear that President Putin is ready to flex his muscles."

"We need to surround our bases with tanks now," growled Rosen.

"For that to work," responded David, "we need to ensure that we select only those we can implicitly trust. Ravid has connections throughout the IDF, with many sympathisers, and many more in the Knesset. With respect, General, I think we need to use stealth here. The evidence we have built up is Ravid's Achilles heel, which is irrefutable, pinpointing his involvement in global assassinations of many prominent people. I regret I am unable to say more other than we know he was part of a group that worked with former Nazi war criminals recruited to work for Israeli Intelligence."

"*Oy Gevalt!*" This time it was Captain Isaac Malkah expressing his shock, "You really have evidence that we worked alongside former Nazis? How could we do that? These people who were responsible for the Holocaust! That is too much to bear." He shook his head, burying it in his hands."

"I'm sorry, but there is more. I can also tell you that we did remove WMD production material from Iraq in 2003, right under the noses of the Americans and the British." There were audible gasps from the military officers present. "Clearly, that was the reason for *Operation Babylon* in 2001, when we sent our air-force in to destroy the Iraqi nuclear reactor, but we have hidden this from the world. One of those who masterminded the secret operation to remove the nuclear material has been assassinated. Ravid was at that time involved, and is now anxious to eradicate all traces of anything or anybody that can threaten his position, status, or ambition. What I can tell you is that we know where this man lives and we think that the best way of avoiding unnecessary bloodshed is to raid his home, and take him into custody. If news then spreads, which we can spread a story through the media, that he had Nazi connections, then those who have associated with him will back away. There is much more that we cannot reveal but the imperative is to strike at the heart of Ravid, who could do irreparable damage to our country, and who puts world peace at risk. I will now pass you over to Lieutenant Colonel Mehedi Saleh who has investigated our mission target." David nodded to Shira, and the screen changed, revealing a schematic drawing of a house and grounds.

Mehedi stepped forwards as David sat down and he felt Shira's hand giving his thigh a reassuring squeeze. Mehedi's style of briefing was brusque and direct. He pointed towards the schematic of the property, "Ravid's house is on Kdoshei Hashoa Street in Herzliya Pituach district. The property is a large six-bedroom villa with spacious grounds stretching fifty metres back from the rear in tiers over a gradient that slopes away from the property. The villa is surrounded by eight-foot walls on all sides. Helicopter landing is impossible because of trees; there are guards just inside the front gates in what appears to be a small barracks. We estimate that he has around thirty armed personnel in the complex. There are heavy metal gates at the entrance and, therefore, in my view, a frontal assault is out as it would require armour and would create a risk of casualties. The central tower in the complex has a squared apex roof but the rest of the villa has flat roof areas, interspersed with ornate framework. Having examined the plans of the property, we know that all bedrooms are on the first floor, which could be accessed via the roof. We have drone footage which will be circulated to you after this briefing. Our intel is that Ravid may be preparing to strike at any moment and, therefore, we think that we should go in as a matter of urgency. We believe that a commando-style operation is the only way. The rear gradient is poorly lit and gives us the opportunity to scale the walls and gain access. Whilst there is an awareness of our investigation, which has cost the lives of two of the victims, they have no idea what we have uncovered, nor will they be expecting any attack, therefore we have surprise on our side. After we have taken the complex, there will be a need for ground reinforcements and I would propose a heavy cordon is put in place externally. I will now pass you over to Colonel Shira Ahava, who has had an outstanding military career and is now working for Aman."

She had a professional presence when she spoke, exuding authority and confidence, "David, Mehedi, and myself would like to go in with the assault team. We are all combat veterans, experienced in paramilitary special forces operations. We possess unique inside information which we can use to persuade Ravid that resistance is futile, and which may prevent further casualties. Ravid is known to me personally, and I want him taken alive. Once we have him isolated, I will need your officers and men to back off in order that we can have privacy with him. I would remind you that he is extremely well connected, and that it is imperative we take him as quickly as possible to prevent him using his considerable influence." She turned to Brigadier General Malachai Rosen. "That is all, sir."

He stood up, straightening his battledress jacket, then, in a deep voice, "You guys in Intelligence always play your cards close to your chest, and then leave it to us to do the heavy work. If it wasn't for my great friend Moshe here, I would be offended by junior officers telling me how to do my job." He smiled at them briefly, and they laughed, recognising the humour in his remark. He looked directly at Major Peretz. "Yosef, we need to deploy 100 special forces personnel immediately, with armoured vehicles, to positions within a block of the Knesset. Inform them, we have intel of an imminent terrorist attack. Get fifty more within a 100 metres of the PM's official residence in Jerusalem this afternoon. Put into effect a military exercise around the nuclear weapons centre at Tirosh with tanks and at least a company with a minimum strength of 250. I want six armoured personnel carriers and fifty heavily armed personnel ready for a frontal assault on Ravid's house, if necessary; we will also need two *Sabrah* light tanks to blast our way in as a backup to the main attack, which I agree should be a special forces operation. We will use smoke grenades combined with teargas to create the initial shock and confusion in the front courtyard, which your force on the ground can launch, once the commandos, under Captain Malkah, are entering the villa. We can co-ordinate by watching bodycam footage of the raid as the operation unfolds. Once the assault is inside the house, your force needs to surround the compound." Peretz saluted, acknowledging the orders. Rosen turned to Captain Malkah, "Isaac, the operation to seize and secure the compound will be under your direct overall command. I want you to draw up plans to involve fifty of your best special forces personnel. As a backup to your operation, I think we need a *Sikorski CH-53* chopper prepared to drop guys in by rope. I suggest we employ stun grenades and non-lethal arms as many of the poor bastards working for this guy probably have no idea what is going on. We can use *M-26* taser stun guns as our first choice backed up by the *Active Denial* pain-beam system. If we can avoid loss of life, that would be preferable. The last thing we want is more press attention with journalists like Yossi Melman and his lot from *Haaretz* sniffing around. Time of attack, I suggest, should be 0300 hours on Thursday, which gives us just thirty-six hours."

28

The Die is Cast

The black Lincoln limousine swept down the boulevard past modest, simple houses and US Ambassador Walworth Barbour mused that this hardly seemed a likely area for the Prime Minister of Israel to live in. He was in his mid-fifties, with greying swept-back hair, and rounded glasses, dressed smartly in a black business suit. Normally, he felt quite at ease in his post, to which he had been appointed by the President two years before, but today was different. His discomfort came from the telephone call he had been woken up to receive from President John F Kennedy that morning at 7am Tel Aviv time.

The friendly soft drawling voice of the President sounded very serious. "Wally, I am calling you from the Oval Office of the White House and I am mighty sorry for contacting you so early in the morning, but it is 11:30pm here. I would not be able to sleep without setting my mind to the achievement of a resolution to the problem that we both recognise we face at this historic time in the history of our relationship with Israel. I deem that this resolution is not only critical for the Middle East, but for the future security of mankind. As you know, I am committed, in conjunction with allies in Great Britain, to reaching agreement with the Soviets on a nuclear weapons test ban treaty. We are close to finalising this but the goal of this entire epic endeavour, towards which we have worked these many years, will be put at risk if we do not stop Israel from developing her own nuclear weapons." His eloquence and conviction, somehow emphasised by his strong Boston accent, were motivating. Ambassador Barbour was utterly committed to the President's strategy; the problem was, the Israeli Prime Minister.

Ambassador Barbour had held meeting after meeting with David Ben-Gurion, who would divert the topic, each time they spoke, to the greater threat from the Arab world, with their professed enmity towards the state of Israel. On rare occasions when Barbour had been successful on obtaining some focus on the nuclear facility at Dimona, Ben-Gurion had waved the matter away by stating that the nuclear plant was dedicated to peaceful purposes only. Barbour had pressed the Prime Minister for dates when US inspectors could visit the Dimona plant to verify its purpose to the world, with more detailed inspections than those previously carried out. He was met with vague responses without any concrete commitment, other than stating such visits were welcomed by Israel. The US had intel that evidenced nuclear weapons development, and that included the involvement of scientists who had previously worked on the Nazi *Uranverein* programme. Visiting consultancy input had been given to the Israelis by Professors Wolfgang Gentner and Erich Schuman, who had worked for the Nazi regime, whilst the CIA had identified that the young Jewish prodigy, Yehudi Krimmer, was a resident scientist working on nuclear missile development. Barbour had raised the issue that Schuman was a former fanatical Nazi who had advocated to Hitler that Germany should use biological weapons against the United States, which, surprisingly, he had vetoed. When the matter was raised with Ben-Gurion, his eyes had assumed a faraway look before responding, "Expedience, dear boy; as Shakespeare said, *'Misery acquaints a man with strange bedfellows'* and no race has encountered more misery than that of the Jewish race in the Holocaust." President Kennedy had sent letters to Ben-Gurion, obtaining similar non-committal responses with platitudes, and his patience was becoming exhausted.

Barbour stated to Kennedy that morning that he was dealing with a man who was impenetrable, and one who would only discuss, in depth, those matters which were part of his agenda, from which *he* would not be diverted. "I regret, Mr President, that his mind is fixated on the security of Israel based upon the foundations of the recent past."

"Then, Wally, he leaves me with little alternative than to destabilise that perception of security. I will draft a message which will leave Ben-Gurion in no doubt as to the United States commitment to peace through non-proliferation. He must understand that America will use force to achieve its aims which are noble and which history will judge to have made a major contribution to the peace of our planet. I pledge that I will not flinch, nor hesitate in the mission upon which I am bound. I am reminded of the great Sir Winston Churchill's words, *'never give in except to convictions of honour and good sense.'* Our cause is honourable and just; we are embarked on a path which will prevent the world from facing a global catastrophe. The message will be wired through to you within the hour, and I want you to deliver it personally to the implacable Mr Ben-Gurion as a matter of urgency."

Ambassador Barbour knew this would not be an easy meeting, as the limousine drew up to the unassuming plain square home of the Israeli Prime Minister. He had called Ben-Gurion's secretary, Liza Shvetz, requesting an urgent meeting. In her usual efficient manner, she had returned his call, within the hour, saying that, despite it being the Sabbath, the Prime Minister had extended an invitation for the Ambassador to meet him at his personal residence. Barbour had read Kennedy's message and for the first time in his career, he felt nervous about the reaction he was about to face. His driver alighted from the vehicle, whilst his secret service bodyguard, who had been in the front, stood outside his car door, his hand inside his jacket resting on his weapon. To his surprise, moments later, the door to the house was opened by David Ben-Gurion himself, with his unmistakeable flamboyant white shocks of hair either side of his head, framing a face which bore a broad smile as he waved. The secret service agent opened the door on the Lincoln and Barbour alighted, carrying his briefcase, feeling the warm air contrasting to the air-conditioned interior of the car. He walked over to the Prime Minister, who held out his hand in greeting then gripped Barbour's with both of his. David Ben-Gurion was small and thickset in build, dressed in an open-neck shirt and baggy trousers, yet his personality somehow made him seem taller. Barbour had seen previously how he could dominate a room, and hold the rapt attention of those present.

"Welcome to my home, Mr Ambassador; please, you are welcome as a valued friend to Israel and to me personally. Let us dispense with formalities in my home, eh, Wally?" He slapped Barbour on the back, who managed a smile despite his apprehension on what would follow. Ben-Gurion led the way up a flight of stairs into a large upper room in which the walls were lined with shelves of books from floor to ceiling. "This is my library," Ben-Gurion announced proudly, "I have no less than 20,000 books here; my life collection in many languages, including ancient Greek, Latin, English, Hebrew, French, Turkish, German, and Russian. I get to know the mindset of friends and enemies by studying their literature. I even have American authors such as Edgar Allan Poe and Mark Twain."

"I trust these books help you recognise the mindset of the United States as your friend," Barbour managed. Ben-Gurion showed him four rooms, each similarly containing bookshelves, and positioned in the last was a small desk and some easy chairs. He gestured to one of them, as he took a seat behind his desk. "Prime Minister," Barbour spoke earnestly, trying to maintain a calm voice, "this morning I spoke with President Kennedy, who impressed upon me the commitment of the United States to the future security of Israel. But, sir, he wishes me to impress upon you that he sees non-nuclear proliferation in the Middle East as inexorably linked to that security. The President says there is a need to demonstrate to the world that Israel has no nuclear weapons, nor has embarked upon their development. To that end, sir, he sees unrestricted inspection of your facility at Dimona as critical to this. He has asked me to stress that the United States will remain a strong ally of Israel, but that your country must understand the strength of our resolve on this issue." He stopped speaking as Ben-Gurion was holding up both hands.

"Please, Wally, I know all this but we must recognise the vulnerability of our nation to the growing threat from Arab states. The United Arab Republic is breaking up, with Syria emerging under an unstable regime, which could become communist. We have the Egyptian threat increasing under the militant Arab nationalism which has been fostered under President Nasser. We need alliances, treaties, assurances or even guarantees to protect our nation, not inspections to placate those who threaten us. You have my assurance that the Dimona reactor has been developed for peaceful purposes, and our relationship must be based upon trust. Imagine, Wally, if I stated to the United States that I wanted to send in teams to ensure you were not developing biological weapons so that the world could trust your commitment!" He threw his hands up in a dramatic gesture, blowing air to emphasise his point before adding, "If our enemies are unsure of our strength, this makes them more careful, no?" He touched his nose as though sharing a confidence. Ben-Gurion's expression became more intent. "In my lifetime, I have seen how the world was able to stand idly by whilst my people were being exterminated under a regime with a commitment to our annihilation as a race. Less than twenty years ago we were being slaughtered not in our thousands, Mr Ambassador, but in our millions." The Prime Minister's use of formal address made Barbour even more concerned about the outcome of his meeting. He attempted to reply, but Ben-Gurion held his hand up, speaking forcefully – "No, please understand me; America lost 400,000 lives in the Second World War fighting; we lost over six million people who were innocent men, women, and children whose only crime was that they were Jewish. We, more than any other race, should be forgiven for wanting to protect ourselves, because never again, never ever again." He buried his head in his hands for a moment in contemplation.

Barbour knew there was no good time; he opened his briefcase with a sigh and pulled out the letter from the President to Ben-Gurion, which he handed to him. "I am sorry, Prime Minister, but I must hand you this message from the President." Although Barbour had already read the contents, he re-read his copy as Ben-Gurion studied the letter.

THE WHITE HOUSE
WASHINGTON
May 18ᵗʰ 1963

His Excellency
David Ben-Gurion
Prime Minister of Israel

Dear Prime Minister:

I welcome your letter of May 12 and am giving it careful study.

Meanwhile, I have received from Ambassador Barbour a report of his conversation with you on May 14 regarding the arrangements for visiting the Dimona reactor. I should like to add some personal comments on that subject.

I am sure you will agree that there is no more urgent business for the whole world than the control of nuclear weapons. We both recognized this when we talked together two years ago, and I emphasized it again when I met with Mrs. Meir just after Christmas. The dangers in the proliferation of national nuclear weapons systems are so obvious that I am sure I need not repeat them here.

It is because of our preoccupation with this problem that my Government has sought to arrange with you for periodic visits to Dimona. When we spoke together in May 1961 you said that we might make whatever use we wished of the information resulting from the first visit of American scientists to Dimona and that you would agree to further visits by neutrals as well. I had assumed from Mrs. Meir's comment that there would be no problem between us on this.

We are concerned with the disturbing effects on world stability which would accompany the development of a nuclear weapons capability by Israel. I cannot imagine that the Arabs would refrain from turning to the Soviet Union for assistance if Israel were to develop such capability--with all the consequences this would hold. But the problem is much larger than its impact on the Middle East. Development of nuclear weapons by Israel would almost certainly lead other larger countries, that have so far refrained from such development, deciding that they must follow suit.

As I made clear in my press conference of May 8, we have a deep commitment to the security of Israel. In addition, this country supports Israel in a wide variety of other ways which are well known to both of us. I will not permit any policy or action which jeopardises the relationship between our two nations but you should understand that the United States will not accept the destabilising effect of nuclear weapons development or deployment in the Middle East by any country. The Soviet Union will be watching, especially after the action we took when they sought to deploy nuclear missiles in Cuba last October. Our policy will be backed by whatever means we have at our disposal including the use of military force. I must impress upon you that this may involve troops on the ground in any Middle East nation which attempts nuclear weapons development.

There is no greater imperative affecting the peace of the world than the prevention of nuclear proliferation. We must take whatever steps are necessary to ensure that the future of mankind is not threatened, demonstrating this inviolate commitment for all humanity.

I can well appreciate your concern for developments in the UAR. But I see no present or imminent nuclear threat to Israel from there. I am assured that our intelligence on this question is good and that the Egyptians do not presently have any installation comparable to Dimona, nor any facilities potentially capable of nuclear weapons production. But, of course, if you have information that would support a contrary conclusion, I should like to receive it from you through Ambassador Barbour. We have the capacity to check it.

I trust this message will convey the sense of urgency and the perspective in which I view your Government's early assent to the proposal first put to you by Ambassador Barbour on April 2.

Sincerely,

John F. Kennedy

He watched Ben-Gurion's expression darken as he absorbed the very real threat couched in careful terms within the letter. The Prime Minister then stood up, and walked over to Barbour with his face set in a grim expression, "I regret, Mr Ambassador, that on this day, I am unable to offer you further hospitality. Our meeting is over."

Less than one month later, on 14th June 1963, Barbour delivered one final sealed message from President Kennedy to Ben-Gurion, the contents of which, even he had not been briefed on. Following the meeting, Ben-Gurion had been heard to express his frustration at an emergency security meeting attended by Deputy Minister of Defense Shimon Peres, the Director of Mossad, Meir Amit, together with Rafi Eitan, and the IDF Chief of Staff, General Tzvi Tzur. In a rare outburst, his propitious words were a misquote from history referring to the English King Henry II about Archbishop of Canterbury, Thomas Becket, "Will no-one rid me of this turbulent man." Two days later, on Sunday 16th June 1963, Israel's first Prime Minister tendered his resignation, saying he "could no longer bear the load," citing that it was "due to personal needs." He spoke to a shocked cabinet, who had not been forewarned, nor had there been any prior consultation.

Wednesday 26th June 1963 – 1:45pm
Rathaus Schöneberg, Tempelhof-SchönebergWest Berlin

His words rang out to rapturous applause and cheers from a crowd estimated to be over 120,000 – *"All free men, wherever they may live, are citizens of Berlin, and therefore, as a free man, I take pride in the words, Ich bin ein Berliner!"* As the President stepped away from the microphone, there was a roar from the crowds, who began chanting, *'Kennedy, Kennedy'*, and he turned to the US Secretary of State, Dean Rusk, with a beaming smile, "I think that went down pretty good," to which Rusk responded, "The Ruskies ain't gonna like it, Mr President; even I'm a little shocked at your departure from the script." The President was elated as he left the platform, shaking hands with the West German Chancellor, Konrad Adenauer, the Mayor, Willi Brandt, and Otto Bach, President of the West Berlin Parliament. As they filed back into the plush interior of the building, with its ornate panelled ceiling and huge chandeliers, the Mayor, who was hosting the event, asked the

President if he could make time for a brief unscheduled meeting. He stressed this should be after the departure of Chancellor Konrad Adenauer, stating that this was a highly sensitive issue of national security. An hour later, five other people joined the President and Willi Brandt in a conference room which included: Secretary of State Dean Rusk, National Security Advisor, McGeorge Bundy, Otto Bach, Heinz Webber of the Berlin Mission, who was acting as interpreter, and Joachim Kruger, who was an administrator in Brandt's office, who would record the minutes.

Willi Brandt opened the meeting, "Mr President, I returned from neutral Sweden after the war, where I had fled to avoid persecution from the Nazis as a result of my membership of the Socialist Workers Party; I found that our country was torn by political intrigue, recriminations, and witch hunts both against Nazis and by Nazis. The Nazis did not fade away in 1945 but re-structured under a new administration based in Argentina. They are highly organised and began a process of infiltration of institutions both here in Germany and in other countries, especially Britain and the United States; there are many sympathisers in both countries who assist them. Their central base is in a place called Bariloche, which they have named *Der Adlerhorst* (the Eagle's Nest) after the secret bunker complex used by Hitler in the war. We know that many former Nazi leaders are now operating from there, including Hitler's former administrator and Head of the Nazi Party Chancellery, Martin Bormann, who we now think is running affairs. This is a matter which we need to keep secret because of the potential to stir up Nazi sympathies, or open up sensitive factions here in Germany. The Nazis are as anxious as we are that their former leaders are not identified, in order to avoid an attack on their base or a manhunt and, therefore, no-one speaks of this. We are in communication with these people through covert channels on matters of mutual interest, but Konrad Adenauer has demanded that such communication ceases. Mr President, the Nazi threat has not gone away. I fear the rumblings of political dissent here in Germany, especially from the young, will be exploited by the Reich in exile if we do not act. We appeal to you for your help as the leader who has brought the beacon of hope in a free world to the new Germany. Your words today have inspired a nation."

The President had been listening intently and he sighed, tapping his hand on the table. "Thank you, Mr Mayor. I have been briefed by the CIA that they have been investigating Bariloche for some time. There are even rumours that Adolf Hitler is in hiding there. I pledge to you that we will apply whatever pressure is needed on the Argentines to eliminate this threat. They are terrified of the former President, Juan Peron, who, despite being in exile in Madrid, still wields enormous influence. He is an admirer of the Nazis, many of whom we know are amongst his social circle. This could be a good time to move to oust them, which will weaken Peron's position."

McGeorge Bundy interjected, "Mr President, the Argentine presidential elections are due this July. Might I suggest that we consider putting some covert units in, under the guise of military advisors, once the dust settles after the election."

As Joachim Kruger noted Kennedy's approval in the minutes, he knew that he needed to contact Walter Rauff, his former SS commander, when Kruger had been a Gestapo administrator in Milan during the war. Rauff was now working for German Intelligence in the BND, but was, in reality, a double agent controlled by Martin Bormann in Argentina.

Friday 5th July 1963 – 3pm
The White House, Pennsylvania Avenue, Washington DC

She had requested a confidential meeting through connections she made when she had met the President in March 1961 at the White House on a visit related to her flying, but to-day was very different. Now the somewhat diminutive figure of Hanna Reitsch waited, sitting beneath a standard lamp in a reception area dwarfed by large paintings of historic figures in an atmosphere of splendour added to by Doric columns. She was dressed in a dark trouser suit and white silk blouse, but had opted that she should not wear the Nazi brooch with diamonds, given to her by the Führer twenty years previously, which she still proudly wore on many formal occasions. Her brown hair was slightly greyed and her blue eyes were sharp and attentive as she waited. After wrestling with her conscience, she had felt compelled to act. "The President will see you now." She looked up to see the smiling face of his secretary, Evelyn Lincoln, who led the way down a corridor into an open area and then to the Oval Office. There, sitting behind a large desk, dwarfed under three floor-to-ceiling windows surrounded by light green curtains, was President John F. Kennedy. He immediately smiled broadly, rose from his chair and walked over to greet her, shaking her hand warmly. He gestured to one of two sofas facing each other either side of a coffee table. She sensed his charisma within seconds. With his boyishly handsome face, his neatly parted thick wavy hair, a ready, disarming smile, he exuded a relaxed, informal style. He was in a shirt and tie, but wore no jacket, which she noticed was hung behind the chair he had vacated.

"I am honoured to meet you again, Hanna." The use of her first name added to the warm informality. "How long is it? I guess it must be a couple of years?"

She responded easily, feeling immediately at ease, "Mr President, it was in May 1961; I was here with the Association of Women Helicopter Pilots. I remember discussing with you my test flight of the world's first helicopter, designed by Professor Focke in 1936. This was when Germany was in its ascendancy." Her eyes lit up with the memory and her words were clipped, spoken with a pronounced German accent.

Kennedy chose not to react to her latter remark. "Hanna, your achievements in the air have become legendary and are admired by the world. I am intrigued, or should I be flattered, that you requested a private audience with me. Normally, I have my brother,

Robert, or my National Security advisors present in meetings but I have respected your request for privacy. I am, of course, hoping that you are not armed." His charm was infectious, with a magnetic confident presence, in which she sensed a slight flirtatiousness. "I have been hearing of your remarkable flying endeavours, setting both world glider endurance and height records. Now I hear you are working for that socialist rogue, President Kwame Nkrumah of Ghana, running a glider school."

"Mr President, that 'socialist rogue' is an inspired man, and he is realising that his strength of leadership may outgrow the constraints of democracy that weakens regimes today."

"Is that a warning to me, Hanna?" Kennedy was laughing. "Here, let me fix us a drink. You gotta try one of my strawberry daiquiris."

He walked over to the large desk, in front of the tall windows, with ornate carvings including an eagle in the centre of the base. The President patted the surface. "This here is *the Resolute desk*. This was presented by Queen Victoria to President Rutherford in 1880. It's made out of the timber from the British explorer ship, HMS *Resolute*, but the most important part of it is this button which sits on the top." He beamed, pressing a large red button mounted on a rectangular box. Seconds later, the door to the Oval Office opened, and a smartly dressed figure appeared in a white jacket. "Hanna, I'd like to introduce you to the most important man in the White House, Eugene Allen. This man serves the drinks, organises food and pretty much everything else I need. Without his input the US government would come to a halt." Allen grinned broadly and bowed to Hanna. "Eugene, can you fix us two large daiquiris, you know what I like and don't go too easy on the rum." Allen chuckled as he bowed again, throwing a friendly glance with a twinkle in his eye to Hanna before leaving the room.

She smiled at Kennedy, "Your manservant reminds me of Heinz Linge with his deferential manner. He was a lovely man who once served the Führer."

Kennedy was aware of her reputation for being forthright, and also that she often spoke openly of her admiration for Hitler, which he decided not to sidestep but to explore further, as he sat in the sofa facing her.

"I visited Germany before the war and went touring there in the summer of 1937 with a buddy, and I recall many people spoke very highly of Hitler back then. That was a different time before the tragedy of war."

Hanna's demeanour suddenly became more serious. "Times have not changed, Mr President; we did not want war with Britain or America. You should have joined us against the real enemy, Russia, and now look at what has happened to the world. We are in another war; the Cold War, which could end in the destruction of civilisation. There are many of us who still believe in National Socialism; not with the terrible excesses of people who went too far like that fool, Himmler, but people who admire strong leadership. Many rue the day that Germany was overrun." Her eyes had a faraway look as she spoke. "In those days we were strong; we had pride; we had a visionary leader and we had a unity of purpose. Those were the greatest times for Germany." Suddenly she looked at him more earnestly. "That is why I am here, Mr President, because we have not changed, and some of us have not adapted. A few days ago, I had dinner with my great friend, whom you know well, Wernher von Braun."

The President leaned forwards. "A great scientist who is helping America fulfil our historic mission to land a man on the moon. I have pledged that we will achieve this within this decade."

"He was also a supporter of the Führer," Hanna retorted. "At this dinner were other former Nazis from that time who now work in the United States. These included Reinhard Gehlen, Hitler's head of Intelligence on the Eastern front, Arthur Rudolph who works with von Braun on your space programme and who was with Wernher working on the V-2 rocket in the war. Also there was Heinrich Müller, the former head of the Gestapo, who now has a new identity and operates under an assumed name; and Hans Kammler, the former SS general who headed up the concentration camp producing the V-2. He also has a false identity and a much-changed appearance." At that moment, the door opened and Eugene Allen entered, carrying a silver tray on which were their two drinks in long glasses, with protruding cocktail sticks on which were stars and stripes flags which he placed on the table between them.

"Two strawberry daiquiris which the bartender assures you ain't lacking in the rum department." The moment seemed somehow lost and irrelevant in the context of their conversation, but Kennedy smiled at him, mumbling a brief, "Thanks, much appreciated."

As the door closed, Hanna continued, "Mr President, there was another at this dinner who was a leading commander of special forces during the war by the name of Otto Skorzeny. Sir, I have to tell you, but you cannot name me as the source, that Müller, who was very drunk, stated that you must be targeted if you attempt to move against the Reich headquarters in Argentina. These men had heard that you discussed eliminating the Eagle's Nest during your recent visit to West Berlin. Skorzeny stated that Müller had given him the perfect motive to assist him in a plan to have you removed. Von Braun and I walked out in disgust, Wernher strongly stating that we did not wish to be witness to such vile talk. I am concerned for your safety, Mr President, because I know what these men are capable of. I came here to warn you. Whilst I may not regret my past, I could never condone or support those who would act in this way. These are the people who tainted National Socialism, and I know that they are serious."

"You choose to mix with some pretty unsavoury people, Hanna," the President remarked drily, then, he picked up both glasses, one of which he handed to her, touching his to hers, smiling disarmingly as he sat back, lifting the tension with his words, "Let us toast our differences because, at least, in a democracy, we are allowed to air them. '*Vive la difference.*'"

"You know, Mr President, I have learned that former adversaries can make great friends and former prejudices can be erased with common understanding. I have a good friend by the name of Yvonne Pagniez, who was a member of the French resistance, and I have forged friendships with many African leaders, despite me knowing that Hitler would have looked down on them."

Kennedy sighed, "The great purpose of my presidency must be to reach out across the world and show those, who may have been adversaries, that America seeks peace and friendship to create a better and more secure future. I can hear the words of Abraham Lincoln, who said, *'Do I not destroy my enemies when I make them my friends.'* Hanna, we live in a democracy but I am grateful for your honesty and the risks you have taken in talking to me. I cannot hide because the world expects more from America, as we bear the torch of liberty, bringing hope, justice and freedom to those in the darkest places. I have been chosen to lead our mission and in that I will not fail, or cower from the forces who seek to destroy me or what I stand for." Before she left, he embraced her, saying, "Once you may have sided with our enemy, but today, I embrace you as a friend."

When Hanna was driven from the White House that day, she felt, for the second time in her life, that she had been in the presence of a truly great leader, and one who had offered the hand of friendship to her; but despite her efforts, the die was cast.

29

The Samson Option

Thursday 27th May 2021 – 2:45am
Kdoshei Hashoa Street, Herzliya Pituach, Tel Aviv-Yafo

Brigadier General Malachai Rosen and Major Yosef Peretz were in a TACCS (tactical armoured command and control shelter) otherwise known as a Rhino mobile headquarters vehicle. They were seated in a large rectangular room they had entered an hour before through a thick armoured door in the rear. Inside there were comfortable chairs around a dozen computers fixed to a table in the centre. All around the top of the interior were screens and communication equipment, whilst a number of operatives were sitting, in uniform, wearing headphones, studying the information displayed. The vehicle had rolled into position on open land bordering Tsvi Propes Street, a quarter of a mile from Omer Ravid's villa. They were joined shortly after arriving by two *Sabrah* tanks and six armoured personnel carriers.

Two large military trucks had pulled up on Shmu'el Shnitser Street, which ran parallel to the rear of the villa. Mehedi, David and Shira were in the lead truck with Captain Isaac Malkah. All of the assault commandos were dressed in black battle fatigues with helmets worn over their blackened faces. Each carried a taser in one holster and sidearms in the other. Mehedi and Shira carried the commonly issued *IDF Jericho 941* semi-automatic pistol whilst David had opted for his favourite Glock 19. Some of the commandos had Tavor assault rifles and many carried stun grenades. Five of them had been issued with the latest *ADS* rifles (active denial non-lethal beam weapon), which looked like long torches but with a traditional shoulder stock to assist with aiming. The plan was that twenty of them would initially scale the walls and attempt to reach the steps near the rear doors of the villa undetected. The rest of the force would be deployed once they had gained access to the villa, and the diversionary attack had started at the front. The strictest emphasis had been given to them in person by Malachai Rosen earlier in the day that they should try to avoid any loss of life. However, in the event of stiff resistance, a 'shoot to kill' policy would apply. Despite the difference in their ranks, both Shira and Mehedi opted for David, as the one who had led the investigation, to be their leader during the assault.

Malachai Rosen ordered troops from two of the personnel carriers be deployed to seal off both ends of Kdoshei Hashoa Street with road blocks. No-one was to be permitted access or to leave the area, including police vehicles. Any security forces other than those under his direct command approaching the road blocks or requesting access were to be detained until the mission had been completed.

A drone was launched from the command vehicle, with infrared telephoto capabilities, and soon they had a view of the villa in sight on one of the larger screens. There were guards gathered by the outer barracks to the front of the property where a number of vehicles were parked, including the Rolls-Royce, which belonged to Omer Ravid. Occasionally the guards would saunter to the rear and then back again. There did not appear to be any evidence of heightened security. Rosen picked up the phone that directly linked to Malkah, who had led the first twenty men, together with Mehedi, David and Shira, to a building near to the rear wall of the villa. "Clear to go – bodycams on and good luck."

"*Root avor,*" (received over) responded Malkah. He turned to face the twenty commandos gathered behind him. "We go in five minutes; we will split into two assault sections; Section One under my command, and Section Two will be led by *Rasar* (Master Sergeant) Elon Segel." He selected who would be in each. "Carry out a last weapons check and ensure tasers are armed. Section One with David, Shira, Mehedi and myself will go first, Section Two will follow on my command." He walked to a further group gathered behind them. "Backup platoon: wait until my signal before coming over."

David looked at Mehedi with a smile. "Like old times, eh; strange how they trust you with a taser considering you Bedouin don't use electricity in the desert."

"Listen, *mefagger* (idiot); as your senior officer, my orders are to kiss my ass."

Shira shook her head at them in mock exasperation then, unnoticed by the others, she gave David a brief smile, nodding her head with a deep look. Even as he felt the adrenalin of their impending mission, he glowed inside briefly, before dismissing all thoughts, other than a total concentration on their mission. Two assault ladders were brought forwards and they proceeded in silence, under the cover of darkness, the last twenty-five metres to the high wall bordering the rear of the villa. The sound of a heavy helicopter high above them could be heard but, apart from that and the odd bark of a dog in the distance, all was quiet. The two ladders were placed in position and David, Shira, and Mehedi followed directly behind Malkah. He paused, peering over the apex of the wall; it was pitch dark on the other side although there were subdued lights to the rear of the house over a patio. Raising his night vision binoculars, he scanned the fifty-metre gradient up to the villa but there were no signs of life. A clump of shrubs about thirty metres in was their first chosen point of cover. Malkah gave a signal to Master Sergeant Elon Segel that they would advance in fives. In seconds, he dropped soundlessly into the villa grounds as Segel raised his assault rifle to cover him, training it on the villa beyond. David, Shira, and Mehedi immediately followed together with one of the commandos carrying an ADS rifle. They reached the first clump and Malkah raised his arm beckoning and seconds later the next five commandos joined them. Two of them assumed a kneeling position either end of the line of shrubs with assault rifles held at shoulder level. Just as Malkah passed a signal back for the next batch to come forwards, a bright flood-light flashed on from the house and they threw themselves flat on the ground, watching as a startled jackal shot sideways desperate to seek shelter. Malkah held up his hand and spoke with an urgent whisper into his radio mike.

"We have a motion sensor light which will probably trigger up to a distance of at least ten metres. Hopefully, it will probably only light for a minute or so. If we edge slowly forwards in the prone position, it may not pick us up. We'll go forwards in twos once the light goes out." They waited and watched for what seemed an age but within less than a minute the light shut off. Malkah picked his binoculars up and watched the villa as two guards wandered into view, looking out across the rear open space. A powerful handheld light was switched on and the beam traversed the grass in arcs towards their position; instinctively, they all ducked their heads. Moments later the light went out and there was a brief sense of relief as Malkah watched through his night vision binoculars and beckoned the rest of the commandos to follow. As the last of the troops joined them, he turned to address both David and Segel in a low whisper.

"When we reach the house, hopefully undetected, you take the first floor by scaling the patio framework with Sergeant Segel and Section Two. I'll secure the ground floor with Section One. There are two balcony entrances which should give you good access. Hopefully, you will take Ravid without too much difficulty. *B'chatzlacha!*' (good luck) He gave the order for them to don their gas masks and to inch forwards in twos with at least a five metre gap between each. "Move like ballerinas;" he whispered, adding with a mischievous smile, "I hope that is not an insult to the ladies present." The faces around him all smiled at the lightness of the moment despite the tension in their mission; their commander was not known for his political correctness.

Malkah inched forwards with another commando two metres to his right. Within minutes all were spread across the open space, edging their way up the gradient towards the villa. David was in the third row, Segel by his side with Mehedi and Shira behind him. As he carefully lifted his head, he could see that Malkah had reached the edge of the patio only twenty metres away without triggering the light and was not moving. "We can do this," Segel whispered, "and take these bastards by surprise." At that moment, the whole area was flooded by a blinding light and all the commandos were totally visible spread across the gradient. David's natural command took over and he turned to Segel. "Let's go upstairs, Sergeant; we'll take the left-hand balcony; you take the right. Follow behind me, Shira and Mehedi!" He then climbed to his feet as Segel waved three from his section to follow David, running with the rest to the right-hand side of the patio. A brief burst of fire from Malkah's assault rifle took out the light and, for a second, they struggled to see in the blinding, disorientating effect from glaring light to sudden darkness. In the mobile HQ vehicle, Malachai Rosen gave the order and from the front of the villa came the sound of a thunderous noise and flashes from stun grenades followed by tear gas, taking the guards totally by surprise. David, Mehedi and Shira were scaling the framework of the patio to an upper balcony with Segel and four of his nine commandos climbing to the far side. He ordered two to remain at the base to give cover. Malkah fired another burst at the French windows of the rear entrance, shattering the glass, and entered the villa. Four guards came running to the rear, coughing from the effects of the tear gas. The first was hit by a taser and screamed, collapsing to the floor writhing in agony, as a second raised his weapon; an ADS pain beam hit him and he shouted unintelligibly as he dropped his gun. The other two stopped in their tracks as they were confronted by five commandos all with their automatic weapons held at shoulder level pointed at them. They were told to lie on the floor. Malkah had ordered the second platoon to enter the compound; they now arrived and began edging their way forwards down the side of the villa, bellowing, "Get down on the floor now; we are IDF security forces; do not resist or you will be killed." Another taser was deployed taking down a guard who had appeared brandishing a handgun.

David reached the balcony first and kicked the entrance door, which crashed open; Mehedi moved inside, his taser held at arm's-length, followed by Shira holding an assault rifle to her shoulder with a light fixed to it. "Room clear!" Mehedi shouted as they entered a corridor, hearing a burst of fire from an adjoining room and over the radio "Two occupants in bedroom – no casualties." Two men in battledress uniforms appeared holding pistols. David shouted, "Drop your weapons or die." They darted into a side door and a commando standing beside David drew a teargas grenade from his belt before throwing it through the door. "We have live grenades…live grenades…exit with your hands on your head." He shouted the last words and the men reappeared in the door-way choking and were told to lie on the floor. They moved to an open landing area above a winding staircase, meeting two commandos who held their thumbs up. From downstairs they could hear the occasional burst of gunfire and more shouts over the radio. "Room clear!" or "one occupant, no casualties", then, seconds later, "Ground floor secured." Suddenly there was the sound of gun-fire from a room off the landing and they crouched to the floor, hearing over the radio, "Two occupants, one casualty, room secure – medic needed!" Segel appeared on the stairway with two of his section, speaking rapidly. "One tried to resist and has suffered gunshot wounds to his legs. We are clear down here with four prisoners under guard. No Ravid." They watched as two commandos approached the last room on their wing of the villa and kicked the door open, screaming, "Down on the floor now," as one fired his weapon into the ceiling, bringing shards of plaster down. There was a further corridor across the landing leading to double doors at the end. David beckoned with his hand, walking slowly towards the passageway closely followed by Shira. Mehedi was behind her with his pistol drawn and was holding it at arm's-length, training it on the doors as they approached slowly. Shira held her Tavor tight into her shoulder, waving it in an arc to right and left, checking for threats, trying to fight off an unaccustomed emotional response to David placing himself in danger. She had seen much combat action and had never experienced such feelings previously of a need to protect, other than that which her professional training gave her to ensure the safety of those under her command. David whispered to her, "If he's in here, stay hidden until I call you." She nodded, her eyes meeting his for a second, drawing the briefest knowing look.

David reached the doors pulling his Glock 19 from his holster and signalled to Mehedi that he was going in low after three seconds. Mehedi stood by the door frame as David stepped back then kicked at the centre of the doors, which flew back as he ducked to the floor with his pistol held outstretched in both hands. The light was on and they were faced with the silver-haired Ravid wearing dark glasses, in a silk dressing gown, sitting by an antique desk with his mobile phone to his ear. He spoke animatedly, "They are here now, Naftaly, you must act."

"Drop the phone...now!" David shouted, walking towards him, his finger on the trigger of his weapon. Ravid complied, laying his mobile on the desktop, but David could see it was still connected. He moved forwards rapidly, pressing the end call icon, keeping his pistol trained on Ravid, who looked at him calmly and dispassionately with cold grey eyes. David took off his helmet and gas mask, drawing an immediate but precise response from Ravid.

"Ah, the tennis player; I have friends in high places and I can assure you that you will suffer for this unwarranted, unlawful, and outrageous intrusion into my home." His voice was icy cold. "Who has authorised this?"

Mehedi glanced around the large bedroom with a queen-sized double bed under an ornate canopy, lit by crystal chandeliers and glass-fronted wall lights, with tapestries depicting classical scenes on the wall. There were long, embroidered, maroon curtains pulled under a matching valance over a huge picture window, and a door with gold trim between built-in wardrobes. He strode to the door, hesitating for a moment, his pistol held at the ready, opening it suddenly to reveal a wet room with white fittings set into black marble with multiple wall-mounted shower heads, a deep sunken bath, jacuzzi, and dual wash basins. Two further doors led to separate lavatories. He shouted back, "Room clear!"

David now spoke. "It's game over, Ravid. We know all about you and your crazy plans for a coup, including your intention to attack the nuclear weapon control centre at Tirosh. Oh, and let us not forget the insanity of a pre-emptive strike on Iran."

"Then your intel is flawed, Mr Stern; we have no need to attack because there are those who will invite me, implore me even, to take the necessary steps to protect Israel. It is you who is out of sync and short-sighted people like you who will never understand the action we must take. Action to prevent anyone ever daring to attack us again, not ever. In the words of the great Prime Minister, Menachem Begin, 'We shall not allow any enemy to develop weapons of mass destruction turned against us.' The state of Iran has refused to co-operate on the issue of nuclear arms, having stockpiled enough uranium to build ten nuclear weapons, and the regime is fanatical. Do you think they would think twice before attacking Israel? You should join us, Mr Stern, and recognise that we cannot defeat pariah states which threaten us with a weak, indecisive democracy.

Decisive leadership is needed and many within our country agree with me, including some of your superiors." He reached for his phone. "Allow me to make just one call and I will surprise you. You will be ordered to withdraw and there will be consequences."

David raised his handgun, pointing it directly at Ravid's head. "Do not use that phone. Place it back on the table…now!" The last word was shouted as a command.

Ravid complied, raising both hands in a placatory gesture. His voice was relaxed and grated on David as he spoke in a slick, patronising tone. "You see, David, and yes, I know your name, even US President Trump recognised the naivety of the nonsensical Iran Nuclear Deal negotiated under his weak predecessor, Obama. In 2018, both Israel and the US proved to the world that Iran had broken the terms of the agreement, and even Iran itself admitted in 2019 that it had breached the agreement in relation to its stockpiling of uranium. This is the time to strike and ensure that no-one will ever again contemplate an attack on this country."

David responded, with slow, measured words, "Your way is no better than that of the Nazis. You would seize power without consent and potentially be the cause of World War 3. You have already taken Israeli lives in pursuit of your goal."

Ravid raised his hand pointing to emphasise his words, "Imagine the number of lives we will lose if we fail to act and Iran obtains a nuclear weapon. Then we will have a fanatical regime whose Revolutionary Guard have already said that erasing Israel off the map is non-negotiable. Even their leader, Ali Khamenei, has stated openly that, and I quote, "Israel's obliteration is certain." They fund Hamas and Hezbollah, who kill our people, and we do nothing. They are committed to the annihilation of Israel. Is that what you want?" Ravid's voice rose. "You call me a Nazi when these people are threatening us like no-one since Adolf Hitler. My purpose is to bring forward the 'Samson option', which we have had as policy for years, which states we would exercise massive retaliation if attacked, and massive…means nuclear. All I am doing is saving lives by ensuring that we strike first. You, David, are standing in the way of one who has the strength and the will to act."

David replied testily, "Your wish is to seize power for yourself and destroy the foundations of our great nation. You have killed seven people that we know of simply to prevent others from knowing who you really are and what you have been involved in."

Ravid shrugged. "There is nothing you or any of your people can do. I know too much."

David interrupted – "It is because we know too much about your past that you can never seize power." He watched the shock register on Ravid's face with his next words. "Perhaps, we should start with Unit 235 and where you were on November 22nd 1963. You are finished, Ravid, and once those around you know about your past, most will back away. We want the names of all those in positions of authority who are involved in this plot. If you co-operate, you will not face trial. If you do not, your guilt will guarantee the death penalty for treason. As a minimum, you will serve out your remaining days in prison."

"I assume you have proof?" He still had an air of arrogance.

"We have irrefutable evidence and, regrettably for you, we have discovered your Achilles heel in your past, which you tried to cover-up by killing your former comrades."

"They were old men and they had blood on their hands too," Ravid shrugged, throwing his hands in the air.

"I think there is someone you need to explain that to," David snarled, shaking his head, "Shira, please join us."

Ravid looked up sharply in surprise as Shira walked in, having also removed her helmet and gas mask. "Oh my God, not you as well," he muttered, then, sneeringly, "You are just like your mother; unable to face reality. Once I wanted the best for you, but I gave up on you years ago. You were not worthy of being my daughter and never will be."

"You bastard!" she hissed, "You ruined my mother's life with your abuse and now I rejoice in helping to bring you down. I detest you and everything you stand for. You are responsible for so much evil, even murder, and you disgust me!" Her voice rose with the release of a passion that she had suppressed for so long.

Ravid held his hands up as if signalling that he could add nothing more.

David interjected, "You even arranged the death of an innocent ninety-five-year-old scientist; a survivor of the Holocaust, living out his last years quietly in England, just to protect your ambition for power."

"Oh that *alte kaker*, he should have learned to keep his mouth shut. He was always poking his damned nose into my life, interfering, criticising, and siding against me with the stupid bitch I married…"

When the first shot came, Ravid's face contorted from shock to surprise and he attempted to lift himself out of his chair, and the second threw him backwards as the chair tipped over. He instinctively lifted his arms as if to protect himself. Shira screamed at him, "*Zaydee* was my grandfather, you scum!" Ravid was hit with three more shots in rapid succession, slumping back and not moving, as Shira continued to point her weapon at the lifeless body. David had rushed across to try to intervene but was too late, as she allowed her handgun to fall to the floor. She stood silently, staring straight ahead, not even acknowledging David, who placed his arms on her shoulders, moving her to a chair.

Mehedi, who still had his helmet on with its radio ear-piece, announced, "We have a situation at one of the road check-points. A number of armoured cars have arrived and their commander is demanding access saying he has authority from General Aaron Cohen of Home Front Command to gain access and assume control of the complex. They are to force their way through, if necessary." David left Shira's side and reached out to take the radio mike from Mehedi; he spoke briefly to Malachai Rosen at the command centre. The General confirmed he had despatched tanks to the check-point together with ground personnel under the command of Major Yosef Peretz, backed by a letter of authority from the Chief of the General Staff. A separate unit was on its way to seek out General Cohen and have him arrested as a precaution.

At the debriefing, held an hour later, in the mobile command post, Rosen confirmed that an immediate press release was to be issued, stating that Omer Ravid was killed, resisting arrest, for alleged connections with international terrorism, as part of an investigation into a money-laundering scandal linked to narcotics. His connections were also under further investigation, as a result of his links with former Nazis. Rosen concluded, "That should be sufficient to quell any would-be sympathisers. I'll leave it up to you guys to square all this with Prime Minister Benjamin Netanyahu. Good luck with that one. I served with 'Bibi' and to put it mildly, he does not suffer fools gladly."

At 8am, David, Mehedi, and Shira proceeded to Moshe Gellner's house. Shira had spent half an hour with medics and had turned down the offer of medication to assist with trauma, insisting that she return with David and Mehedi. Moshe greeted each of them, in turn, with a firm handshake, followed by Benjamin Weiss, who also embraced Shira, saying gently, "You have suffered much, and I know my cousin will be there for you." Moshe led the way to the terrace where they sat for a de-brief, discussing the operation. His home had been added to the operational transmission loop, enabling them to both see events through the bodycams and hear the radio messages during the mission.

As they sat drinking mimosas of sparkling wine, vodka and orange juice, which Moshe had mixed, watching the sunlight in a sparkling dance over the Mediterranean, they reflected upon their revelations and what had occurred. Moshe vocalised their thoughts. "Israel, with all the imperfections that affect every nation, is the heartbeat of our hope and that has been the case for over 2,000 years." Shira began singing the *Hatikvah* softly, drawing the others to join in the haunting melody of the national anthem, their voices rising as they clutched hands around the table.

Kol od balevav p'nimah
Nefesh Yehudi homiyah
Ulfa'atey mizrach kadimah
Ayin l'tzion tzofiyah
Od lo avdah tikvatenu
Hatikvah bat shnot alpayim
L'hiyot am chofshi b'artzenu
Eretz Tzion v'Yerushalayim

(As long as deep in the heart,
The soul of a Jew yearns,
And forward to the East
To Zion, an eye looks
Our hope will not be lost,
The hope of two thousand years,
To be a free nation in our land,
The land of Zion and Jerusalem)

Later, as she lay in David's arms, he stroked her hair, holding her, uttering gentle words of reassurance. She looked up at him, her wide eyes wet with tears, unable to place her thoughts into context. "Please love me...make me belong." Their bodies merged in a mutual expression of their need for gentle union, contrasting with the harrowing events of the night, and in each other, they found solace and joy.

Epilogue

They were seated in comfortable armchairs in a long lounge with a sandy-coloured marble floor over which various rugs were placed. At one end of the room, a large window looked out over the outer buildings bordering the city of Jerusalem, whilst at the other, high glazed doors were set in a rosewood timber partition, beyond which there was a long, polished dining or conference table. There were pictures on the wall of Prime Minister Netanyahu with various world leaders at the residence, representing a who's who of the preceding twenty years, including President Trump, Prime Minister Modi, and President Putin; amongst them was one of Prince William in the same room in which they sat, which caught Shira's eye. "I wonder if we will be featured on this rogues' gallery," she mused to the others, which included Moshe, David, Mehedi, and Benjamin.

David had attended a difficult meeting with the Prime Minister the day after the attack on Ravid's home, at which the Director of

Mossad and the Chief of Staff were present. The Prime Minister had been presented with the dossier of their investigations by David an hour previously, which had been completed by Benjamin Weiss the day before. Netanyahu was furious that he had not been consulted and, as he put it, "This clandestine operation undermined the very meaning of democracy. How could this happen? How could you let this happen? More importantly, we must ensure that there is always democratic accountability and proper consultation." David had countered by being direct, "Forgive me, sir, but you, yourself, have a reputation for cutting corners and using your initiative. You have been in the special forces, serving with distinction, and, with respect, if Israel had always awaited democratic outcomes, or even diplomatic ones abroad, many of our enemies would be more powerful today."

Netanyahu had looked directly at him, then his demeanour had softened with almost a hint of a smile, "Get the hell out of here, David; I want to meet you and your team separately."

That had been the previous Friday and now they had all been summoned to a further meeting. The PM entered wearing a well-tailored mid-blue suit and matching striped tie. They stood as he walked towards them with a broad smile on his face. He shook hands with each of them in turn, placing both of his over Shira's before embracing her. "I have now thoroughly read your dossier containing the report on Unit 235, Lekem, and, of course, the activities of Omer Ravid. I would give you medals but the reason you have earned them prevents this. That dossier and the reports it contains does not exist, my friends, and the history you have uncovered must never be written or referred to again.

"You have done a great service to the democracy of our nation, which, ironically, is the means being utilised by my opponents to remove me. Paradoxically, that which we defend, ensures my demise, but democracy survives me."

Mehedi spoke, "With respect, might I say that perhaps the greatest irony is that our policy towards Iran might be compared to that of Kennedy to us. The Greek playwright Sophocles poses the question whether *'the end justifies the evil'.*"

David sighed, waving both hands at Mehedi in derision, as the Prime Minister responded, "That must be the decision of politicians and reminds me of a great debating question, *'If evil must exist for a greater good, then does the end justify the means?'* You are soldiers of the state but, perhaps, like me, you will be the politicians of tomorrow. One final question which is not addressed in your report. Who fired the shots in November 1963?"

"I regret," said David, "we never found out."

"Perhaps, that is just as well." the PM replied, "Shalom, my friends."

Less than two weeks later, on 13th June 2021, Benjamin Netanyahu was forced to resign as prime minister after a no-confidence vote. The Director of Mossad, Yossi Cohen, retired a few days before. On 29th December 2022, Netanyahu was sworn in, for an unprecedented sixth term as Prime Minister. Five days later, a card was delivered to Moshe Gelner's home saying, simply, '*You may recall my words, "that which we defend, ensures my demise". Now that very democracy, which you and your comrades defended, has delivered a reversal. 'Kismet!' Is that fate or destiny? Shalom, Benjamin*"

The priorities, stated by the incoming Prime Minister, were to end the Arab-Israeli conflict, stop Iran's nuclear programme, and build up Israel's military capacity.

One Giant Leap...

As Neil Armstrong tentatively stepped down from the Lunar Module onto the surface of the moon, he uttered the words, "That's one small step for man, one giant leap for mankind." At Mission Control, Wernher von Braun was ecstatic as he embraced his assistant, Arthur Rudolph, "*Mein Gott*, we did it…the journey began in the Reich, but we have completed it here."

Postscript

CBS soap opera broadcast, *'As the World Turns'* is suddenly interrupted.

Unidentified announcer: *"Here is a bulletin from CBS News:*

"In Dallas, Texas, three shots were fired at President Kennedy's motorcade in downtown Dallas. The first reports say that President Kennedy has been seriously wounded by the shooting."

Returns to soap opera for three seconds…then cuts to:

Walter Cronkite – Anchorman at CBS News:

"This picture has just been transmitted by wire. It is a picture taken just a moment or two before the incident. If you can zoom in with that camera, we can get a closer look at this picture which shows the President as he was shot."

One hour later, this announcement is given by Walter Cronkite, who removes his glasses awkwardly, before replacing them:

"From Dallas, Texas, the flash, apparently official, President Kennedy died at 1pm Central Standard Time, two o'clock Eastern Standard Time…some thirty-eight minutes ago…"

Pause, as Cronkite struggles with emotion, pulling a face, then, in a shaky voice:

"Vice-President Lyndon Johnson has left the hospital in Dallas but we do not know to where he…ah…has proceeded; presumably, he will be taking the oath of office shortly and will become…ah…the thirty-sixth President of the United States."

In Memoriam

To the memory of John Fitzgerald Kennedy ('Jack'), decorated combat veteran and the 35th President of the United States, who was cruelly assassinated at 12:30pm CST on November 22nd 1963, at the age of forty-six, on Dealey Plaza, in downtown Dallas, Texas.

In office January 20th 1961 – November 22nd 1963. Kennedy was a reformer, statesman, a supporter of the civil rights movement, and a charismatic leader who inspired many with his idealism and energy. He committed himself to the cause of non-nuclear proliferation, signing the first nuclear weapons treaty with the Soviet Union in 1963. JFK stood as a bastion against communist expansion and set the goal of putting a man on the moon.

"Ask not what your country can do for you, ask what you can do for your country"

"We choose to go to the Moon in this decade and do the other things, not because they are easy, but because they are hard."

To all who sacrificed so much in the course of the Second World War

"They shall grow not old, as we that are left grow old: Age shall not weary them, nor the years condemn. We will remember them…"

Quotation References

"The development of future space ships will necessarily lead to an extremely powerful new weapon. From a big rocket circling around the earth, bombs can be dropped or guided down to any point of the earth's surface. Facing the existence of the atomic bomb and the fact that such a circling rocket represents an ever-present threat above the head of almost every nation, that nation which first reaches this goal possesses an overwhelming military superiority over other nations"

Wernher von Braun (Former Nazi German rocket scientist who became responsible for the Apollo Saturn V rocket taking men to the moon) in a statement to the US Army

July 1946

"There is no distinction between nuclear energy for peaceful purposes or warlike ones...We shall never again be led as lambs to the slaughter"

Ernst Bergmann (Chairman of the Israel Atomic Energy Commission from 1954 to 1966)

December 1960

"If we are to win the battle that is now going on around the world between freedom and tyranny, the dramatic

achievements in space which occurred in recent weeks should have made clear to us all, as did the Sputnik in 1957, the impact of this adventure on the minds of men everywhere, who are attempting to make a determination of which road they should take.

"…we have examined where we are strong and where we are not, where we may succeed and where we may not. Now it is time to take longer strides – time for a great new American enterprise – time for this nation to take a clearly leading role in space achievement, which in many ways may hold the key to our future on earth.

"I believe that this nation should commit itself to achieving the goal, before this decade is out, of landing a man on the Moon and returning him safely to the earth."

President John F Kennedy Speech to Congress

May 25th 1961

"The Israelis, who are one of the few peoples whose survival is genuinely threatened, are probably more likely than almost any other country to actually use their nuclear weapons."

Henry Kissinger (Then National Security Advisor)

July 19th 1969

"We chose this moment: now, not later, because later may be too late, perhaps forever… Then, this country and this people would have been lost, after the Holocaust. Another Holocaust would have happened in the history of the Jewish people. Never again, never again! Tell so your friends, tell anyone you meet, we shall defend our people with all the means at our disposal. We shall not allow any enemy to develop weapons of mass destruction turned against us."

Prime Minister Menachem Begin of Israel – Press Conference–
A statement that underlined what became known as the 'Begin
Doctrine', underpinning Israel's commitment to massive
retaliation if attacked.

9th June 1981

Global Nuclear Weapons Capability

The following countries possess nuclear weapons:
The United States of America
The United Kingdom
France
Russia
China
India
Pakistan
North Korea
Israel*
Ironically, Germany does not, but has nuclear warheads at its Büchel Air Base under the NATO nuclear weapons sharing arrangements.

*The Israeli government has neither confirmed nor denied that the state of Israel possesses nuclear weapons, in a policy termed 'deliberate ambiguity'

Israel/Iran Historical Perspective

2003 – The International Atomic Energy Authority (IAEA) launches an investigation after an Iranian dissident group revealed undeclared nuclear activities carried out by Iran.

8th May 2006 – Israeli Vice Premier Shimon Peres says that "the President of Iran should remember that Iran can also be wiped off the map."

27th July 2009 – Gabriella Shalev, Israeli Ambassador to the US states, "The Islamic Republic's nuclear program and its support of terrorism pose a threat to the entire Middle East."

25th September 2009 – US President Barack Obama reveals the existence of an underground Iranian enrichment facility, saying, "Iran's decision to build yet another nuclear facility without notifying the IAEA represents a direct challenge to the basic compact at the center of the non-proliferation regime." Israel threatens that harsh international measures against Iran may be necessary if US talks with Iran fail.

7th February 2010 – Iran's supreme leader, Ayatollah Ali Khamenei, says that "the destruction of Israel is assured."

In 2010, assassinations targeting Iranian nuclear scientists begin, which were attributed to Mossad. On 12th January, a scientist is killed by an armed motorcycle rider. On 12th October, an explosion occurs at an Iranian military base, killing eighteen soldiers. On 29th November, two senior Iranian nuclear scientists are attacked, with one killed and one severely wounded.

On 23rd July 2011, another scientist is shot dead in Tehran, followed by a further attack on 11th January 2012 killing both the scientist and his driver.

From 2010 onwards, a number of unexplained explosions begin taking place in and around Iranian nuclear facilities together with control system failures resulting from the hacking of Iranian computer networks.

20th May 2012 – Major General Hassan Firouzabadi, Iran's Chief of Military Staff, declares, "The Iranian nation is standing for its cause and that is the full annihilation of Israel."

18th July 2012 – A bomb blast on a bus carrying Israeli tourists in Bulgaria kills five Israeli tourists and the driver, injuring thirty-two. Prime Minister Benjamin Netanyahu blames Iran and Hezbollah for the attack.

15th August 2012 – The Supreme Leader of Iran, Ali Khamenei, states that "the fake Zionist (regime) referring to Israel "will disappear from the landscape of geography" On the same day, Brigadier – General Gholamreza Jalali, the head of Iran's Passive (civil) Defence Organization says, "no other way exists apart from resolve and strength to completely eliminate the aggressive nature and to destroy Israel."

19th August 2012 – Supreme Leader Ali Khamenei reiterates comments made by President Mahmoud Ahmadinejad, calling Israel a "cancerous tumour in the heart of the Islamic world"

October 2nd 2012 – Hojjat al-Eslam Ali Shirazi, the representative of Supreme Leader, Ayatollah Ali Khamenei, to the Iranian Revolutionary Guard, issues a warning that Iran requires only "24 hours and an excuse in order to eradicate Israel." Shirazi alleges that Israel was "close to annihilation."

5th November 2012 – Israel's Prime Minister Benjamin Netanyahu confirms willingness of Israel to mount a unilateral attack on Iran's nuclear facilities.

1st October 2013 – Israeli Prime Minister, Benjamin Netanyahu announces to the UN that Iran is attempting to produce a nuclear weapon.

31st March 2015 – The Israel Radio reports that the commander of the Basij militia of Iran's Revolutionary Guards, Mohammad Reza Naqdi, has said that "erasing Israel off the map" is "non-negotiable".

3rd January 2020 – Qassem Soleimani, a general in the QUDS, part of the Iranian Revolutionary Guard responsible for clandestine military operations, is targeted in Baghdad, Iraq, and assassinated in a drone strike authorised by US President Donald Trump.

22nd April 2021 – A Syrian missile lands near Israel's nuclear plant at Dimona – claimed by Iran to be a warning after suspected Israeli involvement in an explosion at the Iranian Natanz nuclear site.

June 2021 – The former Director of Mossad, Yossi Cohen, gives an interview after retiring, in which he alludes to the responsibility for a series of attacks carried out by Israel on Iran's nuclear programme. These include the assassination of a top Iranian nuclear scientist and an explosion at the underground centrifuge hall in Natanz. The interview appears to warn other scientists in Iran's nuclear programme, that they too could become targets for assassination.

21st December 2021 – AP News reports that the former Head of Israeli Military Intelligence, Major General Tamir Heyman, has confirmed that Israel played a part in the air-strike that killed Iranian General Qassem Soleimani in January 2020.

26th December 2021 – Iran conducts simulated attacks in military drills, with video showing missile attacks raining down on Israel's nuclear site at Dimona.

15th July 2022 – The Iranian military cautions Israel and the US not to use force against Iran. "The Americans and Zionists" (Israel) "know very well the price for using the words "force against Iran," Iranian media quote Brigadier General Abolfazl Shekarchi, a spokesman for the Iranian armed forces.

Thanks

I would like to thank those who have assisted and supported me in the writing of this book. The input and encouragement of those around me have been enormously helpful factors. You know who you are.

I am also grateful for the fantastic feedback from readers of my previous work, 'The Barbarossa Secret' which, in no small way, motivated me to continue.

Finally, I specifically wish to thank my team of incredibly dedicated proof readers:

Ashley Best

Wendy Munro

Jonathan Spencer

I am so indebted to them for their hugely valuable input in rooting out errors, making suggestions, and their positive feedback.

Reflection

As I unearthed the extraordinary historical background to this story, much of which has been either hidden or suppressed, I reflected whether I could include some very sensitive elements but concluded that these gave a valuable perspective on the tragedy of many events depicted.

We must never hide or censor history, or we will fail to learn from it.

Biographical Index

Avraham Ahituv *née* Gottfried: 10th December 1930 – July 15th 2009. Israeli civil servant and intelligence agent who was director of Israel's security agency, Shinbet from 1974 to 1980. Served in Haganah, a Zionist Paramilitary organisation. Joined Israeli Intelligence in 1948. Later authorized the use of lies in Israeli courts to cover confessions obtained by torture. In March 1962, he met with a former Nazi SS officer, Otto Skorzeny, persuading him to carry out operations for Israel. The date of the meeting was later amended in security files. Accused of having been involved in the bombing of Palestinian mayors in 1980 and resigned.

Eugene Allen: 14th July 1919 – 31st March 2010. Served as both a waiter and butler in the White House for 34 years. He had worked as a waiter for many years, in "whites-only" resorts and country clubs before starting in the White House in 1952 as a "pantry man" rising to become the butler to the President. Allen was particularly affected by President Kennedy's assassination but refused to stop working. He was invited to the funeral, but chose to stay at work to prepare for the reception, because "Someone had to be at the White House to serve everyone after…" Allen never missed a day of work in 34 years retiring as the Head Butler in 1986.

Meir Amit: 17ᵗʰ March 1921 – 17ᵗʰ July 2009) Head of Global operations for Mossad from 1963 to 1968 after which he entered politics holding two ministerial positions. He fought for Haganah in the 1948 Arab- Israeli war. In the military, he became a Major-General. Headed up Mossad and Israeli Military Intelligence and was credited with many Intelligence successes including a network of informants across the Arab world. Master-minded the recruitment of the former Nazi SS commando, Otto Skorzeny to work for Israel.

Mohammed Abdel Rahman Abdel Raouf Arafat al-Qudwa al-Husseini aka Yasser Arafat: ? August 1929 – 11ᵗʰ November 2004 Arafat was born in Cairo, Egypt. Whilst a student, he became an Arab nationalist, embracing anti-Zionist ideals. He fought alongside the Muslim Brotherhood during the 1948 Arab–Israeli War. Served as President of the Union of Palestinian Students from 1952 until 1956. Arafat co-founded Fatah, a paramilitary unit wanting the removal of Israel and the establishment of a Palestinian state. Fatah launched attacks on Israeli targets and in 1967 Arafat joined the Palestinian Liberation Organization (PLO). From its base in Lebanon in the early 1970s, Fatah continued its attacks on Israel, becoming a major target of Israel's 1978 and 1982 invasions. In 1988, Arafat recognised Israel's right to exist and sought to negotiate for a two-state solution. In 1994, he settled in Gaza city and engaged in negotiations the success of which led to him being awarded the Nobel Peace Prize, and he became Prime Minister of the new Palestine National Authority (PNA), resigning in 2003. He died after entering a coma at his home in Ramallah; the cause of his death raised much speculation.

Neil Alden Armstrong: 5ᵗʰ August 1930 – August 25ᵗʰ 2012 was an American astronaut, pilot, aeronautical engineer. and university professor. Served in the US navy becoming a pilot in 1950. He saw action in the Korean war after which he obtained a degree and became a test pilot and was then involved with the American space programme. Flew in space on board Gemini 8 in March 1966 and performed first docking of two spacecraft. On 20th July 1969, Armstrong and Lunar Module pilot, Buzz Aldrin, became first people to land and walk on the moon fulfilling a goal set in 1961 by President John F. Kennedy. After leaving NASA, he taught in Department of Aerospace. He died from heart complications after surgery aged 82.

Walworth "Wally" Barbour: 4th June 1908 – 21st July 1982. A long serving US diplomat appointed as Ambassador to Israel by President John F. Kennedy. He served in a sensitive period during pressure by the USA on Israel over its nuclear development at Dimona, because of suspicion it was being used for weapons development. He was also a diplomat in the UK, Greece, Bulgaria, Italy, Iraq and Egypt, and in the early 1950s he served for a period at the U.S. Embassy in Moscow. He retired from the Foreign Service after he left Israel in 1973.

Hans Baur: 19th June 1897 – 17th February 1993 was Adolf Hitler's pilot during the political campaigns of the early 1930s. He later became Hitler's personal pilot and leader of the *Reichsregierung* squadron. In order to ensure he was respected, Hitler promoted Baur to be a Standartenführer (colonel). During the last days of the war, Baur was with Hitler in the bunker where he hatched a plan for Hanna Reitsch to fly him out of Berlin. During his escape from the bunker, Baur was shot in the legs, and his lower leg was later amputated. Imprisoned in the Soviet Union after the war, he was then held captive by France until 1957.

Karl Heinrich Emil Becker: 14th September 1879 – 8th April 1940. A German weapons engineer and artillery officer who recognised the importance of modern science for military purposes, particularly for advanced weapons development. Served in WW1 as an artillery officer before transferring to weapons development for the army ordnance office. Becker took an interest in both atomic research and the development of rockets assisting in the establishment of the Nazi nuclear programme (*Uranverein*) and rocket research. He was a supporter of the development of ballistic rockets as weapons. He committed suicide in 1940 after suffering heavy criticism from Hitler and was given a state funeral.

Menachem Begin: 16th August 1913 – 9th March 1992 Begin lived in Warsaw and studied Law at University. He was actively involved in helping Polish Jews escape to Palestine. He fled Warsaw when the Germans invaded but was then imprisoned by the Soviet Union until 1941 when he joined the Free Polish army and was sent to Palestine. The leader of the Zionist militant group Irgun, he proclaimed a revolt against the British in 1944 who regarded him as a terrorist banning him from the UK. He founded the political party Likud. Elected to the first Knesset, he was in opposition until 1997 when, adopting less hard-line policies, he gained victory becoming the sixth Prime Minister of Israel. He was awarded the Nobel peace prize for signing a peace treaty with Egyptian President Anwar Sadat of Egypt in 1979. He withdrew Israeli forces from occupied Sinai gained in the Six-Day War. Begin authorised the bombing of the nuclear reactor in Iraq in 1982. He ordered invasion of Lebanon because of militant Arab bases there. Resigned in 1983.

David Ben-Gurion: 16th October 1886 – 1st December 1973. Considered to be the primary founder of the state of Israel becoming the first Prime Minister. He was the pre-eminent Jewish leader in British Mandatory Palestine from 1935 until the establishment of the State of Israel in 1948. He was a major Zionist leader heading the World Zionist Organisation in 1946. He jointly led the fight for an independent Jewish state and on 14

May 1948, he formally proclaimed the establishment of the State of Israel. He led Israel during the 1948 Arab-Israeli war creating the IDF (Israeli Defence Forces) uniting various militias. He was both PM and minister of defense and was determined that Israel should obtain nuclear weapons. He presided over the setting up of state institutions and the absorbing of Jews into the state from across the world. Promoted the development of a positive relationship with West Germany negotiating reparations. Resisted attempts by US nuclear inspectors to closely examine the facility at the Dimona Nuclear facility causing a rift with President John F. Kennedy. Resigned in June 1963.

Ernst Bergmann: Dob unknown 1903 – 6th April 1975 Israeli nuclear scientist and chemist who pioneered the Israeli Nuclear programme. Brought up in Germany, studied chemistry at University of Berlin gaining PhD in 1927. Worked in London and was offered a position at Oxford which he turned down. Emigrated to Palestine in 1934 and worked for the Allies in WWII. Was a close associate of David Ben-Gurion and appointed Chief of Israeli Defense Forces Science Dept in 1948 and then scientific advisor to the Mistry of Defense. In 1952 appointed chairman of the Israeli Atomic Energy Commission working closely with Ben-Gurion and Shimon Peres in developing Israel's nuclear programme. Resigned in 1966 and much of his work was shrouded in secrecy.

Anthony Charles Lynton Blair: born 6th May 1953. A British Labour politician. Prime Minister of the United Kingdom from 1997 to 2007 and Leader of the Labour Party from 1994 to 2007. Led the brand of 'New Labour' which swept the Labour Party to victory in May 1997, when aged 43. He championed the middle ground of politics and initially was highly popular. Introduced private finance initiatives coupling public services with private enterprise. Led Britain into war against Iraq instigated by US

President George W Bush claiming that they had weapons of mass destruction (WMD) which were never discovered by US or coalition forces. He subsequently became Special Envoy to the Middle East in a diplomatic post until 2015. He works for the Tony Blair Institute for Global Change, established in 2016. He is the only Labour leader to form three consecutive majority governments.

Benjamin Blumberg aka Vered: 1923 – 28th August 2018 A highly secretive man who operated at the heart of Israeli military intelligence. He headed up Lekem responsible for gaining scientific and technical intelligence abroad from 1957 until 1981. He had a close association with film producer, Arnon Milchan, who assisted in covering up intelligence operations in the USA. He was a close associate of Shimon Peres and organised covert missions to obtain nuclear material for the Israeli Nuclear Research Centre at Dimona. He was a recipient of Israel's highest defense related award, The Israel Prize for Defense.

Martin Ludwig Bormann: 17th June 1900 – 2nd May 1945? Senior Nazi and Head of the Nazi Party Chancellery. He gained immense power as Hitler's private secretary from 1935, controlling access to Hitler. Joined the Nazi party in 1927 and the SS in 1937. Overseer of renovations at the Berghof, Hitler's property at Obersalzberg. Appointed by Hitler to be Reichsleiter and Obergruppenführer. Controlled aspects of Nazi finance with reports saying he amassed a fortune used to finance post-war activities. Last time officially seen was May 1945 outside Hitler's Berlin bunker. Reports from Argentina claim sightings in the 1950s and 1960s. DNA evidence from a body found in Germany claimed to be Bormann's later discredited.

General Omar Nelson Bradley: 12th February 1893 – April 8th 1981- a US Army General during and after WWII. He served under General Patton in North Africa then commanded a campaign in Tunisia. He commanded the 1ˢᵗ US Army during invasion of Normandy after D Day; he then took command of the 12ᵗʰ US Army Group. He was appointed as Chief of Staff of the US Army and was a Chairman of the Joint Chiefs of staff in 1949. Bradley left active duty in 1953. He continued to serve in public and business roles until his death at age 88.

Wernher Magnus Maximilian Freiherr von Braun: 23ʳᵈ March 1912 – 16ᵗʰ June 1977. Born into a wealthy family, he was both a talented musician, and, after receiving a present of a telescope, from his mother, he became passionately interested in rocket science, pioneering research and development of liquid fuelled rockets. Joined the Nazi Party in 1937. Worked in Nazi Germany's rocket development program and helped design the V-2 rocket weapon which became the first man-made object to travel into space on 20ᵗʰ June 1944. In the latter stages of the war, he was working on a much larger rocket, information about which was suppressed. He was accused after the war of knowingly using slave labour from concentration camps in rocket production. Following the war, as part of Operation Paperclip, he was moved with other Nazi scientists to the USA where he helped develop ballistic missiles and the launch vehicle for the first US satellite, also working with Walt Disney on films about human space travel. In 1960, he joined NASA, becoming a director of the Marshall Space Flight Center, where he was chief architect of the Saturn V rocket which took men to the moon in 1969. In 1975, he received the National Medal of Science.

Field Marshal Alan Francis Brooke: 23ʳᵈ July 1883 – 17ᵗʰ June 1963. 1st Viscount Alanbrooke – Served in WW I on the Western Front with distinction. He was Chief of the Imperial General Staff (CIGS) during WWII and was promoted to field marshal on 1 January 1944. He was the senior military advisor to Prime Minister Winston Churchill. He served as Lord High Constable of England during the Coronation of Queen Elizabeth II in 1953. His war diaries criticised Churchill and were the subject of some controversy.

President George W Bush: born 6th July 1946. An American politician and businessman. Elected 43rd President of the United States serving from 2001 to 2009. A member of the Republican Party, he had formerly been governor of Texas. His father, George HW Bush, was the 41st President of the United States from 1989 to 1993. Considered a reforming Governor of Texas in education, energy and justice. Took America into second Gulf War against Iraq claiming they had WMD, which later proved not to be the case. Launched the Global War on Terror in the wake of the terrorist attacks on the World Trade Center, New York, on 11th September 2001.

Admiral Wilhelm Franz Canaris: 1st January 1887 – 9th April 1945. Fought in the German Navy in World War I, seeing action, evading capture and carrying out intelligence work. Initially attracted to National Socialism for opposing Versailles Treaty and standing up to Communism, but became disillusioned by the early years of World War II. Served as German admiral and chief of the Abwehr, the German military intelligence service, from 1935 to 1944 when he was removed by Hitler and his function replaced by the SS. He was involved in the opposition to Hitler and also intervened to help many Jews escape persecution. Met Allied Intelligence operatives in Spain and Paris to discuss terms for peace if Hitler was deposed. Executed in Flossenbürg concentration camp.

Sir Winston Leonard Spencer Churchill: 30th November 1874–24th January 1965. Distinguished army officer, statesman, politician, writer, historian and artist. Served as a soldier seeing action in India, the Sudan and in the second Boer War. Also worked as a war correspondent. First elected as an MP in 1900 and was an MP over a period of sixty-four years. Served on the

Western Front in World War I before being recalled to government. Various ministerial posts included Home Secretary, President of the Board of Trade, First Lord of the Admiralty and Secretary of State for War. British Prime Minister from 1940 to 1945, and again from 1951 to 1955. Leader of the Conservative Party from 1940 to 1955. Served continuously (apart from two years, 1922–24) as an MP from 1900 to 1964. Led Britain throughout most of World War II and was accredited with possessing highly effective leadership skills whilst inspiring the nation. He passionately argued against 'appeasement' with Hitler in the 1930s, warning of the inevitable outcome of war. Recognised as one of the greatest prime ministers, although not without controversy. He was given a state funeral. Churchill was seventh cousin one time removed to Queen Elizabeth II.

Yosef 'Yossi' Meir Cohen: b 10th September 1961 Served as a paratrooper in the IDF. Studied at University in London. Joined Mossad in 1982. Recruited and handled agents abroad. Appointed deputy Director of Mossad in 2011 and became National Security Advisor to Prime Minister Benjamin Netanyahu in 2013. Appointed Director of Mossad in 2015. In 2018, he organised an operation to steal Iran's nuclear archive identifying secret sites across the country. He has been attributed with organising meetings to improve Israeli relations with neighbouring Arabic nations. Retired from Mossad in June 1991.

Sir John Rupert Colville: 28th January 1915 – 19th November 1987. Known by friends as 'Jock', he was a British civil servant who served consecutively as assistant private secretary under three prime ministers; Neville Chamberlain, Winston Churchill, and Clemant Attlee. His diaries were published proving an insight to the activities inside 10, Downing Street during wartime under Prime Minister Winston Churchill. He served in World War II as a pilot in the Royal Air Force Volunteer Reserve (RAFVR) from

1941–44. He was Private Secretary to Princess Elizabeth 1947–49 and was Joint Principal Private Secretary to Winston Churchill from 1951–55.

Walter Leland Cronkite Jr: 4th November 1916 – 17th July 2009 was a renowned American broadcast journalist who served as the anchorman for CBS Evening News for 19 years from 1962. From his early days building a standing as a highly effective reporter during WWII, he developed an outstanding reputation world-wide. Cronkite reported many events from 1937 to 1981, including the London Blitz, the Nuremburg Trials, extensive bulletins during the Vietnam War, and was anchor when the news broke of the assassination of President Kennedy in November 1963. Other famous broadcasts covered the Moon Landing, Watergate, the Iran Hostage Crisis, and the shootings of Martin Luther King and John Lennon. He was known for the catchphrase "And that's the way it is", followed by the date of the broadcast. After retiring in 1981, he was awarded the Presidential Medal of Freedom. He continued to broadcast occasionally and actively participated in supporting students of journalism.

Jesse Edward Curry: 3rd October 1913 – 22nd June 1980. Police officer who rose from being a traffic cop to become the chief of the Dallas Police Department serving in this role from 1960 to 1966. He was Chief at the time of the assassination of President John F. Kennedy on November 22nd 1963. Curry was in the lead car of the Presidential motorcade and noticed unauthorized people on the overpass and wondered how they got there. He suffered damage to his reputation as a result of lax security surrounding Lee Harvey Oswald at Dallas Police Station when Oswald was shot. Curry was not happy with the findings of the Warren Commission, believing that the fatal shot(s) which killed Kennedy came from the front. His life was threatened after the assassination. In later life worked as a private investigator.

Heini Dittmar: 30th March 1912 – 28th April 1960. Dittmar was a record-breaking glider pilot, trained in Germany in the 1930's becoming the first glider pilot to cross the Alps in 1936. He was a friend of the German pilot Hanna Reitsch, with whom he went on international gliding expeditions. He was a research pilot in Nazi Germany. Dittmar was also a designer and test-pilot becoming the first to fly over 1,000mph and arguably the first to achieve supersonic flight. He died in an air-crash, testing a light aircraft of his own design in 1960.

Grand Admiral Karl Dönitz: 16th September 1891 – 24th December 1980. He served in the German Navy in both the 1st and 2nd World Wars becoming commander in chief of the navy as Grand Admiral in January 1943. In WW1 he commanded U boat submarines and was a POW in Sheffield, England until 1919. He commanded Germany's U Boat fleet in 1930 and organised the devastating attacks on Allied shipping. He continued in this role, even after being promoted to commander in chief. On 1st May 1945, he became Hitler's successor as President of Germany until 23rd May 1945 when he was taken into custody by the British. Tried at Nuremburg, he was sentenced to ten years imprisonment. He was a dedicated, unapologetic Nazi for the rest of his life and remained an admirer of Adolf Hitler.

Major-General Dr. Walter Robert Dornberger: 6th September 1895 – 27th June 1980. A German artillery officer serving in the First World War, he took part in the research into liquid fuelled rockets working alongside Wernher von Braun. During WWII he was in charge of the VI flying bomb and V2 rocket development. After the war, his scientific knowledge was sought by both the UK and the USA. He eventually settled in America developing missiles (including nuclear) and worked on various weapon developments, becoming Vice President of the Bell Aircraft Corporation. He is

credited with inputting to the design of the space shuttle. After
retirement, he returned to West Germany to live.

Allen Welsh Dulles: 7th April 1893 – 29th January 1969 was the
first civilian DCI (Director of Central Intelligence) in the USA
and its longest-serving director. Appointed in 1952 by President
Dwight Eisenhower, he served until November 1961. As head
of the Central Intelligence Agency (CIA) during the early Cold
War, he oversaw the abortive Bay of Pigs Invasion of Cuba for
which he was fired by President John F. Kennedy. In the 1920's
and 1930's, he worked as legal advisor on League of Nations arms
issues, meeting many leaders including Hitler and Mussolini. He
saw service in Switzerland during WWII conducting intelligence
operations against Nazi Germany. Appointed in 1963 by President
Johnson to serve in the Warren Commission investigating the
assassination of President Kennedy, he 'crafted' evidence to suit
the narrative 'coaching' witnesses.

Albert Einstein: 14th March 1879 – 18th April 1955. Einstein
was hailed as a genius Physicist recognised as being one of the
greatest of all time. Recipient of the 1921 Nobel Prize for Physics
he developed the Theory of Relativity and helped develop the
Quantum Mechanics theory. Produced theories on the structure of
the universe and molecular motion. Although born in Germany,
he settled in the USA in 1933 after Adolf Hitler assumed power
because of Nazi anti-Semitism, becoming a US citizen in 1940.
In 1933, he spent much time in Britain meeting both Winston
Churchill and Lloyd George. He assisted in initiatives to assist
Jewish scientists to escape the Nazis. Einstein warned President
Roosevelt of the German nuclear threat just before WWII. He
campaigned for Civil Rights and corresponded with Mahatma
Gandhi. He donated all his scientific papers to the University of
Jerusalem in Israel on his death.

Rafael Eitan: 23rd November 1926 – 23rd March 2019. 'Rafi' was an Israeli politician and controversial intelligence agent. His parents were Russian settlers in Palestine. In 1944 He assisted Jewish refugees fleeing Europe to reach Palestine. He carried out sabotage of British installations as part of a guerrilla war seeking an independent Jewish state. As a Mossad agent, Eitan famously led the operation in 1960 to kidnap the Nazi war criminal, Adolf Eichmann, from Argentina. He was engaged in various clandestine operations to obtain nuclear material for Israel. He served as an advisor to Prime Minister Menachem Begin on terrorism. In 1981, he was appointed Head of the Bureau of Scientific Relations or Lekem, offering a token resignation after an Israeli spy scandal, known as the Jonathan Pollard affair, revealed Isreal's involvement in espionage activities against the USA. He advised UK Prime Minister Margaret Thatcher and MI6 on terrorism issues. After 1993, he became a businessman, noted for several large-scale ventures in Cuba. He was the chairman of the Vetek – the Senior Citizens Movement

Levi Eshkol: 25th October 1895 – 26th February 1969. Born in what was Russia, now Ukraine, he emigrated to Palestine in 1914. As a representative of the Zionist Organisation, he negotiated an agreement with the Nazis in 1933 for the emigration of Jews to Palestine. An active Zionist, he helped obtain weapons for the Jewish resistance organisation, Haganah where he served in the high command. He was an Israeli politician, and led the Labour Party of which he was a founder. Appointed third Prime Minister of Israel on resignation of David Ben-Gurion in 1963. He had previously served in various government roles, including Minister of Defense from 1963 to 1967 and Minister of Finance from 1952 to 1963. On taking office as PM, he annulled military rule over Israeli Arabs. He led Israel during the Six Day War in 1967. Eshkol built a warm relationship with US President Lyndon Johnson being the first Israeli PM to be invited to the White House. He died in office from a heart attack aged 73.

Countess Ilse von Finkenstein: 1918 – 2001. Married into the one of the oldest aristocratic Prussian families. She was a striking society beauty who enjoyed mixing with those in intelligence circles. She worked for German intelligence before WWII spending much time in England. Towards the end of the war, she developed contacts within French intelligence who were anti-communist in order to assist Nazis in post war Europe. She married the renowned former Nazi SS officer and commando, Otto Skorzeny, in Madrid in March 1954. She was extremely wealthy, owning a horse farm, and property in the Bahamas, whilst having a spirit of adventure, enjoying the attention of younger men. They had what might be described as an 'open marriage' in which both had affairs. She notably had an affair with the Israeli agent, Rafi Meidan, who helped broker a meeting in 1962 between renowned Nazi SS war commando , Otto Skorzeny and Israeli intelligence agents during which Skorzeny was recruited to work for Israel.

Generalissimo Francisco Franco (Bahamonde): 4th December 1892 – 20th November 1975. A military officer and dictator of Spain. Became youngest general in Europe aged 23 assuming the rank of Brigadier General. In 1936, he joined the right-wing military faction in the Spanish Civil War, becoming leader and declaring a one-party state. In 1939, he became dictator over all Spain after victory over the Republicans. There followed a period of brutal suppression. He sided with the Axis powers during World War II despite retaining an outward policy of neutrality. Although initially anti-semitic, Franco did provide assistance to Jews escaping the Nazis. He allowed more liberal economic policies to develop whilst retaining a strict leadership centred stance. He appointed King Juan Carlos as his successor in 1969. He also relaxed many strict controls in the later years of his dictatorship. He claimed that his leadership had prevented communism from overcoming Spain. His adoption of free market policies assisted in major economic reform and growth which contributed to a retained core popularity until his death.

Muammar Muhammad Abu Minyar al-Gaddafi aka Colonel Gaddafi: c. 1942 – 20th October 2011 was a Libyan leader who played a dominant role in the Middle East. Born to a poor Bedouin family, Gaddafi became an Arab nationalist at school in Sabha before attending the Royal Military Academy in Benghazi, founding a revolutionary group which deposed the Western-backed monarchy in 1969. Gaddafi became leader of Libya ruling via decree through a revolutionary council where he strengthened ties to Arab nationalism and introduced 'sharia' as the basis of a legal system. He turned Libya into a socialist state but retained most controls in a dictatorship. Remaining head of the military and the police, he ruthlessly suppressed dissent. He sponsored terrorism and was suspected to be behind the Lockerbie Pan Am bombing tragedy of 1988. Libya was subjected to sanctions and Gaddafi became increasingly isolated. In 2011 protests broke out against corruption which degenerated into civil war with NATO intervening taking the side of the insurgents, and he was overthrown and brutally killed by militants.

Alfred/Marceli Galewski – B.? – 2nd August 1943. An engineer by profession, he was one of the main employees in the head office in Warsaw of CENTOS, a Jewish charity organisation. He was deported from Warsaw to Treblinka by the Nazis, where he was selected for work and appointed Camp Elder (*Lageralteste*) by the SS. He was involved in the camp Underground and helped plan the revolt, which took place on 2nd August 1943. He escaped during the revolt, but in fear of being taken alive by the pursuing SS, after running a few kilometres he committed suicide by taking poison.

'Mahatma' Mohandas Karamchand Gandhi: 2nd October 1869 –
30th January 1948. Gandhi trained as a barrister being called to the
bar in June 1891. After attempting to set up a practice in India, he
moved to South Africa where he lived for 21 years. Here he raised
a family and first employed nonviolent resistance in a campaign
for civil rights. In 1915 he returned to India and began organising
protests against excessive land-tax and discrimination. He became
leader of the Indian National Congress in 1921 campaigning for
various civil rights and self-rule. He wore a simple cloth 'dhoti' to
associate with the poor as his dress, undertaking fasts for meditation
and protest. He was a radical proponent of non-violence. He
became a symbol to common Indians and called on the British to
leave India in 1942, serving terms of imprisonment as a result of
his protests. Despite his wish for a multi-religious state, India was
given independence but partitioned into two dominions of India
and Pakistan. In the violence that followed, Gandhi undertook
many hunger-strikes in protest but was seen by many to be too
pro-Muslim and he was assassinated by a young Hindu Nationalist
who shot him in January 1948. He is still revered across the world
for his words advocating peace and non-violence.

Charles André Joseph Marie de Gaulle: 22nd November 1890 –
9th November 1970. A decorated officer who was wounded
several times in WW1. Led an armoured division against the
Germans during their invasion of France in 1940. He fled
to England and led the movement of resistance to German
occupation becoming the leader of Free France. He served as
Head of the Provisional Government in 1944. Advocated State
control of a capitalist economy. Resigned in 1946 on account
of frustration with political opposition. During a political
crisis over the Algerian war in 1958, he returned to politics
and founded the Fifth Republic with a strong Presidency. He
gave independence to Algeria and gradually to other colonies.
He opposed reliance on NATO and adopted an independent

nuclear deterrent for France. He fostered a new Franco/German alliance. He was re-elected President in 1965 but resigned in 1969. He opposed European centralisation favouring an alliance of independent states and vetoed Britain's attempts to join the European Economic Community, later the EU.

Reinhard Gehlen: 3rd April 1902 – 8th June 1979. Served as a lieutenant-general and intelligence officer during WWII for Germany, becoming chief of the intelligence service on the eastern front. He rose to become a Major General but was fired by Hitler for filing defeatist reports about Russia's military. After the war, he began working for the CIA in what became known as the Gehlen Organisation. He recruited former military and SS officers for espionage work against the Soviet Union, and then in West Germany during the Cold War. In 1956, he became the founding President of the *Bundesnachrichtendienst*, BND of West Germany serving until his resignation in 1968. He was accused of patronage in his position and the BND was radically reformed after he left. He retained the highest military rank of Lieutenant-General in the reserve and was awarded the Order of Merit in 1968.

Salvatore Mooney Giancana born **Gilormo Giangana:** May 24th 1908 – June 19th 1975. He was an American gangster who joined 'The Chicago Outfit' in the 1930's becoming boss in 1957. In the 1940's – 1950's he ran illegal gambling, liquor, and political rackets in Louisiana. He influenced the Presidential election victory of John F. Kennedy in 1960 turning against Kennedy because of anti-Mafia moves by the Administration. He was rumoured to have been involved with Kennedy's assassination. Worked with the CIA in the 1960's plotting to assassinate the Cuban leader, Fidel Castro. Imprisoned in 1965, he served one year before fleeing to Mexico. He was deported to the United States, returning to Chicago in 1974. He was due to give evidence to the Church Committee investigating abuses by the CIA. He had stated he had information he wanted to use as plea bargaining for immunity but before he could do so, on June 19th, 1975, he was murdered in his home. No-one was ever charged in connection with the killing.

Paul Joseph Goebbels: 29th October 1897–1st May 1945. German Nazi politician, Gauleiter of Berlin and Reich Minister of Propaganda in Nazi Germany from 1933 to 1945. He was a fanatical admirer of Adolf Hitler. A skilled public speaker, he held extreme anti-Semitic views. Joined the Nazi Party in 1924. He pioneered and was highly adept in the use of media for propaganda purposes. On 30th April 1945, he was appointed Chancellor of the Reich under the terms of Hitler's will, but on 1st May 1945 Goebbels and his wife, Magda. committed suicide after poisoning their six children with cyanide in the Führerbunker shortly before it was over-run by Russian forces. He confessed to having only disobeyed Hitler once, when he refused to leave Hitler's bunker.

Johanna Maria Magdalena "Magda" Goebbels born Ritschel: 11th November 1901 – 1st May 1945. A society beauty admired for her poise and looks. Initially married in 1921 to a wealthy businessman, but divorced in 1929. She became secretary to and then the wife of Nazi Germany's Propaganda Minister Joseph Goebbels in December 1931. A prominent member of the Nazi Party, she was a close ally, companion, and political supporter of Hitler, becoming part of the inner circle of his female friends. She became the unofficial "first lady" of Nazi Germany. She bore six children in the marriage, all of whom were poisoned before she and Joseph Goebbels poisoned themselves.

Mikhail Sergeyevich Gorbachev: 2nd March 1931 – 30th August 2022. Russian politician and last leader of the Soviet Union before the end of Communist rule. General Secretary of the Communist

Party of the Soviet Union from 1985 until 1991. Head of state from 1988 until 1991 and President of the Soviet Union from 1990 to 1991. An idealist, he transformed the Soviet Union with sweeping policies of reform, resulting in many Eastern bloc countries seeking freedom by holding democratic elections and ousting communist control. He decided not to intervene in an historic moment when the Berlin wall came down in 1989, whilst many former Soviet Republics declared independence both of which signified the end of the Cold War. This was aided by the tough stance against communism adopted by British Prime Minister Margaret Thatcher and US President Ronald Reagan.

Hermann Wilhelm Göring: 2nd January 1893–15th October 1946. Decorated air ace in World War I being awarded the Pour le Mérite (Blue Max). Served with legendary air ace Manfred von Richthofen. Joined Nazi Party in early 1920s. Elected President of the Reichstag in 1932, a post he held until 1945. Became Commander in Chief of Luftwaffe (German Air Force). Given rank of Reichsmarschall by Hitler, which gave him seniority over all officers in Germany's armed forces. Was seen as Hitler's successor at the height of his power but was dismissed by Hitler for treason for offering to take over as leader because of Hitler's situation in Berlin in April 1945. He died from purportedly taking poison the night before he was due to hang after being sentenced at the Nuremberg war trials.

Robert Ritter von Greim: 22nd June 1892 – 24th May 1945. A German First World War fighter pilot ace who became an ardent admirer of Hitler assisting Hermann Göring in the building of the Luftwaffe in the 1930's. He commanded units in the Battle of Britain and on the Russian front being promoted to General de Flieger. In April 1945, Hitler appointed Greim commander in chief of the Luftwaffe after dismissing Göring. He is the last person ever promoted to field marshal in the German armed forces. He flew to Berlin for unspecified reasons with Hanna Reitsch in April 1945 to meet with Hitler. In May 1945, Greim was captured by the Allies. He committed suicide in an American-controlled prison on 24ᵗʰ May 1945.

Otto Hahn: 8ᵗʰ March 1879 – 28ᵗʰ July 1968 Hahn was a German chemist who was a pioneer in the fields of nuclear chemistry and nuclear fission. In 1938, Hahn, Lise Meitner and Fritz Strassmann discovered nuclear fission. He studied in London and Montreal before becoming head of the Kaiser Wilhelm Institute for Chemistry in Berlin. Working with the Austrian physicist Lise Meitner, They made a series of ground-breaking discoveries. He served with distinction in WWI on the Western front. Although an opponent of Hitler and Jewish persecution, which resulted in Meitner having to leave Germany, he worked on the German nuclear weapons program. At the end of the war, he was incarcerated in Britain for six months with nine other German scientists. He returned to Germany to continue his research and in 1959 co-founded the Federation of German Scientists, committed to the ideal of responsible science. As he worked to rebuild German science, he became one of the most influential and respected West German scientists.

Ernst Franz Sedgwick Hanfstaengl: 2ⁿᵈ February 1887 – 6ᵗʰ November 1975. He studied in the United States at Harvard before taking over his father's art publishing business based in New York. He was well connected socialising with both Theodore and Franklin Roosevelt. In 1922, after returning to Germany, he heard Hitler speak in a beer hall and was drawn to support him becoming a confidante and friend. He joined the Nazi Party in 1931 but later became disillusioned after Hitler turned on him for clashing with both Goebbels and Unity Mitford. Hitler was also angered by his comments about German troops fighting in Spain. He defected to Britain and in WWII assisted the US in building a profile of Hitler and provided intelligence on other Nazi leaders.

Isser Harel: ? 1912 – 18th February 2003. He was the builder of the Israeli Intelligence Service and the Director of the Mossad from 1952–1963. He emigrated from Latvia to Palestine in 1930 having become a Zionist. In 1948, Harel founded and became the first director of Israel's internal security agency, Shin-Bet and Mossad when it was created in 1951. In April 1960, Harel with a team of Agents, kidnapped the Nazi Holocaust organiser, Adolf Eichmann, from Buenos Aires, and transported him to Israel. Harel was forced to resign from Mossad in March 1963, as a result of the policy of attacks on German scientists working in Egypt on weapons development, for which he recruited the assistance of former Nazis in assassination missions. He had a brief time in politics being elected to the Knesset before losing his seat in 1973.

Sir Arthur Travers Harris, 1st Baronet: 13th April 1892 – 5th April 1984. Often referred to as "Bomber" Harris due to his command in WWII. Born in Gloucestershire, Harris emigrated to Rhodesia. He saw action in the First World War in South Africa. In 1915, Harris returned to England, learned to fly, and joined the Royal Flying Corps serving on the Western Front where he claimed 12 enemy aircraft destroyed, ending the war as a Major. He remained in the RAF after the war and was appointed head of Bomber Command in 1942 where he advocated saturation bombing of German cities causing disquiet amongst many for the indiscriminate civilian casualties resulting, raising much controversy after the war. Nevertheless, the pursuit of a devastating campaign against the German industrial heartlands did have a considerable effect although at high cost in bomber crews and aircraft. He moved to South Africa after the war managing a marine corporation returning in 1953 to live out his days in London. The erection of a statue of him attracted considerable criticism as some labelled him a war criminal.

Werner Karl Heisenberg: 5th December 1901 – 1st February 1976. A highly eminent German physicist and a pioneer of quantum mechanics. Heisenberg was awarded the 1932 Nobel prize for the creation of quantum mechanics. Appointed as a principal scientist in the Nazi nuclear weapons program during World War II. He had attracted pre-war Nazi criticism as a "white Jew"; a derogatory term for those who are "Aryan" but act like Jews. He was appointed Director of the *'Uranverein'* program and in June 1942 he informed Albert Speer that a nuclear weapon could be developed by 1945. After the war, he was appointed director of the Kaiser Wilhelm Institute for Physics which became the Max Planck Institute. He was President and chairman of various German nuclear research organisations. He explored in later life the reconciling of religious teaching and advanced science.

Rudolf Walter Richard Hess: 26th April 1894 – 17th August 1987. German politician, becoming Deputy Führer in 1933 with the rank of Obergruppenführer. Served as military officer and decorated in World War I. In December 1933 he became Minister without Portfolio in Hitler's cabinet. Favoured peace with Britain and on 10th May 1941 flew to Britain on a mission to seek a treaty. He was arrested and there is confusion about his role in subsequent talks, which were covered up and denied in Britain and Germany. Sent to Spandau Prison, Berlin, after the war, with a sentence of life imprisonment. He became the only inmate from 1966. He suffered health issues, complaining of poison attempts and tried to commit suicide more than once. He was guarded alternately by the forces of France, Britain, the USA, and the Soviet Union. He was reported to have committed suicide in prison by hanging in 1987 at the age of ninety-three, despite his Doctor stating he was not capable of achieving this; there is speculation he was murdered by British Intelligence.

Major General Tamir Heyman b.1968 – Had a long and distinguished career with the IDF becoming Head of Military Intelligence from which he resigned in 2021. He is a graduate of the College of National Security and a graduate of the Inter-Force College of Command and Staff. He holds both a Bachelor's degree in political science and economics and a Master's degree in political science. He is currently Managing Director of the Institute for National Security Studies (INSS).

Heinrich Luitpold Himmler: 7th October 1900– 23rd May 1945. Joined Nazi Party in 1923, and the new SS (paramilitary elite guard organisation) in 1925. Appointed Supreme Commander or Reichsführer-SS by Hitler in 1929. Built the SS up to become a huge elite military organisation of fanatical dedicated troops. The SS were attributed with a large number of atrocities and war crimes which Himmler authorised visiting many concentration/extermination camps. He was a principal organiser of "The Final Solution", which created the framework for the mass deportation and genocide of all Jews. He urged the setting up of extermination camps and the horrific mass murders of Jews and others in what is termed "The Holocaust". Himmler attempted late negotiations with the Allies in 1945 when Germany was facing defeat. When Hitler learned of this, he gave orders he should be killed. He was poisoned or took cyanide whilst captured by the British on 23rd May 1945.

Adolf Hitler (born Schicklgruber): 20th April 1889 – 30th April 1945? Politician, soldier, leader of the German NSDAP (Nazi Party) and Führer of Germany. Elected Chancellor 1933, assuming dictatorial powers and becoming Führer in 1934. Born in Austria, he was decorated with the Iron Cross in World War I. In 1921 became leader of the Nazi Party. Attempted to seize power in 1923 in the Munich *putsch*. Jailed and wrote *Mein Kampf* in 1925 whilst in prison. He was a skilled orator and could deliver public speeches to thousands without notes inspiring adulation. He introduced laws which made Germany a one-party state under one leader, or Führer thereby becoming a dictator. Adopted policy of Lebensraum (expansion in the East). Directed military aggression across Europe and Africa, causing World War II. His regime was responsible for genocide, including the extermination of Jews as official policy. Ordered largest land invasion in history in June 1941 when his forces attacked Russia. Official version of death is that he committed suicide in his bunker in Berlin with his newly married wife Eva (formerly Braun) on 30th April 1945 as the Russian forces were closing in. Their bodies were never found there and even the Soviet leader, Joseph Stalin, believed they had escaped. DNA evidence of their bodies in Russia has been discredited.

John Edgar Hoover: January 1st 1895 – May 2nd 1972. Hoover was an American law enforcement administrator who served as founder and the first Director of the FBI remaining in post for 48 years, although this includes a period he was Director of the Bureau of Investigation from 1925. He pioneered the introduction of the most modern detection methods and introduced the national blacklist. He became a highly controversial figure involved in abuses of power including the blackmailing of politicians and harassment of dissidents. He amassed an enormous amount of power and it was rumoured he threatened those in power to achieve his goals. He was criticised for a lack-lustre response to the growing mafia and a failure to properly investigate the assassination of President Kennedy.

Saddam Hussein: 28th April 1937– 30th December 2006 was an Iraqi politician and leader dominating late 20th Century Arabic affairs. After initially studying law, he left to join the revolutionary pan-Arab Ba'ath party. In 1958, the Ba'ath Party led a revolution to overthrow King Faisal. He joined a further failed plot to overthrow the new leadership in 1959 after which he lived in Syria, then Egypt, returning to Iraq in 1963. After a further coup, he joined a plot to assassinate the leadership serving two years in prison. In 1968, he took part in a further successful coup and became deputy President and President in 1979. During this period, the country prospered with new oil wealth. Under his repressive regime, he led the country in the Iran- Iraq war, invading Iran, and subsequently, Kuwait resulting in the First Gulf War. He effectively ousted all opposition ruthlessly, building a virtual dictatorship. In 2003, a US led coalition, invaded Iraq on the pretext the country was building a stock of WMD (Weapons of Mass Destruction) and that it had ties to al-Qaeda. The real purpose was the removal of Saddam. He was arrested, tried, and found guilty of crimes against humanity and executed by hanging in 2006.

Jan Nowak-Jeziorański aka Jan Nowak: 2nd October 1914 – 20th January 2005. A Polish journalist, writer, politician, social worker and patriot. He was a leading resistance fighter during World War II. He performed a vital role working as an emissary shuttling between the commanders of the Home Army and the Polish Government in exile in London becoming known as the "Courier from Warsaw". He participated in the Warsaw Uprising of 1944 and broadcast on the radio in both Polish and English, after which he was ordered to leave Warsaw to evade capture successfully reaching England. After the war he worked for the BBC and as the head of the Polish section of Radio Free Europe. He was a security advisor to US Presidents Ronald Reagan and Jiimmy Carter. He was awarded the Presidential Medal of Freedom by President Bill Clinton.

Alexander Boris de Pfeffel Johnson: Born 19th June 1964. Attended Eton College and read Classics at Oxford. Political correspondent for the Daily Telegraph from 1989 and editor of The Spectator until 2005. Elected Conservative MP for Henley serving from 2001 – 2008 and Mayor of London from 2008 – 2016. Re-elected as MP for Uxbridge and South Ruislip in 2015, serving as Foreign Secretary before becoming Prime Minister and Leader of the Conservative Party and Prime Minister on 23rd July 2019. Known as a Euro Sceptic, he was credited with achieving a vote in a divided Parliament to leave the European Union in 2020 after calling a snap election in 2019. He led the country through the pandemic drawing diverse criticism for both being over draconian and failing to act decisively enough. He had a reputation with some for being colourful and is considered by others to be reckless. Resigned after a cabinet rebellion on 7th July 2022.

President Lyndon Baines Johnson: 27th August 1908 – 22nd January 1973, referred to as LBJ. Served as the 36th President of the United States from 1963 to 1969. He was Vice-President and became President after the assassination of President John F. Kennedy. He won election to the U.S. House of Representatives in 1937 and to the US Senate in 1948. In 1960 Johnson ran for the Democratic nomination for President but ultimately Kennedy made Johnson his Vice-Presidential running mate. He was appointed President in November 1963 when President Kennedy was assassinated. Some believe he was involved in the conspiracy to assassinate Kennedy in a coup d'etat. In 1964, he won the Presidential election against Senator Barry Goldwater. His domestic policies were ground-breaking but there were rumours he was involved in massive corruption both before and after he was elected. He expanded the war in Viet Nam and public opinion turned against him. At the end of his presidency in 1969, Johnson returned to his Texas ranch taking little part in public life.

Hans Kammler: 26th August 1901 –? Kammler was a senior SS officer responsible for Nazi civil engineering projects, particularly those surrounding secret weapons programmes. He oversaw the construction of various concentration camps and was latterly in charge of the V-2 rocket programme. He constructed the underground complex at Mittelwerk for V2 manufacturing in months during 1943, and drew on labour from the adjoining concentration camp at Mittelbau-Dora with many thousands of prisoners dying whilst working on the project. A committed Nazi, he served as head of the Aviation Ministry's building department, and other prominent positions believing that National Socialism was a necessary movement for both change and modern construction. He was considered to be the SS construction chief and assumed a power base in the late stages of the war. Kammler disappeared in May 1945 and there has been much conjecture regarding his fate.

President John Fitzgerald Kennedy: May 29th 1917 – 22nd November 1963 John Kennedy ('Jack') aka JFK served as the 35th President of the United States. He was the youngest elected person to assume the presidency and was considered to be an enlightened reformer. He was a Democrat and represented Massachusetts in both Houses. He was part of a wealthy influential family. His father, Joseph, had been Ambassador to Britain in early WWII. He served with distinction in WWII as a naval officer commanding torpedo boats being decorated for gallantry. He entered Congress in 1947 and was elected to the Senate in 1953 after which he became President in 1960, defeating Nixon. He committed himself to Civil Rights, a manned moon-landing, and resisting the spread of communism. He became enormously popular, championing the cause of freedom during the Cold War, and stood up against the Soviet Union's expansion of its nuclear arsenal into Cuba resulting in the missile crisis of 1962 when the Soviet leader, Nikita Khrushchev. was forced to back down by Kennedy's resolve. Kennedy was determined to prevent nuclear proliferation. He was assassinated in Dallas on 22nd November 1963 and his death is surrounded by controversy.

Henry Alfred Kissinger b: Heinz Alfred Kissinger: b 27th May 1923. A prominent US politician, diplomat, and geo-political authority who remains highly influential. He served as US Secretary of State and National Security advisor under Presidents Richard Nixon and Gerald Ford. He fled with his family from Nazi Germany in1938. He saw combat in WWII and volunteered for covert intelligence duties. He achieved rapid promotion on account of his outstanding administrative abilities. He studied Political Science at Harvard, wrote a number of books on defence tactics, power politics and political strategy. He worked as a consultant to the National Security Council to various government agencies, becoming National Security Advisor to Nixon in 1969 and Secretary of State in 1973. Playing a leading role in foreign affairs in the 1970's, he pioneered a policy of détente with the Soviet Union, and helped negotiate the end of the Viet Nam war. He supported involvement in many controversial foreign policy issues including the support for factions committing war-crimes in the cause of 'real politic'. Seen as highly effective despite the controversy, he achieved many successes in foreign affairs. After leaving office, he has continued to be a powerful voice in US policy and some believe that he wields power behind the scenes.

Aviv Kochavi: b 23rd April 1964 was an Israeli military commander becoming the 22nd Chief of General Staff of the Israel Defence Forces in 2018. He had held a number of senior posts including being the Northern Command commander of the Paratroopers brigade and Military Intelligence Director. He holds a master's degree in Public Administration and International Relations. He has seen extensive military service in combat duties and in 2002 during the Second Intifada while on the battlefield, Kochavi developed the use of a 5kg hammer to break down walls and cross through homes in refugee camps to prevent his soldiers from being shot by snipers. This tactic has been copied by other forces including the United States military. He resigned from the IDF in January 2023.

General Tadeusz Bór-Komorowski: 1st June 1895 – 24th August 1966 (Given name after one of his wartime code-names: *Bór* – ("The Forest") was a Polish military leader. He served as an officer in WW1 in the Austro-Hungarian army after which he was an officer in the Polish Army. An outstanding horse-rider, he was a member of the Polish equestrian team that went to the 1924 Summer Olympics. He took part in fighting against the German invasion of Poland in 1939 after which he helped organise the Polish Underground resistance in Krakow. In March 1943, he was appointed commander of the Home Army. His reputation suffered from taking an antisemitic stance opposing Jewish resistance movements and excluding Jews from the army. During the bitter fighting in 1944 during the Warsaw Uprising, he negotiated a surrender with the Germans in exchange for his troops being treated as prisoners of war. Following World War II, he became 32nd Prime Minister of Poland from 1947-1949 but only of the Government-in-Exile in London after a communist regime was established in Poland backed by Russia.

Heinz Linge: 23rd March 1913 – 9th March 1980 served as Hitler's personal valet from January 1935 until the Nazi leader's downfall and reported suicide in April 1945. He was an SS Officer rising to the rank of Obersturmbannführer (Lieutenant Colonel) He was with Hitler constantly from his rising in the morning until he retired to bed looking after all aspects of the household and was also a member of Hitler's bodyguard. He often escorted guests before introducing them to Hitler. He was captured and taken by the Russian forces to Moscow in May 1945 where he was imprisoned for ten years. He later wrote his memoirs.

Hans Luther: 10th March 1879 – 11th May 1962 was a German politician, and economist. He was briefly Chancellor from 1925 to 1926. As Minister of Finance, he helped stabilize the Mark during the hyperinflation of 1923. From 1930 to 1933, Luther was head of the Reichsbank but on the Nazis assuming power in 1933, he resigned at the request of Hitler after which he became the German Ambassador to the USA until 1937 when he retired from office. After the war, he carried out a number of roles in the banking and financial sector, and chaired the organisation set up to organise the re-structuring of West Germany. In 1958, he was appointed President of the German Cultural Organisation.

Günther Lützow 4th September 1912 – 24th April 1945 was a German fighter pilot ace during World War II. By the start of the war, he had already gained five aerial victories in combat during the Spanish Civil War for which he was awarded the Spanish Cross in Gold with Swords and Diamonds, Germany's highest decoration of the Spanish Civil War. In WWII, he flew over 300 combat missions and was credited with 110 enemy aircraft shot down. He commanded JG 3 (3rd Fighter Wing) gaining 15 aerial victories for which he was awarded the Knight's Cross of the Iron Cross in September 1940. Lützow remained in command of JG 3 in the aerial battles of Operation Barbarossa when Germany invaded the Soviet Union. By October 1941, he claimed his 100th aerial victory being only the 2nd pilot to do so. In early 1945, he fell out of favour with Göring for presenting a series of demands with other senior officers over the conduct of aerial operations. In April 1945, he joined Adolf Galland's 4th fighter detachment and was reported missing in action after a combat mission on 24th April 1945 to intercept US bombers.

Nelson Rolihlahla Mandela: 18th July 1918 – 5th December 2013. Mandela was an inspirational leader of South Africa who started his early life as an anti-apartheid activist. He studied law and started to practice in Johannesburg. Joining the ANC in 1943, and founded its youth league the following year. In 1948, after Apartheid was introduced, the ANC committed itself to overthrow the system. He was repeatedly arrested for sedition and in 1961, despite having been initially committed to non-violence, he founded an organisation which carried out sabotage for which he was imprisoned in 1962 with a life sentence for conspiring to overthrow the state. He served 27 years before increasing protests and the threat of civil war caused President FW de Klerk to release him in 1990 and negotiate an end to Apartheid. In 1994 multi-racial elections resulted in Mandela being swept to power as President. His government emphasised reconciliation under his direction and began major reforms. He stepped down in 1999 when he focused on combating poverty and tackling HIV/AIDS issues. He gained international acclaim for his work, and for his commitment to peace, human rights and reconciliation. He was a recipient of the Nobel Peace Prize. He is referred to as the "Father of the Nation".

Heinrich Arthur Matthes: 11th January 1902 – 16th December 1978. Mathes was responsible for conducting horrific war crimes when serving in the SS as a commander in the Nazi era. He was appointed deputy commandant of Treblinka Extermination Camp during the Holocaust in Poland. Matthes was appointed chief of the extermination area at Camp 2 where the gas chambers were built and managed by the SS personnel overseeing some 300 slave labourers. He periodically shot prisoners at random or for reasons such as failure to clean areas to his satisfaction. He was convicted at the Treblinka trials in 1964 and sentenced to life imprisonment. He died in prison.

Evelyn Maurine Norton Lincoln: 25th June 1909 – May 11th 1995. Famous for being the secretary to President John F Kennedy, she became close to him. She had served as his personal secretary from 1953 on his election to the US Senate. Her father was a member of Congress and she had an ambition to work on Capitol Hill from an early age. She was in the motorcade on the day of Kennedy's assassination on 22nd November 1963. She later stated that she believed Kennedy's death had been a conspiracy organised by Vice President Lyndon B. Johnson, Head of the FBI J. Edgar Hoover, the Mafia, and the CIA. She visited Kennedy's grave every year on the anniversary of his death at Arlington National Cemetery.

Rafi Meidan: DOB and death unknown. A Jew of German descent, Meidan was a prominent Israeli agent working for Mossad which he joined in 1962. He became the head of Amal, the department responsible for Nazi-hunting and purportedly involved in organising executions of former Nazi scientists working for the Egyptians, plus undesirables in South America and elsewhere. Served as Chief of the British Station in London in October 1973 when news of the impending launch of the Yom Kippur War was discovered in an intelligence operation. In 1963, he had befriended and become the lover of Countess Ilse von Finkenstein, the wife of the notorious Nazi SS Commando, Otto Skorzeny, as part of an operation to persuade Skorzeny to work for Israeli Intelligence.

Golda Meir b. Golda Mabovitch: 3rd May 1898 – 8th December 1978. A highly active politician, who served as the 4th Prime Minister of Israel from 1969 to 1974 and the first woman to hold this office. Born in the Russian Empire in Kyiv in what is now Ukraine, she emigrated as a child to the USA, where she became a teacher, and then to Palestine in 1921, joining a Kibbutz and taking up politics. On May 14th 1948 she was one of the signatories of the Israeli Declaration of Independence. She became labour minister and served as a very effective foreign minister. She was elected Prime Minister on 17th March 1969 and was in office during the Yom Kippur war of 1973 during which she was deterred from using nuclear weapons on the intervention of US National Security Advisor, Henry Kissinger. She resigned in April 1974 in the wake of political infighting over the lack of preparedness of Israel for the Yom Kippur war but she was exonerated from any blame.

Elise Meitner aka Lise: 7th November 1878 – 27th October 1968 was an Austrian-Swedish physicist who was jointly responsible for the discovery of nuclear fission in 1938 with her nephew Otto Frisch. She also discovered the radioactive isotope, protactinium-231 in 1917 whilst working at the Kaiser Wilhelm Institute of Chemistry in Berlin. In 1905, she became the second woman to obtain a doctorate in physics from the University of Vienna. A department head and a professor at the Kaiser Wilhelm institute, she lost her position during the Nazi Jewish persecutions and fled to Sweden in 1938, subsequently becoming a Swedish citizen. She coined the term "Fission" in 1939, a process leading to the development of the first atom bomb and nuclear reactors. She was nominated multiple times for the Nobel Prize in chemistry despite which she was never a recipient. One of her scientific collaborators in the discovery of fission, Otto Hahn was a recipient in 1944 which was later deemed unjust. She received many other honours, including the naming of chemical element 109 meitnerium after her.

Willi Bruno Mentz: 30th April 1904 – 25th June 1978. A former milkman, Mentz joined the Nazi Party in 1931, becoming a member of a member of the German SS in WWII, He was a particularly brutal guard in his treatment of Jews and other prisoners working at Treblinka Extermination Camp, gaining the nickname, Frankenstein for his horrifying cruelty. His atrocities included shooting sick, elderly and infirm prisoners in horrific circumstances. He dressed as a Doctor at a fake infirmary behind which he took prisoners before killing them. He was attributed with single-handedly murdering thousands. After the war, he returned to being a milkman in West Germany before being arrested in 1960 and sentenced to life imprisonment. In March 1978, he was released from prison due to ill health and died three months later.

Major General Sir Stewart Graham Menzies: 30th January 1890 – 29th May 1968. Educated at Eton, after which he joined the Grenadier Guards. Decorated army officer in World War I, during which he received DSO from George V. Fought in first and second battle of Ypres. Wounded in 1914 and again in 1915, when he was gassed. Joined British Intelligence in 1917 and then MI6 or SIS (Secret Intelligence Service) after World War I. Served on British delegation to Versailles peace conference. Became deputy director of MI6 in 1929 and director from 1939 to 1952, achieving rank of major general. His work, particularly in organising information obtained from code-breaking, was considered a massive contribution to victory in World War II, during which he had over 1,500 meetings with Churchill. He participated in active contact with anti-Nazi elements in Germany during the war.

Arnon Milchan: b. December 6th, 1944 is an Israeli businessman and an Academy Award nominated film producer with a history of involvement in espionage on behalf of Israel. His father owned a fertilizer company which Milchan inherited at the age of 21. Milchan turned the company into a successful chemical business. He earned a degree from the London School of Economics before being recruited to Lekem, an Israeli intelligence organisation tasked with obtaining materials for Israel's nuclear programme. In 1977, Milchan became involved in the movie business starting his own production company in 1991 producing 130 films. He has a diverse range of business interests in a media empire, is a leading art collector, and is the former owner of Puma sportswear. He was involved in procuring nuclear weapons material covertly and has been involved in organising the financing of intelligence operations abroad. He has been linked to corruption allegations involving the Israeli Prime Minister, Benjamin Netanyahu over legislation enacted to protect his businesses.

Rochus Misch: 29th July 1917 – 5th September 2013. He was a painter in 1936 employed on the Olympic stadium where he saw Hitler speak and, on his call up, volunteered to join the SS. Serving in the Polish campaign in 1939, he was badly wounded and after recovering was transferred to the Führer Escort Command; FBK, the unit guarding Adolf Hitler. Promoted to Oberscharführer, he becoming a courier, and telephone operator. He remained with Hitler in the bunker when Soviet forces entered Berlin and claimed to have seen the bodies of Hitler and Eva Braun (then Hitler) removed from the bunker after their purported suicide. When captured by the Soviets, he was subjected to torture, curiously, to exact information from him about Hitler's demise or escape. He remained loyal to Hitler all his life refusing to condemn him, describing him as a "wonderful boss".

Jules Salvador Moch: 15th March 1893 – 1st August 1985. Moch was born into a Jewish family with a distinguished military heritage. He took an early interest in socialism and was elected a socialist member of parliament serving until the 1940 German invasion, becoming a minister. He criticised the collaborating Vichy French government and was jailed for a time after which he joined the resistance which he helped to organise in Paris. Loyal to De Gaulle and the Free French forces he took part in the campaign to liberate France in 1944. After the war, he played a leading role in French politics including Minister of Defence and Interior Minister. He was deputy Prime Minister from 1949 to 1950 and France's delegate at the UN disarmament commission from 1951 to 1960. He left the Socialist Party in 1975. In 1948, he made a speech expressing his deep concern over the rift developing between East and West and is attributed by some as coining the phrase 'cold war'.

Heinrich Müller: 28th April 1900 – date of death unknown. Having served with distinction as a German pilot on the Western Front in WW1 for which he was highly decorated, he joined the police in 1919. He possessed a unswerving loyalty to the state and, therefore, initially opposed the Nazis. However, after Hitler became Chancellor, he continued serving the state, only joined the Nazi Party in 1939 because he was strongly advised to do so. He rose rapidly because Reinhard Heydrich (Chief of Reich Security) had noted his organisational abilities and his reputation for ruthless efficiency. He became chief of the secret police or Gestapo and was one of the main planners and organisers of the Holocaust attending and playing a leading role in the Wansee conference which set in motion deportation and genocide of all Jews, termed "The Final Solution". He was never captured and was last reportedly seen in the Führerbunker on 1ˢᵗ May 1945.

Gamal Abdel Nasser Hussein: 15ᵗʰ January 1918 – 28ᵗʰ September 1970. Nasser, as he was known, served as the second President of Egypt from 1954 until 1970. Nasser toppled the Egyptian monarchy in the 1952 Egyptian revolution, formed a one- party state and was declared President in 1956, although he had assumed power in 1954. He became highly popular in the Arab world after the Suez crisis of 1958 when Nasser had nationalised the Suez Canal. British, French and Israeli forces were forced to withdraw after invading when the USA opposed the action. Nasser formed an alliance with Syria resulting in the United Arab Republic being formed from 1958 until 1961. After Egypt's defeat by Israel in the Six-Day War of 1967, he resigned but was re-instated by public demand, remaining President until his death in 1970. He is credited with leading reforms for social justice, and Arab unity whilst building prosperity but criticised for violations of human rights, and establishing dictatorial rule.

Benjamin Netanyahu: born 21ˢᵗ October 1949. Longest-serving Israeli Prime Minister. Raised in Jerusalem and attended high school in Philadelphia, USA. Saw active service in the military in the 1967 six-day war and later served in special forces. Graduated in science, he entered politics in the 1980s after serving a period as permanent representative to the UN. In 1993, he was elected Chairman of Likud and became youngest Prime Minister of Israel in 1996 but was defeated in 1999. Served as minister of foreign affairs and finance under Ariel Sharon and is credited with successful economic reforms. In 2009, he became Prime Minister a second time and remained so until 13th June 2021. He was accused of alleged bribery, fraud and breach of trust in legal proceedings which were ongoing in 2022. He was re- elected Prime Minister in November 2022 for a record 6th term.

President Richard Milhous Nixon: January 9th 1913 – April 22nd 1994 was the 37th President of the USA from 1969 to 1974. He graduated in law and saw active service in WWII in the US Naval Reserve. A Republican, he was elected to serve as Californian representative to Congress in 1947, and to the Senate in 1950. He served as vice President from 1953 to 1961. In 1960, he ran for President being narrowly defeated by John F Kennedy. His administration saw the end of U.S. involvement in the Vietnam War, a reduction of tension with Russia and China, and the first man on the moon. He introduced environmental and safety legislation but his second term was ended when he resigned from office due to the Watergate scandal resulting from the cover-up of his awareness of a criminal break-in to Democratic offices involving his staff. He resigned before impeachment proceedings would have forced him from office. He is credited with being a reforming President and one who also made great strides in reducing tensions through his global foreign policy initiatives.

Elizabeth Shakespear Nel née **Layton:** 14th June 1917 – 30th October 2007 achieved some fame as personal secretary to Churchill from 1941 to 1945. Having moved to Canada with her parents after WW1, she attended secretarial college in London working for an employment bureau, then the British Red Cross where she was selected for work at Downing Street. At 10-30pm in late May 1941, she met Winston Churchill who initially was unimpressed with her performance making his displeasure clear, especially as she had failed to use double spacing on his dictation. However, they built up a good working rapport and she travelled with the PM extensively during war-time including visits to the White House. Layton completed her work for Churchill by taking dictation for his VE day speech, and wept with him on his defeat in the 1945 General Election. She married a South African and had her first child in 1946, moving to South Africa. In 1958, she wrote her memoir about working for Churchill. She returned frequently to London to attend various commemorative events.

Barack Hussein Obama II: born 4ᵗʰ August 1961. Civil rights attorney, academic and served as the 44ᵗʰ President of the US from 2009 to 2017. A Democrat, Obama was the first African-American President. Introduced Affordable Care Act and legislation to stimulate the economy. He increased US troop levels in Afghanistan, reduced nuclear weapons and ended military involvement in the Iraq War. He ordered military intervention in Libya contributing to the overthrow of Muammar Gaddafi. He ordered the military operation that resulted in the killing of Osama bin Laden. He increased LGBT rights, attempted gun control legislation and authorised action against the so-called Islamic State. Other foreign policy initiatives included global warming, normalised relations with Cuba and the brokering of a nuclear treaty with Iran. He is credited with being an outstanding public speaker.

Lee Harvey Oswald 18ᵗʰ October 1939 – 24ᵗʰ November 1963. Oswald was a US marine veteran who also worked with US Intelligence. After a troubled family life, he joined the marines at 17. He left the marines in 1959, and visited Russia, defected and gained employment. He married a Russian, Marina, in 1961, had a child in 1962, and returned to the USA being dis-illusioned with communist Russia. He lived in the Dallas/Fort Worth area mixing with anti-Soviet Russians. He was tasked by intelligence to infiltrate a pro-Cuban/Castro organisation on behalf of the FBI. He was subsequently seen distributing pro Castro leaflets (despite being anti-communist). On 16th October 1963, he took a job at the Texas School Depository having been informed there was an opening days before. On 22nd November 1963 President John F Kennedy was assassinated and it was claimed the shots came from the Depository. Oswald was seen by several people around 30 minutes before Kennedy's assassination away from the sixth floor from where the shooting purportedly took place. Other witnesses said no-one was on that floor at this time and no-one saw Oswald there. Oswald was arrested on the day of Kennedy's assassination, accused of the shooting, but was fatally shot whilst being escorted through the basement of Dallas Police HQ. Before the shooting he had claimed he was a "patsy" (someone being set up). There is speculation that his killing was sponsored by organised crime. Many witnesses to the assassination died in mysterious circumstances.

Marina Nikolayevna Oswald Porter née **Prusakova:** b 17th July 1941 was married to Lee Harvey Oswald, the purported assassin of President John F Kennedy. Marina was born in the Soviet Union and met Oswald at a dance in March 1961, marrying him six weeks later. In June 1962, the couple moved to the USA settling in Dallas with their daughter born that year. They had a difficult early marriage but reconciled with Oswald staying weekends. Her testimony was not considered reliable by the Warren Commission and she later stated she was browbeaten to make statements, particularly relating to photos of Oswald holding a rifle which she was told to say she had taken. After testifying, she received monies from anonymous donors. In 1965 she re-married and became a US citizen in 1989. Although she initially testified that Oswald was guilty, she has since retracted this and states he was completely innocent.

Yvonne Pagniez: 10th August 1896 – 18th April 1981. Pagniez was born into a well to do family, studying Philosophy before becoming a nurse in WWI when her area of France was occupied. She subsequently trained as an intelligence agent. After the war, she began writing for which she won awards. In 1940, after the German invasion of France, she joined the Resistance in Paris. In 1944, she was arrested and sent to Ravensbrück concentration camp, escaping before hiding in Berlin shielded by underground agents, then escaped to Switzerland. After the war she continued her writing and also became a war correspondent. In later life she became a friend of the German aviator, Hanna Reitsch, who was a life-long admirer of Adolf Hitler.

Priti Sushil Patel: b 29th March 1972 was home secretary serving in the Conservative government from2019 to 2022 and as international development minister from 2016 to 2017. Elected an MP for Witham in 2010, she is considered to be on the right wing of the Party. Born to a Ugandan Indian family, she studied at Keele and Essex University and was inspired by Margaret Thatcher to enter politics. David Cameron recommended she be put on the A list of candidates. She resigned as home secretary in September 2022.

Shimon Peres b. Szymon Persk: 2nd August 1923 – 28th September 2016. Peres was the eighth Prime Minister of Israel serving from 1984 to 1986, 1995 to 1996. and 2007 to 2014. Peres was passionately devoted to the security of Israel, participating in the covert establishment of the nuclear weapons programme centred and hidden at Dimona. He was also involved in organising covert operations to counter Nazi missile technology being adopted by Egypt in the 1950's. Elected to the Knesset in 1959, he became President in 2007. He was deputy director general of defense in 1952 at the age of 28, and director general from 1953 until 1959. He was passionate about arming Israel with latest defence and weapons technology. In 1963, he held negotiations with U.S.

President John F. Kennedy resulting in weapons being sold to Israel. Under Prime Minister Rabin, Peres won the 1994 Nobel Peace Prize after the Oslo Accords resulting in Arab/Palestinian peace agreements. In 1996, he founded the Peres Center for Peace, promoting understanding in the Middle East.

Michael Willcox Perrin: 13th September 1905 – 18th August 1988. An award-winning scientist, he directed the first British atomic bomb programme, and investigated the Nazi atomic bomb. After studying chemistry at Oxford and Toronto University, he succeeded in creating polythene in 1935. He demonstrated the potential of a nuclear weapon in WWII and became part of the secret Tube Alloys programme dedicated to nuclear weapons development. In later life, he worked for ICI before becoming chairman of the Welcome Foundation.

María Eva Duarte de Perón b. **María Eva Duarte:** 7th May 1919 – 26th July 1952. Peron or Evita was an Argentine politician, activist, actress, and philanthropist who was First Lady of Argentina from June 1946 until her death in July 1952. She was the wife of President Juan Perón. She was from a poor family but at the age of 15, she moved to Bueno Aires to pursue a career as an actress. She married Juan Perón in 1945 and he was elected President in 1946. She was active in promoting worker's rights and ran the Ministries of Labour and Health. She also championed women's rights including suffrage. She became hugely popular and announced her candidature as vice President in 1951. She withdrew after military opposition and health issues as she had cancer from which she died at the age of 33 in 1953. She was given a state funeral and was revered by the Argentine nation for her reforming work.

Juan Domingo Perón: 8th October 1895 – 1st July 1974 was President of Argentina from 1946 until 1955 and briefly from October 1973 until July 1974. He enjoyed popularity with the working class together with his second wife, Eva Perón. His government invested in public works and expanded social welfare. He had admired the regime of Adolf Hitler and many former Nazis were welcomed into Argentina after WWII. Opposition to his leadership was ruthlessly suppressed. His second term after being elected by a wide margin was troubled due to an economic downturn, the death of Eva, his personal life and opposition to measures he introduced on divorce and prostitution by the Catholic Church. In 1955, he was overthrown in a military coup after his repressive measures against the Church and Perón was exiled. He returned to Argentina in 1973 and was re-elected President. His term was blighted by in-fighting between right and left and he increasingly supported the right until his death in 1974. His name was lent to an ongoing political movement known as Perónist.

Sir David Petrie: 9th September 1879 – 7th August 1961 was a former police officer serving in the Indian Imperial Police from 1900 until 1936. He chaired the UPSC (the Union of Public Service Commissions) responsible for recruiting officers to senior posts. In April 1941, he was appointed director general of MI5 responsible for internal UK security. His task was to reorganise the service so that it could improve its efficiency. In the spring of 1946, Petrie retired.

Jonathan Jay Pollard: b. 7th August 1954. Pollard was born to a Jewish family living in Galveston, Texas and worked for US Naval Intelligence. He had a colourful reputation for fabricating stories about his background. As a result of a number of security failings, he gained access to sensitive material which he offered to sell to various countries, especially Israel in the 1980's. His activities were discovered in 1985 and he failed to leave the country despite his Israeli handler, Rafi Eitan, informing him he should do so. In 1987, he pleaded guilty to spying for Israel and received a life sentence. The Israeli government acknowledged a portion of its role in Pollard's espionage in 1987, apologising to the US. It is thought his espionage revealed a huge amount of highly classified and sensitive material, and despite objections from many senior officials, he was released in 2015, emigrating to Israel in 2020 with his second wife.

Vladimir Vladimirovich Putin: born 7th October 1952. Russian politician, former KGB intelligence officer and FSB Director. Favoured by Boris Yeltsin as his successor, he served as President of Russia from 1999 to 2008, then Prime Minister from 1999 to 2000 and 2008 to 2012, before reassuming powers as President. After sixteen years serving as a KGB officer, he then worked for President Boris Yeltsin before being appointed Prime Minister. When Yeltsin resigned, he became Acting President, then President. Re-elected in 2012 and 2018. Promotes conservative policies based on traditional Russian Soviet-style values with little tolerance of dissent. Reduction in democratic values has taken place under his leadership which has strengthened his hold on power, described as dictatorial. There are reports of state sponsored assassinations taking place under his authority including a number of wealthy Russians who have died under very mysterious circumstances, after having opposed Putin or objected to the war in Ukraine. Putin ordered Russia's invasion of Ukraine in February 2022 causing wide dissent at home and abroad. He has raised the threat of using nuclear weapons.

Dominic Rennie Raab: b. 25th February 1974. Dominic Raab is a prominent British politician within the Conservative Party. After studying law at Oxford, he took his Master's at Cambridge. Elected an MP for Esher and Walton in 2010 he has been Parliamentary Under Secretary of State, Brexit Secretary in 2018, First Secretary of State, Foreign Secretary, and served at justice and housing as minister. He ran for leader being defeated by Boris Johnson, becoming deputy Prime Minister and Lord

Chancellor. In 2022, accusations were made of bullying or aggressive bebaviour to colleagues in the workplace. He was re-appointed Deputy PM and Lord Chancellor by Rishi Sunak in 2022. Raab is considered of the most influential members of Government. He has written books and pamphlets on Justice issues and human rights.

Yitzhak Rabin: 1st March 1922 – 4th November 1995. An outstanding general, politician, and statesman, he served as the 5th Prime Minister of Israel in office 1974 – 1977 and from 1992 until he was assassinated in 1995. He excelled in school and fought for Israel's independence. He commanded the Israeli commando unit, Palamach, during the 1948 Arab Israeli war. He was appointed Chief of Staff of the Israeli Defense Force (IDF) in 1964, commanding forces during the Six-Day War of 1967. He helped foster a growing relationship with the USA as Ambassador from 1968 – 1973. After his first term of office as PM, he was Defense Minister from 1984 – 1990. On being re-elected as PM, he pursued an Israeli – Palestinian peace process signing the Oslo Accords and was awarded the Nobel Peace Prize in 1994 together with the Palestinian leader Yasser Arafat. He was associated with a strong policy of Arab - Israeli peace. His assassination was by an extremist opposing the Oslo Peace Accords.

Walter (Walther) Rauff: 19th June 1906 – 14th May 1984 served in the SS and committed a number of war-crimes/crimes against humanity. He had served in the German Navy in the 1920's where he met the future senior SS commander, and co-founder/architect of the Holocaust, Reinhard Heydrich who helped build his SS career. He assisted in the development of vans for gassing Jews and those with disabilities having special responsibility for this in Russia during the German occupation. In 1943, he became head of Gestapo in Italy. After the war, he worked for Syria, then was recruited by Israeli intelligence. He also carried out work for West

German intelligence (BND) As he was hunted for war crimes, he went to Chile and assisted their military remaining there until his death despite there being many requests for his extradition. It is thought he was directly responsible for over 100,000 deaths of Jewish, Roma, and those with disabilities.

Ronald Wilson Reagan: 6th February 1911–5th June 2004. An American actor, union leader and politician who served as the 40th President of the United States, serving two terms from 1981 to 1989 and became an influential voice of conservatism. Initially worked as radio commentator, then an actor starring in some Hollywood movies. He became President of the Screen Actors Guild, where he rooted out communist influence. As Governor of California, he built a reputation for firm leadership and sound economics. Reagan was the oldest person, at the time, to become President of the United States at sixty-nine. He implemented sweeping economic reforms dubbed 'Reaganomics', advocating tax rate reduction to spur economic growth and championed de-regulation. Helped end the Cold War through meetings with Soviet General Secretary Mikhail Gorbachev, supported by the British Prime Minister Margaret Thatcher, with whom Reagan had a strong relationship. In later life he suffered from Alzheimer's disease. His approval ratings made him one of the most popular US Presidents.

Hanna Reitsch: 29th March 1912–24th August 1979. A German aviator and test pilot. She set many world glider flying records before World War II. Tested many of Germany's new aircraft during World War II and received numerous honours. A committed National Socialist, she was an admirer of Hitler throughout her life and was awarded the Iron Cross with Diamonds by him. Flew last plane out of Berlin before the German defeat in April 1945. In the 1950s she set up a gliding centre in India, even flying the Indian Prime Minister. She carried on setting world records for gliding and established the first black African gliding school in Ghana. In 1961 she was invited to meet US President John F. Kennedy at the White House. The rocket scientist Wernher von Braun, who designed the V-2 and the Apollo moon rocket, was her lover and it is rumoured she had an affair with the German flyer, Ritter von Greim. Throughout the 1970s, Reitsch set glider endurance records and won international helicopter flying competitions. She remained an admirer of Adolf Hitler and National Socialism until her death.

Manfred Albrecht Freiherr von Richthofen: 2nd May 1892 – 21st April 1918. A German fighter pilot ace in WW1, he achieved a legendary status and was known as 'the Red Baron'. Although a cavalryman at the outbreak of war, he transferred to the Air Service in 1915 where he showed courage and skill in combat. He was soon given command of his own fighter wing and what later became known as "Richthofen's Circus". He achieved 80 confirmed air combat victories becoming famous in Germany and respected by the enemy. Despite receiving a serious head wound in 1917, he returned to active duty against doctor's advice. He was shot down and killed in April 1918 probably from ground fire, and was buried in Bertangles, near Amiens, by the Allies with full military honours and a gun salute being performed. Memorial wreaths were laid by nearby Allied squadrons one of which said, "To Our Gallant and Worthy Foe".

Generalfeldmarschall Irwin Rommel: 15th November 1891 – 14th October 1944. Respected German general and military theorist. A decorated soldier and officer in World War I, he saw considerable action, gaining a reputation as an effective strategist. Became known as 'the Desert Fox' after commanding the Afrika Korps in North Africa. He organised German defences in France, bolstering the 'Atlantic Wall' defences and was given command of Army Group B. He was highly popular with troops. He was a passive opponent of Hitler but would not participate in the assassination plot with conspirators. On 14th October 1944, after being suspected of involvement in the 20th July bomb plot on Hitler's life, he was confronted. He then took poison in a forced 'suicide' near his home in Herrlingen, Southern Germany, when he was offered choice by the Nazis of a state funeral, with his family looked after, if he committed suicide, or face trial in Berlin with consequences for family.

Franklin Delano Roosevelt: 30th January 1882 – 12th April 1945. 32nd President of the United States, popularly referred to as FDR. President Theodore Roosevelt was his fifth cousin, whom he greatly admired. Became a senator in 1910, then served as Assistant Secretary to the Navy in World War I. In 1921, Roosevelt contracted an illness (diagnosed Polio) which left him paralysed in both legs. He became Governor of New York in 1928 and was elected President in 1932. Instigated social security legislation to protect the poor, the sick, the elderly and unemployed. He was the only President to be elected to serve four Presidential terms, although he died during the fourth. President during World War II and at the time of America's decision to join the war after the Japanese attack on Pearl Harbour in December 1941 which he famously described as "a Day of Infamy". Formed close working relationship with Winston Churchill during World War II and helped to shape plans for a post-World War II Europe.

Arthur Louis Hugo Rudolph: 9th November 1906 – 1st January 1996 was a German rocket engineer who developed early rocket engines in the late 1920's and early 1930's. He met Wernher von Braun in 1932 and subsequently worked on the Nazi rocket programme developing the V2. At the end of WWII, he was taken to the USA under the Operation Paperclip programme to harness German expertise. He worked extensively on both missile technology and the Apollo space programme. In 1984, he was investigated for war crimes and he eventually claimed he had been forced to renounce his US citizenship and return to Germany.

Lieutenant Colonel Clayton A. Rust. No dob. or full background info available. He was battalion commander of the 276th ECB (Engineer Combat Battalion), which was serving at the Ludendorff Bridge spanning the Rhine at Remagen, in Germany. This was captured by US forces during the Battle of Remagen in March 1945 in the closing stages of the European offensive by the Allies during WWII. He was on the bridge when it collapsed on 17th March 1945. He fell into the Rhine, was briefly pinned underwater, and then floated downstream to a pontoon bridge where he was pulled out of the water. He later reported: "The bridge was rotten throughout, many members not cut had internal fractures from our own bombing, German artillery, and from the German demolitions."

Muhammad Anwar el-Sadat: 25th December 1918 – 6th October 1981. Sadat was an Egyptian politician and military officer who served as the third President of Egypt. He attempted to gain support from the Axis powers in World War II to oust the British from Egypt for which he was imprisoned. Sadat was a senior member of the military unit which overthrew King Farouk in the 1952 Egyptian Revolution. He was close to President Nasser and was appointed Minister of State in 1954 becoming Vice President. In October 1970, he assumed power after the death of Nasser. He led Egypt during the Yom Kippur war. In 1978, Sadat and Israeli Prime Minister Menachem Begin signed a peace treaty brokered by US President, Jimmy Carter for which they were awarded the Nobel Peace Prize. In the late 1970's Sadat was a reforming president re-introducing democracy and promoting peace in the Middle East. He was criticised for not consulting with Arab States or considering the Palestinians in pursuing peace with Israel. On 6 October 1981, militants opened fire, killing Sadat with automatic rifles during the 6th October parade in Cairo.

Amos de-Shalit: 29th September 1926 – 2nd September 1969 was a leading Israeli physicist. Born in Jerusalem, he obtained a master's degree at the Hebrew University of Jerusalem. He served in the science corps of the IDF and co-wrote a letter to Prime Minister David Ben-Gurion stressing the importance to Israel of nuclear physics in defence. He was actively involved in recruiting those studying physics to join a group dedicated to nuclear weapons development. In 1954, de-Shalit was asked to establish the Department of Nuclear Physics at the Weizman Institute of Science which he ran for ten years whist working for the Israeli Defense ministry. He died, aged 42, from Pancreatitis.

Yitzhak Shamir b: **Yitzhak Yezernitsky**; 22nd October 1915 – 30th June 2012. Born in what is now Belarus, he emigrated to Palestine in 1935. His parents and two sisters were murdered in the Holocaust. In 1940, he joined the militant anti-British Nationalist group, Lehi, and was imprisoned. He plotted the assassination of the British Minister for Middle Eastern Affairs, Lord Moyne, and was implicated in other terrorist atrocities including the assassination of the UN representative to the Middle East, Count Bernadotte in 1948. He joined Mossad in 1955 and was involved in organising the killing of German scientists working for Egypt. He resigned after his boss, Isser Harel was forced to step down over the assassination programme. He entered politics in 1969 as a hard-liner. He became Foreign Minister in 1980 and was the seventh Prime Minister of Israel serving two terms, 1983–1984 and 1986–1992. He assisted with the Camp David Accords and normalised the relationship with Egypt. He was instrumental in blocking the emigration of Jews from Russia to the USA, favouring Israel as their destination.

Ariel Sharon: Aka Arik 26th February 1928 – 11th January 2014. Sharon was born to Eastern European parents who emigrated to Palestine in 1922. In 1942 at the age of 14, Sharon joined a paramilitary youth organisation and later Haganah, the precursor to the Israel Defense Force. He was an effective commander in the IDF serving in the 1948 Palestine War and took part in many active service missions. He was an architect of many special forces units and initiatives. He was a field commander in the 1956 Suez campaign, the 1967 Six Day War, the War of Attrition, and the 1973 Yom Kippur War. Prime Minister Yitzhak Rabin called him "the greatest field commander in our history" He joined the Likud Party holding ministerial posts including Minister of Defense where he exercised hard line policies being blamed for a massacre in the Lebanon War of 1982. Elected Prime Minister 2001, he served until 2006. After initially favouring Israeli settlements on the West Bank, he later began a policy of withdrawal. After a stroke in 2006, he remained in a vegetative state until his death.

Liza Shvetz: ? 1914 – 6th February 2017. She served as secretary to David Ben-Gurion, the first Prime Minister of Israel. Shevetz was born as Liza Welbel and emigrated to Israel from Poland in 1938. She became the secretary of the leader of the Yishuv, Ben-Gurion, (the Jewish community in British Mandate Palestine), who eventually became the first Prime Minister. She continued to serve as Ben-Gurion's secretary until he decided to retire from political life and move to Kibbutz Sdeh Boker in the Negev. After his retirement, she would often volunteer to go to his home and take minutes of meetings. She verified that he valued the unswerving loyalty of Shimon Peres from which he took enormous comfort. She declared that she had been happy to serve the man she loved and admired.

Otto Johann Anton Skorzeny: 12th June 1908 – 5th July 1975 was an Austrian-born German SS officer. He became a commando in the Waffen-SS during World War II heading up special operations and was involved in several audacious missions, including the Gran Sasso raid which rescued Benito Mussolini from captivity in September 1943. He was a favourite of Adolf Hitler who personally decorated him with the Knight's Cross of the Iron Cross with Oak Leaves. He was involved in secreting the gold taken from the Reichsbank in 1945 by the SS. Skorzeny assisted with the establishment of *Der Spinne* helping former Nazis escape after the war. He was imprisoned after the war but escaped in 1948 wearing a US army uniform. Worked for various countries in military intelligence and training until the end of his life. He was recruited to work covertly by Israeli Intelligence in the early 1960's and implicated in a number of controversial kidnappings and shootings. He spent some time in Argentina helping train the military and was rumoured to have had an affair with Eva Peron. There were some claims he had involvement in the assassination of President John F. Kennedy in November 1963 but there were no proven links. Skorzeny accumulated enormous wealth and owned property in Ireland and Spain where he died of lung cancer.

Berthold Konrad Hermann Albert Speer: 19th March 1905 – 1st September 1981. Speer was an Architect and Nazi politician. He Joined the Nazi Party in 1931 becoming a friend of Adolf Hitler and designed many Nazi buildings and structures whilst also planning the vast imposing arenas in which Nazi Party rallies were held. Appointed German Minister of Armaments and War Production in 1942, he was later accused of adopting a policy of extensive use of concentration camp labour to assist the German war effort. Speer was imprisoned after the war at Spandau Prison, Berlin, with many other leading Nazis. He was released in 1966 and wrote his memoirs, which were highly subjective, attracting much criticism. He died in a London hotel, purportedly of a stroke, whilst visiting England to give press interviews with fresh revelations.

Joseph Vissarionovich Stalin (born **Ioseb Besarionis dze Jughashvili):** 18th December 1878 – 5th March 1953. Born in what is now Georgia, Stalin attended a seminary before joining a Marxist Party. Edited the party's newspaper, *Pravda* and raised funds for Lenin's Bolsheviks via robberies, kidnappings and other crime. After the October 1917 revolution, he joined the Politburo of the new one-party state. He saw military service in the Russian Civil War. After Lenin's death in 1924, he assumed the leadership of Russia. Under Stalin, agriculture and industry were radically centralised, contributing to the famine of 1930-33 which killed millions. He began the 'Great Purge' in 1934 in which over 700,000 were executed for being 'enemies of the state'. By 1937, he was a de facto dictator. He collaborated with Hitler over the invasion of Poland seizing Polish territory. He galvanised the defence of Russia in the Nazi invasion of 1941, eventually counter-attacking to take Berlin in 1945. He engineered the re-alignment of Eastern states post-war into a 'Soviet Bloc' resulting in the 'Cold War' with the West. His regime managed to obtain the nuclear bomb in 1949, which was a threat to the West. His totalitarian rule resulted in the deaths of millions of Russian people in a policy of repression under a strict communist ideology.

Major General Sir Kenneth William Dobson Strong 9th September 1900 – 11th January 1982. Born in Montrose, Scotland, he was commissioned as an officer into the 1st Battalion Royal Scots Fusiliers, serving as an Intelligence Officer, and a Defence Security Officer in Malta and Gibraltar. In the 1930's he worked in the German Intelligence section at the War Office, becoming Assistant Military attaché in Berlin. In March 1943, Strong was appointed Assistant Chief of Staff for Intelligence (G-2) at Allied Forces HQ and in May 1944 he joined Eisenhower's Supreme Headquarters Allied Expeditionary Force (SHAEF) He directed covert operations to ensure advanced German weapons technology was seized by British forces. He played a leading part in the negotiations for Germany's surrender at the end of WWII in 1945. Retiring from the army in 1947, he continued to serve in intelligence until 1966. Strong subsequently played an active role in business and wrote two books.

Margaret Hilda Thatcher, Baroness Thatcher (née Roberts): 13th October 1925–8th April 2013. British politician and stateswoman who served as Prime Minister of the United Kingdom from 1979 to 1990 and Leader of the Conservative Party from 1975 to 1990. Studied chemistry at Oxford, then became a barrister. Elected MP for Finchley in 1959. Appointed Secretary of State for Education in 1970. She defeated Edward Heath in a Conservative Party leadership contest in 1975. She was the longest-serving British Prime Minister of the twentieth century and the first woman to hold that office. She won an unprecedented three election victories. A Soviet journalist dubbed her the 'Iron Lady', a nickname she enjoyed representative of her uncompromising leadership style. Helped negotiate the end of the Cold War in the 1980s with US President Ronald Reagan and Russian Leader Mikhail Gorbachev. Reformed industrial relations by democratising trade union practices and controversially presided over the dismantling of the British coal industry. In 1990, after facing a leadership challenge, she lost senior Tory support and resigned. In 1992, she was given a life peerage, entering the House of Lords.

President Donald John Trump: Born 14th June 1946. Entrepreneur mainly in real estate and media personality serving as the 45th President of the United States from 2017 to 2021. He is a Republican and is viewed as a nationalist and populist figure. He is non-conformist in style and presentation and is critical of establishment politics. He is also highly critical of the media's reporting of politics calling it "fake news". He pursued an America First policy in foreign affairs and withdrew from the Iran nuclear deal and the Paris Climate Change agreement. He also imposed protectionist import tariffs which caused a trade war with China. Domestically, he cut taxes for individuals and business to stimulate the economy but also cut elements of health care established by President Obama. Claimed his electoral defeat in 2020 was fraudulent and, following a riot in the Capitol which he was accused of orchestrating, his social media accounts were closed. Despite controversy surrounding his Presidency, he retained popularity although some label him divisive.

John Ward 15th December 1918 – 29th August 1995. He joining the RAF in 1937 as an Aircraftsman to train as a wireless operator/air-gunner. He was promoted to Flight Lieutenant and decorated twice for bravery in WWII operating behind enemy lines after being shot down and escaping after capture. He served as a BBC war correspondent behind enemy lines and fought with the Polish resistance in the Home Army during the Warsaw Uprising of 1944, during which, he submitted moving reports of what was happening, appealing for help. He was awarded the Polish Cross of Valour by the leader of the Polish Home Army, General Tadeusz Bór-Komorowski who arranged for his passage out of Warsaw. He was captured by Russian forces but escaped and eventually returned safely home where he continued to serve in the RAF.

Simon Wiesenthal: 31st December 1908 – 20th September 2005 was a writer and Nazi hunter who was a Holocaust survivor. He studied architecture and was living in Lwów (then in Poland, now Ukraine) at the outbreak of World War II. He was incarcerated in a number of German concentration camps until his release on 5th May 1945. After the war, he set up an organisation dedicated to tracing Nazi war criminals, bringing many to justice. He assisted in tracing Adolf Eichmann, who was later tried and hanged in Israel. His work aided in obtaining evidence to convict Hans Stangl, the Commandant of Sobibor and Treblinka death camps. He also helped survivors and refugees of the Holocaust in tracing lost relatives.

Carl Friedrich Freiherr von Weizsäcker: 28th June 1912 – 28th April 2007 was a German physicist and philosopher who helped pioneer nuclear research in Nazi Germany during WWII under Werner Heisenberg. He was a member of a prominent German family and was the son of a diplomat. Weizsäcker joined those involved in developing nuclear science for military purposes in Nazi Germany and was mentioned by Einstein in a letter to President Roosevelt warning of the weapons potential of a nuclear bomb. He made a number of discoveries in Nuclear Fission and patented a nuclear bomb process in the Summer of 1942. He also pioneered theories on early planetary development of the Solar System. In later life, he was recognised and honoured for his work on philosophical and ethical matters.

Johanna Wolf: 1st June 1900 – 5th June 1985. Born in Munich, she worked for various members of the Nazi Party before joining Hitler's personal secretariat in 1929. When Hitler became chancellor in January 1933, she became a senior secretary in his Private Chancellery. Although observing strict protocol with his other secretaries, he called her "Wölfin" meaning She-Wolf. She developed a close rapport with Hitler and was fiercely loyal to him even after his death. Wolf was a dedicated Nazi and a trusted member of Hitler's entourage. When Hitler withdrew his headquarters into the Führerbunker in Berlin in 1945, she went with him. On the night of 21st – 22nd April 1945, Hitler ordered her to leave Berlin for her safety, despite her saying she wished to remain. Arrested by the Americans in May 1945, she was released in 1948. She refused to divulge any confidential information about Hitler for the rest of her life and defended his reputation.

About The Author

Christopher Kerr has enjoyed a varied career as a civil servant, marketing executive, and entrepreneur. He now concentrates on writing, which has become a passion, based upon a keen interest in history, politics, and current affairs. Christopher's genre is historical/contemporary fiction, set against actual events, and real people, to give added authenticity, and perspective to human drama.

His debut novel, '*The Covenant*', was published in 2021, which was followed by '*The Barbarossa Secret*' in 2022, and '*Fission*', released in 2023. Christopher lives in a quiet village in North Wales where he is currently working on his next novel, '*Bullion*', which adds a fresh, astonishing new angle to a contemporary crime, exposing an international money-laundering scandal with links to Nazi Germany and the disappearance of a fortune in gold at the end of the Second World War.